Jake stumbled back against the door, slamming it shut, and Pepper gazed into his eyes. He gently pushed her away and held her at arm's length.

My God, he thought, she was attacking him. So be it. Pepper pressed her lips to his, and after a long moment, his arms circled around her. She let her body relax and melt into his. *Finally.* All he'd needed was a slight nudge.

Jake buried a hand in her hair. His lips were hard against hers, and he searched her mouth with his tongue, but it wasn't enough. She wanted more. Heat rippled through every inch of her body, and he complied with such fierce pleasure that Pepper's knees began to buckle. She held on to Jake and gathered enough strength to pull him across the room. They moved as one toward a black leather couch until finally, they stumbled back.

Jake turned just in time for her to fall on top of him. A move that he seemed quite practiced at, she thought. She didn't care. His body was warm and hard and soft all at once, and she wanted all he had to give . . .

Good With His Hands

Alexa Darin

ZEBRA BOOKS
Kensington Publishing Corp.
www.kensingtonbooks.com

ZEBRA BOOKS are published by

Kensington Publishing Corp.
850 Third Avenue
New York, NY 10022

All Kensington titles, imprints, and distributed lines are available at special quantity discounts for bulk purchases for sales promotion, premiums, fund-raising, educational, or institutional use.

Special book excerpts or customized printings can also be created to fit specific needs. For details, write or phone the office of the Kensington Special Sales Manager: Attn. Special Sales Department.Kensington Publishing Corp., 850 Third Avenue, New York, NY 10022. Phone: 1-800-221-2647.

Zebra and the Z logo Reg. U.S. Pat. & TM Off.

ISBN 0-8217-8038-7

First Printing: September 2006
10 9 8 7 6 5 4 3 2 1

Printed in the United States of America

Acknowledgments

Many thanks to:

My agent, Pema Browne, for your encouragement and faith.

My editor, John Scognamiglio, for your advice and for making me feel included.

Gary (Crash) Maynard for your encouragement, love, and especially, your undying patience. You remind me everyday what romance is all about.

My children, Richard and Jennifer, for never doubting me and for letting me be your wacky mom. You've enriched my life beyond my wildest dreams.

Roger Heilman for always being there. Your continued support has led the way to this dream. Thanks to you with all my heart. You're an ex worth keeping.

Tara Wootten for all the girl talk. Your friendship has provided much needed laughter, but you're still a crazy driver.

Two great guys, John Hurney and Ron Stewart, for making my heart beat faster. You make this girl feel like a goddess.

Kerry Ryan for capturing the real me.

James Burton and Ron Grina, you know why.

Chapter 1

"I want a man who wows me." Pepper Bartlett slipped her gym bag off her shoulder and slumped into a chair at a table in Malibu's Beachside restaurant. It was a hot spot among locals and tourists alike, and Pepper was lucky to find herself living and working practically next door.

She perused her friends' plates, but chopped fruit and raw veggies didn't look nearly as appetizing as what she smelled coming from the grill. Mahi mahi, fish tacos and chicken quesadillas. Pepper's mouth watered.

Lucy and Simone looked at her briefly and then went back to eating as though she'd made nothing more than a comment about the weather.

Pepper stretched out her legs, flexing and pointing her toes to relieve some of the tension in her calves. Two kickboxing classes had been added to her schedule at Malibu Health, and they were kicking her behind. It was that time of year, after all. The locals were eager to get into shape for the summer, and the fitness rush made for a lot of overtime.

Good pay and a good body were the benefits for her, and she had no reason to complain.

Pepper glanced over at the double doors that opened to Beachside's Barefoot Bar. The bar's floor, a layer of white sand, beckoned to her. She could almost feel the warm grit massaging her feet. It was just what she needed after spending the last few hours jumping around on a hardwood floor.

A crimson sky settled over the blue water of the Pacific Ocean, making what was left of the day glow like embers from a fire. Pepper gave a quiet sigh. She couldn't wait for when her workday consisted of nothing more than creating exotic sandcastles and watching waves roll in to shore. The sun, the sand, the surf . . . what more could a girl ask for? A sexy man sitting beside her perhaps? Posing for one of her sand sculptures? Easy to imagine, not so easy to make happen. Winning the California lotto seemed an easier task. For now, Pepper would have to settle for moonlit walks along the beach with nothing beside her but seagulls and sanderlings.

"Didn't either of you hear me?"

"How could we not? You're practically screaming at us, *chérie.*" Simone opened a gold cigarette case and took out a Virginia Slim. Propping it between her long, slender fingers, she paused. "This is not news."

The petite French woman reached into her black Gucci bag and pushed things around until she finally pulled out a gold lighter that matched her cigarette case. Tucking her short brown hair behind her ears, Simone put the cigarette to her mouth.

"Not in here," Pepper said, her forehead gathering into a frown. She jutted a thumb over her shoulder, pointing toward the double doors.

Simone pouted and dropped the cigarette onto the brown, lacquered tabletop. "Your dad, he left your mom, yes? That does not mean I will leave. And that does not mean you must always be so mean."

"What's wrong with Henry?" Lucy asked.

Finally, one of her friends showing some concern over her love life. Pepper sat back in her chair and folded her arms across her chest. "Henry failed to mention something very important about himself."

The corners of Simone's lips tugged upward, and Pepper waited for her to say something like, "Three strikes and you're out, *chérie*." Although at last count, it probably came closer to three hundred. When no comment was forthcoming, Pepper figured Simone's latest recipe must have been a hit and she was feeling generously compassionate.

Lucy munched on a piece of cauliflower without so much as blinking. "What didn't he mention?"

Pepper's lips pulled into a thin line. Before she could answer, Simone touched Lucy's hand lightly. "Henry, he does not wow our Pepper. He is like this." She plucked a celery stick from Lucy's plate, snapped it in half, and tossed it aside. "What *chérie* needs is this." Simone speared a juicy slice of fresh peach from her own plate and caressed it with her tongue. After what seemed like ten minutes of watching a triple-X movie, she slowly sucked it into her mouth. Nectar glistened on her lips, and she closed her eyes, licking it away.

Lucy's face glowed as red as her hair, and she stopped chewing. Pepper grinned. Lucy might never be able to eat a peach again. Simone was right, though—a peach was definitely more her style.

"That's exactly what I'm talking about," Pepper

said. She slapped a hand down on the table. Lucy's glass of sparkling water threatened to topple, and she steadied it. "I want a man who turns me inside out, upside down and makes me crazy with desire today, tomorrow, and forever."

Beachside's sexy bartender, Brad, looked her way and smiled. Pepper smiled back, lowering her voice. She had no doubt that Brad was one man who could turn a woman inside out and upside down, but she'd heard too many wild stories about him. She wasn't interested in playing a part in one of those stories.

"What did Henry lie about?" Lucy asked.

Pepper looked into her friend's innocent blue eyes. "I didn't say he lied. I said he failed to reveal some important information about himself." Both Lucy and Simone stared at her.

Pepper knew they expected more of an explanation as to why she'd dumped a man who supported her desire to build sandcastles for a living. She leaned in close and whispered, "Let's just say, after three dates, I've seen enough."

Simone wasn't buying it. She gave Pepper a suspicious look.

"What're you going to do?" Lucy asked.

Pepper settled back in her chair and let out a sigh. "I don't know. Become a nun, I guess."

"No, no, no. Look around." Simone spread her arms wide. "It is a banquet."

Pepper gave the room a quick once-over. The place was full of men. And she'd dated them all. Or at least men just like them. Tall, short, skinny, fat, bald, tanned, pale. It was a regular smorgasbord, but generic may as well have been written across all their foreheads. No *wow* anywhere. Dating was an exhausting enterprise. Always having to be "on." Pepper got tired just thinking about her next date. No more. She wanted to feel *spring* in the air, that sudden jolt that left her breathless. A little thing called magic. Or maybe even love at first sight.

"That's easy for you to say," Pepper said. "You've got Paul. He's not a celery stick." She nodded toward Lucy's plate. "That's all I ever seem to find."

"*Oui*. Paul, he is not celery," Simone said with a satisfied smile. Then her face turned serious. "We must find you a peach, yes?"

Pepper and Lucy looked at her. "What kind of peach?" Pepper asked.

"A luscious . . . m-m-m . . . juicy peach."

Lucy's eyes grew big. If Simone started up with her X-rated show again, Pepper was sure Lucy would flee the restaurant.

"If you want to taste a peach," Simone continued, "don't waste your time chewing on celery."

Pepper put her head in her hands. That moonlit beach walk with the seagulls was sounding better than ever. "Okay, didn't you just say this was a banquet? I'm either too tired to understand or you're talking in riddles. Please just tell me—in English— what you are trying to say."

"Honestly, *chérie*,"—Simone shook her head—"I have never thought a woman such as you should date men who have an exclusive contract with Calvin Klein or, worse, Levi Strauss. Now, Helmut Lang, Armani . . . well, the names speak for themselves."

"Snob," Pepper said.

Simone smiled proudly. "Perhaps. But I am a happy snob." She fingered a diamond pendant that hung from her neck.

"I don't care what a man wears," Pepper said. "Although I find the less he wears, the better. One thing I do insist on—"

"Honesty," Lucy piped up.

Pepper pointed a finger at her in agreement. "Thank you."

"I find the higher the educational degree, the higher the degree of honesty," Simone said.

"Has she been drinking?" Pepper asked Lucy.

Lucy nodded.

"I am quite sure I'm not drunk. If you find a man to lift you above the clouds," Simone said, flinging her hands into the air, "I will toss my cigarettes into the sea."

Pepper perked up at Simone's offer. Cigarettes were what had killed her dad. She'd do just about anything to keep them from killing someone else she cared about. She hitched up her chin. "You know I can't refuse now. You're a cheat as well as a snob."

"Perhaps," Simone said with a smile.

Pepper had her doubts, but if any of her friends could produce magic, it was Simone. The French-woman was little, but she was a force.

"So what advice do you have for me, oh wise one? I spend most days inside a gym, and any remaining time, I spend on the beach. Where do you suppose I'm going to find my Armani-wearing lover?"

Simone held up one finger and reached over to the empty seat beside her. She laid the latest issue of the *LA Reader* on the table and pushed it over in front of Pepper.

Lucy put down her fork. "An *ad?* You said she needed a peach, not a psycho." She turned to Pepper. "What will Henry say? What will your *mother* say?"

"Don't worry about Henry; that's his wife's job," Pepper mumbled.

Lucy's mouth fell open. "His *wife?*" She looked over at Simone, who simply shrugged and shook her head.

Pepper was determined to keep the conversation moving. "And leave my mom out of this. She's got enough problems. Anyway, Simone's not serious," she said. A thick moment of silence hung in the air. "Are you?"

Lucy was still stuck on Pepper's revelation about Henry, mumbling about how could she have been so wrong about him.

"Not in there," Simone said, tapping the front of the paper with a long, pink fingernail. "But yes." She flipped open the paper and pointed to an ad for an Internet dating service.

Lucy sputtered. Her face took on a greenish cast, like she'd been on a boat too long. "Let's not let this get out of hand."

"Henry turned out to be a philandering pig. He's someone else's husband. I'd say it's already out of hand."

Simone stifled a laugh.

"How will an ad help Pepper find a good man?" Lucy asked Simone. "The only guys who answer those things are ones that no sane woman would ever date."

Pepper's head fell back. She stared up at a wooden beam. "Am I asking too much? A nice guy with a good job who isn't married and who has a car that runs at least ninety-nine percent of the time? Is that really too much?" She looked back down at the paper.

Simone finished her bowl of fruit. "An ad," she said, dabbing her mouth with her napkin, "is not such a bad idea. It is how my friend Cecelia found her boyfriend."

Hope rose in Pepper's chest. "Really? You wouldn't lie to me, would you?" she asked. Everything she knew of Cecelia's boyfriend was good. He was kind and gentle, and the woman had never been happier. Or more satisfied.

Simone smiled, nodding. "It is true." She held up two fingers. "Scout's honor."

Lucy stilled a twitch below her right eye. "We're going to get killed. I'm not sure there's a feng shui cure—"

"Relax. Our Pepper will be looking for a man of only the highest quality." Simone scanned the bar, taking inventory of all the men. "Say *au revoir* to all these *betês*."

Lucy looked around the room. "How can you be sure no beasts will answer the ad?"

Simone grinned, and her eyes took on a devilish glint. "It is easy. It must be made clear that our Pepper is interested only in men who are successful."

"What if they're successful liars?" Lucy asked. "Like Henry?"

Pepper wondered that herself.

"A man wears his success like a badge. The bigger the badge, the bigger the man, yes?" Simone turned to Pepper for confirmation.

Pepper's face was a blank. She hadn't a clue what Simone was talking about. And Lucy had a point. Some men *were* great liars. She'd dated at least half of them. Maybe the flip side of blue jeans was the answer. "Maybe," she answered Simone.

Simone grabbed her cigarette off the table and stood. "Then it is settled, yes?" She glanced toward the double doors. "What a shame to waste this beautiful night. Let us go outside and watch the sun set into the sea."

Pepper and Lucy knew that Simone didn't care how beautiful the night was—she just wanted a smoke, and although Pepper didn't approve, letting Simone have her way most of the time was less painful than getting a taste of her withdrawals. With any luck, following Simone's advice would accomplish two things. It'd bring a little bit of magic into her life, and it'd force her friend to give up a nasty habit. Yeah, right. And the cow jumped over the moon.

The women picked up their plates and pushed through the double doors. Warm air cloaked them like a heated blanket. They sat at a table with white plastic weave beach chairs that sank into the sand, and all three women kicked off their shoes. Pepper slouched further into her chair, tilting her face into the waning sun.

Simone lit her cigarette, and the women watched a blue ribbon of smoke curl into the breeze. "I think this is a good thing," she said. She gave Lucy a sideways glance. "If Pepper finds a man, maybe you will be next."

"I don't need a man," Lucy said.

"Every woman needs a man, *chérie.*"

"Maybe all Lucy needs is a peach," Pepper said, and she and Simone laughed.

Simone wrapped her arms around herself. "Do you never wish for a night like this? A man to share a bottle of wine with, to hold you, bring you a bouquet of flowers—"

"I've got my own flowers." Lucy was quick to remind Simone. "That's one of the perks of being a florist."

A waitress set a salad in front of Pepper, and she promptly forked a cherry tomato and bit it in half. Lucy made a face when the guts squished out.

After finishing her cigarette, Simone glanced at her watch. "I must go. Suzanne is coming over tonight. She has agreed to share her recipe for seared albacore tuna with fennel. I hear it is quite a hit at Lucques."

"Suzanne will wait. Besides, this ad thing was your idea," Pepper said in an attempt to guilt her friend into staying.

Simone shook her head. *"Chérie,* when Suzanne Goin comes to share a recipe, you do not make her wait. Besides, she has become such a star that I do not get to see her so much anymore." She pushed away her plate and stood. "I'll see you tomorrow, yes?"

"Yes, tomorrow." Pepper got up and leaned in for an air kiss.

"Au revoir, Lucy." Simone waved and disappeared through the double doors.

As soon as she was out of sight, Pepper turned to Lucy. "Okay, spit it out."

Lucy looked at her blankly.

"You weren't exactly jumping for joy at Simone's idea."

Lucy tucked a lock of red hair behind one ear and looked down at her plate. "It's not for me to judge—"

"Don't give me that it's-not-for-me-to-judge crap. Just tell me what you think."

"I think whatever you want to do is fine . . . so long

as you don't bring any strange men into our home."
She paused. "At least not until I meet them."

"Okay, *Mom*," Pepper said with a raised eyebrow.

"Hey, Pepper!" a man called from the doorway.
"How about a beer?"

Pepper looked. A guy she recognized from Malibu
Health waved at her. "No, thanks." She waved back.
"See? That's the only kind of men I meet."

"It's a bar," Lucy said.

"This is not a *bar*." Pepper spread out her arms.
"This is Beachside."

"What about him?" Lucy nodded in the direction
of a man who had just walked past and settled himself two tables away. He was clean-shaven and well
dressed, his build was slight, and he wore his hair
very short.

Pepper shook her head. "And you want to meet the
men before I bring them home? Luce, he's gay! What
the hell am I going to do with him—play bridge?"

Lucy peered over the top of her sunglasses for a
closer look.

"Don't *stare*, for God's sake," Pepper whispered.
She glanced at the man again, just in time to see another man walk in and sit down next to him.

"So I made a mistake," Lucy said. "Promise me
anyway. Before you bring any strange men home, I
get a chance to look them over."

"No problem." Pepper crossed her ankles under
the table. Lucy still looked skeptical, and Pepper gave
her a warm smile. "I promise."

Jake Hunter sat on a concrete bench at the side
of a tiled pool and gazed down the Malibu hillside
at the Pacific Ocean. As far out as he could see,

blue sky met even bluer sea. Except for the ever present brown pelicans and a scattering of seagulls, the speck of a fishing boat was the only thing in sight. The sun's reflection made the water glisten like a sheet of diamonds, and Jake squinted until his face hurt. He pulled a bottle of water from a large, red ice chest and poured half of it over his shoulders before drinking the rest. The cool liquid helped to quench the anger that had been burning inside him all day. This would have been his and Angela's second wedding anniversary, and Malibu was where they'd talked about coming to live someday. She should have been sitting next to him.

Jake swallowed painfully, remembering how Angela had looked standing on the balcony of their room at the Malibu Beach Inn. Her hair flowing in concert with the waves, the full moon casting a delicate wash over her face, she'd looked like something from heaven, an angel. With the waves crashing against the rocks below their room, she'd declared in child-like wonder that the Pacific Ocean could be their backyard.

The muscles in Jake's jaw tensed. It'd been a perfect dream of a perfect life. But that dream was gone, and all that remained was anger about how it had all ended. How Angela's life had ended.

Jake stared out to sea. No one at the hospital had ever blamed him. They didn't need to. He did enough blaming for the entire world. He held out his right hand, palm up, and squeezed it into a fist. Strong and able, he could work all day on megahomes for the rich, but when he'd needed his hands most, they had failed him. He hadn't been able to save Angela's life.

After drinking an ocean of booze, Jake had awakened with the worst headache of his life. He'd also awakened with the decision that he was never going to call himself doctor again. A year later, so far so good. Construction had proved to be safer.

Malibu would never be his and Angela's home, but somehow, coming to the place where they'd intended to live seemed fitting. Day by day, the sun's warmth, the ocean's thunder had proven to be healing—to a point.

Jake took another water bottle from the cooler and held it out toward the sea. "Here's to us, Angela, and what might've been." He gave the blue expanse a melancholy smile, took a drink, and went back to work.

Chapter 2

Pepper went into the downward-facing dog position. Out of the corner of her eye, she saw Simone walk in and sit against the gym's smooth white wall. After holding the pose for a full ten seconds, Pepper relaxed to her knees and sat cross-legged on the floor.

"I've been thinking about that ad," she announced proudly. Simone had her eyes closed and didn't respond. "Remember? The ad for the Internet service you told me about? For a man who'll rock my world, make me want to eat peaches?"

"Oui, I remember," Simone said, opening her eyes. She rested her chin on top of her knees.

Pepper held out her hands. "C'mon," she said. "Do this next one with me."

Simone rolled her eyes and crawled over to Pepper's blue mat. She kicked off her shoes, and they placed the soles of their feet together. Locking their fingers, Pepper stretched forward while Simone leaned back. Pepper felt a pull in her hamstrings, and she waited until the tightness began to subside. Then it was her turn to lean back.

"O-ow! *Chérie*, I cannot." Simone let go of Pepper's hands and gathered her legs to her chest. "Why do you desire to put your body through all this pain?" She waved a hand around at the other women who lingered in the gym. "Why do you American women torture yourselves?"

Pepper smiled. "You're right. No need for me to torture myself." She rolled up her mat and tucked it under one arm. "Let's go. I'll shower, and then we'll go get a cup of coffee. I want to show you what I've got."

Pepperdine University stood tall, overlooking the Malibu Plaza Starbucks. Because of its close proximity, students occupied most of the tables, their faces crammed into laptops and schoolbooks. One small sofa sat empty over in the corner. After a short wait, Pepper ordered her usual nonfat, decaf mocha, and Simone, a double espresso straight up.

"Don't keep me waiting, *chérie*." Simone tucked her long legs beneath her and settled on a plump cushion. *"Dépêche.* Show me what you've got."

Pepper took a sip of her mocha and set the cup on the table. "Okay, here goes . . ." She wiggled her body, settling deeper into the sofa. "Blue Collar Guys Need Not Reply. Wild child seeks dirty white boy with clean fingernails," she read from a sheet of paper. She glanced over at Simone for her reaction. Nothing. "That's the heading," she explained, "so I can get the attention of the right kind of man."

Simone's face settled into an amused grin.

"What?" asked Pepper.

"Nothing, *chérie*. I think you will find the perfect man. Like my Paul."

"Yes, like your Paul. That's exactly what I want," Pepper agreed. "But, you know, my own Paul, not yours."

"Yes, I know what you mean. My Paul, I don't think he is into *ménage à trois*."

Pepper's smile faded, and she frowned. "That's where I get stuck. I can't seem to get past the opening line. Any suggestions?"

"Yes. Forget all this." Simone took the paper from Pepper and tore it in half, then tore it in half again before handing it back.

"But I thought—"

"Cecelia says all you need to do is answer a list of questions. You post a picture, and the men find you irresistible."

Pepper blew out a relieved breath. "Thank God. It's awfully hard to come up with something really witty when you know thousands, perhaps millions, might read it."

Simone waved a hand. "It is for the man to impress you." She reached over and touched Pepper's chin. "You are beautiful, blond American girl. What man could resist?"

"As far as I can tell, just about every man in this galaxy. All the good ones anyway."

"Pooh. They have only to be in your presence for one minute, and they will fall in love."

Pepper noticed the clock on the wall. "I've got to get home and call my mom. With my dad gone . . ."

Simone gave her an understanding look. "Your mom, she is like you, yes?"

"Like me?" Pepper gave it some thought. "Somewhat, I guess."

"Then she will not be alone forever."

Pepper knew Simone meant well, but her mother joining the dating pool was more than she wanted to think about. No, she was sure her mother had no ideas about finding another man. Hannah Bartlett seemed content to live a quiet life alone.

Quiet. Ha! Who was she kidding? Her twin sister, Cat, lived not more than a mile away from their childhood home. With her around, Pepper's mom wouldn't have time to think about dating.

Pepper smiled, thinking back to when she and Cat were children. Their dad had always said that since there were two of them, they needed to have double the fun, and he'd always plan something special for them to look forward to. A day at the Seattle Center or the Seattle Aquarium. Once, he even booked a trip to Disneyland. Pepper felt a quiet sadness. That was way back when she and her sister were the dynamic duo. Before their dad died. Nothing special had been planned since he'd been gone.

Pepper squeezed Simone's hand. "I'm sure you're right."

They stepped out into the night air and were hit by a gust of wind. Simone turned her back to the breeze and lit a cigarette. Pepper looked down the Pacific Coast Highway. It was ablaze with car lights. Most evenings, the walk to her cottage made for a pleasant end to her day, but tonight, she was tired, and a good soak was in order.

"Take me home, please," Pepper said to Simone.

Although her home was not far, with all the traffic, it was ten minutes before Simone dropped Pepper off at her house. Pepper got out of Simone's car and stopped short on the walkway. Red. Her front door was bright freaking, screaming red! She backed up two steps and looked from left to right, then checked the house number. Sure enough, it was her door. Pepper touched the paint and quickly drew her hand back. Now her fingertips were red. She wiped them on the leaves of a bush, and taking care not to touch the wet wood, she opened the door.

Bells tinkled softly from across the room, and Pepper saw that a small wind chime had been hung from the ceiling outside the bathroom. She shook her head and dropped her gym bag.

"Lucy, I'm home," Pepper shouted in her best Ricky Ricardo voice. "You got some 'splainin' to do." She found the redhead sitting on a small stool in the kitchen with the phone pressed to her ear.

Lucy's eyebrows shot up when she saw Pepper. "She's right here, Hannah. I'll put her on." A smug grin covered her face as she handed Pepper the phone.

Pepper's eyes narrowed. "What have you told her?" she asked in a thin whisper. Lucy shrugged, feigning ignorance, and Pepper hoped Lucy hadn't been foolish enough to tell her mom about her plans to look for a man on the Internet.

"Hi, Mom. I just walked in and was about to call you." Pepper looked over at Lucy and stuck out her tongue. Lucy returned the favor.

"Hi, Patrice. Have you thought about it? Do you think you'll be coming home for your birthday?"

Pepper winced. *Patrice.* Ugh. She wanted to stick her finger down her throat. It may have been the name she had been given at birth, but it didn't fit. In fact, she doubted it ever had.

"Mom, don't call me that. You know how I hate that name."

"How can you hate it? It's your name."

"Thanks for reminding me. About me coming home . . . I'm not sure. Things aren't going so well right now."

"Of course things aren't going well. What do you expect? You just broke up with your boyfriend."

Pepper rolled her eyes and sat down. Already, this was a long conversation. Obviously, Lucy had given her mother the lowdown, but had been kind enough to edit out the part about Henry being married.

"Henry was not my boyfriend, Mom. We just dated a few times."

"That's what people do when they're in a relationship. Honestly, Patrice, if you'd come home, you could get a good job working in a nice office building or—"

"Mom, stop. We've talked about this. I'm not coming home to work in an office. I won't even work in an office *here*. What makes you think I'll come to Seattle and work in one?" Pepper heard giggling behind her back. She turned and saw Lucy over on the sofa holding her hand over her mouth. "Shush," Pepper whispered, putting a finger to her lips.

"What do you mean, shush?" Hannah asked.

Pepper shook her head. "No, not *you*. It's Lucy." Pepper turned around so she couldn't see her. "Where were we?"

"We were discussing your coming home and having a nice office career."

"I don't want to work in an office. I have a good job at the health club, remember? I keep telling you I love Malibu, but you don't seem to hear me."

"Maybe your sister and I could come down there then," Hannah said.

"To *live?* Mom, I don't—"

"Don't be silly. I would never want to live in that mess. No, I mean for your *birthday*, sweetheart. Maybe we could come down there for your birthday."

Pepper chewed on her lower lip and scrunched up her forehead. She calculated she'd have at least two more frown lines by morning. "Down here?" She turned and gave Lucy a plea for help look. Lucy ignored her. "You and Cat? Are you sure?" How the heck was she going to keep her search for a man hidden if her mom and sister were hanging around? Her mom would probably pack her bags and force her to come home, and Cat would laugh at her all the way back to Seattle.

"No," her mother said with a sigh. "But if that's the only way we'll get to see you . . . only, I'm not letting your sister drive me around in that traffic. We'll have to hire a taxi. You don't suppose I could just have one at my disposal, do you?"

Pepper felt her eyes begin to glaze over. Five hours of kickboxing and yoga had left her drained. Right now, she needed comfort, not conflict. "Mom, we'll have to talk about this later. I just came in the door, and I've got to help Lucy with something."

"Okay, dear. Think about it and call me tomorrow?"

Pepper nodded. "Okay. Love you." She dropped the phone and turned. Lucy was gone. If her roommate were smart, her bedroom door would be barricaded. "Oh, no, you don't," Pepper yelled, running down the hall. She opened Lucy's door without knocking. "What was that all about?"

Lucy peered up at her through black-framed reading glasses.

"What were you and my mom cooking up? How much information did you give her?"

"I don't know what you're talking about," Lucy said matter of factly, and she went back to her reading.

"All right. That's it." Pepper jumped onto Lucy's bed and started bouncing. Lucy seemed determined to ignore her, so Pepper bounced even harder. With a loud bang and a crash, both women toppled sideways as the bed collapsed beneath them.

"Oops," Pepper said. She and Lucy stared at each other for a moment, and then they broke into laughter.

Finally, Lucy gasped and caught her breath. "You're sleeping in here tonight. I get your bed." She jumped up and raced to Pepper's room, pushing the lock behind her.

Pepper pounded on the door. "Are you going to tell me what I want to know?" No response. She paused with her back against the door. Suddenly, she had an idea. She knew how to get Lucy's attention. "Okay. Guess I'll have to go unlock a few secrets of my own."

Pepper went to Lucy's room, opened her top dresser drawer, and pulled out a thick black journal. Not that she'd ever really invade a friend's privacy. She slammed the drawer shut, and two seconds later, Lucy ran into the room.

"Okay, okay. Give it back." Lucy grabbed at the journal. Pepper grinned smugly and handed it to her, and Lucy examined the lock. Satisfied that it was secure, she placed it back in her drawer.

"Your mom seemed down in the dumps. I might

have suggested she and Cat come down here for a short vacation is all. That's it. I never specified your birthday. Just a short weekend."

"Luce, you know my mom. Since when does she not sound down in the dumps near my birthday? She likes for all of us to be together on special occasions."

"What was I supposed to do? Ignore her pain?"

"Yes! That's exactly what you're supposed to do," Pepper said. "I do."

"I know, but you're a mean daughter."

"Hm-mf," Pepper said. She got up and patted her stomach. "I'm hungry. You went to the store, I hope. By the way, what's with the red paint?"

"Huh?"

"You know . . . where we enter our abode . . . the front door?"

Lucy smiled. "Red is a powerful color. It offers protection."

"Gee, why didn't I think of that?" Pepper did an eye roll. She opened the refrigerator and found nothing that appealed to her. "Tell me, Luce, what do we need protection from? Men?"

The redhead shrugged. "Maybe."

Pepper opened a cupboard. A jar of reduced-fat, crunchy Jif peanut butter sat waiting to be opened. She grabbed it, and a flash of red caught her eye. An envelope. She picked it up and held it to the light.

"It's got rice in it—for good luck," Lucy informed her with a smile. Her smile quickly disappeared. "Henry called."

"Pig," Pepper said without hesitation. She spread a glob of peanut butter on a piece of whole wheat bread, then licked the knife and dropped it in the sink.

"Are you going to call him?"

"Why should I? I can't imagine being interested in anything he has to say." Pepper took a bite of the bread and licked a dab of peanut butter from her lips.

"Don't you think you should hear him out? If he's calling you, maybe it's all a bad misunderstanding."

"Yeah. Real bad."

"I think you should at least tell him to forget about you and get on with his life."

Pepper swallowed a mouthful of bread and looked at her. "You're kidding, right?"

Lucy gave her a motherly look.

"I'm going to go soak in a warm bubble bath." Pepper had heard enough. She admired Lucy for being so understanding and patient *and naïve,* but there was a limit to the amount of understanding some people deserved.

A few minutes later, Pepper slid into warm water laced with lavender bath crystals. The heavenly scent filled the room, and she closed her eyes with a sigh, forgetting all about Henry. When she opened them, a red star stared back at her from the ceiling.

Feng shui. Pepper didn't know what it meant, but she was sure it was something that would profoundly change her life. Right. She smiled and slipped deeper into the cozy water. Good thing she had Lucy watching out for her.

Brad pulled into the driveway of the modest stucco rambler that he shared with his friend Vic. Vic's girlfriend, Marta, didn't live with them. Not technically anyway. But you'd never know it. Little by little, she'd managed to move enough of her personal items in so that she hardly ever had to return home. Except to get more stuff.

Being in such close living quarters with a hot-blooded woman such as Marta wasn't easy. Her swiveling hips in those short skirts had given Brad ideas, and those ideas had turned into reality on more than one occasion. The last time being last night. Vic was out of town on business.

Their encounter was purely physical. Marta had even convinced Brad to try one of those recreational drugs, claiming they enhanced the sexual experience. He shook his head thinking about it. Enhanced? They'd had a friggin' sexual marathon. And, he didn't know how, but today, Marta sported a large handprint bruise on her thigh. Jesus, how the hell was she going to explain that to Vic? If he ever found out the truth, all hell would break loose. And for sure, his friendship with Vic would end.

Brad played the previous night over and over in his mind. He'd had all day to think about it, and he knew things had to change. Marta was hot, but working as a bartender allowed him to come into contact with plenty of hot women. It wasn't worth it to mess around with his best friend's girl. Not ever again.

His fingers gripped the steering wheel as he considered his options. Telling Vic what'd happened was definitely not one of those options. Any way he tried to spin it, the conversation wouldn't have a pleasant outcome, so what it came down to was that one of them had to go. Living in Malibu was expensive. A bartender's wage wouldn't cut it. Marta was the only clear choice as far as Brad could see. Hell, he'd even rent a moving van and move her shit out himself.

The sun burned through the windshield of the car, and sweat trickled down Brad's back. If Vic was home, it was going to get even hotter. Brad wiped his forehead and got out of his car.

He opened the door and was met by a scrawny German Shepherd pup. Brad had found him wandering around Beachside's parking lot and had taken him home. Even after two baths, the pup continued to scratch like it was a bad habit. The name Scratch had seemed fitting.

Scratch jumped all over him, whimpering and licking, and Brad talked softly to him, rubbing behind the dog's ears. He glanced up and saw Marta out in the backyard, hanging clothes to dry. He went over and watched from the doorway as she stretched to reach the clothesline. Only five feet tall, she had to stand on her toes to hang the dripping clothes. He heard her swear as she held up a pair of jeans that were heavy with water. Great. She was in a foul mood.

"Need a hand?" Brad finally asked. No reason to let their conversation get started on the wrong foot.

The petite, dark-haired woman jumped at the sound of his voice. Caught off balance, she took a step back. Her face screwed up in vulgar distaste as she looked down.

"Son of a bitch," she said loudly, lifting a bare foot. It was smeared with a pasty brown substance. "Aw, shit."

Brad resisted the urge to say, Yep, that's what it looks like. Instead, he grabbed a towel off the line and handed it to her.

"Not one of my *good* towels. What's wrong with you?"

"Just trying to help."

"Well, you're not." Marta looked over at the small white table on the patio and pointed. "Get that rag.

Hurry up!" she ordered as she wiped her foot over and over on the dry grass. "Why can't you clean up after your dog?"

Brad handed her the rag and watched her wipe brown goo from between her toes. "I do," he said. "That pile is too big to be from Scratch. Probably that dog from next door again." He nodded toward the neighbor's house.

"Here. Get rid of this," she said, shoving the rag back at him. "Someday, I'm gonna kill that mutt. Someday, those people are gonna come home, and that mutt's gonna be lying on the ground with his tongue hangin' out." Marta stopped suddenly and gave Brad a curious look. She looked at her watch, then back at him. "What're you doing home so early?"

Brad leaned against the railing on the deck and put his hands in his pockets. "I've been thinking about things." He glanced back at the sliding door. "Is Vic home yet?"

Marta crossed her arms over her chest. "No. He called and said he'd be another couple of days." She moved toward him.

"We're not doing that anymore," Brad said. "I told you it would kill Vic. Besides, I thought you were mad about that bruise."

Her eyes got sleepy, and she ran a hand down Brad's belly all the way to his crotch. "I got over it."

He stepped back and turned to go inside. "I haven't," he said over his shoulder.

"I see. You only wanted to try out the merchandise, huh?" Her voice grew louder with each word, and Brad figured soon, everybody would know their business.

He took her arm and urged her toward the sliding door. "Let's go inside and talk."

Marta crossed her arms and stood firm. She closed her eyes and shook her head. "No. You tell me right here, right now. You got some other woman?"

A head peered out the back door of the neighbor's house and looked in their direction. Brad lowered his voice, hoping Marta would do the same. "I'm not going into this in front of the whole stinkin' neighborhood."

Marta shrugged past him, and she marched into the house. As soon as Brad shut the door, she turned on him. "Okay, I'm listening."

"I tried to explain the best I could. You and me,"— Brad shook his head—"it's over. I don't know what else to say to convince you."

"Fine," she shrugged. "It's going to be uncomfortable though. The three of us living here together in this little house."

"You *don't* live here, remember?" Brad looked around the room. "You've just got your shit piled up everywhere." He scrubbed a hand through his hair. "But you're right. One of us has to go."

"That's okay by me." Marta turned and grabbed some mail off the counter. "Don't forget these." She threw them at Brad.

Bills. Brad tossed them aside.

"Loser," Marta muttered on her way back outside.

Chapter 3

Brad spent the night with a friend. He hadn't been back to the house, and he wasn't sure he should tempt fate even to change his clothes for work. Marta had a way of bringing out the worst in him, and he didn't want to do something he'd regret worse than sleeping with her.

He sat on a bench at the end of the Santa Monica Pier, watching tourists and locals pass by. It was easy to tell who was who. Tourists had two different looks. They either gazed around all wide-eyed, interested in everything, or they looked exhausted, like they were shoving two months' worth of fun into one week.

The locals also had two distinctive looks. There were those who walked with purpose, like they knew exactly where they were going and were late. Then there were those who sauntered along as though they had nowhere in particular to go and forever to get there.

Each group dressed differently, too.

Tourists were clean, their clothes pressed, so they'd look their best, no matter if they were going to the corner store or Disneyland. Locals wore whatever they could scrounge off the floor from the night before. That is, unless they were headed to work. In which case, they wore anything from Armani suits and outfits by Prada to casual wear from The Gap.

The sun bore down on the pier, and Brad rested his back against the warmed bench seat. He saw a woman wearing a bouncy skirt and a tight-fitting tank top walking up the pier toward him. Brad felt a pleasant jolt of excitement. He'd know those long legs anywhere. Pepper Bartlett. The day was already looking better.

"Boy, glad I'm not at Beachside," Pepper said, stopping in front of him. "I'd be disappointed if someone else had to make my drink. Care to share what was in that fabulous concoction you made for me the other day?"

He grinned. "What'll you give me?"

Pepper smiled, looking at him coyly. "Why, Brad, would you be propositioning me?"

"Yep."

Pepper laughed. "Down, boy. My schedule is full at the moment. Work, work, and more work. I'm on my way there right now. How about I see you at Beachside later tonight?"

"Definitely." Things were indeed looking up. "I'll see to it that your drink gets that extra special something."

"I love it when you talk all sexy like that." She put a hand to her chest. "Makes me feel all squishy inside."

Brad chuckled. Pepper was a flirt, that was for sure, but he'd never been able to figure her out. She never brought anyone into the restaurant with her other than that Frenchwoman and her cute little redhead friend. Her roommate, he thought. Lesbians? Not hardly.

"Does that mean you're interested?" he asked.

"Hm-m-m," Pepper said, considering his question. "I'll have to get back with you on that. See you later, huh?"

"Always." He took one of her hands in his and kissed the back of it. She blushed and chewed her bottom lip, and Brad could tell he'd just scored some points.

Brad rubbed the coarse stubble on his chin and watched her walk away. The ocean's breeze blew her skirt between her legs, and he could see the outline of her curves all the way up.

He looked at his watch. He had about an hour before he had to be at Beachside. The baggy shorts and tank top he was wearing probably wouldn't go over well. He rubbed the back of his neck, hating the thought of having to go back to the house with Marta still there. With any luck, she'd be off shopping or at her mother's or whatever she did to fill the time.

Vic would be home soon. Marta had agreed to keep her mouth shut, but that did little to reassure Brad. Maybe he'd save some money. Go up North. He'd heard living was good in the Pacific Northwest. He even had a cousin who lived in Seattle and worked at Microsoft. Maybe he could help Brad get a job.

Brad looked down the pier and out to the water. Santa Monica was his home. To hell with living where it rained three hundred days out of the year. If Marta wouldn't move out, he'd just have to find a new roommate. Closer to work maybe. Maybe in Malibu.

Pepper was the first to arrive at Beachside. She chose the same outdoor table that she and her friends had shared a couple of nights before. Her work day had flown by. A kickboxing class, two yoga classes, and then a vigorous swim in the lap pool. She was ready for a relaxing evening. She immediately kicked off her shoes and dug her feet into the warm sand. The waitress took her order for a margarita and returned with it a few minutes later.

Pepper took a sip and licked salt from her lips. M-m-m. The concoction was different from the usual margarita. Brad was true to his promise. How he loved taunting her. She simply had to find out the secret ingredient. She'd even considered trading sex for Brad's recipes, but good sense always came through to shake her out of a bad decision. Pepper looked his way. Bartender Brad was good-looking—great, in fact, but he was trouble waiting to happen. Guys like him should probably wear some kind of warning label for unsuspecting women. Even so, Pepper had a feeling that she and Brad might be just one step away from doing something she'd end up wishing she hadn't.

After finishing off half her drink, Pepper began to wonder why she'd ever promised Simone she'd give the other half of the male population a try. Three men at a nearby table were checking her out. Two had on blue jeans, and the other, shorts. Simone had better get here soon if she wanted to save Pepper from giving in to her drink-induced desires. With the alcohol factor figured in, Pepper believed she'd be able to hold out about another five minutes. Just ignore them, she told herself. Take a deep breath. They don't exist.

She turned her attention to the show in the sky. Who needed men? Malibu's brown pelican population was out in full force, providing plenty of entertainment. Pepper focused on a particular one. He circled high above the Pacific Ocean, gliding effortlessly over the water looking for his next meal. After a short search, he plunged into the sea to seize his prey.

As the alcohol made its way into her system, Pepper relaxed and pushed aside all thoughts of Bartender Brad and the three men. They were already checking out another woman anyway. That figured.

She scrunched her toes deeper into the sand. Where the hell were her friends? It was a perfect evening for an outdoor meal, and they were missing it. The cloudless afternoon sky slowly turned to burnt orange before quietly melting into the Pacific Ocean's clear aquamarine. There'd been no rain for the past few weeks. June gloom seemed to have passed them by. If the weather held, she'd have plenty of opportunity to practice her sand sculpting once the fitness craze leveled off.

Pepper had nearly finished her drink by the time Simone and Lucy arrived. Simone ordered a glass of wine and a salad, warning the waitress that if the salad didn't have the freshest ingredients, she'd send it back. Lucy opted for a bowl of fresh fruit with spring water. Pepper ordered the same as Lucy. She wanted to be slim and trim when she met the love of her life. She did order another margarita, however.

"Live a little," Simone said to Lucy. "Wine is so very good for you." She pulled a Virginia Slim from her gold case.

"Like cigarettes?" Lucy asked.

Simone stared at Lucy and lit her cigarette, inhaling deeply.

Pepper laid a hand lightly on Lucy's arm. "Don't worry about that. Simone has cooked her own goose. With any luck, I'll have found the love of my life, and she'll be sucking her thumb instead of those nasty things." Pepper gave Lucy an appraising look. "Have you lost weight?"

"Some," Lucy said with a satisfied smile.

"By the end of the summer, all the hot guys will be after you," Pepper said.

"Yes, *chérie. All* the hot ones, including those with blue collars and blue jeans."

Lucy shrugged. "I don't care. I don't have anything against a man who works with his hands."

Pepper agreed. In fact, if a man had a busy mind to go with his busy hands, all the better.

The waitress showed up and placed their orders in front of them. Pepper was feeling good. The alcohol had done its job. She picked up her fork and speared a fresh slice of peach the way she'd seen Simone do. She unashamedly licked off all the juice before attempting to suck it into her mouth. Half of it broke off and landed in her lap. So she needed a little practice on her technique. She should at least get credit for making an effort.

Pepper was eager to tell her friends about the Better Half website, but she was going to refrain until they finished eating. Lucy would probably lose her appetite, maybe even her meal.

Finally, she couldn't wait another minute. "I did it," Pepper said, sitting up straighter and wiggling her butt deeper into her beach chair.

Simone lit a cigarette, and Lucy waved the smoke away. They both looked over at Pepper.

"I checked out that dating website and put in my request for a man."

Lucy's eyes opened wide. "I didn't think you were for real." She turned to Simone. "Is she for real?"

Simone's eyes gleamed. "Is scandalous, yes?"

Lucy's mouth opened and closed a couple of times. Pepper thought she looked like one of the guppies in her mom's fish tank. "Have you gone mad?"

"Yes, I believe I have. And it comes from not having a stable man in my life to keep *me* stable."

Simone sipped her wine with a quiet smile.

"Tell me what you think," Pepper said to Lucy. "Don't hold back."

"I think I'll need to feng shui every room in our house to ward off all the creeps that you'll be bringing into our lives." Lucy stared at her plate.

"What's the matter, *chérie*? Have you lost your appetite?" Simone's titter filled the air.

"We're going to get killed," Lucy said. She popped a peach slice into her mouth and squished it between her teeth.

Jake Hunter and two of his friends walked into a bar a few miles from their current jobsite and sat at a table close to one of the television screens. Gordy Philips was Jake's apprentice and, most times, a real pain in the ass. Jake likened him to a little brother who was always following the older boys around and getting in their hair. Pete Erickson didn't work on the homes. He just drew the plans that the others worked from. When Jake had moved to California, Pete and his wife had taken him in and treated him like family right from the start. They'd pretty much saved him from himself.

A playoff game between the LA Lakers and the Portland Trailblazers was in the third quarter. Even though Jake was a bona fide California resident now, he still rooted for Portland, if only to himself.

"What'll you boys have?" a waitress asked as she placed a small beverage napkin in front of each man.

Jake glanced up at her. He could see why she'd called them boys. She must have been pushing fifty. A nice-looking fifty, but still old enough to consider them boys.

Each man ordered a Guinness, and after she left, Gordy nudged Jake's arm. "Saw you eyeing that waitress."

Jake's eyebrows rose. "Huh?" He glanced over at Pete, but the architect was involved in the basketball game.

Gordy nodded toward the bar where the waitress stood waiting for their order. "Looks pretty good for her age. Nothing to feel ashamed about."

"Maybe it's you that's interested. We all know how you like older women." Jake immediately regretted the sarcasm in his voice. He didn't have a problem with his friend liking older women. It was that they tended to be *married*, older women that he found hard to accept.

Gordy laughed. "Nope. Not me. I got me a woman who keeps me busy."

Both men shut up when they saw the waitress coming toward their table with a tray full of beers.

"Twelve dollars," she said and tucked the tray under one arm.

"*Twelve dollars?* Are you sure that's beer in those mugs?" Gordy said.

"Three dollars each and a dollar tip each," the waitress said with a straight face.

All three men looked up at her. She gave them a sincere, but all business smile. Gordy didn't even make a move for his wallet, but Pete dug into his and pulled out two ones. He stood and fished around in his pocket for some change.

"Wife must've cleaned me out," he said, flipping two quarters onto the table.

"I'll get it," Jake said, throwing a twenty onto the table. He shoved Pete's money back in front of him.

"Thanks, buddy," Gordy said, slapping Jake's back.

"Cheap bastard," Jake murmured.

The waitress managed a smile and left a five and three ones on the table in a puddle of beer.

"She likes you," Gordy said. He picked up his beer and took a long drink.

"She's wearing a goddamn wedding ring," Jake told him. Pete chuckled, but didn't take his eyes off the game.

"Guess I missed that," Gordy said. He was silent for a minute, until a group of women walked in. "Would you look at that? All you got to do is pick one, boss."

Jake glanced at the women and went back to watching the game.

"Course, it's been so long, you've probably forgotten all your old pick-up lines."

Jake grunted. "That coming from a guy who still

thinks women fall for guys who whistle at 'em while hanging from a ladder?"

"Shit!" Pete said to nobody in particular. "Lakers are gettin' their asses kicked." He swung around and turned back to the table. "What's that about women and pick-up lines?"

"I was just telling Jake he hasn't had a woman for so long, he's forgotten how to pick one up."

"I could tell him," Pete said with a laugh.

"How're you gonna tell him anything? You're too old."

"Not too *old*, too *married*. But I can still satisfy my honey," Pete said, taking a quick glance back at the game. "Although he is right, y'know." He looked straight at Jake. "Even my Theresa is wondering when you're going to find yourself a woman so I can stop being your Friday night date."

"Yeah," Gordy said. "And I'm your Saturday night date. My woman's beginning to think I might be two-timing her."

Gordy's words stung like salt water in a wound. And they were true. Jake always figured he'd know when the time was right, but somehow, the time didn't even seem close. Still, being alone was better than inviting unnecessary trouble into his life. Which was exactly what Gordy was doing by chasing after another man's wife.

"Maybe you should," Jake said.

"What was that?" Gordy asked, cupping a hand behind one ear. "They got that TV so loud, I can barely hear your gums flappin'."

"Nothing. Doesn't matter," Jake said, shaking his head.

"You sure?" Gordy asked. "'Cause I coulda swore

you said something about how I ought to two-time my woman."

Jake felt angry words pushing against his teeth. He and the other guys always teased Gordy about the women he got himself involved with, but it was far from a joking matter. Gordy's current love interest had a husband who was well-known around Malibu, and he didn't seem like the type to take it too kindly if he found out.

"You're gonna get yourself killed."

Gordy leaned back in his chair and laughed. "That's rich," he said, shaking his head. "You're gonna give me advice when your love life died over two years ago."

Jake gave him a hard look. He took a long drink of beer and turned his eyes to the television.

"Christ, Gordy," Pete mumbled, glaring at the young construction worker.

"Sorry, man," Gordy apologized to Jake. "I didn't mean that."

"Forget it," Jake said, setting his beer on the table. The mug hit the table harder than he'd intended, and amber liquid sloshed over the side. It was hard enough to face the truth on his own, but hearing it from a friend made it even harder. Even so, it was Gordy's well-being he was concerned with right now.

"Tell you what," Jake said, "you show me you're willing to date a single, *available* woman, and I'll start dating too." Even as he said the words, he wanted to take them back.

Gordy hesitated, mulling over Jake's offer. The waitress returned to their table, and Jake ordered another round. Gordy eyed him suspiciously and then glanced over at Pete, who still had his attention on the Portland–Lakers game.

"What do you guys got goin'?" Gordy asked Jake.

Jake shook his head. "Nothing. I just think you should get out of that relationship you're in—for your own good."

Gordy was quiet while the waitress dropped off three more beers. She said she'd come back for the money. Jake took a swallow from the full mug and, without a word, got up from the table. A minute later, he returned with a newspaper.

"Here," he said, tossing it onto the table in front of Gordy. Gordy stared at the paper without opening it. Finally, Jake opened it for him. He pointed to the Personals.

Gordy shook his head. "Naw, man. I ain't into that. What kind of woman has to put an ad in the paper anyway?" He looked to Pete for backup. "Are you listening to this?" Gordy said, nudging him.

"What?" Jake said. "I'm just trying to show you I'm serious."

Pete glanced sideways at him and raised both hands. "Don't get me into this."

"C'mon. Help me out here," Gordy said to Pete.

Pete scooted his chair around and faced Gordy, his face more serious than Jake had ever seen it.

"Help you? Sounds to me like that's what Jake is trying to do. You finding a woman in the want ads couldn't be much worse than the kind you've been dating. The way you're going, all you're gonna get is a big credit card bill or a big doctor's bill. Or worse."

Gordy winced. "Hey, the only reason I got a big credit card bill is 'cause a guy's got to impress a woman—"

"Yeah, yeah," Jake said, pushing the paper at him. "C'mon. What have you got to lose?"

"Tell you what . . ." Gordy said, eyeing Jake. "You first." He shoved the paper back over to him. *"You look for a woman in there. If you can find one, then I'll consider giving it a try."*

A queasy feeling bounced around in Jake's stomach. His first thought was to tell his friend to go to hell. He clenched his jaw tight. It hurt to even think about dating another woman. The guilt bit into him just like it did every time he lay in bed and wondered how it might feel to hold another woman in his arms. Jake swallowed. He knew Angela would tell him to get on with his life.

"One condition . . ." Jake said.

"What's that?" Gordy asked, his eyes narrowing suspiciously.

"As soon as I start dating, you quit seeing *that* woman."

"*That* woman has a name—Sherry—but, okay," Gordy said with a shrug. "I was about to cut her loose anyway." A smug grin covered his face. He picked up his beer and took a swallow.

Jake saw that the Lakers were out of it. Even with a miracle, they couldn't come back now. He silently cheered Portland's victory.

"Here's one for you," Gordy said. He pointed at an ad that had a dark border around it.

Jake looked. The dark border had a purpose—to make it stand out from all the other ads. "No, thanks." He shook his head. "She's desperate. Just because I agreed to go first doesn't mean I don't have standards." Jake wanted to help his friend straighten out his life, but he could come up with a million excuses for not calling any of the women in those ads.

"Gimme that," Pete said, snatching the paper away from Gordy. "You're looking for the wrong kind of woman for our friend here. Jake's got class. He needs a classy woman, not the kind of woman you'd go after."

"My point exactly . . . which is why I don't look in the classifieds for women," said Gordy.

"There are plenty of good women out there," Pete said. "But you won't find them in here." He poked a finger at the paper. "Get on the Internet."

"You shittin' me?" Gordy said with raised eyebrows.

Pete shook his head. "Nope. Theresa and I were watching TV the other night. We saw three ads in just one hour. Everybody's doing it."

"Great," Jake said. "Now Theresa's in on this. Why do I feel like I'm being set up?"

"Because you have that suspicious nature, my friend," Pete said. "They put pictures on the website. It's like a blind date, but you get to see the goods first."

"It could be love at first sight—like Pete and Theresa," Gordy offered.

"Still is," Pete said. He began looking through the Personals section, squinting as he read.

"Better put on your glasses, old man," Gordy said, and he and Jake laughed.

Pete frowned at them and pulled a pair of glasses out of his shirt pocket. He slipped them on and continued reading.

"You look absolutely scholarly," Gordy told him. "That must be how you got Theresa to marry you."

Without taking his eyes off the paper, Pete stuck up the middle finger of his right hand. After a minute of searching, he pushed the paper back over to Jake. "There you go. An Internet dating service. Let's go back to my place and take a look."

Chapter 4

Pete's wife wasn't home. Jake was relieved. It was bad enough having your friends trying to fix you up without having a woman standing around giving you that look of pity because you can't get a date.

Jake watched over Pete's shoulder as he called up the Better Half website. He even entered Jake's preferences for him. Piece of cake.

After several minutes, Pete stood. "There you go," he said.

Jake sat down to look at the picture of the woman Pete thought he might be interested in. She called herself Malibu Miss, and she had honey blond hair that bounced freely about her shoulders. Her eyes were the color of the ocean, and the corners of her mouth turned up slightly, making her look as though she always wore a smile. Jake looked over to the left side of the screen. She was five foot seven, one hundred twenty pounds. So far, so good. He looked back at her photo. Although only a head shot, the tops of her shoulders peeked into the frame to reveal a splatter of freckles. They complemented those sprinkling the bridge of the woman's

slightly turned-up nose. Classic girl-next-door looks.
Jake liked that.

Under the Comments heading, Jake read about
all the things Malibu Miss liked to do in her spare
time, what she did for a living, and what her favorite
TV shows were. He stopped when he came to the
bottom of the screen. He had to read what came
next—twice. Blue Collar Guys Need Not Reply.
Jake's shoulder muscles tensed.

All three men stared at the woman's request for
a certain type of man. They were quiet for a long
moment.

"Pass," Gordy said firmly. "That's crazy. A woman
writes something like that, and she's got her head
in the clouds."

"You don't know anything," Pete said to Gordy.
"This woman obviously likes the finer things in life.
She wants to bypass all the jerks like you. What's
wrong with that? I'd be willing to bet she's a class act."

"I don't know," Jake said, shaking his head
doubtfully.

"Look at her. She's cute. Blonde." Pete nudged
Jake with his elbow as if he knew that blondes were
a weak spot. "Just think about it," Pete said, tapping
the screen with his finger.

Jake looked back at the woman's picture. He
pushed back from the computer. "She doesn't want
a guy like me."

"Wrong," Pete said. "You're exactly the kind of
guy she wants. She just doesn't know it yet."

Jake and Gordy laughed.

"Better get those glasses checked, old timer,"
Gordy told Pete. He poked at the screen. "She
wants an ed-u-ca-ted man. Someone like you."

Pete shook his head. "Jake's got more than enough education."

Gordy laughed, and Jake shot him a frown. "What's so funny?"

"Nothing. It's just that this woman doesn't indicate any desire for a guy who's educated in the fine art of beer."

"Tell you what," Pete said to Jake, "let's make a bet. You go out with this woman for the summer, and I say you'll be able to convince her you've got what she wants."

"I'm not interested in going out with her. She's not my type," Jake said. His friends seemed to have forgotten the whole purpose behind this was really to get Gordy straightened out. Trying to pull a fast one over on Malibu Miss would only complicate things.

"I'll take that bet," Gordy interrupted.

"How do you know? You haven't even met her," Pete said to Jake.

"He's scared," Gordy said.

"I'm not scared. I just don't see any purpose in wasting my time on a woman who wouldn't be interested in a guy like me."

"Like I said, I'll take that bet," Gordy said. "Jake would have to give up beer. He couldn't do that. Not even for a week. And how would he explain those calluses on his hands?"

Jake shot him a shut-the-hell-up look. "Gee, I didn't think you'd noticed."

Pete rubbed his chin. "What about numb nuts there? Don't you want to see him find a nice woman?"

"Exactly. That's what this is all about. So let's keep looking." Pete and Gordy stared at him. Shit.

They knew he was just trying to make excuses. "Fine. Okay, you win. Fifty bucks."

Pete slapped a hand down on the table. "All you need to do is get a digital picture. How about the one I took of you sitting on the edge of the pool at the new construction site?"

"Yeah, the one with his shirt off," Gordy said with a laugh. "Let Blondie get a good look at how manly Jake is. She might change her mind about the kind of guy she wants."

"Can't we just keep looking?" Jake asked.

Pete shook his head. "This is the one."

"Yeah," Gordy agreed. "You know how much you like a challenge."

"Heck, how about an extra fifty to get her in bed?" Jake offered sarcastically.

"Now you're talkin'," Gordy said.

"It's settled then," Pete said with a grin.

Jake looked back at the screen and read the woman's bio once more. The same feeling he got when he ate an entire pizza mixed with a pitcher of beer settled firmly in his stomach. He was going to need a lot of Tums.

The front door was still red when Pepper got home from work the next day. Good. She didn't feel like deciphering Lucy's actions tonight.

Lucy came out of the bathroom. Her mouth oozed toothpaste, and she had a purple toothbrush in her hand. Lucy always used a purple toothbrush. She claimed purple was the color of prosperity. Okay, so she'd have rich teeth.

Lucy walked over to the kitchen sink and spat out a mouthful of froth. "You're home early," she said.

Pepper brushed past her. "Not many beginners in the new yoga class, so I didn't have to waste time with a lot of explanation." She dropped her gym bag in the hallway and went to her room. She changed her clothes, and when she opened the door, Lucy was standing outside waiting.

"You call him?" she asked Pepper.

"No," Pepper said. "Forget about Henry. I have."

"Don't you think it's better to get closure on these things? Whether you want to believe it or not, one's actions do have consequences. Just as one's surroundings influence one's life." Lucy's forehead gathered into a frown. "You should be thankful that I'm watching out for you and trying to keep you safe."

"Oh, I am. I just figure since you've got us covered, that leaves me free to be as careless as I want, and everything will be fine." Pepper headed down the hall.

"It doesn't work like that," Lucy said. "You have to do your part. I can't follow behind you and clean up your messes." She picked up Pepper's gym bag and put it in the closet.

Pepper made herself a quick sandwich and then went back to her room. She turned on the computer, and in a few minutes, she was logged in to the Better Half website. She opened her account and saw that she had twenty responses. *Twenty.*

"Geez, I didn't realize so many men were into snobs," Lucy commented.

"First, I am not a snob. That would be Simone. Maybe these men are like me—tired of wasting their time." Pepper moved all but one of the responses into a Save For Later file. She clicked on the remaining one. It was from a guy named Jake Hunter.

"You'll like this one," she assured Lucy. "I already checked him out."

Hello, Malibu Miss. Jake Hunter here. My sentiments exactly. Why waste time with someone you can't begin to get serious about? You spend your spare time playing in the sand? Sounds like you live in the right place . . .

"He thinks you like to *play* in the sand? Boy, is he in for a surprise!"

Pepper giggled. Everyone else might call it playing, but she couldn't be more serious about it. "I'll say."

Lucy continued to read. "He actually sounds . . . normal," she said after a minute.

"Normal, but interesting," Pepper said, ready to defend her choice.

Lucy shrugged. "Don't be surprised if he has a third eye in the back of his head."

Pepper clicked on the photo icon to enlarge Jake's picture. Several seconds later, dreamy brown eyes looked back at her from the screen. She was a sucker for brown eyes. Both women leaned in closer.

"Better than normal," Pepper said.

"Maybe," Lucy said. "But it *is* only a headshot."

"Now who's the snob? With those eyes, I'm willing to take a chance," Pepper said as she began typing a response.

Malibu Miss is interested in meeting you for dining, star gazing, playing in the sand . . . call 310-555-14—"

"*Wait!* You're not giving him our home number, are you? Why not your cell phone?" Lucy's voice had risen to pitch five, panic level.

"Calm down. Don't start foaming at the mouth. You'll give yourself a hernia."

"How can I be calm when you'll soon be inviting potential criminals into our home? You might as well write our phone number on all the public bathroom walls." Lucy stood and began pacing.

Pepper swung around in her chair. "Does that man look like a criminal?" she said, pointing at the screen where Jake's image gazed out, almost as big as life. "Besides, if he is a criminal," she said, "he's a white-collar criminal."

"I don't know how you can be so blasé about this. We live in Los Angeles. We can't even go to bed and leave our door unlocked here."

"Gawd," Pepper said. She gave an eye roll and let out an exasperated breath. "Now you sound like my mom. C'mon. Doesn't he sound normal? He certainly looks trustworthy. He's handsome and—"

"Ted Bundy," Lucy said.

Pepper waved her hand in dismissal. She stared at Jake's picture. "I have a feeling. I can't explain it. He's got . . ." She reached up and touched the screen.

"Dreamy eyes?"

Pepper gave her a sideways glance.

"Money?"

Pepper lifted her chin. "Maybe. And if he got it by being a white-collar criminal, then he's probably smart, too."

"Fine," Lucy said, shaking her head. "I can see there's no point arguing with you." She looked around Pepper's room, and her gaze landed on the far right corner. "Since you're so determined to follow this destructive path, it might help if you got rid of that dead plant and put something nice and fluffy—and pink—in its place." She got down on the floor and looked under Pepper's bed.

Amusement played at the corners of Pepper's mouth. Right now, Lucy was staring at a pile of clothes, books, and miscellaneous boxes of junk. She wouldn't be able to sleep tonight.

Lucy sat up and pointed. "That's a problem. How do you expect to attract the love of your life with all that clutter?" She took another peek. "And dust?"

Pepper held up a hand. "That's not clutter. That's my life. And every bit of it is important to me."

Lucy's lips formed a thin line. "Well, it's not very conducive to love." She bent over and pulled up the duvet cover. "You might want to tape a red ribbon along this metal bed frame, too."

"Whatever," Pepper said.

Lucy got up to leave. She grabbed a strand of red hair and twisted it into a knot. "I'll leave you alone while you finish your response to Mr. Hot and Heavy. I've got flowers to arrange."

Pepper gazed at the screen. *Jake Hunter,* she mouthed his name. It was a good, clean name. It was the kind of name that rolled easily off her tongue.

She pushed the send button, and as she was closing up, one more message came in. It could wait, maybe forever. Right now, she needed to experience some mindless entertainment. She intended to sit in front of the TV for the next two or three hours and let her mind blank out. It'd been one of those days.

Pepper plopped herself down on the sofa and grabbed the remote. She turned on the television. "What do you think of the bartender at Beachside?" she asked Lucy.

"Brad? I thought you were trying to get away from that type of man."

"He's pretty hot. Not many women would pass up a chance to be with him."

"Only if they knew him. Or were smart."

"I think he likes me."

"*No!*"

"What if there's more to him than meets the eye?"

"Any more to him is just what's under his clothes, not inside where it counts. Everything about that man is exposed, and if you're not careful, everything about you will be exposed. To him."

Pepper laughed. "Don't get your shorts in a wad. I'm just kidding." She flipped through several channels before finally settling on an old rerun of *Bonanza*. Little Joe was hot.

An hour later, when Pepper felt herself starting to do the head bob, she retired to her room. Two new messages had come in while she'd been watching TV, and she added them to the Save For Later file without reading them. She took one last look at Jake's picture. Now there was an image a girl could go to bed with.

Chapter 5

"You call that woman yet?" Gordy asked as Jake handed him a beer.

"Nope."

"You going to?"

"Don't have her phone number yet," Jake said. He picked up the remote control and started flipping channels.

He stopped on ESPN and gave his friend a quizzical look. "What's it to you?"

"I got fifty bucks riding on it." Gordy twisted the top off his beer. "And I want to win it fair and square, not by default. Not only that, I don't plan to stop dating while you take your sweet time. Lucky for you, Sherry's out of town this week with her husband." He drank half the bottle and propped his feet up on the coffee table.

"You said you were ready to stop seeing her anyway." Jake sucked a long draught into his mouth and swallowed. "Don't you get tired of waiting for seconds?"

Gordy shrugged. "It doesn't feel like seconds when I'm with her."

"Well, you can kiss that fifty good-bye," Jake muttered under his breath.

Gordy grabbed the remote from him. "Let's make it a hundred."

Jake stared at the television.

"Chickenshit," Gordy said. "You don't think you can pull it off, do you?"

"You mean fool her into believin' I'se an educated man?" Jake said. He hung his mouth open like he was too dumb to know which way was up.

"Asshole." Gordy got up and went to the kitchen. He returned a minute later with two old wine glasses that Jake kept around just in case. In his other hand was a bottle of red wine.

Jake looked up at him. His forehead wrinkled. "What's this?"

"Wine."

"I can see that. What's it for?"

"It's what educated people drink," Gordy said.

"You don't know anything about wine."

"I know. But Pete does. He picked it out."

"Screw you guys," Jake said, setting the glass down on the table.

"That's what I thought," Gordy said. "Cluck, cluck."

Jake eyed his friend suspiciously and settled back onto the sofa to nurse his beer. "We'll see about that."

Gordy gave him a toothy grin.

Brad spilled piña colada mix all over the counter. He swore under his breath. That was the third drink he'd dumped this shift, and it would come out of his pocket. Vic was due home today, and Brad still wasn't convinced Marta would keep her mouth shut.

Fucking women today. They had a lot of nerve, always thinking they called the shots. If it was possible, they'd probably do away with men altogether.

He chased his anger away long enough to remember how Pepper's legs had looked through the thin fabric of her skirt. Damn. That was the woman he should be taking to bed. No amount of flirting or special drinks had gotten him any closer to closing that deal though. Maybe he was losing his touch. Or maybe Pepper was just a typical woman, having her fun playing head games with him. He laughed. It made him want her all the more.

Brad shoved a piece of lime onto the rim of a glass and pushed it across the counter. He'd play Pepper's game all she wanted. Eventually, she would give in. "Order up," he called to the waitress.

It was Saturday, and Jake was surprised to find himself in such a state of eagerness. Eager to check his messages on the computer. Eager to speak with Malibu Miss. What surprised him even more was that he'd actually gone ahead and responded to her ad. She'd made a request for a certain type of man, after all. Jake ran a hand through his hair. He didn't know why he'd bothered.

He sat at the kitchen table, cup of coffee in hand, staring at the printout of the blonde's bio. They did have several things in common. Mainly, a love for the outdoors. Of course, living in Malibu made it easy to love the open sky.

Jake finished his coffee and took the cup to the sink. He stared out the kitchen window into his backyard for a good two minutes. If he thought about it long enough, he could probably come up with a long list of things that needed fixing around the house and yard. Anything to keep him busy, too busy to call Malibu Miss.

Jake's backyard was a good size, manageable for one person, complete with patio and built-in barbecue area. A stone wall with a magenta-colored bougainvillea sprawled along one side, bringing some life to the otherwise brown landscape. The other side of the wall, which he shared with a neighbor, was bare, except for the two feral cats that were perched atop it. One of the cats hopped down, and Jake strained to see where it'd gone. Trees blocked all but a small view into the neighbor's yard, and he saw that the old woman who lived there had put out a paper dish with cat food. The cat was there eating. Jake had tried unsuccessfully to get his neighbor to stop feeding them, explaining how her good intentions would do nothing but make the problem continue. She said she felt sorry for them. He was sorry, too, but providing food wasn't the answer.

Jake turned away from the window. His eyes were drawn to his laptop. Malibu Miss hadn't even given him her real name. He took a deep breath and tried to shake off the jitters. He'd never even been this nervous before performing surgery. It's not like he'd never called a girl before. Had to be the coffee.

Jake sat back down at the table. Maybe he had Malibu Miss all wrong. Maybe she'd simply gone out with too many jerks. His anxiety got even worse when he saw that he'd received a message from her. Short and sweet, it said, "Call me." She even gave him her real name this time. Pepper Bartlett. So this was it. Probably too late to turn back now without looking like he was one of those jerks she was trying to avoid.

With a resigned sigh, Jake picked up the phone. Punching in her number took determination. After each push, he told himself to hang up, but finally, he punched in the last number. Someone picked up after the third ring. Really too late to back out now.

"Hello?" a gentle but firm voice answered.

The woman's voice, light and airy, already showed promise, and Jake instantly felt better about making the call. What the hell was he supposed to say now? That he was the man of her dreams? *Christ*, like his mouth would ever utter those words.

"Hello?" the voice said again.

"Ah, hello," Jake began, "I, ah—"

"Yes?"

"What the hell . . . Pepper?" Jake ran a hand over his face. He felt a flush of heat fill his cheeks. "What am I doing?" he mumbled.

"Excuse me?"

"Your ad . . . for a man. I'm Jake Hunter."

"Oh," the voice on the other end said flatly. "You want Pepper."

The mouthpiece was covered, and he heard the woman call out, "Pep-p-p-pe-er-r."

Jake spent the next several seconds wondering what kind of excuse he could use to get himself out of this nonsense.

"She'll be right here," the woman said, coming back on the line.

Several quiet seconds passed, and she spoke to him again.

"Are you by any chance a serial killer or rapist or anything else we should know about?"

"Huh?"

"Nothing. Here's Pepper."

"This is Pepper," a silky smooth voice threaded through the line and into Jake's ear. His grip tightened on the receiver. Any thoughts he'd had about hanging up or making excuses dissolved.

"And this is Jake Hunter," he said, doing his best to sound relaxed and casual.

"Yes?"

"I'm calling about your ad?"

"Yes," Pepper said lightly.

Jake detected amusement. "Damn," he said quietly cursing Gordy and Pete for getting him into this.

"Hm-m," the woman's sweet voice seemed to consider. "I don't know. The man of my dreams might not sound so exasperated."

Jake pulled the phone away from his ear and gave it a perplexed look. If it weren't for the magical lilt in her voice, he'd definitely hang up. He pushed the receiver back up to his ear and tried to sound nonchalant. "Not at all," he said quietly, unable to think of anything else to say.

Pepper laughed. "Well, Jake Hunter, I'm glad you called."

The tension in Jake's shoulders finally eased. Malibu Miss didn't sound like a desperate woman. "Would you like to get together for coffee? Or dinner?" Jake suggested.

"I thought you'd never ask," Pepper said. "Tomorrow night?"

Jake glanced down at his free hand. It looked like it was covered with alligator skin. He shoved it into his jeans pocket, as though she might be able to see it through the phone.

"Well?"

"Uh, yeah. That'll be fine, great," Jake answered. He pulled his hand out of his pocket and looked it over once more. It screamed hard labor. Blue collar. If there was a miracle that could be performed to transform his hands by tomorrow night, he was at a loss as to what that might be. The only solution would be to wear gloves like Michael Jackson. Hm-m. That might not go over so well. Jake hadn't considered what he'd have to go through to pull this off. He could kick himself, and he was damn sure going to kick Gordy and Pete as soon as he saw them.

"You sure?"

"Absolutely," Jake said, but he wasn't.

They settled on seven P.M. He had over twenty-four hours to come up with an excuse to back out or somehow find that miracle. The only miracle worker he knew was Theresa, Pete's wife. As a beauty consultant, she'd know what to do.

Pepper hung up the phone. She'd felt Lucy's glare burning into her back through her entire conversation with Jake. Lucy's arms were folded across her chest, and she was giving Pepper that motherly look.

"You know, I could actually *feel* you standing there behind me."

"We had an agreement," Lucy said. Her face glowed as red as the hair that stuck out from under the white towel she had wrapped around her head.

Pepper's eyebrows rose innocently. "I forgot?"

"No,"—Lucy shook her head—"don't do that. I'm the one who gets away with that, not you. You agreed I could meet these men before you brought them home." She stood, feet planted firmly in place, blocking Pepper from leaving the kitchen.

"You *talked* to him. That's almost the same thing," Pepper reasoned. She went over to the coffee pot and plugged it in. She reached into the cupboard and shoved aside the red envelope for a measuring spoon.

"Not even close," Lucy said, the pitch of her voice rising with each word. "There are freaks out there."

"Oh, Gawd. I'm going to have to limit how much you and my mother talk if you keep that up," Pepper warned. "Besides," she said, picking Lucy's newest feng shui book up off the counter and flipping through it, "I'm sure there's a *cure* in here to ward off most every kind of freak."

Lucy snatched the book from Pepper's hands and held it to her chest. "Yes, and I'm going to go and find it right now." She spun around and stomped away, pausing to flutter the wind chimes outside the bathroom door.

Feng shui. Feng *phooey*. Pepper laughed softly. She loved Lucy dearly, but sometimes, it was hard to take her seriously. She'd never have thought her best friend would be the one to get into all that stuff. When they were younger, it was she who believed in magic and dreams and superstition and all that stuff. But as they got older, Lucy started taking more and more of an interest in unseen forces. She had become diligent in making her surroundings come together in complete harmony, "thereby bringing good luck, happiness, and prosperity into her life."

Pepper had known Lucy since grade school, and this was as happy as she'd ever seen her. If feng shui and believing in things that couldn't be seen was the source of that happiness, Pepper was all for it. Herself? She needed more. She needed to know that decent men still existed. Men who would be there today, tomorrow, and forever. In short, she wanted a man she could depend on.

Three short beeps announced the coffee was done. Pepper poured herself a cup and added a packet of Equal and some half-and-half, then grabbed her cell phone and took it with her out to the deck. She breathed deeply of the fresh morning air. Wind whispered through her hair, and a cool mist cloaked her bare skin. She touched a cushion on one of the beach chairs. It was damp, so she set her coffee on the wood-splintered rail that surrounded the deck and dialed Simone's number.

"Hey, girl. It's me," Pepper said into Simone's answering machine. "The weatherman has promised everlasting sunshine, so come on over. We'll gossip, and you can watch me build sand castles." She pushed the end button and picked up her coffee, taking it down the steps with her to the beach. A flock of sanderlings raced along the shore, moving in and out with the waves as fast as their little legs could carry them. A lone seagull and a few sandpipers skittered among them, hoping for leftovers.

Pepper glanced back at the small house that she and Lucy shared. It brought a smile to her lips and to her heart. Barely big enough for one person, let alone two, it was a haven. The added bonus of having the beach for her backyard and the sea to sing her to sleep was more than she could've ever asked for.

Sunny days, people laughing, kids playing . . . it all helped to cover the day's aches. But over the happy sounds, Pepper could always hear her mother. "All the sun in the world doesn't make living in that mess worth it." She knew her mother was talking mostly about the traffic, but it was also the crime, the different culture—a dangerous foreign land where innocent people were murdered in their sleep. Pepper sighed. California, it was where people came to make their dreams come true. That's why she'd come here, and she wouldn't trade it for anything. Jake Hunter's image came to mind. Well, maybe . . .

Through the wet sand, Pepper felt something hard. She dug with her toes until the object showed itself. A broken shell. She picked it up and tossed it back into the water. A shell that was still intact was a rare find. Most disappeared as quickly as they surfaced, picked up by tourists strolling the beach or reclaimed by the sea. No matter. She had plenty of shells. And what really made her backyard perfect was the abundance of sand. She might not have the perfect man to love, but she was definitely having a love affair—with Malibu.

Pepper strolled along the beach. The ocean's roar filling her ears helped to calm her nerves. She felt the usual apprehension—and excitement—about her upcoming date. Several scenarios were possible. She and Jake could take their time getting to know each other, go places, do things, talk, hold hands, fall in love. Or, maybe there'd be fire from the first moment they laid eyes on each other. Worst case, nothing would happen. No sparks. No wow factor. *That* would be disappointing. She'd be back at square one. Oh, how she hoped for at least pure animal lust. The kind that caused a tingling sensation between her legs all the way down to her toes. A moan escaped her lips.

"Pardon?" a man passing by her said.

"Oh." Pepper felt her face turn red. She put a hand to her mouth. "Sorry. I, um, stepped on a shell." A wave rolled in, and Pepper dipped her hand into the salt water. She rubbed the cool liquid over the back of her neck. If she was already moaning and Jake Hunter hadn't even touched her, what would happen when, or if, he did? Jeezus. She'd been around Simone too long.

Brad bristled at the note in his hand. He wiped a hand down his face. Marta wasn't about to let this thing between them go. All the more reason to find another place to live before all holy hell hit the fan.

He crumpled the note and threw it at a wastebasket that sat in the corner of the living room. It hit the rim and bounced onto the floor just as the front door opened.

"Looks like you need practice," a slender man in his early thirties said. He picked up the wad of paper. Vic.

Brad's throat tightened as he stared at the wad of paper in Vic's hand. Vic tossed it into the air a couple of times and then into the basket. Breathe, Brad. By the grin on Vic's face, Brad quickly surmised that Marta hadn't told him anything.

"You look like you just saw a ghost," Vic said.

"I didn't know you were coming home," Brad said, avoiding eye contact.

Scratch wiggled his way over to Vic and demanded a greeting. He reached down and scrubbed the dog's fur vigorously. "Is it your day off? How come you're not out somewhere trying to get laid?"

"No date tonight. Thought I'd just sit around home."

"Been a long day, huh?"

Long didn't begin to describe Brad's day.

Vic dropped his coat over the back of a chair. "Did you cook me dinner, honey?"

"There's a can of Spam in there." Brad nodded toward the kitchen.

"Speaking of honey . . . where's my woman?"

Brad laughed nervously. "Maybe she didn't want to look at your ugly face."

Vic gave Brad a hand gesture and went into the kitchen. He came out with a bag of pretzels and a beer.

"That's healthy," Brad said.

"Better'n Spam." Vic sank down into a black leather recliner and popped the top on his beer.

Ten minutes passed with Brad and Vic making small talk. Brad kept his eye on the clock. Tic, toc, tic fucking toc. He didn't know how much longer he could sit there. Marta could be home at any minute. She must have known Vic was coming home, and she just hadn't told him. The bitch had a sick sense of humor, that was for sure, leaving that note on the counter. Vic could have easily come home before him and found it. If this was Marta's way of making his life miserable, she was doing a fine job.

Sweat ran down Brad's back. He didn't know if it was the heat or his conscience, but he had to do something. Waiting for the axe to fall didn't work for him. For the time being, their secret was probably safe. Marta needed Vic. She didn't even have a job. Even so, her keeping her mouth shut was a long shot, and it was obvious she'd take every opportunity she could to torture him. Would she risk losing Vic? Who knew? But as long as she and Vic stayed together, Brad knew he'd always be sweating whether or not Marta would suddenly decide to tell Vic the truth.

Fuck. He'd created a fucking monster.

Drops of water rolled down the side of Vic's beer can. Brad swallowed dryly. His tongue felt like it was stuck to the roof of his mouth. He went to the kitchen and opened the refrigerator. Not much food, plenty of beer. He grabbed two cans and went back to the living room. He handed one to Vic. If he kept his friend drunk, Marta could do whatever the fuck she wanted. Vic'd be too shitfaced to care. For the first hour anyway.

Vic stood and grabbed his jacket. "I want to show you something." He reached inside and pulled out a little black velvet box. When Brad saw what was inside, he felt like he was going to be sick.

"Damn, don't get so excited," Vic said. He slumped back into the leather chair. "What's with you anyway? I let you know I'm getting married, and all you can do is give me a long face."

Brad looked up at him. "I'm happy for you, man." He shrugged. "You know my feelings about being tied down to one woman. It's just sad to see it happening to my best friend." He took a swallow of beer, hoping it'd help wash down the bile.

"Yeah, I know. They spend all your money . . . play head games . . . keep you from getting together with your friends." Vic shoved a handful of pretzels into his mouth. He shook his head. "They ain't all like that. Especially not my Marta."

Brad simply nodded. Poor schmuck. Love had made his friend blind.

Chapter 6

Jake showed up at Pete's house looking like a homeless puppy, wearing a navy blue T, jeans that had a rip in one leg, and tennis shoes that were crusted with cement.

Theresa's large brown eyes moved from his shoes all the way up to his hair. "When's this date?" she asked.

"Tonight."

Her lips pulled tight. "I don't know," she said, slowly shaking her head. "It's gonna be tough." Her face warmed into a smile, and she reached out and took him by the arm. "Get in here."

Jake followed her to the kitchen, and Theresa gestured for him to sit at the table. A few minutes later, she slid a bowl filled with green stuff in front of him. She picked up one of his hands and looked it over front and back, making a *tsk-tsk* sound. While the hand soaked in the green liquid, she surveyed his face, squinting and examining every inch, and Jake thought he saw a look he recognized as pity in her brown eyes.

"I'll be right back," Theresa said. She disappeared

and returned a few minutes later with another bowl. This one contained a creamy blue substance. "Close your eyes and relax," she said, gently pushing back his head.

Jake was happy to close his eyes. The blue goo was none too easy on them, and they'd begun to water almost immediately. The odor wasn't all that pleasant either. Peppermint, avocado, and sewer gas.

"Got a gas mask? What the hell is that stuff anyway? I hope it's not toxic."

"Don't worry. Theresa's gonna fix you up all pretty." She finished spreading the creamy mixture over his face, and then she disappeared.

Jake did his best to relax, but the smell was pretty hard to ignore, especially since it was in such close proximity to his nose. He was just glad none of the guys he worked with were there to see him.

"What's this?" a familiar voice said, and then the room filled with laughter.

Jake squinted with one eye and saw Pete doubled over in the doorway. Theresa would scold him if he moved, so the only recourse he had was to give Pete the finger. When Pete finally stood up straight, his eyes glistened.

"Glad you think this is so funny . . . seeing as you're responsible," Jake said.

Pete wiped tears from his eyes. "What the hell are you doing?"

"He's getting a manicure and a facial," Theresa said, walking into the room, "so you can close your mouth now." She walked over and lifted Jake's hand out of the green goo, then placed his other one in the bowl. "By the way, how're your toes?" she asked him.

Jake tucked his feet under the chair, and Pete let out another howl. At a stern look from Theresa, Pete got quiet and sat down at the table opposite Jake.

"What the hell is that? Antifreeze?" Pete's lips trembled as he fought to stifle another outburst.

"You know where you can kiss," Jake said, doing his best not to frown. The mask Theresa had slathered on his face was beginning to tighten, and he had a feeling that messing it up might give her cause to do him great bodily harm.

She slapped him anyway. "Watch your language, gringo. And you . . ." she said, jabbing a finger at Pete. "Leave him alone."

Pete burst out laughing again, and Jake swore revenge.

A few minutes later, Theresa placed a warm towel over Jake's face. It felt pretty good. Great, in fact. Maybe women had the right idea with this facial, manicure, pedicure stuff they were always treating themselves to. Theresa left the towel, and Jake felt the mask begin to soften. After a minute, she gently wiped the goo from Jake's face. He looked over at Pete. Pete looked like a man who was about to have a stroke.

"That's what I get for taking your advice," Jake said. He reached up and touched his face. His skin was silky smooth, almost like a woman's, though he'd never say it out loud. And never in front of Pete. "This woman better be worth it, that's all I got to say."

"Have," Pete corrected him.

"What?"

"*Have*. That's all I *have* to say. You need to think about word choices."

"Right," Jake said, shaking his head. He had a feeling that all this lying stuff was going to be harder than he thought.

"It's not gonna matter with this," Theresa said, grabbing a lock of Jake's hair. She picked a pair of clippers up from the table.

Jake's eyes grew big, and he leaned away from her. "No way. You're not cutting my hair. That's where I draw the line."

"You *need* a haircut." Theresa grabbed his hair and pulled. "Whatcha going to tell her you do with hair down to your shoulders? Now sit still."

Jake sat up straight in the chair before she pulled any harder. He glanced over at Pete. Pete's lips were drawn into a line so tight, they looked about ready to split. Jake mouthed *I'm going to kill you.*

"Just a little. *Please?*" he pleaded with Theresa, holding up his thumb and index finger.

"Don't worry, gringo. You'll be beautiful."

"I'd rather be handsome."

Theresa snipped and cut, and occasionally, Jake saw Pete wince. Closing his eyes was his only defense. He and his long black hair had been together for quite some time, and it was hard enough to say good-bye without getting a blow-by-blow account from Pete's facial expressions.

Finally, Theresa laid down the clippers, and not a minute too soon for Jake. She handed him a mirror, and he took a cautious peek. He turned his head from left to right. Theresa was right. He was beautiful. He reached up and traced the two-inch scar that ran from behind one ear and down his neck. He hadn't seen that in quite some time. Not since he'd grown his hair longer. No hiding it now, that was for sure. He'd been told it gave him character, but would Malibu Miss think so? And would she ask about it? If so, that'd be one more lie he'd have to concoct. *Damn.*

"Have you thought about an occupation?" Pete asked.

Jake gave him a blank stare.

"The woman explicitly said, 'no blue collar guys,'" Pete reminded him.

Jake's forehead wrinkled in thought. After a minute, his lips spread in a smile. "Easy. I'll be an architect."

Pete studied him for a minute, then shook his head. "I don't know . . ."

"Perfect, huh? Anything I might need to know, I can ask you." He slapped Pete's back. "Besides, how hard could it be to pretend for a summer? I can wow her with my knowledge of tensile strength, penalty clauses, blueprints . . ."

"You don't become an architect overnight. I went to college for my education," Pete said proudly.

"Yeah, you've told me all about your education. From what I recall, it involved more *sex* education than book education—" Pain suddenly shot up the front of Jake's leg, thanks to a swift kick from Pete.

"I'm glad to see you're so enthusiastic. A couple of days ago, you didn't want anything to do with this. What's changed?"

Jake rubbed his hands together. "I guess having my hands soft as a baby's butt and with hair that's looking so good, I feel I owe it to myself to meet this woman and see how she likes the new me."

Theresa rolled her eyes.

"Yeah, well, if it turns out she's a psycho, I don't want her knowing I was your teacher," Pete said.

"Don't worry, pal. Pete Erickson University will be our little secret." Jake looked into the mirror again. "I'm gonna miss the hair, but I guess it beats having to wear a ponytail when the thermometer rises."

"Yeah, you're beau-tee-ful," Pete said, blowing him a kiss.

"One last thing." Jake turned to Pete, his face serious. Pete looked worried. "Relax," he said. He rested a hand on Pete's shoulder. "Since this was your idea, I must insist on borrowing your car."

Horror replaced the worry on Pete's face.

"My Audi? No way." Pete shook his head vigorously and looked to Theresa for support. She grinned. "You could help here, you know," he said to her.

Theresa threw up her hands. "A smart woman never gets in the middle of her man's deals."

Pete turned back to Jake. "What's wrong with your truck?"

"A truck?" Jake said. "C'mon." He gave Theresa a wink.

"Give the gringo your car," she urged her husband.

Pete turned and glared at her. "Why not *your* car?"

"Too small. It's a woman's car," she said with a warm smile. "At least that's what my husband said when he bought it for me."

Pete reluctantly grabbed a set of keys from the kitchen counter and removed one key, tossing it to Jake. "That car has no scratches, no dents—"

"Honey, what about that new dent in the passenger side—"

"What?" Pete said, his voice shrill.

Jake and Theresa laughed.

The silver Audi was Pete's new baby, and Jake knew he'd better return it in perfect condition. The thought of what Pete might do to him if it wasn't made him consider giving up this crazy bet and taking the fifty-dollar loss—for about two seconds. He pocketed the key.

"How do I look?" Pepper asked Lucy. She made a full turn in front of the mirror. She wore a black formfitting dress that hung gently from the outer edge of each shoulder. A low-cut neckline revealed just a hint of plump flesh. She smoothed the dress, turning this way and that before stopping to face Lucy.

Lucy took a bite of her Red Delicious apple and gave Pepper an appraising eye. "Too short," she said, swallowing a mouthful.

Pepper instinctively reached up to her hair. She'd just been to the hairdresser, and she was lamenting the loss of more than two inches. "I knew I shouldn't have gotten it cut—"

"Not your hair. Your *dress*."

"Huh?" Pepper looked down at the hemline. It rested just a scant six inches above her knees. "Are you kidding? This isn't short. And anyway, short is in, Luce."

Lucy shrugged. "You asked, I told."

Pepper stretched out a foot adorned with one of Kate Spade's finest strappy sandals. "It only seems short because my legs look oh so long in these new shoes."

Lucy finished her apple and wrapped it in a paper towel before throwing it into the wastebasket.

"If it looks short, it is short. What're you going to do—carry your shoes so they won't make your dress *look* short?"

Pepper stuck out her chin defensively. "Well, *I* think my legs are fabulous." Her forehead wrinkled into a frown. "It's my hair that's too short." She fingered the clipped edges, fluffing them out to make her hair look fuller.

Lucy waved a dismissive hand. "It'll grow back." She gave a quick sideways tilt to her head. "Anyway, shorter is easier to take care of."

Pepper pulled her bangs down as far as they would reach, then finally gave up and dropped her hands to her hips. "I don't care about easier. Easier isn't always better, Luce."

Lucy leaned around Pepper and looked at herself in the mirror. She pushed her short, red hair behind her ears and smiled. "Easier *and* better."

Pepper reached out and stuck her fingers into Lucy's hair. With a frenzied swish of her hand, she tossed it like a salad, then stepped back. She put her hands on her hips and looked at Lucy's hair appraisingly. "There. Now *that's* better."

She took a quick glance at her watch. "Jake will be here any minute. So much to do, so little time," she said, hurrying to the kitchen. She looked inside the refrigerator's vegetable and fruit bin and pushed aside apples, some little bags of carrots, and a head of leafy lettuce. Her search grew more frantic with each passing second.

"Is this what you're looking for?" Lucy held out a plump yellow lemon.

Pepper put a hand to her chest and blew out a relieved breath. "I was getting worried." She took the lemon from Lucy and sliced it into fourths, then squeezed its juice into a bowl and dipped her fingertips into it. She whisked her hands through her hair, then dipped her fingertips once more. This time, she ran her hands over her legs and all the way up under her dress.

"Expecting a visitor down there, are you?" Lucy asked her with raised eyebrows.

"Relax, Luce. I just don't want to overwhelm the guy. A little up front, a little hidden," Pepper explained, "and I smell like a fresh spring day."

"I don't know if you could consider it hidden under *that* dress."

Pepper ignored the remark and skipped happily back to her room. She opened her closet and reached up to the top shelf, pulling down a small, black sequined evening bag. She emptied the contents of her day purse onto her bed and spread everything out. She picked out a tube of lipstick, a tiny mirror, breath strips, her driver's license, and a wad of cash. It was a tight fit, but as long as she didn't use anything, it would all fit into the small bag.

"There," she said, snapping it shut. "I'm good to go." She turned and looked in the mirror once more, making sure everything was in place.

The doorbell rang, and a million butterflies did a frenzied dance inside Pepper's stomach. She felt like a schoolgirl waiting for her first kiss. She put a hand to her chest. Here she was getting so excited over a date when just a few short weeks ago, she'd sworn off men. Things certainly could change in the blink of an eye. After her dad had died, leaving her mom alone, Pepper had sworn never to let any man get close enough to have the kind of hold on her heart that could break it.

But here she was, actually looking forward to meeting this mystery man. Getting to know him, having him treat her like a princess . . . Of course, that's how it always started. Guys had the first couple of weeks down pat. Wining and dining and dancing and romancing . . . It made a girl feel like she was on top of the world. Then, suddenly, an earthquake or a landslide or something equally disastrous would happen, and all the good stuff turned into sitting in front of the TV and going to fast food joints and sex, sex, sex. Not that she didn't like sex. But guys didn't get it. If they wanted to continue having sex, sex, sex, then they needed to keep up the romance, romance, romance.

"Luce, go let him in."

"He's not *my* date."

"This is no time to be difficult. *Please* . . . let him in. I'll be right there. Go, *go*," Pepper said, pushing Lucy out of her room.

A minute later, the sound of a man's voice, deep and rich and intellectual-sounding, resonated down the hall. She took a deep breath and smiled. Time to meet this potential man of her dreams.

Pepper walked to the end of the short hallway and stopped to peer around the corner. What she saw made her look up at the ceiling and whisper, "Thank you, God." Jake was tall, and he was built like he could have played football. He certainly surpassed every physical requirement. And here she thought that men in suits were mostly nerdy-looking fellows who could only discuss things like stocks and bonds and how much their Ferraris cost.

Her gaze wandered up and down Jake's broad back, and she tried to imagine how he might look in blue jeans. She might be ready to try the flip side of blue jeans, but it was still important for any man she dated to look good when he was bent over the hood of her car. From where she stood, Jake had definite potential. She couldn't wait to see what the front of the package looked like.

His hair, full and dark, was cut to just above his ears, and it had that freshly trimmed look. A lawyer perhaps? Or *maybe*, Jake Hunter was in the entertainment business. Visions of cameras, lights, and dressing rooms whirled through Pepper's head.

"She's in her room making sure she's perfect," Pepper heard Lucy tell Jake.

Pepper put a hand to her mouth, stifling a gasp. What would Lucy divulge next? Did she intend to reveal her darkest secrets? Time to put a stop to this. She'd spent considerable time in front of the mirror perfecting her smile, and now she plastered it on and whisked herself into the room.

"You must be Jake." Pepper walked toward him with an outstretched hand. Dark-haired and delicious turned. His smile was wide, his teeth were white and perfect, and his eyes crinkled at the corners. Get out the butterfly net. Pepper felt an entire swarm take flight. If that thing about chemistry was true, she was infected. No cures, please.

"Excuse me," Lucy said, clearing her throat. "I'm going up to the roof to pick some flowers."

Pepper barely acknowledged Lucy, giving her a quick nod. Introducing her best friend to Jake didn't even occur to her. Lucy disappeared, and she and Jake were alone.

Jake's gaze roamed discreetly over Pepper from head to toe, though she noticed he was careful not to allow his eyes to linger on any one body part for too long. Pepper had gotten looks from other men. Like they were undressing her with their eyes. Jake's look was different. Like they'd known each other their entire lives. Pepper blushed. Warmth filled her as he stared into her eyes.

"You're beautiful," Jake said, offering her his hand. "Shall we go?"

Pepper took his hand. His touch was warm and cozy, and she felt safer than she had . . . probably ever. Pepper felt her heart swell, just like the Grinch when he finally found Christmas. *You're beautiful,* Jake had said. Not you *look* beautiful. But *you're beautiful.* Without a doubt, *you–are–beautiful.*

She did a quick mental calculation. At this rate, she and Jake would be planning a wedding in about two weeks. Her better sense interrupted that dream. He'd simply said three little words. And they weren't even the three little words a woman longs to hear. Still, her insides were feeling all gushy and mushy, and she prayed her condition was incurable.

Jake took her hand, and they stepped out into the cool night air. Jake paused on the porch and looked up to the rooftop. "Nice to meet you, Lucy," he yelled to her.

Lucy looked down at them. She gave him a genuine smile in return. "Nice to meet you, too."

Jake led Pepper over to a brand spanking new Audi. Under the streetlights, the car's silver paint shimmered like winter frost. Its curves were as sleek and sexy as some of her clients at Malibu Health.

Jake opened the passenger door, and she sank into the car's soft black leather upholstery. She watched him walk around the front of the car to the other side, unable to take her eyes off him. A gust of wind blew his dark hair up and feathered it back, and she noticed the faint outline of a scar along the side of his neck. Entertainment? Stuntman perhaps? Pepper started a mental list of questions to ask later.

Jake slid into the driver's seat, and Pepper swore she could feel the heat of his body. Although, it could've been the heated seats, too. Jake was so much more than she'd dared hope for, and she made another mental note to thank Simone for her wisdom.

"Have you ever been to the Buffalo Club?" he asked.

Pepper gave him her sweetest smile. "No. I've never heard of it." Excitement rushed through her faster than drinking on an empty stomach. Actually, experiencing any place with the man seated next to her would be exciting. She wasn't used to dating a man who didn't need to discuss with her where they were going, and his take-charge attitude was more refreshing than a morning swim in the Pacific Ocean.

Jake brought the Audi's engine to life, and a half hour later, they were driving through the streets of Santa Monica. Pepper used the time to examine Jake thoroughly. His hands were strong and curiously tan. Perhaps from being out in the sun, directing movie stars. Black hair, black suit, maroon pullover. The man looked like an ad from GQ.

Ten minutes after entering Santa Monica, they rolled up to the front of a building that resembled a deserted warehouse Pepper had seen in one too many movies where nothing good ever happened. She looked around. A cautionary chill ran up her spine when she saw that the street, too, had that certain "you don't belong here" look.

Chapter 7

Jake had never been to the Buffalo Club either, but Pete promised he and Pepper could look forward to an enchanted evening. Enchanted wasn't exactly the word he would have used to describe how he felt when he pulled up in front of the old building. Its gray exterior looked as though it hadn't seen a coat of paint in years, and the windows were covered with thick grime. The name Olympic Club was barely visible above a white door, and a sandwich board sitting next to it had the name Buffalo Club painted on both sides. He guessed the Olympic Club hadn't done so well—what a surprise—and the Buffalo Club had taken over.

What the hell did Pete have them walking into? His friend had never steered him wrong, and he wasn't the kind of guy to try and make a fool of a friend, but Jake wasn't feeling all that good about how things were going so far.

Jake checked the address twice on the directions Pete had given him. They were definitely at the right place.

If he had ever driven past this place, it would have

never occurred to him to stop in for a bite to eat or to have a drink. He glanced around the street looking for drunks and drug dealers—maybe a gangbanger or two—and was relieved not to see any.

Jake and Pepper looked at each other. He saw that she didn't have high expectations for their first date. Despite how things seemed right now, he had an amusing thought. If this date were to turn into a lifetime romance, it would be a great story to tell their kids someday.

After they'd sat at the curb for ten or fifteen seconds, the white door opened, and a man came out. He was well-dressed in a black suit and red tie. He approached Pepper's side of the car, then opened her door and offered her his hand. Since the man seemed to know exactly what his job was, Jake didn't see any cause for alarm.

Another man appeared at Jake's side of the car. He wished him a "good evening" and then relieved him of the car keys.

The men walked over to the door, and one of them held it while Jake and Pepper entered a dimly lit foyer. A cherrywood bar polished to a high gloss sat on the left, and a small lounge area lay on the right. The interior looked a good sight better than the outside of the building, but so far, it hadn't reached enchantment level. The place was quiet, except for a few hushed voices, and overhead, Mick Jagger sang "Angie" through some hidden speakers.

Jake and Pepper followed one of the men down a narrow hallway, and Jake was pleasantly surprised when he brushed shoulders with one of his favorite actors, James Caan. The actor had a beautiful woman draped on each arm, and the small group passed them and went into the lounge area. Things were beginning to look up.

They continued on through another door, and the sky opened above them as they entered a small courtyard. Brick walls covered in trumpet vines and red flowers circled the perimeter, shutting patrons off from, and making them forget, the outside world. Miniature lights twinkled like fireflies atop the brick wall, and Chinese lanterns glowed overhead, strung from one side of the wall to the other. They swung gently in the cross breeze. The space in the middle of the courtyard was limited, and it had only a dozen small tables that were each adorned with a floating candle.

Every detail spelled romance.

Jake looked over at Pepper. Her face was like a child's on Christmas morning. She was indeed enchanted.

The man who had escorted them that far disappeared, and they were greeted by a waiter in a red blazer. He directed them to one of the small tables. Jake paused before sitting to pull out Pepper's chair. When he looked across the candlelit table, her face had a warm glow, partly due to the candle, but mostly because she was beautiful. He took a really good look at her. Her online photo hadn't done her justice. Indeed, she was far more than he'd expected, and already, more than winning some stupid bet, he wanted to get to know the woman behind the impish smile.

Their eyes held, and a disturbing thought hit him. If by some chance, he and Pepper hit it off, them having this damned lie between them was no way to begin a relationship. And it would probably squelch any chance of them having a lifelong romance.

Jake certainly couldn't blame Pete and Gordy for the situation he found himself in. All they really wanted was for him to get out and have some fun, to get on with his life—so they could get on with theirs. Pete and Gordy had both spent many a Friday night baby-sitting him, and Pete had recently joked that Theresa was threatening to hire someone to follow him to make sure he wasn't cheating on her. Pete cheat? That was laughable.

The waiter returned for their drink order, and Jake hesitated. The guy at the next table was drinking a microbrew. Jake swallowed. He wanted one so bad he could already feel it sloshing down his throat.

Pepper ordered some kind of girlie froufrou drink that he thought looked like the same stuff Pete's wife had made him soak his hands in.

It'd been a while since he'd had anything to drink besides beer. Popping a top was just plain easier than mixing up some exotic concoction that required remembering a recipe.

"I'll have a Knob Creek," he told the waiter.

Their drinks came, and Jake took a large swallow. His stomach was empty, and the alcohol spread quickly through his system. The bourbon was just as smooth as he remembered. Better than smooth. It soothed his chiseled nerves, and he even managed to convince himself that since he was lying for a good reason, it wasn't so bad.

"I liked your ad," Jake said in a pathetic attempt at making small talk. He wanted to kick himself. It'd been a while since he'd had to say anything witty to someone of the fairer sex. If he'd just given it some thought, he was sure he could have come up with something better, like, "Nice weather, huh?"

"You didn't think it was . . . offensive?" Pepper asked, looking a bit sheepish.

Jake shrugged. "You know what you want." He felt himself relax as the bourbon continued doing its job. A bell clanged in the distance, and he wondered if Pepper enjoyed sailing. A couple of mornings ago he'd stood at the back of the construction site and looked out over the Pacific Ocean. In the distance, he'd seen the glimmer of light from a ship through the overcast sky, and it had reminded him of a falling star.

Jake stared into Pepper's eyes. Even the brightest falling star couldn't compare to the sparkle he saw in those eyes.

"So, what do you do?" Pepper asked.

There it was. Her first question to his first lie. And just when things were going so well. Jake's heart thumped, and he felt like it would come to a complete stop. His mind groped for any answer that wasn't a lie. He'd never realized that deception required so much energy and thought.

Pepper's slender fingers twisted the edge of her cocktail napkin. She was nervous, too. Maybe because of her own secrets. Probably, he should find out what her story was before he kicked himself for what he was doing. Jake picked up his glass and emptied it.

"Architecture. I'm an architect," he said. The words lay bitter on his tongue, and he knew that no amount of bourbon, no matter how smooth, could wash away that bitterness.

Jake thought he saw a fleeting look of disappointment on Pepper's face. How could she be disappointed? He drove an Audi, for crissakes. Or rather, Pete did. But he *could*. Seconds later, the look disappeared, and she gave him a genuine smile. Which only made him feel worse.

"There've been some great homes built up on the Malibu hillside. Were any of them your work?" She'd sufficiently mauled the corner of her napkin, and now her hand rested lightly on the side of her glass.

Jake remembered all the homes in the Malibu hills that he'd worked on. There were many, including his current project.

"A few." He ordered another bourbon as the waiter passed their table. The more alcohol, the easier the lies. If lying really caused nose growth, his would soon be out the door.

"How about you? What do you do?" Jake asked. He already knew, but he was desperate to direct the conversation elsewhere. It was going to be a long summer.

"I teach yoga. And kickboxing. Five long days a week," Pepper said with a long sigh.

Jake searched her face and detected nothing but honesty. Of course, the truth was right there in front of him. Pepper Bartlett was the picture of perfect body fitness. He smiled through his guilt. He was the only liar at their table. He wished for a tidal wave to swoop in and wash the restaurant away.

"You don't enjoy what you do?"

"It has its perks," Pepper said. She went to work on her napkin again. "It allows me time to pursue other things."

Jake waited for her to continue.

"I, um, build sand castles. Professionally someday— I hope."

Jake smiled. Well, if that's all the woman had to hide . . .

Chapter 8

Pepper burst into Lucy's room and flipped on the light. "I'm in love." She raised her arms in the air and spun around. "Absolutely, positively in love."

Lucy peeked out from under her pink duvet cover and squinted through the sudden flood of brightness. "Huh?" She sounded like an old bullfrog. One eye peered over at the clock on her nightstand, and she squished her lips together. "It's late," she said, pulling the covers back over her head.

Pepper plopped herself down on the edge of Lucy's bed. "No wonder you wake up with headaches," she said. "You're air deprived." She grabbed the bedding and pulled it away from Lucy's face.

Lucy raised an arm and crossed it over her eyes. With her free hand, she attempted to regain control over the covers, but Pepper held tight. Groaning, she rolled over and smashed her face into her pillow.

Pepper began to bounce lightly on the bed. "C'mon, Luce. Don't you want to hear about my date?"

"Tomorrow."

Pepper bounced harder for a minute, and then

she lay down on her side next to Lucy. She stared until Lucy pulled her face away from the pillow.

"That's how you get wrinkles," Pepper said.

"You're not going to leave, are you?"

"Not for a while. I have some important stuff to tell you."

Lucy moaned and then yawned. "Fine, but only a synopsis."

"No laugh, no smirk. Not one ounce of amusement did Jake reveal when I told him about my dream of becoming a professional sand sculptor."

"That's nice. 'kay, g'night." Lucy patted Pepper's hand.

"He's an architect, and I'm in love." Pepper raised her legs in the air and began pointing and flexing her toes.

Lucy dropped her arm away from her face. She looked over at Pepper. "That's it? That's what you woke me up for? He's an architect, and you're in love? Boy, the two of you will have kids in college soon." She rolled over and hugged her pillow. "Okay. You can turn off the light and leave now."

"Fine." Pepper ruffled Lucy's hair and got up. "I'll fill you in on the rest tomorrow."

"Gee, I don't know if I'll be able to sleep," Lucy said into her pillow. She was already drifting back to la-la land.

"I guess old Pete was right. Not all ads are placed by desperate women," Gordy said.

"I guess not." Jake sat on the sofa and screwed the cap off a bottle of Fat Tire beer. "By the way, it's gonna cost you more."

"Why? If anything, it should be worth more for *me*. If it wasn't for me, you'd have never met her."

"Wasn't it Pete who found Pepper's ad?"

"Yeah, but it was *my* seeing Sherry that convinced you to go for it," Gordy said, a satisfied grin covering his face.

"Good point."

"Anyway, why do you say it's gonna cost more?"

Jake shrugged. "It's not easy, this lying business. And like you just said, it's because of you that I even agreed to do this. I had to take drastic measures to get you on the straight and narrow." He took a long drink of beer. It was good, but the memory of the bourbon from the night before still lay smooth on his tongue. He could get used to that.

Gordy laughed once, shaking his head. "Just remember one thing . . ."

"What's that?"

"Women are always on their best behavior in the beginning. As soon as you get caught in their web, the fangs come out." Gordy grabbed his crotch. "Then you have to hide your gonads."

"You don't know what you're talking about. There're plenty of good women out there, and I'm pretty sure I've found one. And if I have to lie to her all summer, it's going to cost you more than fifty bucks."

Gordy laughed. "What the hell are you gonna do when summer's over? Tell her the truth? Course, I guess by then, she'll be so charmed by the great Jake Hunter it won't matter that you're just another sweaty, smelly blue-collar liar."

Jake pointed at Gordy's beer bottle. "You done,

dickwad?" Gordy nodded, and Jake took the empties to the kitchen.

"It is funny, don't you think?" Gordy said, following him. "If you tell her the truth now, she won't give you the time of day, and if you wait, she's gonna toss you out like those empty beer bottles."

"I'm glad you find it so amusing," Jake said. "Don't worry. I'll figure it all out soon enough. What about you? I've lived up to my end of the bargain. Seems to me, it's your turn to get online."

"Not so fast. You've only taken Malibu Miss on one date. *I* could even fool the woman for an hour."

Jake laughed. He wasn't so sure about that.

Gordy squeezed Jake's shoulder. "We'll see what happens in the next couple of weeks. Hey, if it don't work out between you two, maybe I could entertain the lady."

Jake gave him a hard look. Pepper was a nice girl. She tried to put on a tough façade, but he'd seen through that in the first hour. Somewhere under that hard shell was a sensitive young woman, and she didn't deserve to be lied to—not even by him. No way would he ever turn Gordy loose on her.

He shrugged Gordy's hand from his shoulder. "I can do fine on my own." His feelings of protectiveness surprised him. Only one other woman had ever caused him to feel that way.

"Hey, I got an idea. Why don't you ask her if she's got a friend? We could double date."

Jake shot him another look. This time, one of disbelief. Gordy was one of his best friends, and he wasn't bad-looking. He even had a certain youthful charm. The problem was, along with being crude and even rude at times, he lacked the social skills that it would take to convince any woman he was anything more than a construction worker. No, as bad as he wanted Gordy to find a nice, unattached woman, Pepper's roommate wasn't going to be his test case.

"You're kidding, right?" Jake asked.

"What gives? If your Malibu Miss is so special, it stands to reason that she's got some nice friends. It's a win–win deal. I get a woman, you get a woman."

"If you're so sure I can't pull this off, what makes you think you could?"

"Easy. No lies. Just tell her I'm one of the guys that work for you. The truth always works best for me."

Jake imagined his hands wrapped around Gordy's scrawny neck, his eyes bugging out of their sockets. If Gordy didn't shut up, he might be tempted to make that image a reality. Jake twisted the top off a fresh beer. "I'll see what I can do," he said. "I'm not promising anything."

As soon as Gordy was out the door, Jake tossed the idea of a double date aside. Hell, he wasn't even sure he should introduce Gordy to Pepper, let alone her roommate. Guys like Gordy only cared about three things: their next beer, their next lay, and whether or not they can find their tool belt the next morning—in that order. Jake wasn't sure that Pepper would believe he was any different. Especially since just about everything he'd told her up until now was a lie. He was pretty sure a good woman could change Gordy, but right now, it was a risk he wasn't willing to take.

"He's an architect, and she's in love," Lucy said to Simone.

Simone had just walked in the door, and she hadn't even had a chance to sit down. She looked at Pepper with raised eyebrows.

"Is this true, *chérie?* I am crushed that you did not tell me."

Pepper hesitated. During and right after her date with Jake, she'd been floating on air. But now, after a good night's sleep, she realized it might be a bit premature to call it love. Why did Lucy have to take everything she said so literally? After all, everyone knew it wasn't like her to let a man get under her skin that fast. No, love was too strong a word to use just yet. Lust was probably a better description of how she was feeling.

Pepper shrugged sheepishly. "I don't know. It was late. I was tired. I don't remember."

"You said you were in love," Lucy reminded her.

Pepper shot her a frown. "How do you know? You wouldn't even wake up long enough to talk me out of thinking that way." She twisted a lock of her hair around a finger. "Let's just say, Jake appears to be . . . well . . . perfect."

"Oh, *chérie,* tell me more," Simone said. "I so want to hear a good love story. It is like Cary Grant and Sophia Loren on the houseboat, yes?"

Pepper held up a hand. "Slow down. I wouldn't say it's gone that far."

"You said you were in love," Lucy reminded her again.

"Thank you so much," Pepper said.

"So you're not ready for the houseboat, but tell me everything," Simone pleaded.

"What can I say? He's a perfect gentleman. And smart. Like Lucy said, he's an architect. He's worked on some of those megahomes up there on the hill." Pepper waved a hand in the direction of Malibu Hills.

"And tell me, what does this gentleman look like?" Simone asked.

Pepper settled onto the sofa and took a sip of her iced tea. Where did she start? She'd only memorized every detail about Jake. His hair was the color of dark chocolate. Oh, how she loved dark chocolate. He had the kind of shoulders that a woman could lean on, and he had laugh lines—just enough—around his eyes, proving he's a man who knew how to enjoy life. Yet somehow, they were etched with sadness. Like he'd had one too many heartaches. That gave him a sexy kind of vulnerability.

Pepper remembered his hands on the steering wheel as he drove. So large, so tan, like the color had been baked into them. She'd already spent considerable time imagining how they would feel holding her.

"Tall," Pepper said.

"Very tall," Lucy chimed in.

"He has near black hair—" Pepper continued.

"Perfectly coiffed—" Lucy added with a dreamy smile. She fluttered her eyelashes.

Pepper and Simone looked at each other. Pepper wondered if Lucy had an inner woman that no one knew existed?

"He's charming," Pepper said.

"The kind of charm that makes a good girl want to go bad—" Lucy continued.

"Okay, enough," Pepper said, holding up a hand. "Maybe you were right. Maybe I shouldn't be bringing these men to our house." Lucy smiled smugly, and Pepper realized that her roommate was simply mocking her state of mind from the night before. "Very funny," she said, sticking out her tongue.

Simone looked from Pepper to Lucy and back. "Hair, *charme?* That is not what I want to hear." She leaned forward and lowered her voice. "Tell me, is he well-endowed?"

Warmth filled Pepper's cheeks, and an unexpected tingle flittered through her thighs. "I wouldn't know." She hitched up her chin. "It was our first date."

"Oh, *chérie,*"—Simone waved a hand at her— "don't tell me you couldn't feel something when he stood close. Dancing perhaps?"

"We didn't stand close enough for that. Nor did we dance." Pepper took a long sip of iced tea. The cool liquid quenched her thirst. She only hoped it had the added benefit of flushing the heat from her face. "But I'll make a mental note to let you know when I find out."

She glanced over at Lucy, who was suddenly quiet. "Oh, now you don't have anything to say?"

"I have a lot to say, but when do you ever listen to me? Besides, I concur. Jake seems like a good guy. I can understand why you came home in such a state."

"No lecture?"

Lucy shook her head and did a zipping motion across her lips.

"Tell me, *chérie* . . . this white shirt-wearing man, he wows you, yes?"

"So far, on a wow scale of one to ten, he's an exquisite eleven."

"Then I must have details. Hold nothing back. It may be the only sex I get for a while."

"What are you talking about? You've got Paul.

That's more sex than Lucy and me put together will ever have."

Simone waved a hand lightly and laughed. "Yes, Paul, he is a lot of sex." A pout settled on her perfectly painted lips. "But he has gone home, and he won't be back for a month." Simone rested her head in her hands. "An entire month. It is more than I can bear."

Pepper gave her friend a sideways glance. "I feel for you."

"Pooh. You're just like Paul. You don't even care that I'll have no one to kiss me to sleep at night."

"You can kiss me." Pepper puckered her lips.

"If you introduce me to this white shirt man, then maybe I let him kiss me."

"Not a chance," Pepper said, shaking her head. She wasn't sure she ever wanted Jake to meet Simone. Simone had a way of making even a beautiful woman look like a mud hen. Pepper was convinced that if she possessed only one-third of Simone's sexiness, she'd be lying in Jake's arms right now.

She looked at her watch. "I've got a few hours until I have to be at work—just enough time to do some damage on the beach. How about the three of us go dig in the sand?" Pepper wanted to change the subject before Simone forced her to promise she'd keep her informed about Jake's manhood.

"I've got to go up to the roof and clip some flowers," Lucy said. She went over to the kitchen table and grabbed her pruning shears.

"And I must go meet Suzanne. She and I are going to the Santa Monica market. *Bonne chance* with your perfect man, Pepper." She tucked her short brown hair behind her ears and waved a hand at Lucy. *"Au revoir, chérie."*

Pepper walked Simone out and watched her drive away, red scarf blowing in the wind. Simone was like a butterfly, flitting about and touching down in one spot only long enough for a quick glimpse. Pepper wondered how Paul had ever captured her.

After changing into cutoffs and a hot pink bikini top, Pepper smoothed on plenty of SPF 30 and then grabbed her bucket of kitchen utensils, aka sand sculpting tools. She stood on the steps that led down to the beach and paused to watch a brown pelican plunge from the sky into the sea. Two seagulls fought for position next to the large bird, crying for leftovers.

The sand glistened wetly and sparkled like fairy dust. Waves gently rolled toward shore, depositing a line of white foam, the high tide line. Now to find an area that was relatively clear of debris, which was really just about anywhere.

With a couple of hours available for practice, Pepper decided on something that included small details. A castle with turrets and a winding staircase should do nicely. She dropped her tool bucket onto the beach, then knelt and began mounding sand to form a pyramid shape. She'd recently read about a new technique called drip castling that she'd been wanting to try, so she added plenty of water to the mound. Then she grabbed a handful of the wet sand and allowed the grainy mixture to run through her fist. It plopped like mud pies onto the base, and the water drained downward. Pepper worked slowly, patiently, careful not to hurry the process, which could cause her structure to weaken and then become vulnerable to caving in or falling over.

Eventually, after many fistfuls, she had a large enough form to create her castle. She added more water to the top of the pyramid and allowed it to drain into the center and percolate down to the water table, thereby ensuring a stable building base.

Two hours later, Pepper put the finishing touches on her sculpture. She sprayed it with sea water for an additional buildup of salt crystals, then sat back to admire her work. The winding staircase didn't exactly wind, and the windows weren't square. She needed a lot more practice.

"Hey, sun goddess," a voice called out.

Pepper looked and saw Lucy waving from the open doorway.

"Phone," she yelled.

Pepper gathered up her tools and tossed them into the small bucket. She took one final glance around before leaving the beach.

"Hey, Sis," Cat said into Pepper's ear.

"Hey, you. What's up?" Pepper continued into the house.

"It's almost our birthday. I thought we'd surprise Mom and get you up here," Cat said.

Pepper paused. What was wrong with this picture? Not so long ago, Cat wouldn't have even been concerned about them getting together.

"Listen, I just came in from the beach and need to get cleaned up for work. Could I call you back later?" She really would call Cat back. She just wanted to have a drink in her hand when it happened. She ran a hand through her hair and felt gritty sand on her face. "Damn," she muttered.

"Pardon?" Cat said, hurt inflections in her voice.

"Nothing. It's the sand. It's everywhere."

"Okay. I get it. Call me back when you're not so busy."

"Sure." Pepper hung up the phone and turned around.

Lucy's lips formed a thin line as she tried to force one more bird of paradise into a tall ceramic vase. She didn't say anything, but Pepper knew that look.

"What?"

Lucy continued working on the flower, finally jamming it into place. She looked at Pepper almost apologetically. "Why do you keep putting your mom and sister off? They want to see you. Is that so bad?"

Pepper squeezed her pail of tools to her chest. "I'm not putting them off. I just need to get cleaned up. I told Cat I'd call her back." She shook her head. "Geez."

"He was Cat's dad, too. And he was like a father to me. Are you going to start avoiding me?"

"That's ridiculous. I talk to them." Pepper waved a hand at the phone, and she shook her head. "I can't do this right now." She spun around and disappeared down the hall.

She sat in her room with the door closed for a long time. It wasn't that she didn't want to talk to her mom and sister. Things were just all mixed up right now.

The truth was she partially blamed her mom for her dad's death. It didn't make any sense, she knew, but she couldn't help but feel that if her mother had been stronger, meant what she said . . . Pepper wiped away a tear. It didn't matter now. All those years her mom had tried to get her dad to stop smoking had been futile. She'd nagged and scolded and even resorted to throwing those damn cigarettes away.

Once her mom had even threatened to leave her dad, but he never took her seriously because he knew, ultimately, she wouldn't. Unfortunately, her dad finally left all of them.

Then there was Cat. Dear, sweet Cat. Cat hadn't been sweet since grade school. Somehow, over the years, she'd changed into dear, selfish Cat. When their dad lay dying at the Evergreen Hospice, Cat was too busy to visit. She spent all her time partying with her friends. She wasn't even there on the day their dad died. Dear, sweet Cat. Right.

Pepper knew she couldn't avoid their phone calls forever. And with her birthday coming up . . . well, it would almost be impossible. She blew out a big breath. Time to suck it up for her mom's sake.

The next morning, Pepper woke up exhausted from tossing and turning all night. She shuffled into the kitchen. The aroma of fresh coffee filled the cottage. Caffeine was exactly what she needed. She found Lucy, all perky, sitting at the table, putting together another flower arrangement.

"You look like you've been up all night. Dreamin' about Mr. Dreamy Eyes, I suppose?" Lucy said.

"I was. And no, you suppose wrong. It was that phone call from my sister." Pepper ran her fingers through her hair. "Am I a bad daughter? And sister? You did tell me I was mean, after all."

Lucy took a moment to ponder Pepper's question. "I think you're just confused."

Pepper gave her a quizzical look.

"You don't know what to do or say when your mom is feeling bad, so you don't do anything. Then *you* feel bad." Lucy worked a sprig of jasmine into the vase. "Insomnia can be caused by a lot of things.

I don't think you should avoid your mom just because you feel helpless. She'll get over her loss a lot sooner if she knows her daughters are there for her." She gave Pepper a warm smile.

"Leave it to you to make sense of this whole damn mess," she told Lucy. Not that what Lucy said made her feel any better.

Pepper poured herself a cup of coffee and took it with her out to the deck. The chairs were damp, as usual, but she sat anyway. A westerly breeze blew off the Pacific Ocean, and a salty mist swirled through the air. The sun made an attempt to peek through the clouds, but the sky remained gray. It matched her mood. Her upcoming birthday, a new guy in her life, keeping up with Lucy's feng shui stuff, it was all zapping her energy.

One thing she did know was that she loved her mom. And despite their differences, she loved her sister, too.

Brad stood behind the bar wiping glasses dry. A bad taste filled his mouth when he saw Marta come through the door. Right behind her was Vic. They were both smiling. That was good, he guessed.

"Hey, guys. What's up?" he asked.

Vic sat on a stool and ordered two beers. One for himself and one for Marta. She sat next to him and held up her left hand for Brad to see. The ring Vic had shown him sparkled delicately from her finger. Brad felt sick. Marta gave him a smug grin and then excused herself to go to the ladies' room.

"Obviously, she said yes," Brad said to Vic. He looked away and studied the ocean waves as though they held some sage piece of advice he could give his friend or something he could say that would convince Vic to change his mind. "You sure about this?" was all he came up with.

"Hell, yeah. She's the one." Vic slapped Brad on the shoulder.

Brad placed two mugs of beer in front of him. "On me," he said. "Congratulations. I wish the two of you all the best." And good luck, you'll need it. He hoped it was a long engagement so his friend might come to know the real Marta and have a chance to change his mind. It was hard enough to have his best friend dating and living with a woman like that. But to *marry* her?

Marta returned, and Brad poured himself a shot of whiskey. It would take more than a mug of beer to wash away the bad taste of what he'd done to Vic.

"To you," he said to Vic and Marta.

Chapter 9

After one of the laziest days she'd had in a long time, Pepper felt revived. She'd taken full advantage of having the day off, just hanging around the cottage, watching a couple of old movies. She didn't even work on her sand sculpting. To top off her day, Jake had called and asked her out on another date.

"Since you like Jake so much, does that mean you're going to cancel your ad?" Lucy asked Pepper.

"Would you marry the first guy who asked?" Pepper stood in front of the mirror and applied lipstick, a natural peach color. After blotting it with a Kleenex, she added a swipe of darker pink on top. "What do you think?" she said, puckering her lips.

"Red would be better," Lucy said.

"Red?" Pepper frowned into the mirror. She looked in her makeup drawer and shook her head. "I don't think I own any. Why red?"

Lucy gave her a smile and did a little shrug.

Pepper didn't need to ask again. Feng shui. "Forget it. That's your thing." She stepped back and admired her figure in the new white dress she'd picked up last week at The Grove. It had barely there straps and a hemline cut high enough to make Lucy blush. It complemented her white sandals perfectly, but it wasn't very complimentary to her checking account.

The doorbell rang. Pepper and Lucy looked at each other. "It's Jake. He's early. What man is ever *early*?" She gave Lucy a *please* look. "Keep him entertained while I get my lemon fix?" She rushed from the room and slipped into the kitchen before Lucy opened the front door.

Pepper heard Lucy talking to Jake as she shoved aside a head of leafy lettuce in search of the little yellow fruit. She found one and sliced it into fourths. Instead of squeezing the juice into a bowl, she held the lemon over the sink and squeezed it over her fingers. Citrus smell infused the air. Sunshine in the kitchen. She ran her fingers through her hair and then did a quick swipe over the backs of her legs.

Pepper rinsed and dried her fingers and then made her entrance. Remembering her conversation with Simone the day before, her eyes were immediately drawn to Jake's crotch. She felt a warm flush and had to force her eyes to look elsewhere, anywhere. The floor, the wall, the ceiling.

Jake reached for her hand, and Pepper thought for a moment that he was going to shake it like she was nothing more than a casual acquaintance. She was relieved when, instead, he gently pulled her to him and brushed his lips across her cheek. Her knees went weak, and she squeezed his hand tightly for support.

"Sorry," she said, still holding his hand. "I was feeling a bit dizzy. I guess I'm hungrier than I thought." Hungry didn't begin to describe the way she really felt.

Lucy rolled her eyes.

"Shall we go?" Jake offered her his arm.

"Let's." They turned for the door, and Pepper smiled when she saw him take a deep breath.

"Do you smell lemons?"

"Lemons?" Pepper looked at Lucy. "No. Uh-uh." Lemons. Nature's secret weapon.

Jake drove down Pacific Coast Highway a while, and Pepper thought she'd fall asleep before they got to their destination. He was quieter, different from two nights before. In her experience, only a couple of things could make a person who was outgoing and self-assured unusually quiet. One of those things was schizophrenia. Lord, please don't let this gorgeous man have a problem like that. Pepper glanced over and gave him a scrutinizing look. Could be that he had something heavy weighing on his mind. Not a nice alternative, but the better of the two evils. If that's what Jake suffered from, she hoped for his sake it wasn't anything too heavy.

Pepper was pleasantly surprised when their destination turned out to be a dance club at Universal City Walk. She was also glad that Jake seemed to recover and was back to his old self.

The club had ceilings that reached the sky. Wooden beams stretched across the center and gave it a wilderness cabin feel. They were assaulted by sounds of people talking and laughing, their voices echoing off the tall ceiling. The lively tinkle of piano keys filled in any leftover space. And the smells. Pepper took a deep breath of something that was cooking on the grill. It was greasy and good, and Pepper had to have whatever it was. She looked up at the menu. No salads, no soy burgers, no health food in sight. Pure heaven. For once, she had a good excuse to eat something really bad and not feel guilty.

After getting their meal out of the way, Pepper and Jake went on to more serious things. Dancing, talking, making goo-goo eyes at each other. Well, maybe Jake wasn't making goo-goo eyes, but Pepper was making good use of every minute they spent together.

Throughout the evening, Jake was attentive, his eyes only on her, even though the club was full of beautiful, scantily clad women. Pepper was additionally impressed with how he handled a situation that could have turned out sticky. During one dance, a man who'd had far too much to drink bumped into her several times. From then on, Jake made sure he positioned himself between her and the intoxicated man. No harsh words spilled from his mouth; he simply dealt with the problem without making a scene. Big bonus points.

Between dances, they talked. Jake asked more about her sand sculpting, and she probably told him a lot more than he really wanted to know. Still, he didn't look the slightest bit amused. She'd gotten all kinds of reactions in the past when she told men about it. Most didn't take her aspirations seriously. Not even when she informed them that professional sand sculpting was considered one of the nation's top twenty professions.

Every now and then, Jake turned quiet, and it was beginning to pique Pepper's curiosity. Who was the real Jake Hunter anyway? Had he been acting differently on their first date just to impress her? She noticed he wasn't drinking as much tonight. Had it simply been the alcohol talking? "It's the quiet ones you have to watch out for," Lucy always told her. But whatever Jake had on his mind, he did his best to see that Pepper had a good time.

And she did.

Finally, the moment Pepper had been waiting for arrived. The music softened, and Jake drew her close. She was lost in his arms. Her heart raced, and she was sure he could feel it thumping, hard and fast, against his chest. He looked into her eyes, and she melted.

"You dance very well," he said.

Pepper laughed. She didn't know how, seeing as she couldn't even feel her feet. She—and they— were floating on air.

"Ballet and tap. My mother insisted I take them so that I could grow up into a graceful young woman."

"I'm glad to see it worked."

"I try." Pepper swallowed, and her lips parted. *This is where the guy is supposed to kiss you,* she told herself.

"Tell your mother she's a very wise woman."

Pepper watched Jake's lips move as he spoke, anticipating what was supposed to come next.

It didn't.

"I'm sure she'd be glad to hear that." Especially from a man like you. Pepper smiled.

The dance got over too quickly, and so did the evening.

When Jake took her home, he walked her to her door, and she was hoping this was another one of those moments she'd been waiting for. She held her breath and waited for Jake to make his move— then, he thanked her for the great evening and kissed her lightly on the cheek.

Pepper went inside and stood with her back flat against the door. She couldn't help feeling disappointed. *Disappointed?* He might as well have told her she had bad breath. She reached up and breathed into her hand. No. Bad breath didn't seem to be the problem.

After her shower, Pepper slipped between her five-hundred thread count sheets. They usually worked like a sleeping pill, but tonight, her mind jumped all over the place. She lay there for over two hours, replaying the last few days over and over in her mind. Her pulse raced just being near Jake. Had she been seeing and feeling things that weren't there? Surely he felt something, too.

Tired and frustrated, she tried to blank out the way his mouth moved when he talked, while he ate, when he smiled, but it was useless. All evening, she'd anticipated the moment his full lips would touch hers, and then it had never happened. She deserved that kiss, dammit.

Chapter 10

A week passed, and another weekend stared Pepper in the face. Her muscles ached, and she lay in bed, eyes focused on the ceiling. Another hour of sleep would be nice. She still wasn't getting much rest, what with all the tossing and turning and dreaming about Jake.

A slice of sun peeked through the blinds, meaning that no clouds were draped over the sky. Pepper sat up and stretched her arms toward the ceiling, leaning to the right, then over to the left. Nine o'clock glowed on her nightstand clock. Lucy had let her sleep in. At least the weekend was off to a good start.

The locals' frenzied fitness craze continued, with yet another kickboxing class added to her schedule. How much exercise could a body take, for crying out loud? She'd come home from work each night and barely have time to catch her breath before she had to go back. She hadn't seen this kind of determination since January, when everybody had signed up for exercise classes to fulfill resolutions made while under the influence of alcohol.

Pepper looked forward to when summer was in

full swing. Outdoor activities would increase, and things would slow down. Californians didn't know how good they had it. When the weather suddenly became cold and wet, which wasn't often, everyone ran for cover. If that would have been the case in Seattle, people would never get anything done— they'd never leave their homes. As far as Pepper was concerned, Malibu's weather was good enough for year-round outdoor activity, even when June gloom hit.

With fewer classes, she'd be able to spend more time working on her sand castling. She'd also be able to spend more time working on Jake.

Even with her busy work schedule, Pepper had still managed to carve out time to see him twice during the week. Once for a quick drink and once for a movie. Lucy told her that technically movie dates didn't count because they didn't allow much opportunity for talking and getting to know each other.

That was a bunch of hooey as far as Pepper was concerned. Going to movies might not allow much talk, but she'd gotten to know some guys pretty darn well sitting in the back of a theater. She'd also been known to get a few kisses. For some reason, that still hadn't happened with Jake, and it was well past due. She practically knew him well enough to bear his children, for crying out loud, or at least to have gotten past cheek kissing. His resistance made her more determined than ever.

Invigorated by that thought, Pepper jumped out of bed and slipped into her blue silk robe and a pair of fluffy bunny slippers. She found Lucy at the table eating a bowl of MultiGrain Cheerios.

Pepper poured herself a bowl.

"Our landlord doesn't like the red door. He wants us to paint it back to white."

"Bastard!" Pepper said with feigned indignation. "Didn't you inform him that we single girls need all the protection we can get?"

Lucy nearly choked. "Did I hear you correctly? Are you saying you finally believe what I've been telling you?"

"You mean about all that feng phooey stuff?" Pepper checked the date on the milk carton before pouring it over her cereal. "No."

Lucy threw up her arms. "If I can't even get my best friend to understand, how am I going to get our landlord to appreciate the protection that a red door provides?"

Pepper sat down with her bowl of Cheerios. "Yes, it's quite a conundrum, isn't it?"

"That's okay." Lucy held up a piece of red cord with a tiny bell attached to one end. She shook it. It emitted a barely audible tinkle. "I'm going to hang this on the inside of the front door." Lucy's face exuded as much excitement as a scientist who'd just discovered penicillin.

Pepper gave her a blank look.

"It'll warn of intruders," Lucy explained.

"I hate to tell you this, Luce, but I don't think that little bell would wake up either one of us. Have you thought of getting a dog?"

Lucy went over and looped the cord over the doorknob, tying it securely. She opened the door and swung it back and forth a few times. "I can hear it just fine," she said.

"Wait until you start snoring."

Lucy frowned. "I don't snore."

"I have a question for you . . . do I have bad breath?"

Lucy's forehead wrinkled. "Where did that come from?"

Pepper sighed. "I don't know. I think I may be losing my touch with men. I've been out on four dates with Jake—five, if you count the night we met—and he has yet to kiss me."

"No kisses?"

"Not where it counts."

Lucy's eyebrows arched. "I hope you're meaning your lips." She shrugged. "Maybe he's more of a gentleman than you're used to, and he doesn't believe in real kisses until the *sixth* date." A devilish grin quickly covered her face. "*Maybe* he doesn't even believe in sex before marriage."

Pepper pursed her lips and narrowed her eyes. "We'll see about that," she said. The phone rang, and she reached across the table.

It was Jake.

"I've got the day off and was wondering if you'd like to get together?"

Pepper's heart felt as though it had sprouted wings. YES! YES! YES! she wanted to shout, but she somehow managed to keep her enthusiasm down to a three on the Richter scale.

"Sure," she said with forced nonchalance. "I'm free all day." She turned her back to Lucy and lowered her voice. "What did you have in mind?"

"You decide," he said.

Pepper glanced outside. The sun was bright, and the beach beckoned. She hadn't had time to practice sculpting all week. "I'll let it be a surprise."

Jake laughed. "Okay. I'll see you soon."

Pepper hung up the phone and took a few bites of her now soggy cereal. No matter. She'd suddenly lost her appetite. Jake seemed to have that effect on her. She jumped up and rinsed the cereal down the drain, then snapped the lid off a Flintstone vitamin bottle. "Say good-bye, cruel world," she told an orange Pebbles, popping it into her mouth.

"That must have been the dreaded nonkisser," Lucy said, nodding at the phone.

"Yes, it was, but I'd never use the word *dreaded* to describe Jake."

"Better brush your teeth three times if you plan on getting that kiss."

"I'll do better than that. I'll even gargle."

Jake stepped into the shower and turned the turbo shower head to full force. Hot water pulsated over his shoulders. He turned his head from one side to the other, stretching his neck down and around, back and forth. He'd been plagued by tense muscles for a week. Probably stress from this ridiculous lie he was living. Water spilled down his chest and onto the tile floor. He thought of Pepper and what it would be like to shower with her, touch her nakedness, run his hands over her soap-slickened body. It made him hard, and he turned up the cold water. That didn't help much. It only made him imagine Pepper's nipples hard and erect. If he was ever lucky enough to see her naked, he was going to take it slow, savor the moment. It took a long time standing under the cool water to bring him back to reality.

Jake finished his shower and stood in front of the mirror. Right after he spread shaving cream on his face, he heard a knock at the front door.

Gordy stood on his porch with a bloodied nose and swollen lip.

"What the hell happened to you?" Jake asked.

"Spent the night with *that woman*," Gordy said.

"Hold on . . ." Jake held up a hand. "I thought we had an agreement."

"I'm human. She called and said she needed to see me."

"I bet. Then what? She wake up this morning and decide she no longer needed your services? Told you to leave and you wouldn't?"

"Nah. Nothing that simple. She forgot to tell me her husband would be home early. He thought I should leave—out the bedroom window." Gordy lifted an arm, exposing a raw scrape.

Jake grimaced. "Youch." He poked a finger into Gordy's chest. "Stupid son of a bitch, I keep telling you, you keep fooling around with that woman and you're going to get yourself killed."

"I think I might love her."

"Are you insane?" Jake shook his head. "Look, I'd love to stay here and give you a lecture, but I've got a date. You going to be okay? You don't have any broken bones or anything, do you?"

Gordy shook his head "no" and followed Jake down the hallway to the bathroom.

Jake stretched his jaw tight and dragged the razor up the side of his face. He finished one cheek and then went to work on the other.

Gordy looked thoughtful. "Let's see, how long has it been?"

"Barely two weeks." Jake rinsed the razor and wiped his face with a towel. A dot of blood appeared, and he blotted it with a piece of tissue.

"Damn," Gordy said, "you look good enough to kiss." Gordy moved toward Jake, and Jake pushed him away. "You ask Pepper about her friend yet?" Gordy asked.

"Give up that woman, and we'll talk about it." Jake walked out the front door and locked it. "How would it look for me to have a friend who's chasing after another man's wife?" He got into Pete's Audi and rolled away from the curb.

A lock of hair came loose from Pepper's ponytail and hung alongside her face. She started to tuck it back into her hair band, but on second thought, liked the way it softened her jawline and added a touch of sexiness. She pulled the strand of hair forward and smelled lemon.

Jake showed up an hour after he called. His eyes brightened when he saw her. His smile was warm, his lips inviting, and Pepper felt a knot twist tight inside her stomach. He had on jeans and a navy blue T-shirt. She probably should have told him they'd be playing in the sand. She glanced out the back sliding door, and a smile played on her lips. Jake might be dressed a little warm for the beach. At the very least, he'd have to remove his shirt. The thought of him baring his chest made her tingle like she was taking a bath in champagne. She admired a man who took good care of himself. It took commitment, and from what she could tell, Jake was very committed.

"All set. Let's go," she said, leading him toward the sliding glass door.

"Out back?"

"To the beach. We'll be spending all morning out there. You game?"

Jake laughed. His brown eyes crinkled at the corners. "Sure. I've played in the sand. When I was a kid."

"That was then," Pepper said, looking straight into his eyes. "This is now. This is serious business." She grabbed her tool bucket.

"I see," Jake said. Light danced in his eyes, and he gripped her hand tighter. A jolt of electricity shot through her. "What are we waiting for, then?"

Pepper's heart started pumping. She glanced over and waggled her eyebrows at Lucy. For sure, this was going to be her lucky day.

After finding a clean area above the high tide line, Pepper sat on the sand, and she had Jake sit directly across from her. She pulled several small tools out of her bucket, and after giving Jake a short course in sand castling 101, she formed her hands into a scoop and went to work dragging sand toward her. As she did so, she imagined Jake's hands on her, massaging her entire body with long, even strokes. Whew! The sun wasn't even high in the sky, and she was already overheated.

Focus, Pepper told herself. Soon, she had a mound large enough to begin creating. She moved over in front of the mound and proceeded to form a five-foot-long rectangular base.

Pepper glanced over at Jake every now and then, half expecting to see his eyes glazed over from boredom. They weren't. Instead, his gaze was fixed on her hands as though he were a student fascinated by her artistic skill. She continued to work, pulling sand away here, adding some there. Twenty minutes later, she had the basic shape of a mermaid.

She continued at one end, all the while conscious of Jake watching her every move. In a short time, she switched to a melon baller for working on the mermaid's scales. With the proper tools, they'd take less time and effort, but having to make do with kitchen utensils forced her to be more resourceful. Once her skills improved, she intended to reward her efforts by purchasing the best sand sculpting tools she could find.

When Pepper looked up, her cheeks burned, and it wasn't from the sun. Jake had taken his shirt off. She swallowed hard.

With him sitting there half-naked—and looking absolutely delicious—concentration became near impossible, but she managed to complete a few more scales. She continued working, scraping away excess sand, leaving plenty for the mermaid's head and hair, and finally, it was time to start with the details on the upper body.

Pepper stopped for a minute to give her back a break. "It's your turn," she told Jake.

He held up his hands and shook his head. "I'm not very creative. I don't think you want me to get my hands into your sand."

That was for sure. She wanted Jake's hands elsewhere. Everywhere, in fact. His fingers were large. Manly. They looked as though they'd seen a lot of hard work. Pepper took one of them in hers and squeezed. It was firm and strong.

"Liar," she said. "You're an architect. You wouldn't be in business if you weren't creative."

Jake gave a nervous laugh. "I guess what I really

meant is that I haven't had much experience using sand as a building material."

"It's easy once you get started." Pepper looked him squarely in the eyes. "And I've got everything you need. Don't be afraid. I'll help you."

"I'm sure that's true."

A smile tugged at the corners of Pepper's mouth as an idea formed in her head. She crawled around the base of the sculpture and sat close to him. "First," she said, "we need to finish these two small mounds." She added a small nob of sand to the top of one and told Jake to do the same to the other.

He gathered a small bit of sand between his fingers and set it on top of the mound, rolling it and tweaking it just so, until it closely resembled the one Pepper had finished.

Oh, how Pepper wished she were that mermaid right now.

When Jake finished his assigned task, she sat back and gave it her appraisal. "Perfect," she said.

Jake nodded like he'd just gotten the joke. "Breasts."

"You're very perceptive." Pepper looked up at him through long lashes. "Shall we continue?"

Jake leaned back onto his forearms, his biceps and chest glistening in the morning sun. Dark brown hair fanned out from the center of his chest, with a thin line running halfway down his stomach. Pepper hadn't seen muscles ripple like that in, well, forever. It'd be awfully nice to have a few clients like him in her kickboxing class.

She offered him the melon baller. "Want to, um, try making some scales?"

"I'd rather work on her hair." Jake reached up

and tugged playfully at the lock of hair that hung alongside Pepper's face.

"Um, maybe we should stop for now. Go inside, get cleaned up." Pepper knew that if she didn't get away from Jake's bare chest in the next few seconds, she might do something very enjoyable . . . like dive on top of him. She imagined them being locked in an embrace, rolling around in the sand. Anyone who walked by would get a front row seat. Even Cher would probably hear about it and give her dirty looks when they passed each other in the aisle at Ralph's Market. She'd be forced to move to another beach to escape the gossip.

Pepper tossed her tools into the bucket, and Jake held out his hand and pulled her to her feet. Their faces were inches apart, and Pepper found herself staring into dark brown pools. Boy, would she love to drown right now. In anticipation of the moment their mouths would come together, she licked her lips.

"Did I say something wrong?" Jake asked.

Pepper wiped her forehead. "It's just that it's getting hot out here," she managed between quick breaths.

"Would you like to go somewhere and have a cold drink, maybe something to eat?"

Pepper released his hand and nodded. "After I get cleaned up."

Jake brushed sand from the back of his jeans. "Me, too. After you change, we'll go back to my place."

"You look fine," she said, her voice almost squeaking as she watched him pull his shirt back on.

"You okay?"

"It's just the sun . . . so hot . . ." She fanned herself.

* * *

The ride over to Jake's was quiet. Pepper was too busy thinking about their imminent kiss to do much talking. She imagined it over and over until it seemed real. His lips on her face, nibbling her neck, her . . . oh my.

"Could you turn up the air conditioning, please?" Pepper's voice was an octave higher than normal, and it came out all breathy. She hardly recognized it as her own.

"You okay?"

"Oh . . ." She waved a hand. "It's just so unbearably hot suddenly." Get a grip, she scolded herself. It's just a freaking little kiss.

The rest of the ride over to Jake's, Pepper did her best to wipe all thoughts of kissing out of her mind. She also tried not to think about Jake's naked chest pressed against hers. "No sense worrying about something that might not even come to pass" is what Lucy would tell her. It was a futile effort.

By the time they walked in Jake's front door, Pepper was ready, willing, and able, and he had only two options: He could either give her the kiss she'd been longing for, praying for, for God's sake. Or he could give her some kind of explanation. She turned to face him and took a step forward. A big one. Her toe got hooked on the carpet, and she was going down. Jake's shirt was the only thing available to grab, and she did so with both hands. He had a surprised look on his face when he caught her in the biggest, strongest arms that she'd ever had the pleasure of falling into. For the first time in her life, Pepper was glad to be a klutz.

Jake stumbled back against the door, slamming it

shut, and Pepper gazed into his eyes. He gently pushed her away and held her at arm's length.

My God, he thought, she was attacking him. So be it. Pepper pressed her lips to his, and after a long moment, his arms circled around her. She let her body relax and melt into his. *Finally*. All he'd needed was a slight nudge.

Jake buried a hand in her hair. His lips were hard against hers, and he searched her mouth with his tongue, but it wasn't enough. She wanted more. Heat rippled through every inch of her body, and he complied with such fierce pleasure that Pepper's knees began to buckle. She held on to Jake and gathered enough strength to pull him across the room. They moved as one toward a black leather couch until finally, they stumbled back.

Jake turned just in time for her to fall on top of him. A move that he seemed quite practiced at, she thought. She didn't care. His body was warm and hard and soft all at once, and she wanted all he had to give.

Without removing his lips from hers, Jake performed another move that impressed her—he slipped a hand under her tank top and made her see fireworks. An explosion of color. Oh, Gawd . . . blue . . . green . . . red. Pepper gulped for air, and her chest heaved just like the heroine's did in the romance novel she was currently reading. *Yes, yes, I'm ready.*

Jake wasn't. As quickly as the fireworks began, they fizzled. Jake had doused them. He pulled his hand out from under her tank top and stopped kissing her. Feeling more than a little silly, Pepper composed herself and sat up. She rearranged her clothes and tucked the lock of stray hair behind her ear.

She searched Jake's face. Then a horrible thought occurred to her. Maybe he had a *problem*. No. He'd just lain on top of her. No, from what she could tell, this man did not have *that* problem. Oh, Gawd. What if Lucy was right? What if the white-collar half of the male population had some secret rule about waiting a certain length of time to have sex?

He'd had every opportunity to kiss her right there on the beach. Why hadn't he? She blew out a frustrated breath and gave him a sideways glance. Could he be gay? *No.* Not that man. Besides, he wouldn't be with her right now if he were. *Would he?*

Pepper got control of her breathing. "What is it? Don't tell me you just want to be *friends*," she whispered.

Jake shook his head. "No, baby," he said, nuzzling the words into her hair.

"Good answer," Pepper said. She reached for him, ready for another round of kissing. Anastasia's song, "Don'tcha Wanna," screamed through her head, but Jake didn't make a move.

He let out a long sigh. "I think we should wait a while. Not take things so fast."

Pepper folded her arms across her chest. "We've gone out several times, and you've never so much as kissed me. You've never even acted like you wanted to. Until today," she said.

"I guess it doesn't pay to be a gentleman, huh?"

"I wouldn't say that, but a woman does like to feel desirable." She traced a finger down his chest and paused at the top of his jeans.

Jake smiled gently and took her hand. He drew it

to his mouth and kissed the back of it before placing it back down, but higher on his chest, away from the danger zone.

Pepper's virtue had never been safer, and she had never been more frustrated.

Chapter 11

Jake watched Pepper make her way to the bathroom, her golden legs glowing in the dim light and her hips swaying gently from side to side. There goes a woman comfortable in her own body, he thought. Not like so many who wanted to change everything about themselves.

Pepper closed the door, and Jake rested his head against the back of the sofa. The room smelled of citrus. Intoxicating, alluring Pepper. God knows he did desire her. He wanted to run his hands over every inch of that fit body. It'd been a long time since he'd taken a woman into his bed. Never, since he'd moved into the small stucco house he now called home. Never, since his wife.

Jake had plans for the small house, like expanding the master bedroom and adding another bathroom. Right now, it was big enough for two, but if children were in his future, he'd need more space. *Children.* The thought made him smile—and ache. He and Angela had planned to have three. That wasn't going to happen with her, but he still intended to have them someday, with the right person.

Jake tried to picture what a child of his might look like. If it was a little girl, would she have dark hair? Red? Or might she resemble the woman who occupied his bathroom? That was a definite possibility if things continued on the way they were. But taking advantage of Pepper's feelings right now, making love to her without her knowing the truth, wasn't something he could bring himself to do.

Pepper returned a few minutes later and snuggled close to Jake. He turned his face into her hair and breathed deeply of the lemon scent.

"Careful," she said.

"Of what?"

"I think I could get used to you being a gentleman."

"Enjoy it while it lasts," Jake said. He kissed her once more, this time tender, gentler. The hunger from before was gone, replaced with a deep longing to fill the emptiness that had haunted him for so long. He kept his kisses light, not wanting to push himself past the point of no return, but Pepper wanted more, and she was a hard woman to resist. Jake was almost glad when the phone rang.

Pepper caught his arm as he reached for it. "Let it ring," she whispered in his ear.

Jake considered her request for about a second. Letting the machine pick up was out of the question. It could be someone from work. When the time came for Pepper to know the truth, Jake wanted it to come from him, not a machine.

He kissed the tip of her nose. "Sorry, it could be important." He leaned away from her and picked up.

"Hey, Mr. *Architect,* how about going out for a couple beers tonight?" Gordy said on the other end. "You can fill me in on *things,* if you know what I mean."

Jake paused. "I'll have to get back to you on that," he told Gordy.

"You're kidding? Since when do you pass up free beer?"

"I didn't say anything about passing. How about eight? Our usual place?" Jake said. He squeezed Pepper's hand.

Gordy laughed. "I can tell you're preoccupied right now, so I'll let you go. See you then."

"Sure."

"Hey, wait—before you go . . . did you ever ask Pepper about her roommate?"

"I'll do that," Jake said, impatience forcing out the words. Gordy was persistent.

"When?"

"Right now," he said and hung up.

"Right now what?" Pepper asked him.

"Huh?" Jake looked at her blankly.

Pepper gave him the same kind of look that he'd gotten from his mother a million times.

Jake's head fell back, and he stared up at the ceiling. He'd hoped to hold off letting her meet any of his friends for a while longer. Like the entire summer.

"That was a friend of mine. He's been bugging me about meeting your roommate."

"Lucy? Why?"

Jake shrugged. "I guess he figures since I like her, then she's probably a good woman. He hasn't had much luck finding nice women."

Pepper laughed. "Tell him to look on the Internet. Doesn't he know that's how I found you?"

"He's interested in Lucy because I mentioned what a nice girl I thought she was."

"Hm-m. You like Lucy?" Pepper asked, feigning jealousy.

Jake looked over at her and felt his heart do a little flip-flop. This lie had to end—and soon—just as soon as he figured out a way to tell her the truth without losing her.

"Not as much as I like you."

Pepper gave him a coy smile. "Careful; you could be in danger of losing your virginity."

"I'm counting on it," Jake said. His fingers got lost in her hair, and he pulled her to him. Heat spread through him like a slow-burning fire.

Suddenly, a grating croak blasted its way through the room. Pepper's body stiffened, and she jerked her head around. The source of the noise stared at her from the doorway of Jake's kitchen.

"A-agh-h!" she shrieked, yanking her feet from the floor. She scrambled up onto the back of the sofa. "What the hell is that?"

Jake laughed. He'd never seen anyone move so fast. "Pepper, meet Gilligan," he said, extending a hand toward a large, brown-feathered bird. "Gilligan, you sure know how to ruin a good time."

The creature, a brown pelican, flapped its wings once and then rested its head in an S curve atop its neck. It croaked again.

"Is that . . . a . . . pelican? In your *house?*" Pepper remained crouched on the back of the sofa, her knees pulled to her chest and her body pressed firmly against the wall.

Jake nodded. "He must've come in the back door. Sorry." He got up, hands outstretched, and walked

toward the gangly creature, herding him back toward
the kitchen. "C'mon, Gilligan. You know you're not
supposed to be in here."

Gilligan wasn't moving. His yellow eyes focused
on Pepper.

"I think he likes you," Jake said.

"You live with a pelican? In your *house?*"

"Yeah, I think we already established that. I do try
to limit the living arrangements to the backyard
though. Can be kind of messy having him indoors,
if you know what I mean."

"I would imagine." She waggled a hand at the pelican. "You know, I think those things are endangered."

Gilligan waddled closer to the side of the sofa
where Pepper was perched, and she scooted farther
down, making sure to stay out of reach.

"Yeah, I know. But I don't have the heart to turn
him away." Jake walked around to the other side of
the coffee table, and Gilligan protested with nu-
merous deep-throated croaks as Jake pushed him
along. He finally persuaded the bird to go back
outside.

Jake returned and gently pulled Pepper down
from the back of the sofa. "It's safe now."

She kept her eye on the kitchen doorway.

"Don't tell me you're frightened of a bird. Pelicans are all over your backyard," he reasoned.

Pepper nodded. "Yes . . . I'm used to pelicans. I
enjoy watching them soar across the sky"—she
waved a hand above her head—"up there. Outside.
But being this close to one . . . in a house . . . in *your*
house—how on earth did you come to own a brown
pelican? It must be against the law."

"You gonna turn me in?" Jake asked with a grin.

"Maybe," she said, hitching up her chin.

Jake laughed. "I found him when he was but a youngster. He'd been injured, couldn't fly. I brought him home, took care of him. I never expected he'd stick around. It's been six months, and here he is."

"I'm sure they have places for injured animals," Pepper offered.

Jake shrugged. "He's no bother. I like having him around. He came into my life at a good time. And until you came along, Gilligan kept me out of trouble."

A croak sounded through the window, and Pepper jumped. She moved closer to Jake, and he circled his arms tightly around her.

"Don't worry. You're safe with me," Jake said. His heart warmed at the trust he saw in her eyes.

"Is he able to fly now?" she asked.

Jake nodded. "He always comes back."

"Maybe he thinks you're his dad," Pepper teased.

"Maybe," Jake agreed. "Now . . . forget that bird." He leaned over and pressed his lips to hers. Her moans told him she had.

Later, Jake walked into the Right Stuff Bar and Grill and saw Gordy over in a corner, already settled at a table working on a beer. Even before he sat down, Gordy began to question him about Pepper's roommate.

"Did you ask her?"

Jake nodded and signaled the waitress for a beer. "I did. She's okay with it. I'm not so sure *I* am."

Gordy looked hurt. "What? You think I'm going to mess up what you got goin' with your lady?"

"That's exactly what I'm afraid of." He looked

Gordy over. "Look at you. You're a mess. Dirty fin-gernails . . . holes in your jeans . . ."

"Hey! You're the one who's got a lie to pull off. Just 'cause Pepper has a thing against hardworkin' guys doesn't mean her roommate does." He looked Jake up and down. "Besides, you had some help gettin' your stuff together."

Jake cursed Pete under his breath. He should have known word of his makeover would get around. Damn. No telling how many of the guys knew he'd gotten a facial.

"You could use a little help yourself," he told Gordy.

"Shit," Gordy said. He slouched low in his chair.

Jake looked and saw a man and a woman come in and sit three tables away. The woman was tall, brunette, and slender. Sherry. *That woman.* She was on the arm of an even taller man. Gordy scooted around so that his back was to them.

Jake kicked his chair. "Sit up straight. You need to quit this bullshit. You can't be hiding whenever you go out. You keep this up, and you won't be able to go anywhere."

"I'm not hiding," Gordy said. "Let's get the hell out of here."

Brad's bedroom door opened, and Marta shoved Scratch through.

"Take care of this dog. He ain't my responsibility."

Brad reached down and scooped up the pup, rubbing him gently behind the ears. "This little guy isn't hurting anything."

Marta's eyes glared cold and hard. She hadn't wasted any time showing Brad the consequences of him calling their affair quits. Darn. And he thought they could at least remain friends. He'd hoped her attitude would change after Vic popped the question, but if anything, she was worse. Now she acted like she was some kind of goddamned queen bee.

"I told you a hundred times, I ain't no dog sitter." Marta slammed his door shut, and Scratch jumped. Brad lay back on the bed, and the pup began to gnaw gently on his fingers.

"Don't worry," Brad told him. "I won't let her hurt you. She's just mad. Women get like that sometimes when they don't get what they want."

Scratch looked up at Brad through large hazel eyes. Brad liked that the pup wasn't afraid to hold his gaze. He stroked the pup's thick fur, and Scratch curled up into a ball next to Brad. Soon, he was snoring in a soft rhythm that made a gentle vibration against Brad's leg.

"C'mon, Scratch," Brad said, picking him up. "We stay here, and we both might get a bad case of lice."

He went out to the living room and stood in front of the TV, purposely blocking Marta's view. She looked up at him with contempt.

"It's been three weeks, so I assume you've decided against telling Vic what happened between us," he said.

"And you haven't moved out yet, so I assume you've decided you're not." Marta settled deeper into the sofa and propped her feet up on the coffee table. "I told you I wouldn't say anything. But I could change my mind if you plan on stayin' here much longer."

"You really going to marry him?" Brad asked.

"You meet a lot of women. You could move in

with one of them." Scratch jumped up on the sofa, and Marta pushed him off. "You and that flea-bitten mutt have worn out your welcome here."

"Let's not forget who was living here first. C'mon, Scratch." Brad grabbed his car keys from the table and headed for the door.

"Oh, Bradley," Marta called after him, and he turned. She held up her left hand and wiggled her engagement ring. "Let's not forget who Vic has chosen to spend his life with."

"Fuck you, Marta," he said, closing the door.

Brad sat in the car and lit a cigarette. He opened the ashtray and saw Pepper's business card at the bottom. He wouldn't mind having her for a room-mate. Her smell reminded him of the lemon drops that his mother used to give out to the neighbor-hood kids. He'd sure like to wrap his hands around her lemons. Fat chance of that happening though. She was a tough chick to crack.

Maybe he could get her to go to a movie or some-thing. Movies weren't hard. Not much talking involved. Then afterward when he took her home, he'd kiss away the taste of salt on her lips from the popcorn. He'd lick them clean, and then he'd take her home and lick her breasts. He was dreaming. That probably wasn't something Pepper Bartlett would let him get away with.

Brad slipped her card into his shirt pocket. He'd been meaning to stop in at Malibu Health and see her. He could use a little muscle toning. Course, he could just accidentally run into her at the beach. A little rolling around in the sand sounded like fun, too.

He knew she lived somewhere along the Pacific

Coast Highway near where she worked. She'd mentioned how she enjoyed sitting on her deck with her morning coffee and watching the waves roll in and out, so he also knew that her place was right on the beach. It shouldn't be too hard finding her on that stretch of sand. He wondered what she would think if they should run into each other while she was out for a morning stroll. That might not go over so well, especially if she was with her wacky roommate. Maybe a visit to Malibu Health would be better, after all. He was pretty sure Lucy wouldn't be there.

Chapter 12

The weekend was over far too soon. Pepper needed more sleep. She needed more of something else, too. At least she'd accomplished one thing. She no longer had to wonder what it would be like to kiss Jake. It was even more amazing than she'd dreamed about. She'd lain in bed half the night reminiscing about it.

That man. That wonderful, sexy man. She wanted desperately to make love with him. He wanted to wait. And that made him even sexier. To find someone who really cared enough to want to wait until the time was right for both of them was refreshing—in a frustrating sort of way.

Pepper had only one class today, and she dragged herself to work fifteen minutes late. Her kickboxing students were already there and warming up without her, which was just as well. She was having a hard time focusing. She forced herself through the motions though, and in no time, class was over. Most everyone cleared out, but a few remained huddled over in one corner talking.

Pepper lay on her mat, thinking and stretching

and thinking some more. After a few minutes, the others left, and Pepper was alone. She lay there for a while in the quiet of the gym, letting her body cool down, remembering her rendezvous with Jake. She'd never wanted a man so badly, and the more she thought about him, the deeper and faster her breathing became. A few more minutes, and she'd be orgasmic.

Someone cleared his throat, and Pepper sat up.

"*Brad.* What are you doing here?"

"I've been thinking about taking one of your classes. Looks like I got here just in time."

Pepper's eyebrows raised in question. She glanced around. Couldn't he see the place was empty?

"You looked like you'd fallen asleep and were having a bad dream."

Bad dream? Hardly. Pepper laughed. "No, I was just resting my bones." She looked around the gym. "As you can see, class is over. I had only one today," she said. She rolled up her mat and tucked it under one arm.

"Maybe you could give me a private lesson."

"Uh . . . I'm not sure that's possible. I mean, I really do have to get home." Pepper was sweating more now than she did while teaching class.

"But you're here, I'm here. Couldn't you teach me a few moves?"

"Moves?" Pepper gulped. Sweat trickled down her back. Where the hell was the air-conditioning when you needed it?

Brad smiled. "I'm a quick learner."

Pepper licked her lips. God, her mouth was dry. Why couldn't Brad have shown this kind of interest three weeks ago? She shook her head slowly. "Really,

I can't. Maybe you could come by another day and check things out."

"You sure?"

Pepper nodded.

"Then I guess that's what I'll do." He smiled and started to walk away, but then stopped. "I had another reason for coming here," he said. "I wanted to ask you if you'd like to get together tomorrow after I get off work. Maybe have some dinner?"

Pepper's brow wrinkled. Despite his reputation, she was tempted. Or she would be if it weren't for Jake. She had a strict rule about dating only one hunk at a time.

"I've already got plans," she said. "Sorry. How about we have a drink together one night this week when I come in to Beachside?" She knew Brad wasn't allowed to drink during working hours, but maybe if she was there late one evening and he got off a little early, she could spare a few minutes. That way it wouldn't really be a date. No chance of hurting Jake's feelings or making him feel like she was seeing other men.

"I understand. See you then," Brad said.

He left, and Pepper blew out a breath. Boy. She prayed he didn't join one of her classes. She didn't need any more distractions.

When Pepper walked through the front door, she heard the faint tinkle of bells.

Lucy came down the hallway smiling smugly. "See, it works. I heard you come in."

"Really? It couldn't be that I slammed the door?" Pepper dropped her gym bag on the floor and headed for the kitchen. Her eyes grew big, and her

mouth fell open when she saw two dozen red roses displayed on the table in a crystal vase. Her heart skipped as she grabbed the small, white envelope that was propped among them.

"They're from Brad," Lucy told her before Pepper could read the card.

A frown appeared on Pepper's brow. *"No.* Not *Brad.* We've never even dated. I just saw him over at the club. He didn't mention anything about sending flowers." She almost felt bad about giving him the brush-off.

"They have thorns. Shall I throw them out?" Lucy offered, reaching for the vase.

"No." Pepper swatted at her hand. "Why would you do that?" She leaned over and inhaled the spicy scent of the velvety petals.

Lucy shrugged. "Thorns are sticky."

"They're beautiful." Lucy gave her one of her looks. "Bad feng shui?" Lucy nodded, and Pepper rolled her eyes. "I don't care." Pepper shoved the vase back to the center of the table and stood back. She lightly clapped her hands and spun around to the refrigerator. It made a girl feel good to know she had options. She pulled out a can of Sprite and leaned against the counter, looking at the roses. Jake and Brad were two pretty good options.

"What if Jake sees them? He might think you're seeing other men. He'll think he's not the only wolf in the pack," Lucy said.

"It's good for a guy to know that sometimes. Speaking of men . . . Jake says one of his friends wants to meet you. I thought the four of us could go out to dinner tomorrow night. What do you say?"

"Why? You're the one who's looking for the man of your dreams."

Pepper took a long drink. "So what shall I tell him?"

"Can't hurt, I guess," Lucy said with a shrug. "A woman's got to live on the edge now and then." She took Pepper by the arm. "Come and see what I've done to help you with *your* love life."

"Luce, tell me you didn't feng shui my room," Pepper protested.

"I did, and you're going to love it." Lucy led her down the hall.

"I can hardly wait."

"Really?"

"No."

Afraid of what she might encounter, Pepper opened her bedroom door just a crack, enough for a small peek. It was like the sun had risen in her room. It glowed all rosy and warm like a summer day. She swung the door open wide. Fresh flowers were on the nightstand, one of the walls had been painted soft pink, and a fluffy white rug had been placed alongside her bed. Prisms of light twinkled over all four walls from a crystal that hung from the ceiling. It made her want to put on the Bee Gees and do the hustle.

She turned around and around, amazed at how a few simple changes made such a big difference in the look of a room. Pink wouldn't necessarily have been her choice, but it did give the room a subtle warmness. Good for the complexion, too. This time, she decided, Lucy had done good.

"It's beautiful," Pepper said, slowly turning in a full circle once more. She walked over to her bed and picked up a small, red heart-shaped pillow. "I think I might let you keep this." She handed it to Lucy. "Since you'll be meeting Jake's friend, maybe it could go on your bed."

Lucy took the pillow and clutched it to her chest. "That's okay. I knew you wouldn't want it. I really bought it for me anyway."

Pepper kicked off her shoes and rubbed her feet over the shaggy, white rug. "O-o-o, this is exactly what I needed. Thanks, Luce."

"I'm glad you're beginning to see things my way."

"I wouldn't go that far." Pepper looked around the room. "But it is a nice change." She jumped up and brushed past Lucy. "I've got to call Jake and tell him you've agreed to meet his friend."

Jake had mixed emotions when Pepper called to tell him Lucy had agreed to a double date. He was happy that Gordy was finally taking that first step toward finding a nice, *available* woman. But he had a sick feeling that the whole thing was nothing but a ticking bomb ready to blow up at any second.

Having Gordy spend an entire evening in Pepper's presence was going to be stressful. He'd have to remember to bring a roll of Tums. If Gordy could control his motor mouth just this once, he might consider giving him a raise.

Jake made reservations for six o'clock at Gladstone's. He'd been there a few times, and it provided a nice view of the Pacific Ocean, but the best thing about it was that it wasn't far from Pepper's cottage. If Gordy proved to be too much to handle, Jake could simply feign a headache or something, and in just a few minutes, he'd have Pepper and Lucy back home, safely out of harm's way. Then he'd set about kicking his friend's butt.

The evening started off smoothly. The pelicans were entertaining, and the conversation easy. At least it was for three of them. An hour into the evening, Jake was beginning to worry about Gordy. He hadn't uttered but a dozen words. Jake had warned him about talking too much, but he hadn't intended for him to become a mute.

Maybe his apprentice was afraid of coming across as an idiot. Or maybe Gordy was totally taken by Pepper's cute little friend. That could be trouble. If the two of them hit it off and continued going out, he didn't want to have to play chaperone just so he could make sure Gordy was behaving himself.

They all chose the House Special—grilled salmon with cucumber dill sauce—except for Gordy, who ordered steak and crab legs. He was clearly taking advantage of Jake's generosity. That was okay. Jake didn't mind treating a friend to a good meal. It was probably the only one Gordy'd had in a month, unless you counted a mixture of tomato sauce and high-fat ground beef, topped with cheddar cheese. Jake remembered those days of eating like a bachelor. Nothing was off-limits, unless it took an oven or a stove to prepare it. But then, along came Angela. She'd changed all that. They'd made a deal to share in the cooking, and she'd shown him several easy dishes to prepare when it was his turn. Long hours at the hospital hadn't allowed him to prepare anything gourmet, but what she taught him did allow for healthy, tasty meals.

Jake looked over the wine list, and he saw one that he'd recently read about in a magazine. He ordered it, and the smile on Pepper's face told him he'd chosen well.

Everything was perfect, all the way from the crab cake appetizers to the dessert. Jake and Pepper shared a piece of Big Fat Chocolate Cake and Gordy ordered a whole piece for himself. Lucy opted for raspberry sorbet. After dinner, Pepper suggested the four of them go to Beachside for drinks and to watch the sun set.

"They make the best piña coladas," she said. "We can even have the bartender add a float of Captain Morgan's Spiced Rum."

"Sounds tasty," Gordy agreed.

Jake gave his young friend a stern parental look. After two glasses of wine, Gordy had loosened up somewhat. If he had much more to drink, he'd really relax and open up. That was a frightening thought.

The drive to Beachside wouldn't take long; traffic was unusually light. The evening was ripe with romance—the sky was clear, the stars bright, and a warm breeze washed through the open windows of Pete's Audi. Jake almost forgot he had two passengers in the back seat.

He felt Pepper's eyes on him, and when he looked over at her, she gave him a slow, easy smile that melted him from the inside out. She took his hand and began stroking it softly and with purpose. It made Jake want to pull over and do something he hadn't done since high school. The lady had him under her spell, and he didn't want to break it, but he needed a diversion before he drove all of them off the road.

He looked in the rearview mirror. Gordy and Lucy were sitting close, and Gordy had a big grin on his face. "It's awfully quiet back there," he said, feeling somewhat like Ward Cleaver.

"We're enjoying the ride," Gordy responded.

Lucy smiled.

So much for Gordy saying he was in love with *that woman*.

When they arrived at Beachside, Jake couldn't help noticing the look that passed between Pepper and the bartender. Not exactly the kind of look that would make a man worry he might have some competition, but, still, a look. And a couple of times, he even thought he caught the bartender staring at Pepper. The hair on the back of his neck bristled, and he thought maybe he should growl or something.

Jake passed on having a piña colada and, instead, ordered a glass of merlot. Gordy went along with Pepper, and Lucy ordered a sparkling water with a lemon twist. By the time they were halfway through their drinks, Gordy had begun to open up.

"Captain Morgan sure put some kickass into his rum," he said with a laugh.

Jake's foot connected with Gordy's leg under the table.

Gordy rubbed his shin and continued. "Has Jake ever told you about the time he saved a guy from drowning?" He pointed to the beach below. "Right out there."

Pepper and Lucy looked at Jake and waited to hear more. When he didn't oblige, Gordy continued for him.

"We were working on one of those houses right down there on the beach, and all of a sudden, we heard screaming and yelling and carrying on—"

"It was nothing," Jake said, waving a dismissive

hand. "The ladies don't want to hear any of our boring work stories."

"Don't listen to him. He's being modest. And it wasn't work. It was above and beyond the call of duty."

Jake kicked Gordy harder this time and threw in a glare for good measure. Doctors didn't consider saving a life going above and beyond the call of duty, but Gordy wasn't aware of his past. The only thing any of his friends knew was that his wife had died and he'd moved here for a fresh start.

"Damn," Gordy said, once again rubbing his shin. "Keep those size thirteen dogs on your own side of the table."

At that moment, Jake considered picking Gordy up by the scruff of his neck and tossing him over the railing. Instead, he did something more civilized. He shifted sideways in his chair and got gut punched when he saw one of the guys from work walk through the door.

Chapter 13

Eric Burnham, youngest guy on the crew. If it was possible, he had an even bigger mouth than Gordy. Jake turned back to the table, hoping Eric wouldn't see them.

"Hey," Gordy called out, waving to Eric. He was next to their table before Jake could think of anything to do to stop him.

"Hey, Gordy, Jake . . ." Eric greeted them. He gave Pepper and Lucy a polite nod. "Glad I ran into you guys. Pete stopped by after you guys left. Said the client had a request for that other house we're just gettin' started on. Looks like we're gonna have to put in a ramp to accommodate someone with a disability."

Eric had baby blue eyes and a shock of blond hair that hung over one eye. He looked like he should be carrying a surfboard under one arm. Instead, he stood at their table in work boots and jeans that were crusted with cement, paint, and a host of other unidentifiable materials. Everyone at the table sat in silence while he talked. Finally, Eric paused and took a look around the table. A wide grin spread across his face.

"What the hell are you drinking, boss?" Eric reached for Jake's wineglass, but Jake stopped him. "Is that *wine?*" he asked. *"Dang,* I've never seen you drink anything but beer."

Jake gave Pepper a quick glance. Her forehead creased into a frown. It was definitely time to rid her of Eric's presence. He stood and patted the kid's back, then ushered him through the double doors. A couple minutes later, Jake returned— alone. He hoped that the incident would pass without any further explanation. No such luck.

"Where's your friend?" Pepper asked.

Jake looked over at Gordy, who gave him a slight shrug. "He had to leave," Jake said.

"He seemed to think your drinking wine was pretty funny," Lucy pointed out.

Jake's face filled with heat. He'd managed to keep the lies to a minimum over the last couple of weeks, but tonight, there was no escaping them.

"That guy?" Gordy asked, jutting a thumb over his shoulder. "He wouldn't know the difference between wine and a jug of piss."

Jake appreciated Gordy's efforts to come to his rescue, but he had a feeling that if he let him continue talking, things would only get worse. All he wanted at that moment was to slide under the table and slither out the door like the snake he was.

Fortunately, the rest of the evening passed without incident, and Eric's visit to their table seemed to have been completely forgotten by the time Jake and Gordy dropped the women off. Jake was even

more assured when Pepper's kiss was just as warm
and as inviting as ever. She teasingly bit his lower lip
and whispered in his ear, "See you soon." He looked
over at Gordy and smiled when he saw him plant a
kiss on Lucy's cheek. Even under the porch light, he
thought he saw her blush.

On the way back to Jake's, the men were quiet.
Finally, Jake spoke up. "I'm thinking I should tell
Pepper the truth," he said. He looked over and saw
a vacant look on Gordy's face. His friend was either
daydreaming or just plain shit-faced. It took a
minute, but what he said must have finally regis-
tered because Gordy's head snapped around and
he had a look of panic on his face.

"*What?*"

"It's hard lying all the time, trying to keep everything straight," Jake explained.

"Don't be going all goody-goody on me," Gordy
said, desperation creeping into his voice.

"What's it to you? It'd be a sure fifty bucks in your
pocket."

"Yeah, but I think Pepper is good for you. You
should wait until you're sure you've got her wrapped
around your you know what."

Gordy was giving his concerned-for-a-friend act a
good run. Jake considered what he'd said the rest
of the way home. It wasn't until they pulled into his
driveway that it hit him.

"You're full of it," Jake said.

"What?" Gordy asked.

"You don't care two cents about whether or not
Pepper is wrapped around anything. It's her friend
you're worried about."

"*What?*"

Jake unlocked the front door and went straight to the kitchen. "Lucy," he said, chuckling. "She's already got you wrapped around all of her freckles."

"Now you're the one who's full of it. She hardly even noticed me."

Jake took a beer from the refrigerator. He scowled at its bitterness.

"What's the matter?" Gordy laughed. "You drink a couple glasses of wine, and now you're turning your nose up at your favorite drink?"

"It doesn't taste right." Jake set the bottle on the counter. "If Lucy didn't like you, what was she blushing about?"

Gordy picked up Jake's beer and smelled it. With a shrug, he took a large swallow. "She blushed 'cause she liked what she saw."

"Yeah, wait'll she gets a dose of your charm and wit. She'll be all over you," Jake said. "Frankly, I'm surprised you got away from her with all your clothes still on."

"Ha-ha. I can be a gentleman, too, y'know. At least she likes me for who I am."

Jake shot him a sharp look.

"Sorry, boss. I know it was me and Pete who put you up to this . . ."

That was true, but Jake wasn't about to blame anyone else for his lies. No one forced him, and now he had to figure out how to get himself out of this situation without having Pepper run the other way. Jake grabbed his beer back from Gordy and finished it off.

"Maybe you just get her hooked on beer. After all, it seems like you've already got her hooked on you."

"Let's hope so," Jake said.

***

"So what do you think?" Pepper asked Lucy.

"He has potential," Lucy said.

"Oh, *c'mon*. You know you like him. You should have seen your face when he kissed you. I swear it turned the color of your hair," Pepper teased, and Lucy's face flushed pink. "See, there it goes again."

"It's the wine," Lucy said. "You know how it makes my cheeks and ears red."

"Liar. You only had a sip." She reached out and brushed Lucy's hair away from one of her ears. "Hm-m. They don't look red to me." Lucy batted her hand away, and Pepper went into the kitchen. She pressed the button on the answering machine.

Pepper, it's Brad. I've been thinking about you and just wanted to see if you might change your mind about getting together tomorrow. Let me know.

She pressed delete, then listened to the next one.

Pepper, it's me again. Guess you're still out. Sorry, I didn't realize you were seeing somebody else when I left that other message.

Lucy looked at Pepper with raised eyebrows. "Is that *Brad* the *bartender?*"

Pepper chewed her lower lip. "I'm afraid so. And don't give me that look." She shook her head. "I don't know what's suddenly gotten into him. I've been going to Beachside for nearly three years, and now, suddenly, he wants to go out on a date."

"You must've done something to encourage him." Lucy wagged a finger at her. "Your mother would force you to move back home if she knew you were getting involved with a man like that."

"Who said anything about getting involved?" Pepper threw up her hands. "I don't know what's going through his mind." She smiled. "At least I know he's interested, in case Jake and I don't work out."

"Lord help us." Lucy walked to the hallway and fluttered the wind chimes that hung from the ceiling outside the bathroom.

Pepper rolled her eyes and pressed the button to hear the last message.

Pepper, it's Cat. I'm calling about Mom. Before you get too excited, she's all right, but I wanted you to know she had a problem with her medication and had to go to the emergency room. Like I said, she's all right, and they'll be releasing her in the morning. I'll be at the house tonight if you want to talk.

Fear washed over Pepper like a huge wave, and Lucy reached out to her. She looked around the room, dazed, not knowing whether to sit, stand, or run to her room. Finally, she went and sat on the sofa. Lucy sat next to her and put an arm around her.

Pepper scrubbed her hands through her hair.

"I better call her," she said after a minute.

Lucy nodded, giving Pepper's shoulder a gentle squeeze.

Pepper's fingers shook, and she paused, frowning, as she struggled to remember the number she'd been dialing for years.

"What's wrong?" Lucy asked softly.

"The number. I can't remember it."

Lucy took the phone and dialed for her. She handed it back, and Pepper gave her an appreciative look.

Cat must've been waiting by the phone because she picked up after only one ring.

"How's Mom?" Pepper said, trying to keep her voice under control.

"You got my message?"

"Yes. What's this about a problem with her medication? *What* medication?" Pepper's voice cracked, and she took three calming breaths. She waited for her sister to explain, but what she really wanted to do was scream. This was her fault. If she'd been home where she belonged, none of this would've happened. Her mom had been trying to get her to come home ever since she left. Oh, God, don't let it be too late to fix things.

"Mom's been taking sleeping pills and—"

"*What?*" Pepper shrieked. "Since when?"

"For a while now. She's been having trouble sleeping, and her doctor thought he'd have her take them for a short time until she could adjust—"

"*Adjust?* Adjust to what?" But Pepper knew. It was everything. Her dad dying, her moving to California, too much change.

Cat tried to explain. "Her doctor says all that she's had to deal with in the past couple of years has finally wore her down."

Oh, God. It *was* her fault. Pepper rubbed a hand over her forehead. She began pacing the kitchen. Her mom's sleeping problems had started the day her dad died. Why couldn't she have waited a while before moving out? If anything happened to her mother, she'd never forgive herself.

"Pepper, you're not at fault here," her sister said as though she was reading her mind. "Yes, it was hard on Mom when Dad died, and yes, it was hard on her when you left . . ." Cat grew quiet. "It was just a lot of stress for her to deal with all at once."

Pepper gripped the phone so tightly her fingers ached. Tears filled the corners of her eyes, and she wiped them away. A light touch on her shoulder made her turn, and Lucy handed her a Kleenex. A hard lump filled her throat, and she tried to swallow it away, but the pain simply moved into her chest. Sleeping pills? What had they all done to her mother? Fear filled her as an unspeakable thought gathered in her mind.

"Cat?" Pepper's voice was barely a whisper, as though speaking too loud would make what she was thinking more real. She paused before continuing. "You don't think . . . Mom wouldn't have been . . ." The words were lying thick and painful on her tongue. She leaned against the wall, trying to gather strength, and Lucy stood next to her, giving her support. Thank God for best friends.

Cat didn't wait for Pepper to finish. "No, not at all."

Pepper allowed that to be enough for now, even though she wasn't convinced. "I'm coming home. You said she'd be out of the hospital tomorrow?"

"Yes, but you don't have to—"

"Of course I do. We both need to be there for her."

"I just meant that I'll be here, and I know she wouldn't want to think she'd disrupted your life. You know how she is."

Pepper did know, but she couldn't sit around and wonder why this had happened. She had to see for herself. She needed to look into her mom's eyes and try to see the truth.

Chapter 14

It was morning, and Pepper had barely slept. The phone rang, and a minute later, her bedroom door opened. Not quite ready to face the day, she pretended to still be asleep. After getting the news about her mom, she'd lain there all night in the dark, imagining the worst. It'd be hard to face her mom with a smile after all that had happened, especially since she felt like she was a big part of her mom's unhappiness.

"It's Brad," Lucy said softly.

With no energy and heavy eyes, Pepper willed herself to sink deeper into the mattress. Maybe it would swallow her up. She considered asking Lucy to tell him she wasn't home, or better yet, to go to hell, but Brad was her problem, and she wasn't going to make her friend lie for her. She reached a hand out from under the covers and picked up the phone.

"I didn't wake you, did I?"

"I was about to get up," Pepper said. "I have to leave for the airport." Her voice shook as thoughts of her mom swirled around in her head. She wiped a tear from her eye.

"I just wanted to say I'm sorry about calling you last night. You told me you were busy, and I should've listened. Still friends?"

"Of course. I'll be out of town for a couple of days, but when I get back, you can make me a good, stiff one." She'd need it after spending a couple of days with Cat.

Brad didn't ask where she was going, and she was glad. She wasn't in the mood to explain about her family's problems. Pepper hung up and let the phone drop to the floor. She swung her legs over the side of the bed. When she looked up, Lucy still stood in the doorway.

"What?"

Lucy's lips drew into a thin line. "Stalker."

Pepper let her head fall back. "He's not a stalker. He just wanted to say he was sorry for being so persistent." She reached for the phone and held it between her ear and shoulder while she tugged on a pair of jeans. Jake's line rang five times, but no machine picked up for her to leave a message.

She finished getting dressed and was ready to go in less than an hour. Pepper tried calling Jake once more when she got to the airport. Still no answer.

She stuffed her bag in the overhead bin across the aisle from where she sat. Row eleven. Lucky eleven.

After getting settled in her window seat, Pepper turned on the overhead air dial. A blanket lay in the seat next to her, and she pulled it over onto her lap in case she got cold later. She closed her eyes, and almost immediately, her thoughts turned to Jake. She was disappointed she hadn't been able to talk with him before leaving town. What if the plane crashed and she never had the chance to say good-bye? What if they never got to share another kiss? Her mouth drew into a thin line. And then she smiled, remembering how Jake had tried to herd that pelican out the door. She could even see herself enjoying the big bird's company once she got used to the idea.

Pepper'd been ready to make love, and Jake had turned her down. His hands had been on her body, under her tank top, touching her bare skin. How could any man turn back from there? She'd anticipated his touch, wanted it so bad. And then it'd finally happened, and she'd wanted to scream, *"Just do it."* But Jake Hunter was the type of man who wanted to take his time. Replaying the whole scene through her mind, Pepper put a hand to her chin and smiled with a little shake of her head. He was full of surprises.

"Are you okay, honey?"

Pepper looked into the face of the elderly woman who was sitting next to her. She felt a flush of color in her cheeks. "Just a little nervous about flying, that's all."

No way she was going to tell granny the truth— that she was practically orgasmic at the thought of a man's hands on her. The woman would probably have her thrown off the plane. Hm-m. That's a thought. At least it'd get her out of having to go to Seattle. She pushed that thought away. Her mom needed her. Jake and his hands would be here when she got back.

"Don't worry," the old woman said, patting Pepper's arm. "Flying is quite safe now with all that new security in place against the Tannenbaum."

Pepper smiled. Yes, the *Tannenbaum* was a frightful thing. She stared out the window as the plane taxied the runway. It picked up speed, and rather than watch the blur of the tarmac, she closed her eyes to pray for a safe flight. Ever since she'd read that takeoffs and landings were the most dangerous part of flying, it'd become a ritual. As soon as the plane was safely in the air, Pepper finished her prayer with an *Amen* and opened her eyes.

Cat picked Pepper up from Sea–Tac airport two and a half hours after she boarded the Boeing 737 in LA. Forty-five minutes after that, she was in her old bedroom, lying on her bed, staring up at the ceiling, wishing that instead, she was back in Malibu with a particular dark-haired man. She'd told Lucy if he called, to tell him she'd be back in a couple of days. Nothing more. He didn't need to know about her family's problems. Not yet anyway.

Pepper pushed Jake to the back of her mind. Right now, she wanted to focus on her mom, make sure she was all right.

Cat tapped lightly at her bedroom door.

"I'm leaving to go pick up Mom now. Want to come?"

Pepper didn't need any time to consider. The less time she and her sister spent together, the less likely the visit would turn sour. She and Cat had different views on life, and Pepper felt bad about leaving her mom with only her sister for comfort and support after their dad died. Cat wasn't exactly the supportive type. She was more the needy and demanding type.

"I'll wait here," she told Cat. Pepper listened for the sound of her sister's car leaving before reaching for her bag. She had enough clothing for a week stuffed inside, but come hell or high water, in no more than three days, she was determined to be on a plane headed for home.

She hung a black sweater in the closet, dropped her makeup bag on the bathroom counter, then went out to the kitchen. The refrigerator was stocked with what had been her favorites: orange soda, cheese for sandwiches, half-and-half for her morning coffee, lunch meat, and several different flavors of yogurt. These days, soy milk had replaced soda, fruit had finally made its way into her diet, string cheese had displaced fattier cheeses, and she now used fat-free half-and-half in her coffee. She smiled wistfully. It was almost as though she'd become a stranger to her family. Hadn't she told them she was into fitness now? Hadn't her mother listened when she spoke about her job at the health club? Hadn't they noticed all the work she'd put into losing what they'd always referred to as baby fat? Pepper glanced down at her thighs. Well, maybe not all of it, but close.

Pepper opened the vegetable drawer and spotted a bag of grapes. She grabbed a handful and stood at the kitchen window looking down the street. So much had changed since her last visit. What used to be acres and acres of forest and horse pastures and barns was now a huge construction site. No more hidden places for a girl and boy to walk together, hold hands, sneak a kiss. She'd sneaked more than one herself in those woods. And though she'd gotten used to, and rather liked, hectic Malibu, she always looked forward to coming home where she could count on a slower pace and tons of green. From the look of things, that would soon be a thing of the past. Too bad. Pepper shook her head with a sigh. Things changed. Development always had a way of catching up, even in Washington. Even on the Eastside.

Pepper looked out at the driveway. The last time her mom had been in the hospital was for gallstones. She had stood in the same spot she was standing right now, waiting for her dad to bring her mom home. They'd pulled up in her dad's new, white BMW, and she'd watched him get out and hurry to the other side of the car to help her mother. They'd walked from the car and come up the steps together, her dad holding her mom gently with one arm, making sure she didn't slip on the pavement. They were like newlyweds. Frank Bartlett had loved his wife, and he wasn't afraid to show it. He was a true gentleman. Always treated her mom like a lady. He was the kind of man she'd always wanted. It'd take quite a guy to live up to the standards her father had set.

Remembering that day made Pepper's heart ache, and she turned away from the window. Her dad had left them far too soon, and she couldn't help thinking something more could have been done to prevent it.

Pepper's mom and sister walked through the back door a half hour later, and Pepper made sure to wipe away any lingering tears. Her mother certainly didn't need any added stress after what she'd been through.

Hannah's eyes danced at the sight of her daughter. "Pepper," she said, holding out her arms.

Her mother's embrace was just what she needed. It warmed her and made her feel all cozy and loved, and she completely forgot why she'd stayed away so long. After a long minute, she stepped back to see for her-

self that everything was okay. Her mom didn't look like
a woman who'd just tried to commit suicide. Relief
lifted the weight from her heart. Maybe it really had
been an accident. After all, her mother had always
been strong, always the one to go to with her troubles.
Pepper bit her lip. Who could her mom go to with *her*
troubles? Whatever had happened, she had only three
days to find out and try to make it better.

"Let me look at my sweet girl," Hannah said. She
looked Pepper over like she was one of her prize
dahlias. "Skinny." She turned to Cat. "Doesn't she
look skinny?"

"Yeah, skinny," Cat agreed. She pulled out a chair
for their mom and nudged her to sit, but Hannah
moved toward the refrigerator.

Pepper did an eye roll. She knew what was coming.
Food . . . and lots of it. By the time she went back
home, she'd be carrying an extra five pounds. "I'm
not skinny. I'm fit."

Her mom waved a dismissive hand. "You're too
young to be *unfit*." She scanned the contents of the
refrigerator. "I see your sister went to the store and
picked up a few of your favorite things. Are you
hungry?" she asked, turning to Pepper.

"I'm not here for you to wait on me, Mom. I'm
here to make sure you're okay. So you can stop
trying to fatten me up—both of you." Pepper stood,
facing her mom and sister with her hands planted
firmly on her hips. "Now, Cat," she said, "as much as
I like you being here, I'd sure like it if you could run
to the store." Pepper reached into her jeans pocket
and pulled out a piece of paper. "Do me a favor, and
go get these things."

Cat didn't put up a fuss or roll her eyes or anything.

She sure seemed to be on her best behavior. Either that, or she, too, was feeling her share of guilt. It made Pepper want to laugh. Given enough time, she was sure her sister would go right back to being that spoiled little brat she'd been since, well, forever. It'd take a lot more than one day of feigning concern to make Pepper believe Cat had finally grown up. At the moment, Pepper didn't care about the reason; she was just glad they were both there to help her mom.

"Have you looked in here?" Hannah pointed into the refrigerator. "Look. All the things you like."

"Used to," Pepper said. She gave her sister a little wave, and Cat left. "I don't eat those things anymore. That's why I'm *skinny."* She took her mother's arm and led her back over to the table. "Now sit. Tell me what's going on with you."

A flicker of pain filled her mother's eyes, as though to speak of it would open a wound that had not yet healed. Almost immediately, Hannah sat up straighter, and the twinge of pain, or whatever it was Pepper thought she had seen, was gone. Her mother, brave and proud, would never admit to being so hurt that she would dare to take her own life.

Pepper knew it was no use, but she had to ask anyway. "Mom? What was this accident with your medicine?"

Hannah looked away briefly, and then her gaze locked onto Pepper's.

"You know how I am. I simply forgot I'd already taken my pills." She shook her head lightly. "I get so busy and have so many pills to take . . . Sometimes, I forget." Hannah got up and went over to the window. "Did you see what they're doing over there?" she said, nodding toward the street. "It's a shame. The traffic will be awful."

Pepper went over and stood next to her mom. She obviously thought she'd successfully changed the subject. But dammit, she could be determined too. They would talk later.

"Yes, it's a shame."

"Let's go. I'll show you," Hannah said, turning to her daughter. "Even though I hate that all those beautiful trees have been chopped down, it's fun walking through all the new houses." She headed for the door without waiting for Pepper's response.

"*Wait*. Are you sure?" Pepper asked. "Aren't you supposed to be taking it easy?"

Hannah waved a hand at her. "Those doctors don't know anything. Let's go."

Pepper ran to her room and grabbed her coat. She caught up with her mom halfway down the street. "Gee, thanks for waiting."

Hannah smiled and kept up her brisk pace. They got to the end of the street and waited a long minute for the light to change before crossing. As soon as they reached the other side, Hannah turned off onto a path that veered away from the street.

"At least they've left these trails so I can still enjoy my walks," she said.

Pepper looked around. She and her mother were surrounded by trees. "I thought we were going to look at houses."

"We'll walk through here for a bit first," Hannah said, slowing her pace only slightly.

"You don't walk over here alone, do you?"

"Who else am I going to walk with?" Hannah's voice had an edge, and she grew quiet.

Pepper hated to make her mom face any more pain, especially right after getting out of the hospital, but this might be her only chance to find out what was really going on. "How're you and Cat getting along?"

Hannah stopped and turned to Pepper. "We're fine. We're getting along just fine." Again, her mother had put on the brave front she was so well known for, and any hint of pain was pushed aside. Hannah continued walking, but Pepper caught her arm.

"Wait. Why won't you talk to me?"

"We are talking," Hannah said, looking back defiantly. "What did you think? That you'd come here and *fix* things? What's happened can't be fixed. Just like your sister having a streak of the devil in her can't be fixed."

She laughed. "What do you want to hear, Patrice? That I'm so sad I wanted to kill myself? Then what?" Hannah flung out her arms. "What would that change? Would that make your dad come back?"

Feigning anger at her prying was her mother's way to cover the pain that was eating away at her heart. Although Hannah Bartlett was still a striking woman, life, not always easy, had claimed her face like a sorrowful story. Is that what she had to look forward to?

She'd seen firsthand how life's events had a way of robbing a woman of her youth. Where did it go? It seemed that the woman who remained beautiful throughout her life was the one who had truly found "happily ever after." That would explain why some of her clients at the club looked like they could use the name of a good plastic surgeon instead of a good workout.

The spark her mom's eyes had once held was

gone, and Pepper knew that her mom didn't think anyone was aware of that. But her mother's brave front didn't fool her. Still, she knew that if pressed, her mother would dig in her heels and be more determined than ever to hide her true feelings.

"Do you still want me to come up here for my birthday?" Pepper asked.

"Of course. It would be nice to see Lucy, too. How's she doing with her flowers? Has she met a man yet?" Hannah spoke as though their previous conversation had never taken place.

"It just so happens that Lucy and I went on a double date the other night."

"With you and Henry?"

"No. I don't see him anymore, remember?"

Hannah nodded. "I just thought maybe you two had patched things up."

"No. I don't think his wife would appreciate that. And before you start, I didn't know he was married. That's why I stopped seeing him."

Hannah gave her a sympathetic nod.

"It's okay though. I've met a great guy. It's early, but I think he could be the one. And if Lucy comes up, you can grill her about our date." Pepper took her mother's arm as they continued walking.

In a few minutes, the forest opened to a clearing. Pepper recognized it as the place where a meadow full of wildflowers used to grow when she was a child. She'd pick a bunch and run home with them, and her mother would put them in a vase. A bit further, a field where horses once stood grazing was now filled with new housing construction, some finished, some not. Pounding hammers echoed through the still air. So much change, so sudden. Or had she simply been away that long?

When they got back to the house, Cat had returned from the store. Pepper checked to see that her sister had gotten all the items on her list. To Pepper's surprise and delight, Cat had even picked up a few extra things that she thought Pepper might like. A *Cosmopolitan* magazine to read in bed, some scented lotion for after her shower, and raw almonds for snacking on late at night. Raw almonds? Maybe her sister *had* been listening. She certainly did seem to be making an effort.

That night, her mother prepared a dinner that could have fed five people. Salad with homemade blue cheese dressing, baked potatoes, buttermilk chicken, fresh snap peas. It was more food than Pepper was used to, and most of it was loaded with carbs. Pepper remembered when she could have really made a dent in a feast like this, but now, as she looked around the table, she wondered how anyone could eat this much food. Her mother had gone through so much effort though, that Pepper was compelled to at least take a small helping of each item.

When they were finished with dinner, Hannah brought out decaf coffee and blueberry cheesecake for dessert.

"I'm not sure I can fit anything else inside here," Pepper said, gently rubbing her stomach.

"You used to eat a lot more," Cat reminded her.

"I used to be a lot different," Pepper said with a laugh. "So did you."

Hannah reached over, lightly touching Pepper's arm. "We're all older and wiser."

* * *

Brad was up early, intending to get out of the house before Vic woke up. Much more having to listen to talk about wedding plans and how much his friend was looking forward to married life, and he was going to hurl. With any luck, he'd have a new roommate soon and be able to move out.

He pulled a piece of paper out of his wallet. One of his female customers had given him her phone number and address. Alena Hamilton. She'd been coming into Beachside for the last couple of months, and she had made it clear she was interested. When she gave him her address, she told him just to show up. She'd be waiting by the pool. If things went well, Pepper might have to wait for that drink. He even told his boss that he might be late to work that night.

Brad left the house and headed up the Pacific Coast Highway toward Malibu. Just before reaching Pepperdine, he turned right and drove three miles up the winding road into Malibu Canyon. After driving around up there for forty-five minutes looking for Alena's address, he was beginning to get frustrated. Finally, he pulled over to the side of the road and let Scratch out for a pee break.

He looked out over the brown hillside of scrub brush and dry grass. It was ripe for fire. A gentle breeze blew up the hillside, but it provided little relief. If it weren't for the view of the Pacific Ocean, Brad wouldn't see any point in living up there. The dry air made his lips dry, and he licked them. He hoped Alena was prepared with plenty of refreshments. Until he found her place, plain old water would have to do. He took a bottle of water from the backseat and finished half of it.

Brad leaned his head against the headrest. With the car stopped, the inside heated quickly. He turned up the air-conditioning and put his hand to the vent, feeling for cool air. It was practically nonexistent.

"Great," he said, flipping the switch from side to side. Brad lowered both windows, but that wasn't much help considering it was hotter outside than it was in the car. Perspiration ran down his temples, and he wiped it away. Scratch jumped back in the car, and Brad continued up the meandering hillside road.

With the temperature rising and no end to the winding roads, his patience began to wear thin. He slammed a hand down on the steering wheel. Scratch looked up at him and lowered his head like he was in trouble. "It's fucking hot in here," he said to the dog. He noticed a construction site up ahead. Maybe the men working there could help point him in the right direction. That is, if they spoke English.

Jake dropped an empty water bottle on the ground next to the cooler and dug another out from under the ice.

"There's beer in there, too," Gordy said. He grabbed a towel and wiped sweat from his face. "Oh, that's right. I forgot. You don't drink beer anymore. You're into wine now." He chuckled.

"Wine's good for you," Jake said, taking a long, cool drink of Dasani. He looked out over the terrace, where a pool rested on the edge of the hillside, making it look as though it dropped directly into the Pacific Ocean. A work of art.

"So's beer." Gordy leaned back and rubbed his bare stomach. "It's got barley and hops and all kinds of healthy stuff in it."

At twenty-five, Gordy was well on his way to having one of those bellies like those fat little smiling statues. Jake jabbed Gordy's abdomen with his water bottle. "So is exercise, but I don't see you out jogging."

Gordy straightened up. He sucked in his stomach, but a small pouch continued to hang over his belt. "Hey," he said, "I could get rid of this, no problem."

Jake finished his water and grabbed another. "I'm going inside to work on that staircase."

"I'll be out front. I need to make a phone call." Gordy kept his eyes focused on the ground.

"I thought we had a deal," Jake said.

"We do. You convince your woman for the entire summer that you're what she wants, and I stop seeing *that woman*."

"That wasn't the deal, and you know it. Besides, what about Lucy?"

"Sorry, but I got needs, and I don't think that cute little redhead was all that into me," Gordy said, and he walked away.

"I think you're wrong," Jake yelled after him. "But she sure as hell won't look twice at you if she finds out you have a fixation on other men's women."

He tossed the water bottle on the ground. A dozen brown pelicans, looking like mere specks from where he stood, soared high above the water, and every few seconds, one of them plunged into the sea. Jake wondered if any of them might be Gilligan. His feathered friend had been gone for a couple of days, probably out looking for some female companionship. Jake chuckled, remembering the look on Pepper's face when she first saw the bird. He should have warned her.

He stretched his arms to the blue sky. He'd woken up with a kink in his back, and as the day wore on, it hadn't gotten any better. He'd considered going to one of Pepper's classes. All that stretching and twisting might be of some help, but he wasn't about to be the token male in a class full of women.

Jake put his tool belt back on and entered the house through a French slider. He stopped by the front staircase and looked out front. Gordy was still on his cell phone.

"I hope she's worth it," Jake muttered.

A car approached, and he saw a guy, maybe late twenties, get out of a newer model Mustang. Probably looking for work. Jake thought he looked like he could handle the heavy lifting required for the job. He glanced over at the rest of the crew. They were still on break, sitting under a cypress tree. He didn't need another body taking up ground space and drinking all the water. He went to work on a piece of railing, and a minute later, Gordy called to him.

Jake went to the open door frame, and a truck sped past, leaving a flurry of dry dirt in its wake. He waved the cloud of grit away from his face, and when he looked back, Gordy and their visitor were doing the same. The trapezius muscle in Jake's back clenched tight. It was the bartender from Beachside.

"This guy's lookin' for an address." Gordy walked over and showed Jake a piece of paper.

Jake shook a towel out of his back pocket and dragged it across his face, wiping off sweat and some of the dirt the passing car had left behind. He gave the paper a brief glance. "It's up the road another mile."

Brad looked in the direction Jake pointed. "I've been up there. Twice. The road forks off, and there's no street sign."

"Yeah, that's a problem," Jake said.

"Hey, weren't you guys at Beachside the other night?" Brad looked over at Gordy. "You guys came in with a couple of women."

"Yeah, they were pretty hot, huh?" Gordy said, grinning widely, but Jake didn't see anything to grin at.

"Guess I'll drive back up there and take another look," Brad said. He got back into the Mustang and drove off.

Brad pressed down on the accelerator and drove in the direction Jake had pointed. He looked in his rearview mirror as he left the two men behind. So that's the kind of guy who interests Pepper. He'd never have guessed. He figured her more the attorney type. Hell, if she was willing to go out with a guy who swings hammers for a living, what was wrong with him? He shook his head. She could do better than that.

Brad's car crested the hill, and a little farther, he came to where the road forked. Going left would lead him to a dead end. And right, to a small older neighborhood. He turned that way and had been driving around for another ten minutes when he finally came to a narrow cobblestone street with houses that were probably older than his grandmother. Well-kept yards, most with pools. When Alena had told him she lived in the Malibu hills, he pictured it being in a more upscale neighborhood.

He found her house near the end of the street,

and true to her word, she was indeed waiting for him out by the pool. Naked. He looked up when he saw her and mouthed, *Thank you.*

Alena had long, stick-straight blond hair and breasts that poked straight up into the sky. Probably manufactured in a lab somewhere. She looked up when he stepped off the grass and onto the brick walkway, and Brad swore her nipples hardened immediately. They stood all perky at attention as though a general had just entered the room.

Brad reached into his pocket and fingered the plastic bag that contained two hits of joy, although it was entirely possible they wouldn't need to use them. Alena seemed ready for action.

An hour later, Alena kicked Brad out the door.

"Son of a bitch," she said. "How dare you try and slip drugs into my drink."

She slammed the door in his face, and Brad stood there, perplexed. What the hell had happened? He was usually pretty good at reading women, but he'd obviously misunderstood her for the type to enjoy a good high with a good roll in bed.

Damn.

Chapter 15

From the moment Pepper stepped off the Boeing 737, she felt more relaxed than she had in a long time. Lucy met her when she walked out of the restricted area, and she was only slightly disappointed that Jake wasn't with her. Having him there would have meant a perfect homecoming. Still, it was good to be home.

When they got back to their cottage, Pepper quickly unpacked and changed her clothes. She dropped her dirty things in the hamper and breathed a sigh of contentment when she looked out and saw a brown pelican dive-bomb from the sky. It was almost like she'd never left.

Except she had. And she'd had a nice visit with her family. Her mother looked well despite having been in the hospital and being forced to eat that food for two days. And although Pepper remained skeptical, she'd enjoyed her time with Cat, too. As well as the visit had gone, however, it was twice as nice being home. Pepper was eager to get back to her daily routine of playing in the sand, watching the sun set with her friends at Beachside, and making kissy face with Jake.

Pepper went out to the kitchen to find Lucy. The sliding door was open, and she went outside. Lucy was up on the roof with a watering can, tending her flowers.

"You going to be up there long?" Pepper yelled to her.

Lucy looked down and put a hand to her ear. It was high tide, and the waves slapped against the shore, making it near impossible to hear each other.

Pepper shouted, "Never mind," and waved a hand at her. She went back inside and stopped at the kitchen table to go through a pile of mail. Three credit card offers, a *Coastal Living* magazine, and a bright yellow flyer that could easily have been mistaken for junk mail. It was her monthly newsletter on upcoming sand sculpting competitions. She sat down to read it, and a few minutes later, Lucy knocked at the sliding door with her arms full of fresh flowers. Pepper let her in, and there was another knock, this time at the front door.

"Could be Mr. Reed," Lucy whispered. "He dropped by unexpectedly twice while you were gone."

"Geez, that's worse than having a parent live nearby," Pepper said. She figured he made unscheduled visits to see if he could catch them doing something against the provisions in their lease. Pepper suspected if he ever did, he'd try to use it as an excuse to evict them so he could get more money for the small house. She couldn't blame him. Malibu beachfront property usually went for four times what she and Lucy paid for a cottage like theirs. Mr. Reed had only agreed to let them live there so cheaply as a favor to his son, who left Malibu a year ago to go to New York and become a stock trader. But a lease was a lease, and in it, he had agreed not to raise their rent for three years. Sorry, Mr. Reed, two years to go. She wasn't about to do anything to lose their rent-controlled dwelling.

Pepper put an eye to the peephole.

"Brad," she whispered to Lucy. What the heck was he doing there? Mr. Reed would have been a welcome sight. She turned slowly, quietly, keeping her back pasted against the door, so he couldn't see her through the side window. She gestured for Lucy to hide in the kitchen, who for once did as she was told. What now? She couldn't stay with her back plastered to the door all day. Her brow furrowed. What made him think he could just show up on her doorstep any time he felt like it? And not only that, how did he know where she lived?

Pepper had a mind to make it clear that this kind of intrusion was unacceptable. She'd only just gotten home from a traumatic weekend with her mom and sister, and she was in no mood for this kind of behavior.

Pepper stepped away from the door and swung it open, poised to give Brad a few choice words. Instead, her mouth just hung open.

"For you," Brad said, holding out another bouquet of flowers. This time lilies. White, beautiful— and not that she'd ever say it out loud—but they rivaled any of the flowers Lucy had brought into the house.

"I hope you don't mind me showing up like this.

I spoke with Lucy last night, and she told me about your mother. I thought these might help."

Thanks, Lucy. Although Pepper was in no mood to see her favorite bartender, she couldn't help but be touched by his thoughtfulness. She stepped aside to allow him in.

"I know you said your schedule was busy, so I won't keep you," he said, his voice full of apology. "I hope your mother is feeling better."

Brad's concern for her mother touched Pepper. "That's very sweet of you," she said. The coffeemaker chimed, and a rich, earthy aroma wafted into the living room.

"Would you like some coffee?" Offering him a cup was the least she could do to thank Lucy for not warning her.

"No, thanks," Brad said. "I just wanted to drop these off. Better get them in some water."

Pepper put her nose to the petals. A smile crept to the corners of her mouth as she thought of Lucy's reaction to the last bundle of flowers he'd brought. These flowers were thornless. Nothing objectionable to these.

Perhaps she'd been too quick in judging Brad. How could a woman not like a man who brought her white lilies? Jake hadn't even reached the stage of swiping a flower from the garden and presenting it to her. And when she'd asked about him, Lucy told her he hadn't called once while she was away. She smelled the flowers again. Either they were working some voodoo on her, or she was beginning to take a liking to Brad the bartender.

"Are you sure?" Pepper asked, walking over to the

Zebra Contemporary

To start your membership, simply complete and return the Free Book Certificate.
You'll receive your Introductory Shipment of FREE Zebra Contemporary Romances,
you only pay $1.99 for shipping and handling. Then, each month you will receive
the 4 newest Zebra Contemporary Romances. Each shipment will be yours to
examine FREE for 10 days. If you decide to keep the books, you'll pay the preferred
subscriber price (a savings of up to 30% off the cover price), plus shipping and
handling. If you want us to stop sending books, just say the word... it's that simple.

If the FREE Book Certificate is missing, call 1-800-770-1963 to place your order.

FREE BOOK CERTIFICATE

Yes! Please send me FREE Zebra Contemporary romance novels. I only pay $1.99 for shipping and handling.
I understand that each month thereafter I will be able to preview 4 brand-new Contemporary Romances FREE for
10 days. Then, if I should decide to keep them, I will pay the money-saving preferred subscriber's price (that's
a savings of up to 30% off the retail price), plus shipping and handling. I understand I am under no obligation to
purchase any books, as explained on this card.

NAME _____

ADDRESS _____ APT. _____

CITY _____ STATE _____ ZIP _____

TELEPHONE (_____) _____

E-MAIL _____

SIGNATURE _____

(if under 18, parent or guardian must sign)

Offer limited to one per household and not to current subscribers. Terms, offer and prices subject to change.
Orders subject to acceptance by Zebra Contemporary Book Club. Offer Valid in the U.S. only.

Thank You!

CN096A

THE BENEFITS OF BOOK CLUB MEMBERSHIP

• You'll get your books hot off the press, usually before they appear in bookstores.

• You'll ALWAYS save up to 30% off the cover price.

• You'll get our FREE monthly newsletter filled with author interviews, book previews, special offers and MORE!

• There's no obligation —you can cancel at any time and you have no minimum number of books to buy.

• And – if you decide you don't like the books you receive, you can return them. (You always have ten days to decide.)

Zebra Contemporary Romance Book Club
Zebra Home Subscription Service, Inc.
P.O. Box 5214
Clifton NJ 07015-5214

PLACE
STAMP
HERE

table. "I make good coffee. At least that's what I'm told."

Lucy did an eye roll and pretended to be absorbed in her flower arrangement, but Pepper knew her roommate was hanging on every word that passed between her and Brad. Lucy tucked a stem of some exotic flower with a name that Pepper couldn't pronounce into a large ceramic vase.

"Maybe next time," he said.

Brad stepped into the kitchen, and he and Lucy greeted each other with a polite "hello."

An uncomfortable silence hung in the air. Pepper didn't care. That was their thing to work out. She took a vase from under the sink and filled it with water, then added a few drops of bleach before placing the flowers in one by one. When she was finished, she pushed the vase to the center of the table and stepped back. Not a bad job of arranging, if she did say so herself. Lucy's work must be rubbing off on her.

"Guess I'll be going." Brad turned to leave, and Pepper followed him to the door. She watched while he got in his car. That man would have potential, she thought, if only it weren't for his questionable reputation.

Pepper poured herself a cup of coffee and sat at the table to finish looking through her mail. She estimated she could get through at least half of it before Lucy would be forced to say something about Brad's visit.

Surprisingly, Lucy remained fixed on her flower arrangement. The concentration in her blue eyes told Pepper that no lecture was forthcoming. What a shame her roommate couldn't keep her opinions to herself more often.

Lucy took a sip from Pepper's cup. "Please tell me this is decaf. It tastes so good I couldn't stand it if it wasn't."

"Decaf it is," Pepper said. She was still waiting for Lucy to start in about Brad. Nothing came. She continued reading her sand sculpting newsletter, but the information just went inside her head and floated around without sticking. Lucy's silence was unbearable.

"That's it. Spit it out."

"Spit out what?" Lucy gave her an innocent look. Pepper stared at her.

"Okay," Lucy said. "I thought you were done seeing guys like Brad. Forever." She took another sip of Pepper's coffee.

Pepper shrugged. "He doesn't seem so bad—why don't you pour your own cup?" She crossed her arms over her chest. "And besides, I have no aversion to guys like Brad. I think we both know I only made that deal to get Simone to stop smoking."

Lucy reached up and rubbed the back of her neck. "I didn't sleep very well last night. Nightmares."

Pepper rolled her eyes. *Here it comes.* "Go ahead. Give it to me."

"I dreamed I ate an entire box of Hostess cupcakes."

Pepper eyed Lucy suspiciously. "Yuck. That is a nightmare."

"That isn't the bad part. None of them had any cream filling. I was robbed. I mean, if I'm going to dream of eating that stuff, I'd like to at least be able to enjoy all of it, not just the empty shell."

"I hear you," Pepper agreed. She studied Lucy's face. It was then that she noticed the dark circles under her friend's eyes.

Nightmare or not, it wasn't like Lucy not to speak her mind. She felt bad for Lucy not getting her cream filling, even if it was only a dream, and she pondered what it could mean.

"Maybe you're worried about gaining all that weight back and having Jake's friend not want to see you again," Pepper offered. She smiled, pleased at her analysis. Generally, she considered it good if she could figure out what her own *waking* thoughts meant.

"I don't think so. I think it's my subconscious urging me to warn you away from men who are all fluff and no substance. In other words, empty shells."

The phone rang, saving Lucy from a neck wringing. Caller ID showed it was Jake. With the long reach, Pepper lost her balance and fell over, chair and all. Lucy looked down at her and waited to make sure she was okay before answering it herself.

"Hi, Lucy. Is Pepper there?"

"Yeah, Jake. She's falling all over herself to talk to you." Lucy smiled and held out the phone. Pepper got up off the floor, brushed her hair back from her face, and turned her back to Lucy's amused grin.

"I was hoping I'd hear from you today. Sorry I didn't get in touch with you before I left town," Pepper said.

"Left town?"

"Didn't Lucy tell you? I went to see my mom." She knew Jake hadn't spoken to Lucy, but she was hoping it might prompt him for an explanation as to why he hadn't called.

"To tell you the truth, I've been so busy I haven't had a chance to call. Everything okay?"

Busy? Pepper chewed her lip. Was she putting too much energy into this relationship?

She looked over at Lucy, who had finished with her flowers and was now pretending to look over the morning paper's coupons.

"Everything is great. Me, my mom, and my sister all had a good visit. We took a few walks in the rain; I wished I was back home in the sun. You know, a typical Pacific Northwest vacation." Pepper didn't see any point in going into details about her mom, especially with a man who hadn't even noticed she was gone.

"I don't suppose you feel like leaving town again so soon? For the weekend? I could use a change of scenery, some fun," Jake said.

Fun? Okay, all was forgiven. Pepper remembered the *fun* they'd had the last time they were together. A river of warmth flowed through her all the way from her head to her toes. Her pulse raced. Fun was for kids. What had happened between her and Jake was a lot more than a ride on a Ferris wheel.

"Fun sounds good," she said, speaking quietly into the receiver. She could feel Lucy staring a hole into her back.

"I'll be there in an hour," Jake told her and hung up.

Pepper quickly gathered up her mail. She twirled around and took her coffee cup over to the sink.

"Jake's coming over?" Lucy asked with raised eyebrows. She glanced at the flowers Brad had left. "What're you gonna tell him when he sees these?

He's going to know that Gordy didn't send them to *me*."

"He's a guy. He won't even notice them."

"Speaking of Gordy . . . are you going to see him again? Have you heard from him?"

"Nope." Lucy sipped her coffee daintily. Her face gave nothing away. Pepper didn't know if that was good or bad.

"Do you *want* to hear from him?"

"Maybe." Lucy picked up a pair of scissors and clipped a coupon.

Pepper ran her fingers through her hair. "Well, if you do, I hope he calls," she said, practically bouncing out of the kitchen. "I've got a date to get ready for."

"Thorny flowers are bad," Lucy yelled after her. Pepper paused, and Lucy raised her hands, shrugging. "You really should let me at least throw the roses away. That's all I'm saying."

Jake opened the door and was surprised to see Gordy on his front step.

"Bad timing. I was just on my way out."

Gordy followed him down the walk. "Got a hot date?"

"Yeah, something like that." Jake opened the Audi's door and threw in his brown leather jacket and a small bag.

"How long you figure Pete's gonna let you keep his ride?" Gordy asked, leaning against the car.

"I'm taking it back to him after this weekend. Don't be scratching the paint. I don't want to get blamed for any damage—especially by Theresa," Jake said. He remembered the slap to the back of his head all too well. The woman packed a punch. "I don't want her climbing all over Pete's back either."

Gordy laughed. "Pete was in trouble the day he got married—he's so kitty flogged, I'm surprised she lets him go out for beer with us."

Jake looked at Gordy and shook his head. "You don't get it."

"What?"

"Pete happens to be in love. But don't worry, pal, you'll find that out when you meet the right woman."

"*Really*? Like you?"

"Maybe."

"Damn, you're both kitty flogged."

"And you're jealous."

"Hardly," Gordy said, shifting from one foot to the other. "What do you mean, you're taking the car back?"

"I'm taking Pepper away for the weekend. Then I'm telling her the truth."

Gordy shook his head. "I'd try to change your mind, but I gotta say, that date last week was stressful. All that havin' to be careful what you say, I don't know how you do it. Have you figured out how you're going to convince Pepper you're still a nice guy after lying to her all this time?"

Jake stared ahead. There was an answer. He just didn't know what it was yet. "It'll be a problem, but I'm hoping she'll be understanding. You know, guys will be guys, that sort of thing? If all else fails, I'll just blame it on you and Pete. Don't worry. You don't have anything at stake since you're still seeing *that woman*." Jake got in the Audi and stuck the key in the ignition. He looked up at Gordy.

"I thought you and Lucy made a connection.

Guess I was wrong. If you're lucky though, she'll still be there if you ever get your shit straightened out."

"I never said I was worried."

"I know."

"Right on time," Pepper said. "I like that."

Jake grabbed her by the shoulders and pulled her to him. "I've been thinking about you." Out of the corner of his eye, he saw Lucy. She got up from the sofa and moved quietly down the hall, and he heard her bedroom door close. "Sorry. I didn't see her sitting there."

"She's okay. She's probably just wondering how come your friend isn't here doing the same thing to her."

Pepper slid her arms around him, and he held her firmly against his body until she squeaked. He hadn't figured on having to make excuses for Gordy, and the best he could come up with on such short notice was to mumble something about Gordy being all screwed up.

"If you've been thinking about me, how come you didn't even know I was out of town?" Pepper asked.

"How come you didn't tell me you were leaving?"

"Fair enough," she said, running a finger up Jake's chest. She stopped at the top of his shirt and played with the dark hairs that peeked out the top. "I'll let you make it up to me all weekend. Where're we headed?"

Jake squeezed her tighter. "I told you, somewhere fun." His blood pulsed through his body, and he knew hers did as well because he could feel her heart beating hard against his chest.

Chapter 16

Pepper couldn't wait to see what Jake had in store for them. It'd been quite some time since she'd been on an adventure, and the anticipation of what might happen between them was agonizing. She shifted eagerly in her seat when they got on I-5 headed south. San Diego Zoo maybe? Sea World?

"How much longer?" she said after only one hour.

"Patience," Jake said.

After riding quietly for another ten minutes, Pepper leaned close to Jake. "What's it gonna take to get you to tell me what I wanna know?" she said, using her most sultry voice. She looked up at Jake through thick eyelashes and fluttered them shamelessly.

He laughed. "I bet you were a terror at Christmastime."

"Yes, but I could be even more so if that's what it'll take to make you spill."

Jake kept his eyes focused ahead. "I'm a rock."

"We'll see about that," Pepper said. She walked her fingers toward his stomach.

Jake took her wrist gently in his hand, massaging

it for a moment before placing her hand back into her own lap. "Like I said, I'm a rock."

"Pooh," she said. She looked in the backseat and grabbed a novel she'd brought along to read, just in case Jake still had ideas about taking things slow. After a few minutes, she leaned her head against the headrest and let the blur of scenery hypnotize her to sleep.

After what seemed like only a few minutes, Jake woke her up. She sat up with a yawn and arched her back like a cat. Her breasts strained against the fabric of her shirt, and she smiled to see Jake taking notice.

Pepper looked around at her surroundings just as they passed a sign welcoming them to the small community of Imperial Beach. She looked back at the sign, straining her neck to make sure she'd read it correctly. "Do you know where we *are?*"

"I think so," Jake said.

"*Yes.* But it's also the home of the largest sandcastle competition in the country." She was quiet for a minute, trying to take it in. "My God," she said. "This is *the* weekend. Do you know what you're in for bringing us here? On this weekend? Not to mention we'll never find a room."

"That's already been taken care of," Jake assured her.

"*How?* Reservations have to be made so far in advance—"

"Magic," he said, giving her a wink.

Pepper nodded her head vigorously. "It'd have to be, especially since we haven't known each other long enough—" She gave him a sideways glance. "That is, unless you've had this planned for some time." She grew silent.

"What?"

"Have you had this planned for some time? With someone else perhaps?"

Jake laughed and shook his head. "Only since last week—"

"But how?"

"I've got a friend, lives down here, owes me a favor. He's out of town right now. He hates the crowds, the traffic. I asked him if I could use his house for the weekend."

"Lucky you," Pepper said as she continued looking around.

A few minutes later, they pulled into the driveway of a small stucco rambler. The outside was painted a burnt sienna color, and it had a brown lawn with a splash of color provided by a couple of large potted plants. It wasn't exactly the Westin, but Pepper wasn't about to complain. After all, she was about to spend three days at a place she'd only dreamed of with a man who made her ache for his touch. She didn't even care that she'd have to share him with some 300,000 other people.

"You weren't kidding when you said you were taking me away for some fun. This is more than I could have imagined," Pepper said, purring her approval.

"Come with me." Jake held out a hand, and Pepper was happy to take it.

The house had a distinct seaside charm. An open design, it had plenty of windows, and the walls were aquamarine. The floors were hardwood with plenty of throw rugs scattered about. The kitchen cabinets were a soft blue, along with all the appliances. It reminded her of a beach house she'd seen in *Coastal Living*. Shelves had been built into every available space, and old books filled them. Pepper ran a finger lightly over their worn spines, taking in the titles. *Moby-Dick, Call of the Wild, Treasure Island.* All classics. All nature.

The sofa was a relaxed piece with a heavy wood frame that was painted white. It had large, puffy blue cushions, and its companion side chair also had a puffy cushion in green. It seemed to beckon one to come, sit, sleep.

Sleep. She'd done that in the car. Now was the time to explore. Pepper looked over at Jake. Exploring him was definitely high on her list.

"We're even in time for the Annual Sand Castle Ball," Jake said, reading from a small pamphlet. "It's tonight."

"But, sir, I don't believe I packed a ball gown."

"Don't you worry," Jake said, placing a finger under her chin and tilting her head up. "You'll be the most beautiful woman there, no matter what you wear."

Pepper blushed at the compliment. Men had certainly told her she was beautiful, but never like that. Never with such absoluteness. It touched her heart and scared her all at once—she dared to consider for just a split second that she might find the same kind of forever that her mom had found with her dad.

Jake took their bags to a bedroom that was located at the end of a short hallway, and he dropped them on the floor next to a queen-sized bed that nearly filled the room. The only other piece of furniture in the room was a small dresser. A vase of fresh lilies sat on top of it. Pepper grimaced, feeling slightly guilty. At least they weren't white.

"Nice touch," Pepper said, touching her finger-tips to the flowers.

Jake waved a hand. "I'd like to take credit for them, but my friend who owns this place is a romantic. I might've let it slip that I was bringing a woman with me. Sorry, the room is a bit small—"

"Don't," she said, gently placing a finger over his lips. "Don't you dare apologize. There's no other place I'd rather be."

A sour look flashed across Jake's face. He took a step back and turned, opening a drawer. "You can put your things in here," he said.

Pepper's forehead creased. "All right." She touched his arm. "Did I say something wrong?"

"Not at all." Jake checked his watch. "Would you like to shower before we go to town?"

Pepper nodded. Whatever was wrong, he was determined to keep it to himself.

Jake waited until he heard Pepper turn on the shower before opening his bag. He reached inside and carefully pulled out a peach-colored floor-length gown. It had skinny little straps and a ragged hem-line, with a slit up one side. He imagined Pepper walking along the pier, sea air blowing through her hair, the dress flowing softly about her legs. It was made of some kind of light, silky material that Jake had no idea what it was. All he knew is that it felt smooth between his fingers, and he was sure it would feel just as good wrapped in his arms.

Jake laid the dress on the bed where Pepper would see it as soon as she came out of the bathroom. It'd been a perfect choice, and he had Pete's wife to thank.

Jake walked over to the window and rested his arms on the sill. Several children were playing out in the street. "No other place I'd rather be," Pepper had said to him. He winced. It was almost like being stabbed in the heart. Those were the words Angela had spoken to him the last time he'd held her in his arms. He tried to shake it from his mind. Pepper wasn't Angela. Still, those words had made him turn away from her when all he'd really wanted was to gather her in his arms and kiss her. He ran a hand over his face. Was the secret he carried going to cost him another woman he loved? Damn Gordy and Pete. Damn the bet. Before the weekend was over, he had to tell Pepper the truth.

Several minutes passed, and Pepper came out of the bathroom, followed by the faint scent of honeysuckle.

"What's this?" she asked when she saw the dress on the bed.

"For you. I thought you were probably a size six." The look on her face told him it was perfect.

The entire evening was a blur. Music, dancing, laughter, long minutes of gazing into each other's eyes. It was a most enchanting evening, but all Pepper could think about was what she hoped would happen later that evening. Being held in Jake's strong arms for the last few hours had made her feel like Cinderella, except when the time finally came to return to the house, she didn't have to run away and leave her Prince behind. He was right beside her. With any luck, there he'd stay.

She was intoxicated with the idea of making love with Jake. She thought he was finally ready, too. It would be different this time. This time, it was more than lust. As far as she could see, only one thing might stand in their way. Jake had been perfectly sweet, surprising her with a beautiful gown, holding her in his arms all evening, but whatever had happened earlier at the house, whatever she might have said, she sensed continued to bother him, even though he'd done his best to pretend it didn't.

When they got back to the house, Jake opened a bottle of merlot and poured a glass for each of them. They sat in the small living room on the puffy blue cushions, and Pepper felt something like an electric current flowing between her and Jake.

"Thank you for the best evening I've had in a very long time," Pepper said.

"It was my pleasure. Although I'm sure you're just being kind. After all, I did step on your toes half a dozen times."

Pepper smiled. "I must have missed that."

Jake brushed a lock of hair from her face. "A woman such as yourself is probably not lacking for dates."

Pepper gave a little shrug. "It's not that getting a date is hard, but getting the right date is a bit like winning the lotto. My last one had a wife he failed to tell me about." Pepper took a long sip of her wine. She shook her head. "Too many lies, not enough *fun.* I'd just about given up."

"I'm glad you didn't." Jake took her glass and set it on the coffee table. Then he kissed her.

Pepper felt good all over. They'd had a couple of drinks in town and now the wine. Her body felt like it was floating. She could have spent the entire night on the dance floor in Jake's arms. She suspected her euphoric feelings had less to do with the alcohol and more to do with the chemistry that existed between her and Jake.

He kissed her again and ran a hand up her back to the top of her zipper. Oh, Lord. This was it. Only now she felt sick to her stomach just like the time a boy she liked in the third grade kissed her for the very first time. It had to be lovesickness. If so, she never wanted a cure. She'd waited for this moment, relived it over a thousand times since that day at Jake's house.

Pepper felt herself falling, and it took all her strength to resist. She wanted everything about tonight to be perfect.

"I think I'll go get comfortable," she told him. Her voice quivered, as did her entire body. "Want to help?" She batted her lashes at him. Without waiting for his answer, she got up and disappeared down the hall. A minute later, Jake walked into the room and stood behind her, his body heat warming her like a smoldering fire. God help her, she was more than ready to ignite. Keeping her back to him, she asked him to unzip her dress, and he let his fingers graze the back of her neck until he smoothed her hair to one side. Pepper's knees were like Jell-O when his lips brushed across her bare skin. They burned into her flesh, and she so desperately wanted to turn and feel those lips on hers, but still, she waited.

Her dress fell to the floor, and she stood almost naked, still with her back to him. A cool breeze blew in through the open window and washed over her body, but nothing could extinguish the fire that was building between them. Pepper had never desired any man the way she did Jake, not even that day they were *having fun* rolling around on his sofa.

Jake smoothed his hands down her arms, and it was like a feather being drawn across her skin. His hands continued moving, and he slipped his hand inside her panties, finding the vulnerable spot between her legs. Pepper gasped, unsure of how much longer she could remain standing.

After what seemed like too many minutes of torture in which her mind was a flurry of feelings she had yet to grasp, Jake turned her around and swept her up into his arms. He carried her over to the bed and laid her down, and the torture continued when he made her wait and watch while he undressed. Blood pulsed through her thighs while Jake removed his shirt. His body was awash in the pale moonlight, and he paused to light a candle. The flame flickered delicately, giving the room a soft glow and accentuating his muscular frame. He continued to undress, removing his pants next. By the time he kicked them aside and lay down next to her, Pepper's breathing was heavy with anticipation.

Patience, she told herself. It was hard, and he was hard, and it wasn't any easier when he rested a hand lightly over one of her breasts. Kiss after kiss, Jake moved his lips slowly from her stomach all the way up her body.

He took his time, stopping at each breast, nuzzling her nipples, and Pepper moaned her desire as she let her legs fall apart.

Just do it, for God's sake, she wanted to scream. Instead, she continued to endure Jake's slow tease while he moved his mouth back down her abdomen.

He paused between her open legs, and Pepper arched her back.

"Stop!" Her voice was heavy and thick, and desire pulled at her in a delightful, painful kind of way. "I can't take it. Please . . . now. I need to feel you inside me now."

Jake rose up and covered her body with his. His movements were slow, purposeful, and everything he did was heavenly. But she'd had enough. No more waiting. She wanted to have some goddamn fun! Pepper grabbed him and pulled him to her, and her hips rose to meet him. She guided him into her, and it was like a sudden rush from a rogue wave. *Yes!* He'd finally gotten it. Passion was what she needed. Hot, fiery passion with a punch.

Screw tender and easy.

With every thrust, she rode the wave higher and higher until a final surge engulfed them both.

"Oh-h, oh-h, oh-h . . ." Pepper's voice crescendoed, and her back arched, her toes curled. The tingling intensified, and she forgot where she was, who she was, and why. She was floating in a free-fall, tumbling head over heels, until with one long breath, their bodies relaxed into the mattress. The sensation continued with each wave becoming smaller and smaller until she lay exhausted in Jake's arms. They lay still for a long time, and Pepper was conscious of her breathing as it eventually slowed and became steady again. She rested for a minute, and then she opened her eyes. Jake was gazing at her. He pulled her to his chest.

"Wow," he said, exhaling long and slow.

"Yeah, wow," Pepper responded weakly.

They both laughed.

"How do you do that?" she asked. "How do you turn me into a crazy woman? Just the sight of you . . ." She blushed. "Let's just say, what I want to do isn't very ladylike." Her face flushed, and she hoped the color would be lost in the flickering candlelight. They were quiet for another minute. Pepper felt like Raggedy Ann, all floppy and soft and light as a leaf blowing in the wind. Mind-numbing orgasms had a way of doing that to a woman, she'd heard. Now she knew for sure.

"I'm not usually that blunt, but it *is* true," she continued. "I do want to do things with you that I've never done with any man—each and every time I lay my eyes on you."

Jake raised himself up on one elbow and leaned over her. His mouth melted onto hers, and he moved his tongue slowly in small circles and then back out and across her lips.

"Okay," Pepper whispered. "Screw my brains out again. Right now." Jake smiled and kissed each side of her face.

"I'll do my best."

Jake reached into her hair and kissed her fiercely. He'd obviously taken her cue. Slow, easy sex was for later. Much later—when they were old and gray and had no energy for crazy passion. That's when they could slow down.

Once again, they rode the wave, and the way it made Pepper feel confirmed in her mind that Jake was the only man she wanted in her life.

Afterward, they lay in the dark and watched the candlelight flicker on the walls. No more words were spoken between them, yet everything was said. Whatever he wanted, she was ready to give. And it scared her. She was in love.

Chapter 17

Their lovemaking left Pepper ravenous. She slipped out of bed during the wee morning hours but found nothing to eat in the small kitchen except some old cereal—expiration date three months ago—and a partial loaf of bread that looked like it had been growing a second crust for quite some time.

She woke Jake up early, starving and eager to see and do as much as possible in the short time they had in Imperial Beach.

The Chamber of Commerce sponsored a pancake breakfast, but Jake and Pepper chose instead to go to a place called Grandma's Pantry Restaurant and Bakery. Popular for its homestyle cooking, it came highly recommended by Jake's friend.

Throwing all caution aside, Pepper ordered bacon, eggs, and toast. Bacon had never tasted so good, and she was sure that she and Jake would more than burn off any extra calories. This was the first breakfast she and Jake had shared, and she sat across from him, watching him eat. He licked syrup from his lips, and Pepper wished they were back in bed. She wouldn't mind having him lick her lips like that every morning for the next fifty or sixty years.

After breakfast, they walked along Seacoast Drive and perused all the craft booths. On display was an assortment of homemade items, things that would only gather dust and clutter up her small cottage. Paintings, leatherwork, pottery, knick-knacks. Something for just about everyone. Pepper bought nothing. Jake bought a small hand-carved wood pelican. He named it Gilligan.

They stayed in town throughout the morning to watch the Sandcastle Parade and afterward, Jake suggested they take a break. Pepper readily agreed. The small community had become like a beehive, with swarms of people arriving all day until it seemed no more could fit. But fit they did, and it was exhausting just being in the middle of all the frenzied activity.

Pepper may have been exhausted, but she was nowhere near sleepy. She and Jake made love once more, then had a quick snack of fresh strawberries and cream that they'd purchased in town.

By mid-afternoon, Pepper fell asleep in Jake's arms, and when she woke up, he surprised her with dinner—the best seafood salad she'd ever had. Mostly because he'd made it. Big chunks of Dungeness crab, Oregon Bay shrimp, plump black olives, tomatoes, and hard-boiled eggs served over a bed of gourmet salad greens. And if that wasn't enough, he'd even made homemade Thousand Island dressing. A recipe he claimed that had been handed down since his great grandmother.

Pepper sat quietly as Jake filled bowls with more salad than she would ever be able to eat. He plucked an olive from his bowl and offered it to her, and she took it between her teeth and held it there until he bit off half.

"I'm impressed," she said, giving him a warm smile.

"Me, too. I managed to put all this together without waking you." Jake poured two small glasses of champagne and handed one to Pepper.

"What's the occasion?"

"You."

Their eyes held, and Pepper felt the words "I love you" forming on her lips.

"Jake, I . . ."

"You're not going all mushy on me, are you?" Jake asked with a nervous laugh. He took a large drink from his champagne glass.

"Mushy?" Pepper swallowed. She studied his face for a moment. He wore that look that men always got when things were moving too fast. "No, I was just noting the time. We'd better get back to town. It'll be time for the fireworks soon."

Intense color burst into the ink-black sky. Blue, red, green, gold, and silver splashed onto the night's canvas like an artist gone wild. Each color burst was followed by puffs of white smoke, and the air smelled of sulfur.

The exhibit rivaled anything Pepper had ever seen back home in Seattle, including the annual Fourth of Jul-Ivar's celebration. Pepper was conscious of Jake's arm around her waist all during the show, and its warmth settled around her heart. She couldn't think of any time she'd ever enjoyed a day so much.

Soon after the grand finale, the crowd began to

disperse, and Jake turned to her. "I better get you back to the house."

"Do I have a curfew?" Pepper said, giving him a devilish smile. "Or did you have something else in mind?"

"Always that, but, no, I was thinking of something more practical—sleep."

Pepper gave him a curious look. "Do I look that bad?"

Jake laughed. "Never. But since we're getting up early for the competition, we might want to get some sleep."

Pepper's lips curved into a broad smile. "I guess we better." She shook her head. "I still can't believe I'm here—*we're* here."

They started walking, but after half a block, she stopped and faced him and took both of his hands in hers. "This is something very special you've done for me. *You're* something very special."

Taking her face in his hands, Jake kissed her, and she looked forward to another evening like the last.

Guilt from the lie that stood between them bit viciously at Jake. He wasn't going to spoil Pepper's time here, but after the competition tomorrow, he was telling her the truth. He'd seen hurt in Pepper's eyes when he'd asked her if she was getting all mushy, but it was better than the alternative—hate. He'd sensed what she was about to say, and it made his guts churn like they were inside a cement mixer. He couldn't let her say the words until she'd heard the truth. Though it wasn't some life-altering lie, he didn't want her ever to regret telling him she loved him.

Pepper managed to convince him that she'd

sleep so much better if he'd accommodate her wishes just once more. He was powerless against her desires.

Afterward, Pepper lay on her stomach, and he gently rubbed her back. It all seemed so right, so natural, as though this was the way they were meant to be. A few minutes later, Pepper's breathing became soft and steady.

Sleep. Lately, it had been hard to come by. He'd lie awake, staring up at the ceiling only to eventually drift off in the dead of night. Usually, it was a problem with a construction site that gave him sleepless nights. Not so now. Lies had a way of winding themselves into the fabric of a person's life until they didn't even know what the truth was anymore. He knew this relationship had nowhere to go as long as it was based on a lie. He smiled sadly. If Pepper hated him, at least he'd have the four-hour ride back in the car with her to try to explain.

He gazed at her sleeping face. Enough moonlight peeked through the blinds to allow him to see the curve of her cheek. Even in slumber, her lips turned up at the corners. Who was this woman? He'd have thought it impossible that anyone could make him forget all the hurt of losing his wife. Jake swallowed painfully at the thought of being lost yet again, and he watched Pepper for a long time, wanting to relish the moment, because God only knew if they'd ever be like this again.

Morning came too fast, and Jake had been unable to come up with anything that sounded like an explanation Pepper would be willing to accept.

"We should talk," she said as she cleared their breakfast dishes from the table.

Uh-oh. When a woman said, "We should talk," it usually didn't have a happy ending for the man.

"We can talk," Jake said cautiously.

"I can't help but notice you've got something on your mind. Is there something wrong? Between us maybe?"

The truth was like a lump of dry sand in Jake's mouth. He was tempted to tell her everything right then, accept the consequences, but this was her day, and he wanted her to enjoy every minute of it. There'd be plenty of time later to see the disappointment on her face when he admitted what a dog he was.

"Just work problems." He squeezed her hand. "Nothing for you to worry about."

Pepper was one of those smart blondes, and Jake saw that she wasn't buying it. Only one thing to do . . . move on to another subject.

"I was thinking that next year, it'll be you out there competing," he said.

Pepper laughed. "Or the year after. Or the year after that. It takes a very long time to be good enough to compete with any of the pros we'll see out there today."

Jake gave her a reassuring smile. "I have great faith in you." He pulled her onto his lap and kissed her. "Are you ready to see what you'll be up against?"

"M-m-m," she said with a purr. "I think I know what I'm up against."

"I'd give you a preview," he said, glancing at his watch. "But we'd be late, and we'd miss everything." He kissed her again. He wanted to swallow the moment. Never let it go.

***

This was the biggest sand sculpting event Pepper had ever attended. She'd only started seriously thinking about sculpting when she moved to Malibu, but now it seemed like a dream she'd had forever. She'd only been to some of the smaller competitions in her area, and she had no idea there could ever be so many people gathered together in one place. Everywhere, thousands of people. It reminded her of an ant farm, with everyone in a frenzied rush to get from here to there and back. Getting through the crowd was slow going, but Jake eventually managed to forge a way through so they could get down to the beach.

More than forty teams were on hand to compete, with each Division and team hoping for their share of prize money. Amateurs, too, had their own categories based on specific themes, with a top award of $1,000.

Pepper wished she had known in advance that she'd be attending. She might have practiced more and then entered as an amateur. Certainly she was good enough for that after all the sand pieces she'd built.

Each team or individual sculptor had a designated building area and was restricted to using only biodegradable decorative materials such as shells or seaweed. Water containers had been filled ahead of time and were stored outside each plot.

Limited to only five hours, each team was well into their sculptures by the time she and Jake arrived.

Mermaids, dragons, and castles—all the standards one would expect to see at a sand sculpting event—along with much more difficult sculptures lined the beach. The detail work was amazing. Castles weren't just castles with turrets. They had drawbridges, murder holes, windows, curtain walls, stairs, scalloped roofs. Dragons breathed fire; had fangs, ears, and feet with claws. Mermaids had scales; long, wispy hair that curled about their shoulders; and breasts that would put any woman to shame, including Pepper. One mermaid was so anatomically correct and beautiful that Pepper wondered if her creator might have a second job as a plastic surgeon. She smiled, remembering the day she tricked Jake into putting a nipple on her mermaid's breast.

"Look." Pepper grabbed Jake's arm and pointed to one of the sculptors. "That's Russ Leno. He's from Everett, Washington." She fluttered her hands together in a delighted clap. "Isn't this exciting?"

Jake nodded, and the look on his face told her he really was enjoying himself and not just going through the motions.

"Oh, Jake," she said, wrapping her arms around his neck, "thank you so much for this. It means everything to have you support my interest in sand sculpting."

"Anything for you, babe."

At that moment, Pepper wanted to gather Jake into her arms and shout, "I love you," for all the world to hear. But she remembered how he had accused her of becoming all mushy. Jake obviously wasn't ready to hear what her true feelings were.

They continued down the beach, trying to get close enough to examine every single sculpture, and Pepper took mental notes on all that she observed. Seeing all the activity, the hard work, the attention to detail, it gave her new inspiration. After all, in what other job could a person play on some of the most beautiful beaches in the world and get paid for it?

They came upon a team building a castle with a

dragon's head sticking out the top, and Pepper liked it the best. One of the amateur teams was working on a life-size Volkswagen Bug, complete with boy, girl, and surfboard sticking out the window. Jake chose that as his favorite.

The hours ticked by faster than Pepper would have liked, and soon it was time for the winners to be announced. A complicated sculpture of a wizard with a long, flowing robe and a straggly beard won the amateur first prize, and a chorus of angels singing won the Master's. Both deserving of their titles, Pepper felt.

Soon after, Jake was eager to get away from the crowd and go back to the house. Pepper hoped his eagerness had something to do with her.

After showering, they made love, and he lay next to her without talking. He'd gone to that quiet place again.

The sweet smell of honeysuckles filled the room from Pepper's freshly washed hair. She usually smelled of lemons, and he'd come to know it as her scent, but this was nice, too.

If only he had the power to go back in time, change how they met. Or maybe fast forward past the hurt and anger that was sure to come so they could get on with their lives.

Pepper drifted off to sleep, and Jake slipped out of bed. He stood at the window and stared into the night sky for a long time. The moon was full and light, and he was able to see all the way down the street to a small section of town. Lights blinked on and off, and for a few fleeting moments, thoughts of Angela filled his head. If only—he quickly stopped himself from going down that path. It had been a dream. Dreams had a way of being spirited away, and he wasn't so sure his heart wasn't about to feel that pain all over again, even if he did deserve it. He closed his eyes and said a silent prayer that this time, the outcome would be different.

A minute later, Pepper's slender arms circled him from behind. He turned and looked into her soft blue eyes. Her honey-colored hair glistened like spun gold in the moonlight against her tanned skin. He reached up and brushed back a lock from her face. His heart swelled, and right then, if the entire world disappeared, he wouldn't have even known—or cared. Not as long as this moment never ended.

Jake took Pepper's hand and led her back to the bed. She laid her head on his chest and slept, but it took him half the night to find enough peace for sleep.

Morning came quickly. It seemed like Jake had just closed his eyes ten minutes ago. He stayed still and let Pepper sleep a few minutes more. He wasn't in any hurry to get on with the task at hand.

His cell phone started to hum, and Pepper stirred. He reached over and picked it up from the nightstand.

"Gordy's in trouble," Pete said to him without so much as a "hello" or a "good morning."

Jake's stomach turned. If Pete was calling him this early on the weekend, he knew it couldn't be good. "What's going on?" he asked with forced casualness. Pepper got up from the bed and went into the bathroom.

"It's that woman he's been seein'."

An icy hand gripped Jake's chest. "How bad?"

"He's at Saint John's Health Center. I think you'd better get here."

Jake glanced at the nightstand clock. "I'm about four hours away. Tell him I'm on my way." He slapped the phone shut. What he really wanted to do was slap Gordy, but from Pete's tone, it sounded like someone had already beat him to it.

Pepper came out of the bathroom, and the speech he'd been preparing for her was forgotten. The truth would have to wait a while longer.

"It's Gordy," he said. Her brow raised in concern, but now wasn't the time to go into Gordy's mating habits. "We've got to go."

Chapter 18

When Pete gave Gordy Jake's message, he attempted a smile, but it wasn't happening. Pete wasn't even sure Gordy could make sense of what was going on around him through all the medication that had been pumped into him.

He stared at Gordy's bruised face, his swollen eyes, wanted to touch his hand, but decided against it. The guy didn't need any more pain.

After a while, Pete wandered out into the hallway. It was quiet, as though a sign had been lit, hushing everyone into silence. A couple of empty chairs were lined up along the wall. They'd been occupied earlier by a man and woman whose son had been in a car accident. Pete knew it'd been bad, and he wondered about the outcome. The woman had looked as though she was going to faint when the doctor came out and began talking to them.

Pete looked at his watch. Jake would be there soon. God only knew what his reaction would be when he saw his friend bruised and looking like someone had used his face for batting practice. He looked through the window to Gordy's room and rubbed a hand down his face.

He wasn't ready to go back in there. The sight of all those tubes and the smell of antiseptic permeating the air like it was coming out of the walls had him feeling like *he* was going to need a doctor. Walking the halls seemed like a better idea.

A vending machine was down near the elevators, and Pete stopped for a coffee. He punched the buttons for sugar and waited while the dispenser did its thing. It was quick, state-of-the-art vending machine coffee at its best, supposedly. He removed the Styrofoam cup from the window and took a large swallow. Rancid, like tar clinging to the back of his tongue. It made him grimace. The machine might be state of the art, but the coffee was pretty typical. Black, bitter, way past strong. He walked over to a waste can and tossed it inside. No amount of weariness could make him drink that shit. It was bad enough that the people here were already under stress, feeling bad. At least give them a decent cup of coffee.

Another fifteen minutes went by, and Pete finally went back to Gordy's room. He sat on the small, plastic guest chair, head in his hands, eyes on the floor.

"I really screwed up this time, didn't I?" a voice scratched through the hum of medical equipment.

Pete looked up and saw that Gordy's eyes were finally open. Or at least one of them. The other one was swollen to twice its normal size and was a mere slit in a fold of flesh. He wanted to scold the kid, ring the little bastard's neck. Instead, he nodded, giving Gordy his sternest father look.

"Yeah, you really screwed up." He reached for

Gordy's hand and once again stopped himself. Gordy's fingers were swollen, and they had been wrapped in white gauze. Pete guessed he'd either put up a good fight or someone had stomped on them pretty good.

"Sherry?" Gordy said through thick lips and a wired jaw.

Pete bristled at the woman's name. He wanted to tell his battered friend to forget that bitch, but right now wasn't the time for a parental scolding. "She's fine." His lips drew into a thin line. "She's just fine."

A shadow moved outside the window, and Pete heard Jake's voice.

"Be right back." He touched Gordy's shoulder, the only place that seemed safe. Out in the hall, he found Jake talking to the attending physician. Pete waited until they were through.

"What the hell took you so long?"

"I got here as fast as I could. I wasn't next door, for crissakes." Jake looked through the blinds into Gordy's room. His face bunched into a tight grimace. "Goddamn—"

Pete grabbed him by the arm and pulled him aside. "You know what they say . . . it looks worse than it is."

"I fucking hope so." Jake took another look at Gordy. "Sherry's husband?"

"And then some," Pete said, nodding. Jake's hands clenched into fists, and Pete could almost see his friend's blood pressure rise.

"He gonna be okay?"

Pete nodded.

"Tell Gordy I'll be back," he said, but Pete had him by the arm again.

"What do you think you're gonna do?"

"I'm going to fix this once and for all." Jake yanked his arm away.

"That's a load of crap, and you know it. The only one who can fix this is him." Pete jutted a thumb over his shoulder. "What do you think? That you're gonna go tell Sherry's husband, 'Hey, my friend really wants to screw your wife. Do you think you could look the other way?'" Pete ran a hand over his face and shook his head. "Gordy's got to be the one to fix this. Not you. Not me. Him."

Jake slapped the wall, let out a long breath. "How many times do you suppose this is gonna happen before *he* knows that?"

Pete shrugged. "Hell, I don't know. Maybe now. Maybe he's finally got the message." He looked through the window at Gordy. "All I know is there's nothing we can do to help him if he's determined to chase after another man's wife. All we can do is be here for him."

"Yeah," Jake said. He took a resigned breath and walked into the room.

"I'm ready," Gordy managed through his wired jaw.

"For what?" Jake asked. He'd prepared for this moment, knowing it would eventually come, but now that it was here, all he could do was feel sorry for his young friend.

"For you to give me hell."

"I guess I figure you're already in hell." Jake leaned forward, concern etching his forehead. "Tell me what happened."

Gordy turned away from Jake's probing stare. "It was like you always said—husband comes home; I get my ass kicked." He shifted in the bed and winced from the pain.

"I thought we had a deal."

"It was an easy deal for you. You're getting what you want." Gordy looked straight at Jake with his one good eye.

"Christ, is that all a relationship is to you? Sex?" Jake could feel a lecture forming as he spoke.

Gordy rolled his head slowly from side to side. "She told me her husband had moved out."

"So? What did you think was going to happen next? That you and she were going to get married, have a happy little family?" Jake sat back in the chair and rubbed the side of his face. His whiskers were full-blown stubble now. He'd been in such a hurry to get back after receiving Pete's phone call that he'd skipped shaving.

"Married? Who said anything about getting married and having a family?"

"Just tell me you're finished with her," Jake said.

Gordy lay quiet for a long minute. "Yeah, it's done."

Jake stayed with Gordy for another hour until he drifted off to sleep. It gave him a little too much time to think. God help him if Pepper found about about this. She already knew Gordy had been hurt, but he hadn't gone into any details. Now, he not only had to worry about the outcome when she found out about him lying to her, but also to have her best friend go out on a date with a guy who was having an affair with a married woman? He could only imagine the outcome. After what she'd said about the last man she'd dated, it wasn't going to be good.

* * *

When Jake dropped Pepper off, Simone's little red Mazda Miata was out front. Mouthwatering odors met her as soon as she walked through the front door, and she found Simone in the kitchen with Lucy. Simone was hovering over a large, steaming pot.

"You're just in time. She's making us lunch," Lucy announced proudly, as though she had something to do with the creation.

"It is from Suzanne's restaurant," Simone said, waving a wooden spatula.

"I hope it's got alcohol in it," Pepper said.

"*Cioppino* with shrimp and lobster." Simone went over to the sink and pulled out an angry-looking creature that was still very much alive.

"Oh, Gawd. Is that a live lobster? In my *sink?*" Pepper walked over to get a closer look. Another crustacean with the meanest-looking claws she'd ever seen was awaiting his demise. No wonder they were angry. Darn things knew what their future held.

Simone stood over the boiling kettle and plopped the creature in. "Live, yes, but only for a moment."

Lucy looked away, and Pepper winced. Seeing the decapod being lowered into the pot reminded her of a scene from a Vincent Price horror flick. Not an image she wanted to go to bed with.

"Aw . . . must you torture those creatures in my house?" Pepper moved away from the stove. She sank into a chair and averted her eyes from the boiling pot, imagining the terror that the poor lobster was enduring.

Simone rinsed and dried her hands, then set a five-minute timer. She perched on the edge of a stool. "Lucy tells me you spent the entire weekend with your white-collar man. Is this true?"

Pepper nodded and her face relaxed into a contented smile. "It's true."

"And?"

"*And* it's just like I first suspected. Jake is perfect."

"Don't stop there, *cherie*. My Paul is still away, and I fear I won't remember how to make love—"

"Okay, you can stop." Lucy covered her ears and shook her head. "I don't need—or want—the details. Save it for when the two of you are out for coffee or something."

Simone pulled one of Lucy's hands down. "There is a cure for this," she said. "Is called sex. Perhaps the young man who is friend to Pepper's lover will accommodate you."

Lucy scrunched up her nose, and Pepper laughed. A little sex might be what Lucy needed to loosen up. The only problem now was that Gordy was hurt, so it wasn't likely he'd be doing anything for Lucy anytime soon.

Just thinking about the look on Jake's face sent a nervous chill through her. He'd been quiet all the way back from Imperial Beach, and she hadn't wanted to press him, but she'd gotten the idea that it must be pretty bad.

The timer dinged, and Simone transferred the lobster in the pot to a large bowl of ice, then dropped the next one into the water.

"You may not hear from Gordy for a while. This morning, before we left, Jake got a phone call." She gave Lucy's hand a gentle squeeze. "Gordy's been hurt."

Genuine concern filled Lucy's eyes. "How?" she asked.

Pepper shook her head. "Jake didn't say."

"Oh," Lucy said quietly. She picked up a dried flower petal off the table and rolled it between her fingers.

Pepper gave her an encouraging smile. "I'm sure he'll be okay." She looked around the room. "Hey," she said, "where are my roses?"

"They died," Lucy said with a shrug.

Pepper gave her a sideways glance. "They wouldn't be dead after only a couple of days." She looked at the crumbled red petal Lucy had dropped on the table and had a pretty good idea that her roses had met a fate similar to the lobsters in the pot. Normally, she would have protested, maybe even made her friend dig them out of the trash just for punishment, but not tonight. She was far too tired, and it didn't matter anyway. Jake had stolen her heart, and he was the only one she wanted buying her flowers.

Pepper looked over just as Simone wrestled the tail and claws off the lobsters. Definitely not a sight she wanted in her dreams. Simone cracked the shells and removed the meat all in one piece.

Though what she'd just witnessed repulsed her, hunger overrode any sympathy Pepper might have had for the creatures, and she went over and stood next to Simone as she sliced off the tails.

"I hope this isn't an all-night recipe." Pepper eyed the lobster meat. "Maybe we could eat it as is," she said, reaching for a piece.

"Not yet." Simone slapped her hand away. "Here," she said, handing Pepper a stalk of celery. "It will be worth the wait."

Pepper wrinkled up her nose and handed the celery to Lucy, who promptly went over to the cabinet and spread peanut butter inside its green valley. Now more than ever, Pepper was sure Lucy was worried about Gordy.

The *cioppino* was worth waiting for, but the meal didn't do much to help Pepper sleep. She suffered bizarre, chaotic dreams that she was sure were a direct result of witnessing the demise of the two lobsters.

Jake hadn't called, and by the time morning came, both women were worried. Pepper considered calling him, but thought better of it. If something terrible had happened, she didn't want to intrude, especially since he hadn't seemed very eager even to talk about what had happened. Jake would call when he could.

She spent a little time out on the beach, but didn't tackle anything difficult. Her mind was on Jake and the weekend they'd shared. At eleven o'clock, she went inside to get cleaned up for a lunch date she'd made with Simone at Beachside.

As Pepper hurried toward the restaurant's heavy wooden door, she could almost hear Simone's lecture about being late. She rushed inside and ran smack into Brad. Boy, was he one solid piece of manflesh.

"*Brad.* Sorry! I didn't mean to run you over." She looked around him to the barefoot bar. "I'm supposed to meet Simone. Is she here yet?"

"Not yet. Grab a table, and I'll bring you a drink. What'll it be?"

She smiled. "Surprise me."

Pepper continued through the double doors and

picked a table in the full sun. She sat facing away from the bar so that she could avoid looking at Brad and imagining the muscles she'd find under his shirt. Sadly, their flirting must come to an end. Obviously, he'd begun to take it too seriously.

He brought her a drink that was a rich, frothy mixture topped with whipped cream. "I was concerned that maybe you were mad at me," Brad said, setting the drink down, in front of her. "You usually come in on the weekend. I didn't see you and thought maybe I'd pissed you off. You're a good customer. I don't want to ruin that."

Pepper felt bad. Brad really hadn't done anything wrong. He'd just made his interest known at the wrong time.

"Do you have a minute?" she asked. Brad nodded and sat down, and Pepper did her best to explain the situation with Jake.

Chapter 19

"So you see, it's not that I don't find you attractive," Pepper told Brad. "I'm just currently pre occupied, and I think it could be serious. I feel a real connection with Jake. He's someone who I might consider marrying." The more she talked, the more she felt like a blathering idiot. "I want stability," she finally said. Pepper put a hand over Brad's. "Can you understand?"

Brad smiled. "Of course. I guess you're hoping that the housing market doesn't go south then."

Pepper looked at him with raised eyebrows.

"I guess construction must pay pretty good, though. He's probably got plenty stuck away for a rainy day."

"I suppose," Pepper said. "But I think as an architect, he'd still have plenty of work, even if the housing market goes bust." She felt her hackles rise. She didn't know why she felt the need to explain anything about Jake to him.

"Architect? He's a construction worker, I thought." Pepper gave him a blank look.

"I better get back to work." Brad stood and touched Pepper's shoulder. "If you ever change your mind . . ."

He started to walk away, but Pepper stopped him. "Why would you think he's a construction worker?"

Brad paused. He scratched the side of his jaw. "I was driving by a building site the other day, looking for an address. I saw him."

"So?" Pepper's curiosity was beginning to lean toward impatience. "Jake's an architect. Of course he'd be at a building site occasionally."

"He was wearing a tool belt."

Pepper stared hard at him for a long moment.

"My mistake," Brad said. "Sorry I said anything."

Just then, Simone rushed up to the table and sat. "So sorry, *chérie*. I had trouble getting up. Paul and I had phone sex last night, and I was up late."

Brad walked away.

"What was that about?" Simone asked.

Pepper waved a dismissive hand. "A misunderstanding."

"Is there something you want to tell me?"

"Nothing." Pepper refused to believe the man she'd just spent the weekend with would lie to her. She shook her head.

"Okay. Then I will tell you about *my* date last night." They both ordered a salad, and Pepper only picked at hers, taking a bite every now and then while Simone relived the details of her phone date.

"What is wrong, *chérie*? Are you unhappy I was late?"

Pepper shook her head.

"Is it that bartender? Did he say something nasty to you?" Simone started to get up. "I will give him a piece of my mind."

"No," Pepper said. "Would you mind awfully much if we rescheduled? I have an errand to run."

She could have told Simone the truth, but that wouldn't have helped anything. Simone would have only used the opportunity to light up a smoke. Not that she'd completely quit, but she had managed to cut back to about half of what she'd been smoking.

When she got home, she checked to see if she had any messages from Jake. Nothing. She paced the kitchen and tried reasoning with herself. Who cares if he's a construction worker? She'd dated a lot worse. She continued pacing for the next five minutes, working herself into a state. If he lied about what he does, what else had he lied about? "Once a liar, always a liar," Simone always said. Certainly, that had some merit. Oh, Gawd, please don't let him be married, too.

Pepper wrapped her arms about herself and stared at the phone. She could easily clear up this misunderstanding right now by asking Jake if what Brad had said was true. She reached for it and then pulled back her hand. No, she wasn't going to call him. What she needed right now was to feel warm and safe, and the only thing that came close was a bath. Well, there was always Brad, but she didn't want to jump the gun.

As she soaked, Pepper tried to put what Brad had told her out of her mind, but images of Jake pounding nails into boards and taking beer breaks with his buddies while they catcalled to all the female passersby filled her head. It didn't make sense that he'd lie to her. Why would he? It's not like being a construction worker was anything to be ashamed of. She sank deeper into the water, letting its warmth curl gently over her body and closed her eyes.

Her ad!

Pepper sat up straight. Blue collar guys need not reply. Jake lied because of her ad. She didn't even care if he wore blue jeans to work. She loved blue jeans. It was a stupid, stupid lie.

Pepper slipped back down and let the water envelope her. It felt good, but it only made her remember how safe she'd felt in Jake's warm arms. The very thought of him, the love they'd made, his whispered words of seduction in her ear, but now Brad's words intruded on the memory, and she couldn't push them aside. By the time she climbed out of the tub and dried herself off, Pepper had herself convinced that the only thing to do was investigate.

Brad walked up the steps, still in a foul mood from Pepper's rejection. First Alena, now Pepper. What was going on anyway?

He heard a yelp come from the backyard and rushed around to the side of the house. Another yelp. A happy one. No cause for alarm. Scratch must've heard him pull up. Brad went through the gate and found the dog tied to the fence. No water, no food, no shelter from the sun. He rushed over and was met with wiggles, licks, and happy whimpers.

"Hey, boy, what're you doin' out here?" Brad said to the pup. He untied the dog, and it jumped gratefully into his lap, its joyous wiggle uncontrollable. Brad scooped him up and took him inside for a bowl of water. Scratch finished the first one, and Brad gave him a second, which he also finished.

Marta was in the living room sitting in a black

recliner. Quiet snores came from her, and she had a drink in one hand that was about ready to spill. Brad tried to pass by without waking her.

"I don't want that mutt left in this house when you're not gonna be here to watch him," Marta grumbled just when Brad thought he was home free.

He stopped and gave her an icy glare. "You could've given him some water," he said, even though he knew that was a joke. Ever since their falling out, Marta had made it clear she wouldn't lift a hand to make anything easier for him or his dog. He continued to his room. He wasn't interested or in the mood to listen to anything she had to say.

"Sorry, boy. I thought we might have a new place to stay soon." He ruffled the dog's fur and tossed him a toy.

He grinned. Pepper hadn't wanted to let on, but he wasn't fooled by her little act. It was clear she hadn't known that loverboy was a construction worker.

"Architect, my ass," he mumbled. The guy might have her fooled, but he knew what he saw. With any luck, maybe she'd be in the market for a new man soon. "Yep," he said, rubbing Scratch's belly, "maybe it'll work out after all."

Jake's porch light was off, but Pepper knocked anyway, just in case he might be home and in bed. No answer. Operation catch-the-bastard-in-a-lie was a go. The dark made it hard for Pepper to see what she was doing, but it was nice for hiding from neighbors. Now she understood all the things she'd heard about bushes and the dark and burglars. Luckily, she'd thought to bring a penlight.

"I don't know about this," Lucy said. "We could get thrown in jail."

"My virtue is at stake. Just hold this," Pepper said, shoving the small light at Lucy.

"I hate to tell you this, but your virtue hasn't been at stake for a very long time."

Pepper stopped and looked at her friend. "I'll ignore that remark, but only if you be quiet and do as I say."

Lucy rolled her eyes and followed Pepper around to the back of Jake's house. Years of forgetting her house key and not wanting her parents to know she was out late was finally going to come in useful. Pepper had the door open in two minutes.

"I don't want you to be afraid—" Pepper whispered, quietly shutting the door.

"Of what?" Lucy said loudly. "We're already criminals just being in here."

"Jake's got—" That was as far as Pepper got before a noise that sounded like a thousand bullfrogs came from the corner of the dark kitchen.

"AUG-GH-H-H! God help us!" Lucy wailed. She flailed her arms about and jumped around the room as though whatever had made the croaking sound might be slithering around at her feet.

Lucy flapped around Jake's kitchen like she was about to take off and fly. It made Pepper laugh so hard she nearly peed herself. She covered her mouth to stifle her laughter, but it was no use. She leaned on the counter for support, gripping it as tears filled her eyes.

"We've got to get out of here!" Lucy screamed. A Swiffer was leaning against the wall, and she grabbed it.

Pepper put out a hand to try to stop her. Lord knows she didn't want that poor bird to get hurt. "It's okay," she sputtered.

"It's not *okay*. Did you hear that?"

"Stop—I can't stand it—sh-h-h." She put a finger to her lips and wrapped both arms around Lucy.

"Let go," Lucy cried, trying to free herself. "Can't you see it? It's . . . it's flapping." Lucy took a swing, and the brown pelican hopped to one side, croaking indignantly at the attack.

"Yes, it's flapping." Pepper grabbed the Swiffer from Lucy. "It's okay. It's Gilligan." Pepper leaned over and took a second to catch her breath. She wiped tears from her eyes. "He's Jake's pelican."

Lucy backed up against the door, her eyes wild in the dim light. "Jake's got a *pelican?*" Her face instantly changed from a look of horror to one of confusion.

"Yes," Pepper said, nodding and wiping her eyes some more.

"What's he doing with a pelican? It could be a protected species . . ."

"I know. Now forget about it." Pepper took Lucy by the arm. "We're not here to investigate his harboring a protected bird."

"But—"

"Never mind."

They made their way down the short hallway to Jake's bedroom. Lucy reached for the light switch, but Pepper batted her hand away.

"No lights. Give me that." Pepper grabbed the penlight from Lucy. She circled it around the room and stopped, focusing on Jake's closet.

"It'd be so much easier to have a light on."

Lucy was right. Especially since the tiny light was growing dimmer by the minute, but Pepper couldn't take that chance.

"What if the neighbors see?"

"See what?" Lucy asked. "A light on? Gee, I guess they might think Jake was in his bedroom?"

Pepper stopped short at the sound of a car, and Lucy ran into her, stepping on the back of her heel. "Hey, give me some room." She clicked off the light and held her breath, waiting.

"*See?*" Pepper said.

"See what?"

"Don't give me 'See what?' You were just as worried as me that it was Jake coming home." She turned back to the closet and clicked the penlight back on, but it only emitted a faint yellow glow. "Great. How are we supposed to see anything now?"

Pepper shook the light, and the room was suddenly flooded with brightness.

"*Shit!*" both women shrieked and turned.

"Hello, ladies." Jake stood in the doorway of his bedroom, arms folded across his chest.

He looked from Pepper to Lucy and back. "Something I can do for the two of you?"

Lucy took a step forward, her face becoming as red as her hair. "We're so sorry—"

"I can speak for myself," Pepper said, her face showing no shame at being caught.

"And embarrassed," Lucy said. "Please don't call the police. She talked me into this. I would never—"

"Thanks, *friend.*" Pepper stepped past Lucy, giving her a dirty look. "Like I said, I can speak for myself. Where have you been?" she asked Jake.

Jake stared at her for a long second. "At work."

"You didn't call me last night."

"I got home late."

"Gordy?"

Jake nodded. "He's going to be okay."

Jake's weary face almost made Pepper forget why she was standing in the middle of his bedroom clutching a fading penlight. Almost, but not quite.

"I have something to ask you," she said.

"I'll wait for you in the other room," Lucy mumbled, heading for the door. She peeked into the hallway first.

"He's harmless," Jake told her and turned back to Pepper. "The answer is no."

Pepper gave him a curious look. "No, what?"

"No, I don't have another girlfriend. Or, no, I wasn't with another woman."

"What?" Pepper shook her head. "I never said anything about another woman."

"No, but I figure the only thing that can make a woman act this crazy is the suspicion that the guy she's in love with is cheating on her."

"The thought never entered my mind," she said. Her eyes opened wide. "And who said I was in *love?*"

"Okay," he said, rubbing a hand down his face. "Suppose you just tell me because I'm dead tired and I have an early day tomorrow."

"Work, huh?"

Jake nodded and yawned.

"I suppose it's hard work swinging a hammer . . ."

He started to nod again, but caught himself.

Hurt burned inside Pepper's chest. He'd made love to her and lied. And she'd believed him. Hurt quickly turned to anger. "So it's true? You're nothing but a construction worker?"

Jake paused, closing his eyes. He nodded slowly.

"I don't know how you found out, and it doesn't matter. I was going to tell you this weekend; then the phone rang, and we had to leave. I never got the chance."

"It was a *three-day* weekend. You couldn't find time to tell me the truth in three whole days? Or how about the entire last month?" Pepper waited for his response, but what could he possibly say? He'd betrayed her.

Pepper's mind raced. Signs. There must have been signs. God, it was true—love was blind. No wonder he'd been so anxious to get rid of that friend who had shown up when they were at Beachside. He was worried his little game would be ruined. *Bastard!* She fought back the tears that threatened to flow. She wanted to hit him, to tell him she hated him, but she couldn't force the words from her mouth.

Jake reached for her. "I can explain."

Pepper put up a hand. "I've heard that line so many times." She brushed by him, but he caught her arm.

"Wait. Listen to me."

Pepper searched his dark eyes. They were gentle eyes. Not the kind that could look straight at you and lie. Yet that's exactly what he'd done. He said he'd intended to tell her the truth, and instead, he'd made love to her all weekend. Now he wanted her to listen. Maybe during the throes of passion, she would have. Right now, she knew she had to get out of there. No way was she going to let him see her cry.

Pepper yanked her arm free, and Jake followed

her, still trying to explain. Her anger blocked out everything that came out of his mouth. She wasn't hearing any of it. Lucy jumped up from the sofa when she came down the hall, and without a word, they left.

Chapter 20

"You're a good friend, Luce," Pepper said when they got back home.

"Why? Because I broke into a man's house with you?"

"No. Because you haven't given me one of your looks."

Lucy walked over and leaned her head against Pepper's shoulder. "The night is young. Besides, you haven't told me what went on back there."

"The bastard lied," she said, flinging her hands into the air. "He *lied!*"

A frown formed on Lucy's forehead. "Bastard? Are we talking about Jake?"

"For God's sake, Lucy, where the hell do you think we just came from? Yes, Jake. He lied to me." Pepper poked a finger into her own chest.

Lucy's frown grew deeper. "Are you sure?"

Pepper slumped onto the sofa. A lump formed in her throat, and she tried swallowing it away, but it was an irritant, like a grain of sand that no amount of swallowing would get rid of. It made her even angrier.

She'd only known Jake for a short time. It didn't make sense, having a broken heart over him.

Lucy sat at the other end of the sofa and was quiet.

"What is it about me anyway?" Pepper asked. She turned halfway around and pointed to her back. "Check, will you? Is there a sign back there that says calling all losers?"

"I don't know because basically, you haven't told me anything," Lucy said.

Pepper took a deep breath and released it slowly through pursed lips. "Jake and I were having the most perfect morning after the most perfect night . . ." She looked over at Lucy and paused. Her friend probably didn't need every little detail. "I don't want to offend your virgin ears with the highlights," she said with a dismissive wave. The memory of those highlights brought back the heat of passion from two nights before, and warmth spread through her all the way from her toes to her heart. The lump in her throat grew even larger, and she wondered if she'd been too hasty. On second thought, no! He'd lied to her.

"So if it was perfect, what ruined it?"

"As it turns out," Pepper said with a sigh, "Jake is nothing more than a construction worker." Even as she said it, she realized how ridiculous it sounded. She was in love with him, and it didn't matter what he did for a living.

Lucy's lips formed a thin line, and she shook her head. "Imagine that, a common construction worker." She gave that disapproving mother look that Pepper had thanked her for not giving earlier.

Pepper leaned back against the arm of the sofa,

and a pout formed on her lips. "I should've known you wouldn't understand." Her chin tipped upward.

"I understand completely," Lucy said.

"You obviously don't. He *lied* to me. L–I–E–D." Pepper folded her arms across her chest.

"Lied. Right. I see. What I don't see—if you love him—is why it matters. He's going to have to do something a little worse than tell a fib if he's going to make the top of my dog list."

Pepper's mouth dropped open, and her arms spread before her. "Who said anything about love? What is it with you and him and this love business?"

"You love *me*."

"What's that got to do with—with anything?" Pepper was at shriek level. Dealing with Jake's lie and now having Lucy be so damn logical was too much.

"I've lied to you," Lucy said. Pepper gave her a sideways glance. Lucy nodded. "That's right. Remember the time your mom came in and asked who'd eaten all the cake? And remember we ate it because I had told you your mom said we could?"

"*So?*" Pepper looked at her friend incredulously.

"So I lied to you, and you still love me," Lucy said matter of factly.

"That's so completely different that I'm not even going to try to explain it."

"Nope. A lie is a lie. I've heard you say that yourself." Lucy's mouth turned into a smug line.

"He's a construction worker. That's about as blue collar as it gets. Get it?"

"Got it," Lucy said, nodding. "But who cares? Dating a suit was Simone's idea, not yours." Lucy shook her head. "I could have told you that a suit doesn't guarantee honesty. Ever heard of embezzlement?

Extortion? Some of the biggest crimes have been committed by men who wear suits."

Pepper mulled over what Lucy was saying, but she couldn't get past the glaring reality that Jake was a big, fat liar. She folded her arms across her chest.

"So now what? Another flight on the Internet skyway?"

Pepper shrugged. "There's always Brad," she said resignedly.

Lucy's lips scrunched together liked she'd sucked a lemon. "Maybe you should give Henry another chance? I hear his wife is divorcing him."

Pepper rolled her eyes. "I'm going to go crawl into bed and pull the covers over my head and sleep so I don't have to think about Jake or Brad or any man." And Jake better not even think of invading her dreams.

Morning came, and Pepper didn't feel refreshed at all. She hadn't slept more than an hour or two. She'd need some toothpicks to get through this day. When the sun poked its roundness through the overcast sky, she got up and threw on some cut-offs and a lime green bikini top. She could at least put her anger to good use by building a sandcastle. More than likely, it was the only castle she was ever going to have anyway.

She pulled her hair up into a ponytail and grabbed some lemonade on her way out to the beach. As soon as she stepped outside, the morning sun warmed her face, and she paused on the bottom step. A foam stain marked the high tide line, and she stepped down into the sand. With the way things were going, a monster wave would probably come along and wash all her tools out to sea today.

Pepper dropped her bucket and knelt on the beach. She scooped and scraped, using both hands to pull sand toward her and from the hole. She packed it into a pile and pounded the top flat, aiming for depth rather than width, and after several minutes of vigorous digging, she hit water. Only then did she take a breath and sit back on the sand. She leaned from one side to the other, feeling tense muscles give as she held each stretch for at least ten seconds; then she gave her legs a good shake before resuming a crouch position.

Pepper slowly poured a small amount of sea water on top of the pile. When it evaporated, salt crystals were left, forming a thin crust over the surface to serve as a bonding agent. Every few minutes, she sprayed the sand to add even more buildup.

With the sun warming her back and the sound of the waves crashing against the shore, Pepper had a temporary respite from thinking about Jake's deceit. Although she hadn't had much luck finding a good man, she had no regrets about moving to Malibu. Well, maybe one . . . that she wasn't closer to home so she could help her mom get through her hard time. Her forehead creased as she considered all that had happened in the last couple of years. She sighed. Her mother would be fine. She'd looked good during her last visit, and Pepper had finally believed that the thing with her mom's pills truly had been an accident.

Staring into the sand, she recalled the last time she and her sister had been close.

It was late May. Spring had sprung, the days were

longer and warmer—life was good. Except Pepper had a bad cold and wouldn't be going to the prom. Pepper's chest ached, remembering how she'd felt that night, so filled with envy at seeing Cat—or Christine as her mother insisted—come down the stairs in her prom gown. Because she was sick, she wasn't in the car with Cat when it careened off the road, hitting a light pole.

They'd had their share of sibling rivalry, but in their hearts, she and Cat were connected in such a way that Pepper thought she'd die when she heard the police at the door telling her parents about the car accident. She remembered Cat lying in her hospital bed, looking up at her and whispering, "You're the best sister a girl could have." Even now, thinking about how close she had come to losing her sister caused such pain that it clogged her throat like a thick fog.

If Cat died, they'd never have the chance to make things right between them.

Tears filled her eyes, and she tilted her face to the warm sun. "You too, Cat," she said, swallowing away the fog. A breeze blew across her face, and her lips curled into a smile. Somehow, she knew it was a kiss from her dad.

Life was okay now. With the exception of not being able to find that one special man, she'd say it was almost perfect. Unfortunately, all that'd happened with her mom proved that everything good could be whisked away as if it had never existed. Still, Pepper was determined to find the same kind of man who would grab her heart just as her father had her mother's. With Jake, she thought she'd found him.

Pepper smashed a fist onto the mound of sand.

Shit! Men were more trouble than they were worth. Maybe she'd be better off if she just dated and never let herself get emotionally involved. After all, that policy seemed to work for most men.

Pepper sighed and went back to work on the block of sand that lay before her. Starting at the top, she began carving, working first on one side, then doing the same to the other, making sure she kept the structure balanced.

It didn't take long to form a cone shape, and in a few minutes, she was at a point where she could begin to practice on some smaller, more detailed work.

Lost in creativity, all thoughts of her mom and dad and, most importantly, Jake were kept in check. She continued working, adding small scalloped shingles to the roof of her castle, and before long, she needed to stop and stretch again. She rested back on her forearms and closed her eyes. The soothing rhythm of the waves relaxed her until she thought she'd fall asleep.

Footsteps behind her made her open her eyes, and a flutter began in her stomach. *Jake.*

Just as quickly, the flutter disappeared. She was angry, dammit. How dare he show up without giving her a chance to think things through, without even giving her a chance to miss him.

She scooped up a bucket of sand and spun around on her heels. Luckily for her visitor, spinning around from a crouching position proved difficult, and she fell backward, spilling sand all over her chest.

"A-ag-gh-h," she said, brushing the gritty matter out of her bikini top. "This is *your* fault." She looked up against the blue sky, where a figure stood above her in the sun's glare, and she had to shield her eyes to see who it was.

Tall. Hunky. "Brad?"

"Sorry," he said, reaching out a hand to help her up. "Guess I should've said something."

"No. *I'm* sorry. I thought you were someone else. I was out here working . . ." She gestured toward her sculpture.

Brad glanced at her work and nodded. "I came by to tell you I'm sorry for butting into your business with your friend. I'd like to make up for it by taking you down to the Santa Monica Pier. We could have a drink, get something to eat," he said, his gaze pausing at her sand-covered chest. "After you get cleaned up, of course."

Pepper looked down. The sand, already dry, glittered against her chest. The itching inside her bikini top begged her to pull it up and whisk the sand away from her breasts, and she might have if it'd been Lucy or Simone—even Jake—standing there.

"Of course," she said, managing a smile. A rebound date didn't sound half bad right then. It would at least get her mind off Jake.

"I blew it," Jake said. He dropped Pete's car keys and a crisp fifty-dollar bill on the kitchen table. Theresa walked in and snatched up the money before Pete had a chance to pocket it.

"Hey," Pete said to her, "that's mine." He attempted to grab it from her, but she slapped his hand away.

"Ha!" Theresa tucked the bill down the front of her blouse. "Who cut his hair and shaved away an inch of callus from his hands?"

"Whose car did he use?" Pete retorted.

"Ours," Theresa answered smugly.

"She's got a point there. Community property and all," Jake pointed out. Pete didn't dare argue with that.

"And let that be a lesson to you gringo boys," Theresa said, jabbing a finger at the two men.

Pete pulled her into his lap and bent her backward. "What lesson would that be, my little black-haired vixen?" Theresa halfheartedly tried to squirm away, but Pete held on.

"Never lie to a woman," she said, managing to sit up. "Not if you plan to win her heart." She slipped off Pete's lap and patted her chest where she'd tucked the money. "For that little piece of advice, fifty dollars."

"And good advice it is," Pete agreed. Theresa left the kitchen, and he turned his attention back to Jake. "So now what? You just gonna give up?" He leaned over to the refrigerator and pulled out two Budweisers.

"When are you gonna start drinking real beer?" Jake asked, turning the can in his hand. He popped the top and took a long, cool drink. It wasn't a microbrew, but it would do in a pinch.

"Don't change the subject. What're you going to do about that woman who's got you tied in knots?" Pete pressed him.

"I lied to her. What can I do? She walked out without giving me a chance to explain." He picked at the woody grain on the tabletop.

"From what I hear about the two of you—"

"From who? Gordy?" Jake shook his head and gave a sarcastic laugh. "Gordy's finally got a chance to be with a woman who's available. A nice woman.

He chooses to chase after someone who's likely to get him killed." He slapped a hand to the table. "Doesn't matter. He'll be glad to get his fifty bucks."

"I don't think so. Although," Pete said with a chuckle, "he doesn't have a wife that he has to share it with. Not that I mind sharing," he added, Jake supposed for Theresa's benefit, in case she overheard.

"What makes you say that?" Jake asked.

"I think he's tired of livin' life on the run from angry husbands and boyfriends." He, too, began rubbing and picking at a knot in the wood.

Theresa came back and slapped him in the back of the head. "I don't want to have to buy a new table with that money I just got." She turned to Jake. "I think you're the one whose *corazón* dances. Go to her, Jake. Get down on your knees and beg her to forgive you," Theresa commanded him. She tapped the side of her head lightly. "Trust me, *mi amigo,* if she loves you, she will listen."

Jake looked at Pete.

"Couldn't hurt. Most women won't listen though. Not long enough for a man to apologize anyway." Theresa took the opportunity to slap the back of his head again. *"Hey,"* he said, rubbing his head, "what's that for?"

"For encouraging his behavior in the first place." Theresa nodded in Jake's direction.

Jake's lips pulled into a thin line. He knew better than to laugh when Theresa was riled.

"And you . . . you should be ashamed." She pointed a long finger at him. "Both of you." She gave each man a look of disapproval, and they hung their heads like dogs that'd just been caught digging holes in the yard.

Jake thought it best to get out of there before Theresa found a reason to slap him, too. Pete could get into enough trouble with his hot-blooded woman on his own. He kissed Theresa on the cheek, and Pete walked him outside.

"Let's hope you're right about Gordy. I don't think his ass can take too much more kicking," Jake said. He smiled, but he was dead serious. This time, Gordy had escaped with a bruised kidney, a broken jaw, and two blackened eyes. Next time, he might not be so lucky.

Jake got into his truck and rolled away from the curb. The inside of the cab was hot, and the air, stale. He rolled down a window, but it didn't help much. The outside air was just as bad. After a few blocks, the cab had cooled, but the back of his shirt was dampened with sweat. At the next red light, Jake pulled it over his head and tossed it onto the passenger seat. When the light changed to green, a horn honked behind him. He considered giving the driver behind him a hand gesture, but then thought better of it. There'd been a recent news story about a man being pulled from his car and beaten for doing the same thing, and today, nothing was going to stop him from getting to his destination.

Most days, it was hard to find a parking space along the Pacific Coast Highway, but today, he managed to nab a spot right in front of Pepper's cottage. He took that as a good sign. With the temperature rising, he left the windows open. The salt air might help make it smell better, too.

As he stood on the doorstep of the small house, he

had the sudden feeling that he should've stopped to buy some flowers as a peace offering. Too late now—the door was opening.

A fist pounded inside Jake's chest while his stomach flip-flopped. His first impulse was to run, but his legs were rubber.

The pounding became so furious, the nausea so immediate, and then Lucy's freckled face peeked out at him.

"Lucy," Jake said, his voice touched with relief.

"Good to see you, too, Jake," Lucy said.

She took a good look at his bare chest, and he thought he saw her blush. Kinda hard to tell through all her freckles.

"Pepper's not here." Her bright blue eyes looked at him without judgment.

"Sorry, I didn't mean to . . . I was hoping—"

"I know. Sorry, she really isn't here."

"Do you know where I might find her?" he asked, ready to hunt her down, if necessary.

Lucy stared down at the stoop as though pondering his question. Finally, she raised her head and looked him in the eye. "I'm not sure I should tell you. On the other hand," her lips curved mischievously, "she didn't tell me not to. She's gone down to the Santa Monica Pier."

Jake grabbed both sides of Lucy's head and kissed her forehead. "Thanks, Lucy; I owe you," he said as he bounded off the front porch.

"But, Jake," she yelled to him.

He turned and looked back.

"She's not alone."

"No?" he said. "Can I take him?"

Lucy smiled, and a hundred freckles squished together in her cheeks. "I'd bet money on it."

Jake was sure he broke a speed record getting down to Santa Monica. He slipped his shirt back on and walked down one side of the pier, scanning the crowd for Pepper's face. By the time he got to the end, he still hadn't found her. He stopped for a few minutes and watched the crowd, then returned back down the other side. When he got back to where he'd started his search, frustration was beginning to set in. Maybe she hadn't come here after all. One more look, and he was leaving.

This time, he'd take it slower, really look at all the women with honey-colored hair. He was aware of a few women giving him looks back, some that made him feel exactly like the kind of man he knew Pepper didn't want. Then there were those who seemed to enjoy being leered at, and they gave him long looks back. He even stopped and waited across from the women's public restroom to make sure Pepper wasn't inside, only to slip out after he walked down the pier. After a couple of minutes, he moved on.

Jake stopped across from the Pacific Park entrance and gazed into the water. It was murky and green, and as he stared, he remembered the hurt on Pepper's face when he admitted he'd lied to her. An excited shout made him look over to where a couple of men were fishing. One of them pulled a perch from the water and held it up appraisingly.

Jake turned around and faced the park. He read a sign that said, "A day at the beach has never been this fun." Pepper? Having fun with another man? Not if he had anything to say about it.

Maybe she'd already come and gone. Maybe her date had taken her back to his place. For some fun. Jake closed his eyes and remembered the way her nude body looked as it was caressed by soft candle-light. Her easy curves and mocha-colored skin, compliments of Malibu Beach, were enough to fill any man with ideas. Jake brought a closed fist down onto the railing. Dammit! He refused to allow him-self to consider that Pepper might be intimate with anyone else. A small child standing nearby jumped, and her mother quickly ushered her away.

Jake continued up the pier, trying to think of where to look next. He heard a familiar laugh. It was the kind of laugh that stood out from a crowd. All throaty and sexy, and it made a person turn to see what was worth that kind of laughter.

He looked and spotted a couple with their back to him. The woman's hair was pulled into a short ponytail, and she had a heart-shaped butt with long, tan legs sticking out from white shorts. He'd know that laugh anywhere, but even more, he'd know that ass.

Adrenaline pumped through him, and a quick assessment of the guy told him Lucy was right. He could take him.

Jake started toward the couple, but hesitated when the man slipped an arm around Pepper's waist. He was filled with a rage he'd never experi-enced before, and he envisioned walking over and breaking the guy's arm. Yep, the guy's arm dan-gling limply by his side was something he wouldn't mind seeing. But he seriously doubted it was some-thing Pepper would enjoy. And it would only serve to make her think he was a madman as well as a liar—and an uneducated caveman.

A loud clatter further down the pier made him turn just in time to see a boy who looked about twelve years old getting ready to skate off the top of the steps onto the walkway below. His friend stood at the bottom with a video camera. Jake was convinced the boy was going to kill himself. He wanted to stop the kid, ask him if his mother knew what he was doing, but it was too late. The kid launched himself off the steps, and Jake held his breath, watching, waiting for the aftermath of brains splattered on the cement. When the boy landed with both feet still on the skateboard, Jake let out a long sigh of relief. Stuntman in the making.

Jake turned back to Pepper and her escort. They were laughing and standing way too close. The way he saw it, he could either walk over to them and act civilized and ask to speak with her, or he could walk away and forget about her. Jake dragged a hand down his face. Forgetting about Pepper wasn't an option. Damn Pete and Gordy and their bet anyway. He didn't know what he was going to say, but he knew he'd had enough of watching another guy put the moves on his woman. He stepped off the curb to cross the street.

Pepper laughed, tilting her face upward. A breeze whipped her ponytail from side to side. Maybe Brad wasn't such a bad guy after all. Underneath his suave exterior, he seemed to have a vulnerable side. And he was easy to be with. She felt no pressure to talk about what was bugging her, no pressure to explain her feelings. It was almost like being alone. *Alone.* What a concept. She never thought she'd find anything good about being alone. But after all that had happened, maybe that's what she should try for a while.

Simone had always told her that a good man was like fine wine. You could always stick with what you knew and never be surprised, or you could wait until a good one happened along and savor it. Pepper shook her head. She didn't understand then and didn't understand now, but somehow, it seemed like good advice.

She glanced over at Brad and considered whether she would ever date him for real. He might have a bad boy reputation, but he also had a sense of humor. Plus, he was good for taking her mind off Jake. But boy, would Lucy have a fit if he was constantly hanging around.

Brad slipped an arm around Pepper's waist, and she felt her body tense. She shifted, pulling away slightly, but he didn't seem to notice. His arm didn't even budge. In fact, she was almost certain he pulled her closer. It wasn't that it was unpleasant—it was more that she felt like she was cheating on Jake. It was Jake's arm that belonged around her waist, not Brad's.

Jake was a flame to her chocolate, and together, they made fondue. When he held her, she melted into him. They were a perfect fit, and she missed him terribly. Why did Jake have to go and make love to her with a lie? Why did every man she met have some fatal flaw?

Pepper turned suddenly and grabbed Brad's face with both hands. She pulled him to her and planted her lips on his. After a long minute, she let him go. The kiss wasn't nearly as satisfying as she'd hoped, but judging from Brad's reaction, it was more than he'd imagined would happen between them today.

Pepper put her fingers to her lips and backed away. "Sorry," she said. "I don't know what came over me."

"You don't need to apologize," Brad said. "It was nice."

He leaned toward her, poised for another kiss, and she knew she'd made a mistake giving him any encouragement. It'd been hard enough keeping him at bay. What was she thinking?

Pepper glanced at her watch. She needed an excuse to put him off. Failing to come up with something good, she fell back on what she always used.

"I've got to go. I have a class soon." And actually, it was close to the truth. Her class just wasn't until later.

Brad backed off immediately. He looked confused.

The two of them walked toward the end of the pier, and all the while, Pepper tried to think of a way to avoid the good-bye kiss that she felt coming.

"Pepper," a voice called to her.

Either she was having a heat stroke, or what she saw was simply a mirage. Jake was walking across the street toward her.

Brad's arm immediately dropped from her waist as her mirage got closer.

Nope. It really was Jake. Pepper's heart skipped. She wanted to run to him, wrap her arms around him, get lost in his lips. But she stayed put. Nothing had changed. He was still the liar who took her to bed and made love to her like no one ever had or probably ever would again.

Jake stepped up onto the curb, and she lifted her

chin in defiance, hooking an arm through Brad's. Brad's arm stiffened, but she held tight.

"What do you want?" she asked.

"I thought we might talk," Jake said.

"We don't have anything to talk about." She gripped Brad's arm even tighter.

"Then let me talk, and you listen." Jake reached over and touched her shoulder.

Brad shifted his body so that he stood between them, and Pepper was surprised when Jake's voice deepened to a growl.

"Back off," he said to Brad. Without missing a beat, he turned his attention back to Pepper.

"I . . ." she began, but Brad's arm tightened over her hand. "I can't. I've got to get to work."

Jake gave Brad a better-not-get-involved warning look. "Don't do this," he said to Pepper. "Come with me. Let me explain."

His voice was so gentle, so reassuring that Pepper had trouble holding on to her anger. But the hurt wouldn't rest, and she closed her eyes and shook her head. "I can't."

She held Brad's arm, and without another word, they continued off the pier.

Chapter 21

"What's eatin' you?" Vic asked Brad, knocking his foot off the coffee table. "Woman trouble?"

Brad looked up at his friend. He chuckled dryly. "Yeah, woman trouble." He drank the last of his beer and went to get another. It pissed him off that his best friend was marrying a woman like Marta. He didn't even want to think about it, and he didn't know how long the friendship could possibly last once she and Vic were married.

"No, really. What's been troubling you? Marta says you've been bitchy as hell to her."

Brad grabbed the TV remote and turned up the volume, and Vic stepped in front of the screen, his thin frame barely blocking it.

"What the hell do you want? I'm trying to watch the game."

"Whatever's bothering you, you need to stop taking it out on Marta. Look, man, if you and she had some falling out, maybe it might be better if you found another place." Vic jutted a thumb toward the door.

Brad turned off the TV and looked up at him. He

couldn't believe what he was hearing. "You kicking me out?"

"I ain't saying that. But I'm getting married, and I can't have this hostility between you and Marta. She says it's stressing her out."

Stressing Marta out? What did Vic think it was doing to him?

"I can't make it living here in Malibu without a roommate on my salary. But as a matter of fact, I have been seeing this woman, and I might be moving in with her soon." If that SOB who tracked her down at the pier stayed away. He'd hated the way Pepper had grabbed his arm to make her boyfriend jealous. Game playing. But maybe her little game would turn out in his favor.

"Serious? You're finally gonna become domestic and live with a woman? Hey, man, that's great. Sorry if I came across as trying to get rid of you. Marta's been on my ass. You know how it is." Vic laughed. "Or you will soon enough. Tryin' to keep them happy is a bitch."

Brad laughed. Vic had a point there. He tossed the remote control onto the coffee table and got to his feet. "Either way, I'm looking for a new place. Marta will have you all to herself." Brad brushed past Vic and went to his room. He heard the front door slam a few minutes later and then the rattle of pots. Marta had come home, and she was in the kitchen scrounging around for something easy to fix for dinner.

He sat on the bed, and Scratch woke up. The pup started licking his fingers, and Brad rubbed a hand roughly over the dog's head. Vic was right. It was time for him to get busy and find a new place to stay, because if he didn't, something bad was going to happen.

Pepper took a look around the gym. One of the other instructors had asked Pepper to take over her aerobics class, so she'd combined it with one of hers. Space was tight as it was, and then five walk-ins had arrived wanting to give working out a try before signing up. Pepper didn't relish the thought of another class being added to her schedule, but she wasn't going to stress. Walk-ins rarely joined. Even if they did, they usually didn't last more than a few sessions. These were people who happened to look in the mirror one morning and were shocked to see a roll of flab around their middles. That, in itself, was shocking.

In Pepper's opinion, there was a long warning period before a person was considered obese. When clothes begin to fit a little tighter, that's when you take a look at what you can do to fix it. You don't go out and buy the next larger size and pretend you still look good.

With most of the participants being relatively new, Pepper decided to take it easy on them. Nothing too difficult. Almost effortless. Sidesteps, squats, lunges . . . nothing too taxing. Just enough to make them reconsider.

After fifteen minutes, a couple of the walk-ins couldn't keep up, and a few of the regulars were breathing hard. Too bad, she thought. If they could only see what might be in store for them when they got older, they'd probably be more likely to stick with it.

Pepper's grandmother had spent the last ten years

of her life caring for her grandfather because he'd never taken an interest in any kind of physical activity. She'd always told herself that she'd never spend her golden years playing nursemaid to a man who had health problems simply because he was lazy. Lucky for her, the two men who were interested in her right now were both great physical specimens.

After an hour of pushing the neophytes into near exhaustion, Pepper let up and finished with a five-minute cooldown. Watching some of them gulping for air and seeing the sweat roll down their padded cheekbones made her long for the day when she'd spend her time traveling to the world's finest beaches to build sand sculptures. Teaching kick-boxing and yoga had its advantages, and she'd continue to do them anyway, with or without teaching a class, but playing in the sand? Nothing could be better than that.

With only a few more stretches to go, Pepper noticed someone come in on the other side of the gym. Her heart raced when she saw who it was.

Jake.

She dismissed the grateful class and picked up her mat. Unfortunately, the ladies' locker room was also on the other side of the gym, and she had to walk past Jake to get to it.

"Do you have time to talk now?" he said to her when she got close.

"What are you doing—stalking me? I told you that I didn't want to hear what you had to say," Pepper said. She kept walking.

"I know what you said. I figured it was partly because you were with your bartender friend." He caught up with her and had her by both arms.

Pepper didn't attempt to pull away. She'd never admit it, but she enjoyed the sensation of his fingers pressing into her flesh. Instead, she looked into his face at his ready smile. And God, he smelled good. He was close, so close all she had to do was rise up on her toes, and her lips would be on his. Just do it, she told herself. Reach up, kiss him, forgive him . . .

As though he'd read her mind, Jake suddenly pulled her to him and pressed his lips to hers. Oh, how she wanted to let herself go, melt into him, but she'd had her fill of liars.

"No." She pulled herself free. "How dare you? You think you can just come in here and force yourself on me and everything will be better?"

She continued walking toward the swinging doors . . . almost there . . . she could make it . . . a few more feet. Pepper reached out a hand to shove the door, but Jake came up behind her. He wrapped her tightly in his arms.

"Yes, I do. I do because I haven't done anything for you to treat me this way."

Pepper gasped as his lips met hers once more. This time, she was determined not to enjoy herself, but his tongue in her mouth was so sweet. So perfect.

After a long time—but not nearly long enough— she found the strength to push him away. Their eyes locked, and then she backed through the locker room door.

Pepper stopped just inside and leaned her head against the wall. She was safe. The Jake she knew wouldn't dare enter the ladies' locker room with naked women walking around. But then, she didn't *really* know him. She chewed her bottom lip. *Please come in. Keep chasing after me, and I swear I'll let you catch me.* He didn't.

Hot tears filled her eyes. She stripped off her workout clothes and stood in the hot shower with her face turned up to the showerhead, hoping it would make her forget the burning imprint of Jake's lips on hers. Love wasn't supposed to hurt this much.

Pepper got home and paused at the front door. A wreath in colors of green and red hung from a hook. It smelled of pine and roses. What was Lucy up to now? She had no desire or energy to make sense of it. No doubt, it was some kind of cure for evil. The colors made her think of the holidays. Christmas would be here soon enough without Lucy helping things along.

What would the holiday season be like this year if she couldn't share it with the man she loved? Pepper hated to admit it, even to herself, but she wasn't looking forward to another tomorrow without Jake, let alone an entire winter.

"What's with the wreath?" Pepper asked. "It looks like Christmas is here early," she shouted over the TV.

"Since we couldn't have the door painted red, I thought red flowers would suffice," Lucy explained and then went back to her movie. She was hugging a bowl of popcorn, and Pepper hoped this didn't mean that her friend had given up on her diet.

As though reading her mind, Lucy said, "Low fat."

Pepper slumped onto the sofa and eyed Lucy suspiciously. "I don't suppose you know anything about Jake finding me at the pier earlier today?"

"Seemed like you could use some help," Lucy said. She grabbed a handful of popcorn and popped a couple of kernels into her mouth.

"And you were oh so happy to oblige," Pepper said with a bite of sarcasm, even though she was glad Lucy had a big mouth. She wasn't going to admit it though. Limits had to be kept on Lucy's interference in her life.

"I told you he *lied* to me—"

"We've been over this already," Lucy said. "We all lie to those we love."

"*Who?*"

"Your mom."

"I never—"

"Yes, you have. Don't make me start naming times. You have. So does that mean she shouldn't talk to you anymore?" She looked at Pepper defiantly.

No response.

"I thought not." A smug smile curved Lucy's lips upward.

"Who's this for?" Pepper asked, bending over to smell a flower arrangement on the coffee table.

"Someone you've lied to, but since you've lied to her, I guess she wouldn't want it."

"Who?" Pepper said. She pulled the vase of flowers toward her, but Lucy snatched the card before she could take a look. "C'mon, let me see."

Lucy struggled to hold on to the card, but Pepper grabbed it and opened it.

"*Cat?*"

"Her birthday is coming up in just a couple of weeks. Just like yours."

Pepper tossed the card back to Lucy. "I forgot. Guess I've had a lot on my mind."

The next morning, Pepper sat at the kitchen table with a glass of orange juice. She wanted to go out to the beach, but she didn't know if she was in the mood. Malibu was thick with summer; tourists were everywhere. It was the time of year when she could expect passersby who were out for their morning stroll along the beach to stop for a few minutes and watch her build. Not that she minded. What she could do without was all their questions. "What kind of tools do you need?" "How long does it take to become really good?" "What's your favorite thing to build?" Never "What's a nice girl like you doing sitting out here on the beach all alone building castles?"

It'd been only one day since she'd seen Jake, and already she missed him like crazy. Pepper pressed her fingers to her lips, remembering the sensation of his mouth on hers. The thought of spending the rest of the summer without him was torture, but the pain of his lies made her more determined than ever to get over him.

With a little help from Malibu Health, she could fill her time by working herself into a frenzied fitness freak. Exercise was good for stress release.

And sleep.

Unfortunately, that's probably when the real torture would begin. Dreams filled with lovemaking: Jake's arms around her, his hands roaming over every inch of her body. She sighed. In that case, her love for him would only continue to grow.

"Gee, that must be some good orange juice," a tired voice said.

Pepper jumped. "What?"

Lucy walked up to the table. She had on pink cloud pajamas and blue stay-at-home socks. Her red hair was smashed to one side like a splatter of paint, and she didn't even care.

"Nice hairdo," Pepper said.

"Thanks. You been working out?" Lucy asked. She filled a cup with water and stuck it in the microwave.

"What makes you ask?"

"You're glowing. The only time you glow is when you've been working out or when you've had a particularly eventful evening." Lucy waggled her eyebrows and looked around the living room. "I don't see Jake or, God help us, Brad, so I assume it's a workout."

"That shows how much you know. I was simply thinking about how nice it'll be to get the summer over with," Pepper said.

"Liar," Lucy said. The microwave dinged and she made herself a cup of hot chocolate. She sat at the table with her hands wrapped around the cup and sucked whipped cream off the top. Even on days that promised to reach eighty degrees, Malibu mornings could be cool enough to enjoy a warm drink.

Someone knocked at the front door, and Pepper was glad for the interruption.

"That's probably Mr. Reed coming early for the rent," Lucy said.

"Or maybe he's finally going to evict us for entertaining men in our home."

They both giggled.

Pepper tiptoed over to the door and peeked through the peephole, half expecting to see Brad. It was Simone.

"*Bonjour chérie,*" Simone rushed in like the Santa Ana wind, her arms full of packages and bags hanging from fingers on both hands. She paused to air kiss Pepper's cheek and continued over to the sofa, where she dropped everything.

"What's all this?" Pepper asked.

"Birthday gifts for you," Simone said, flinging her arms out wide.

"Must you remind me? Before you know it, I'll be celebrating my thirtieth, and I'll *still* be looking for Mr. Right. You know my birthday isn't here yet." Pepper peeked into the bags and saw several small, brightly colored packages. "I don't suppose there's a vacation in there anywhere?"

Simone waved a hand at her. "You have no need for a holiday. We are surrounded by sun, sand, and sexy men. What more could you want? Now," she said, "let me show you what I found at The Grove." She proceeded to take packages out of the bags and pile them on the coffee table. The last item she removed from the bag was a bottle of expensive merlot.

"Okay, if there's no vacation, then is there at least a sexy man in one of those packages?" Pepper asked.

Simone looked at Pepper with one raised eyebrow, then turned to Lucy. "What does she say, *chérie?*"

"*Chérie* is saying that she has tossed her sizzling sexy one aside and is now dating a potentially dangerous heartbreaker."

Simone looked at Pepper for confirmation.

Pepper put up a hand. "I had a very good reason. He lied to me."

Simone looked at Lucy, and Lucy shrugged.

"Lied?" Simone laughed. "Everybody lies, *chérie.*"

"He's a construction worker," Pepper said.

Simone's lips squished together like she'd just bitten into a piece of sour fruit. "Construction?"

Pepper nodded. "'Fraid so."

"And who is this dangerous one Lucy speaks of?"

"He's not dangerous. He's just—"

"—Potentially lethal," Lucy piped in. Her eyebrows rose, and her lips pulled into a thin line.

Simone paused a moment, then looked over at the packages. She picked out a red one with a white bow and tucked it under her arm. "I'll keep this one until your Jake comes back."

"You might as well take it back to wherever you got it then, because he's not coming back," Pepper said. "Ever." She stood and faced both her friends with her hands on her hips, daring either one of them to disagree with her.

"*Chérie,*" Simone said, "Jake makes the bed sizzle, yes? He will be back."

Pepper felt her face fill with blood. She glanced at Lucy, who was busy rolling her eyes.

Simone pointed to a bright green package with pale green, curling ribbons. "Open that one first." She smiled sweetly with a devilish light in her eyes. "Something to make you feel like a woman."

"Great," Pepper said. "Just what I need . . . to feel like a woman when I don't even have a man."

Jake sat on his back step in the cool early morning air. He reached into a metal bucket, scooping up a handful of herring, and tossed them to Gilligan.

"That's it, pal," he told the brown pelican. The gangly bird waddled over and stuck his long bill into the bucket. Seemingly satisfied that it was empty, he croaked loudly, and his neck settled into an S curve over his back.

"Isn't there a pretty female out there you'd rather spend your time with?" Jake asked.

The pelican's yellow eyes stared back at him.

"No? Okay, I guess it's just you and me then." He stroked Gilligan's head once and went inside. Gilligan followed him.

It was time to go pick up Gordy and take him for a checkup.

Jake was thankful he'd been forced to work overtime while Gordy was on the mend from his injuries. That was about to change. Two weeks had gone by and Gordy was ready to come back to work, which would give Jake more time to ponder where he'd gone wrong. He shook his head. "Why in hell are women so stubborn?" he asked Gilligan. The bird didn't have an answer. Jake grabbed a jacket and ushered the pelican back outside. Gilligan croaked in protest.

Jake thought about Pepper all the way over to Gordy's. He hadn't given up on her yet, but he hadn't quite figured out how to get through to her. With any luck, she'd get tired of trying to make him jealous with the bartender and realize how much she missed him.

Several times, he'd picked up the phone to call her, but each time, he stopped, figuring that if she could say goodbye so easily, he was better off getting over her. She was just another crash waiting to happen.

Jake waited in the lobby while Gordy got his checkup, browsing through magazines about parenting skills, health advances, and a host of other things he no longer had any interest in. Each time he looked up, one of the nurses at the front desk smiled at him. After he'd flipped through half the magazines, she finally walked over.

"Sorry for the long wait. We're backed up today," she told him.

Jake looked at her name tag. Missy Loveland. It sounded like one of those made-up names that a woman might choose thinking it might help her break into the entertainment business. She had a pleasant smile, and what the hell, he hadn't heard a peep from Pepper since he'd gone to see her at the club. Maybe Missy Loveland could fill some of his spare time, as well as help to mend the hole in his heart.

By the time Gordy came out of the exam room, Jake was in possession of Missy's phone number. He'd also made a date with her for later that night.

"What are you doing?" Gordy said, glancing back at the buxom brunette as they left the hospital. "I thought you cared about Pepper."

"I did. I *do*. She doesn't care about me."

"She's a woman."

"What's that supposed to mean?"

"It means she's gonna need at least a week for every week you lied to her." Gordy propped a foot up on the truck's dash. "So let's see," he said, counting on his fingers. "By my calculations, she's got another two weeks before she'll be ready to call and beg you to come over."

Jake laughed. "Where the hell did you come up with that theory?"

"Experience."

"Yeah, well it's been my experience from

watching you that you don't know what the hell you're talking about."

"Okay," Gordy said, nodding. "You'll see. Don't blame me if you blow it by being caught with your pants down."

"That's your job," Jake said. "Just because I go out with a woman doesn't mean my pants automatically come off."

Gordy shrugged. "I just don't want to have to say 'I told you so.'"

Chapter 22

Some women posed a challenge, but Brad had never thought it'd be this hard to gain Pepper's interest. Admittedly, he hadn't exactly been using all his charm. Just an occasional mixed drink made especially to suit her tastes and a special look between them now and then. Subtle flirting. The kind that goes no further until one of them wants it to. Vic was breathing down his neck hotter than the California sun, and he needed to do something about it. Stepping up his attention level to Pepper was high on his list.

Brad drove home from work in a funk, knowing that if Marta was home, she'd be ready to strike with her sharp tongue as soon as he went in the door. She'd hold off, let him grab a beer, but as sure as the sun came out every day in Santa Monica, the shit would start to fly. "When are you gettin' outta here? What about that woman?" Vic had told her about him seeing another woman, and that had only served to get her even more amped up.

Brad wiped the day's heat from his forehead. He

didn't have answers to any of her questions. Not ones she wanted to hear anyway.

He rolled up to the curb and sat there in front of the old, dirt brown stucco house. The street was void of anything resembling a human being, and not even a feral cat could be seen slinking around. Brad looked up at the house. Yellowed curtains hung haphazardly from the windows, and a single light emitted an eerie glow from inside. If it wasn't a rental, he'd give it a new coat of paint and add a little outdoor lighting.

The yard was nothing but dried grass, and even the weeds, which seemed to have an ability to grow anywhere in any climate, were brown. The house sat back on the lot, making it look bigger than it really was. Big and empty, he hoped.

Even though the house was a rental, you'd think a woman would do something to fix it up, make it more homey. Not Marta. Of course, she didn't really *live* here, he reminded himself. God, he didn't know what Vic saw in her.

Brad silently cursed himself for his lapse in judgment concerning Marta. All she did for him now was remind him of a bad day. He'd be glad when it was over. Tense muscles pulled in his left shoulder, and he twisted his head down and around to relieve some of the tightness, but it didn't help.

He got out of his car and by the time he reached the front door, he sensed that something was off.

Brad shoved open the front door and listened for Scratch's familiar welcome whine, but it didn't come. It was unusual for the pup not to have heard him drive up.

Marta was sitting in the recliner with her usual

afternoon toddy, and she didn't even look up. The shopping channel was busy trying to sell her a ten-piece cooking set.

"Where's my dog?" Brad demanded. Marta continued to ignore him. Only when Brad stood in front of her did she acknowledge his presence.

"My dog." Brad's voice filled the room, drowning out the television. "Where is he?" He hoisted Marta up by her sweater.

She jerked away from his grasp. "I ain't responsible for your damn dog. He was out there yippin'. After a while, he finally shut up. Good thing, too. I was getting damn tired of hearing that noise." Marta slumped back down into the recliner and turned up the volume on the TV.

Brad moved quickly toward the back door and stopped. The German Shepherd pup lay still in the grass. No wagging tail. No leaps in the air to greet him. Brad rushed outside, and he heard Marta shout behind him again that Scratch wasn't her responsibility. He crouched next to the dog, laying a hand on his still warm body. Brad could tell there was no life remaining in the little dog. He turned him over, and bile rose in his throat when he saw that Scratch's side was concave.

Jake took Missy out for dinner and drinks, choosing a place outside of the Malibu and Santa Monica area. Not to sneak around, though God knew Pepper had made it clear she didn't want to see him. Maybe never. His choice of where to take the nurse was purely to savor his memories of Pepper—where they'd gone, things they'd done. He didn't want to muddy those memories with another woman.

Missy was fond of dirty martinis with three plump olives. She'd plop them into her mouth, roll them around on her tongue, and finally crush them between her teeth. The way she kept her eyes on Jake while performing this ritual made him feel like she had ideas about feasting on him. One drink turned into two; two into three; and when his judgment became sufficiently clouded, he suggested they go back to his place.

Missy wasn't interested in why he had a brown pelican in his house. She wasn't even concerned. The only thing that concerned her was the location of his bedroom. So that's where they headed as soon as they arrived. As they walked down the hall, Jake remembered what it was like the first time he'd brought Pepper home. Her passion, her desire. She had plenty of it. So did Missy. But it was one-sided. Hers. She wasn't Pepper—not even close. And bringing her into his bedroom didn't feel right. For that matter, it didn't feel right bringing Missy into his house. He tried talking himself into it, but getting groped by any woman other than Pepper just didn't hold much appeal.

"C'mon, baby. Work with me, will ya?" Missy pleaded. Her fingers fumbled with the buttons on his shirt, and she finally managed to get half of them undone.

Jake took her wrist firmly in his hands and stopped her. "What's your hurry?"

Missy backed off and looked up at him through thick, dark lashes. She tossed her hair and faced him square on. "Seems to me this was your idea. A man dances with a woman, holds her close the way you held me . . . I thought this was what you wanted," she said with a seductive tilt of her head. She leaned in and brushed her lips lightly over his while pressing her hips against him.

Jake's head swam with the effects of alcohol and desire and guilt. He'd thought he'd known what he was doing. Back at the restaurant, he'd even managed to convince himself that holding Missy in his arms was the first step in getting over Pepper. But now, all it did was make him want her even more. A man could change his mind, couldn't he? Suddenly, he knew how it felt for a woman to be called a tease.

"Sorry. I don't think I can do this," he said. He sat on the edge of the bed, and the room started to spin. Nausea twisted through his stomach, and he didn't know if it would be better to keep his eyes open or close them. It quickly became clear he had two choices: he could either try to make it to the bathroom, or he could lie down and hope for a quick, painless death. He chose the latter.

Pepper woke up to an obnoxious *tr-ri-il-l-l*. She covered it with her spare pillow, but the noise continued. Where the hell was Lucy? With a groan, she reached for the phone.

"Good morning, sweetie," her mom sang in her ear.

Pepper frowned. "Mom?" She raised her head and opened one eye to look at the clock. "It's too early," she moaned, letting her head drop back onto the pillow.

"I wanted to make sure I caught you before you

were up and out of the house. I'm sure you have a full day planned—"

Pepper took another look at the clock. "Not at eight AM on a Friday." She stared up at the ceiling. Sleeping in was out of the question.

"What about work?"

"I have Fridays off," Pepper said with a loud yawn. She hoped her mother would offer to call back after she'd had a chance to wake up, perhaps give her a chance to take a shower.

"What about your friend? I'll bet he has something special planned for you today," Hannah said, maintaining the singsong lilt to her voice.

Pepper would have accused her mother of being on drugs, but she knew better. Not after her recent scare. No, something else was causing her mother's chipper mood, like maybe she'd finally turned a corner. Hope somersaulted inside Pepper.

"Mom? What's going on?"

"What do you mean, Patrice?"

"I *mean,* why are you so happy? Did you win the lotto?"

"No," Hannah said. "I'm just in a good mood. The sun is out. The birds are singing . . ."

"Oh, really? Since when does that make you happy? Last time I was there, you were threatening to kill the birds because they were waking you up at four AM with their singing."

Hannah laughed. "Oh that. I found a cure for their singing. It's a wave machine. I've got the sound of ocean waves playing all night in my bedroom. Works like a charm. Anyway, what about your friend? Do you still think he's the one?"

Pepper closed her eyes and saw Jake's face. "I don't think so."

"But why? From what Lucy told me—"

"Lucy doesn't know everything. Besides, when was the last time you and she talked?"

"A couple weeks ago, when you told me you weren't coming home for your birthday," Hannah said, her voice dropping in disappointment.

"Old news, Mom." Pepper sat up and scrubbed a hand through her hair. "Listen, maybe I will come home after all."

"Really?" Hannah said, her voice returning to a high-pitched glee.

Pepper heard her mother cover the phone. She was talking to someone, but Pepper wasn't able to make out what was being said. She looked at the clock again. Who, other than her sister, could be there so early?

"When?" her mother said, coming back on.

Pepper blinked her eyes, trying to think through the fog that still clogged her mind. "I don't know. Tomorrow, if I can get a flight." She could feel her mother's smile through the phone.

"Great. We'll have a birthday party," Hannah said.

"No party, Mom. Just a nice visit."

"Okay, Patrice. A nice visit."

Pepper hung up the phone and lay there with the strange feeling that she didn't know the half of what she would be walking into.

Jake woke up with Pepper on his mind and a large lump next to him in the bed. He frowned, trying desperately to remember what had happened the night before. It'd been a long time since he'd had so much to drink that he couldn't remember the night before.

The lump lying next to him was covered from head to toe, and from the smell of perfume that continued to linger in the room, he had a pretty good idea who it was—and a pretty good idea who it wasn't.

The lump stirred, and a minute later, Missy Loveland's brunette head peered out from under the sheet. She gave him a sweet, heavy-lidded smile, and Jake thought he'd be sick.

"Hey, baby," she said with a yawn.

Jake took a quick peek under the covers. He wasn't naked. Relief surged through him, and he let his head relax onto his pillow. He tried to remember what had gone on the night before. Something that might explain why Missy was still there and in his bed. It hurt his head to think that hard.

After a brief moment to gather his strength and his wits, Jake got out of bed and tugged on a pair of jeans. Hung over or not, he wasn't spending another minute in bed with Missy. When he turned around, she was sitting up, breasts bared and glowing like gazing balls in the dim light. Amusement played at the corners of her mouth.

"Relax, sugar," she said. "I didn't take advantage of you while you were under the influence. That would be against the law now, wouldn't it?"

Didn't take advantage of him? Please, God, let that mean they hadn't done the horizontal mamba. Jake rubbed a hand over his face and into his hair, trying to smooth it into place.

"Oh, honey, that's not gonna help."

Missy got up from the bed. She wasn't completely

nude, just topless. Jake wanted to look away and stare, all at the same time. He compromised, staring for about two seconds and then turning his head.

"I'm going to use the little girl's room," she said, "then it's all yours."

Jake watched her curvy body glide into the other room. A man would have to be in love if he didn't want to take advantage of that. He looked around for his shirt and found it at the foot of the bed. He started to put it on until the smell of Missy's sickeningly sweet perfume clogged his sinuses. Jake threw the shirt to the floor and pulled a clean one from a drawer.

"Maybe by the time I come out, you could have some coffee on," Missy yelled from the bathroom. "Maybe you'll have gotten your voice back, too."

By the time she turned off the shower, not only did Jake have coffee ready, but he'd also managed to scrounge up some carrot muffins from the freezer. The least he could do was feed her after a night of he didn't know what. He thawed three and piled them on a plate.

When Missy came into the kitchen, she looked as fresh and clean as a nun. Jake knew better. A little makeup and a lot of perfume, and she'd be that temptress who'd tried to seduce him the night before. At least she was a classy temptress, refusing to take advantage of a man while he wasn't in his right mind. He set the plate of muffins before her and gave her a sheepish look.

"I found these in the freezer, if you're hungry," he said and pointed to the plate.

"Thanks, no," she said. "Just coffee." She sat at the table and brought the cup to her nose and inhaled deeply. "M-m-m. Smells good." She took a sip. "Tastes good, too. Not many men can make a good cup of coffee."

Jake didn't care if it was good or not. The woman had said they didn't have sex. That's all he cared about. He sat at the table feeling awkward, like a teenage boy who had just had sex for the first time with a prostitute and was now trying to figure out how to get rid of her before his parents came home.

"About last night—"

Missy held up a hand. "You don't have to explain again." She set the cup down and placed a hand over his. Her wide brown eyes were kind, nonjudgmental. "It's okay. I was in love once, too."

Jake's eyebrows rose. Missy seemed to know more than he did about what had gone on between them. He didn't know how much she knew, and he didn't care. What he did care about was that he believed Missy when she said they hadn't done anything. Thank you, God.

Chapter 23

Brad placed the small bundle into the ground. He'd have to return with a grave marker. That meant a return trip to Catalina, but he didn't mind. Catalina held many fond memories from his childhood. Once or twice a year, he and his mom had taken a special trip to Avalon "just to get away from life," she'd say. Brad figured it was really to get away and have some adventure since his dad was mostly a distant figure in their lives.

He gently packed the rich earth and placed some flowers on top of the mound. After a few minutes, he turned away and went to another grave not far away. The marker on this one was broken and barely legible. He'd have to bring a new one for that one, too.

Pepper arrived in Seattle the following afternoon. Her mom looked better than she'd seen her in a long time. But then, the sun was shining, and that had a way of lifting the spirits of just about anyone.

"Wait till you see the recipes I've found for us to try

while you're here," Hannah said. She took Pepper's bag and started down the hallway. "C'mon, I'll show you to your room."

"Okay, Mom, but I do know where my room is."

Hannah laughed. "I guess you do, but I'll show you anyway."

Pepper followed her mother down the hallway, and they passed what used to be her dad's den. Her mom had turned it into a sewing room, but everyone knew it was still Frank's den. And as long as her mother lived there, it always would be. Hannah had refused to remove anything. All his books, bowling trophies—everything remained the same as the day he left them.

"Here you go," her mother said, stepping into Pepper's room.

Pepper smiled. Her mother didn't give up easily. Not if she wanted something bad enough. That must be where she got her determination from. Twenty minutes later, she was settled in as though she'd never left.

That afternoon, Pepper helped her mother with the potato salad, chopping pickles and providing taste testing. It was the best potato salad she'd ever had, and her mom always tried to have a large bowl waiting in the refrigerator whenever she came to visit.

Pepper stood next to her mother as she finished mixing everything together. Hannah put an arm around her, giving her a good squeeze.

"I'm happy to be here," Pepper said. She kissed her mother's cheek and gently wiped a smudge of lipstick from her soft skin.

"Hm-m . . . I was beginning to wonder. You don't seem all that happy."

Pepper leaned her head against her mother. "It has nothing to do with you," she said.

"Man trouble?"

"Is there any other kind? I'm beginning to think that they're more bother than they're worth."

"Oh, honey," Hannah said with a sigh, wrapping an arm around Pepper's shoulder. "If you find the right one, it's worth everything." She stepped over to the refrigerator. "Can I get you anything? Water, juice, vodka?" She pulled out a bottle of water for herself.

Pepper smiled. Some things would forever be the same. Her mother had been offering guests vodka ever since she could remember, and she had always wondered what her mother would do if anyone ever took her up on her offer.

"Nothing right now, thanks," Pepper said. She searched her mother's eyes. The sadness she'd seen during her previous visit was gone. In fact, she thought she saw a hint of the old spark. For the first time since her dad died, Pepper saw a rosy glow on her mother's cheeks. She raised a quizzical eyebrow.

"You believe there's more than one love in a person's life?" Pepper asked, and she swore the rosy glow on her mom's cheeks grew even rosier.

"Perhaps," Hannah answered warmly, putting a hand to her chest.

The way her mom looked, Pepper thought maybe she was going to swoon like the women did in those old movies. She gave her a suspicious look. If she didn't know better, she'd swear her mom was in love. Pepper couldn't even consider that possibility. Her parents had been together so long, and after what she had gone through, it didn't seem worth it to put her heart out there again.

Still, the twinkle in her mom's eyes was unmistakable. Something was up.

If it *was* a man causing that twinkle, who? And how had her mom found him, for God's sake? *She* couldn't even find a man.

Maybe it was a sex thing. It was almost too weird to consider, but she'd read that a lot of women reach their sexual peak later in life, like in their forties. Her mom was in her early fifties. Close enough. But visions of her mom with any man other than her dad disgusted Pepper, and she forced the thought from her mind.

"What's going on with you? You seem . . . well, happy. Don't get me wrong, I'm glad to see you feeling good . . . I'm just curious." When her mother didn't answer right away, Pepper felt like she'd pried into an area where she had no business being. "Sorry," she said, but she was dying to know.

Hannah moved around the kitchen, putting things away and wiping the countertop. Pepper watched her. Her mom had a little smile on her lips, and that only made Pepper more curious. Finally, she couldn't take it anymore.

"Have you met someone?" She immediately wished she could take back her ridiculous question. Of course her mom hadn't met anyone. She was still in mourning over Pepper's dad. When Pepper saw her mother's face flush to a warm glow, she felt her stomach churn.

Her mom looked over at her and opened her mouth to answer.

Pepper held up her hand. "Wait. I'm not sure I'm ready to hear this."

Hannah shook her head. "I doubt I'll ever really

get over your dad." She put a finger under Pepper's chin and looked into her eyes. "The truth is I have met someone."

"What?" Pepper shrieked. She wanted to grab her mother by the shoulders, tell her to come to her senses. After all, her dad had only been gone less than two years. Horror filled her as she thought about how she'd met Jake. She looked into her mom's eyes and quickly shoved that absurd idea aside. "So you're dating?"

"Well, it's not that simple. It's a little bit more than dating," Hannah said.

Pepper put her hands over her ears. "I can't hear this." She felt like her brain was going to explode. She couldn't believe she and her mom were having this conversation. She also couldn't believe she was having such a fit over it. Her mom getting back into life was all she'd wanted for a very long time. But her mom with another man wasn't the way she wanted it to happen. It made her head swim.

Her mother's warm smile turned serious. "Listen . . . I have needs, too."

"I'm not ready to hear this," Pepper said.

Hannah stood straight, proud, and raised her chin. "Well, I am. I'm ready to live again and love again. I'm just like you, and I want to share my life with someone."

Pepper highly doubted her mother was just like her. She rolled her eyes. "That's no excuse to do it so soon."

"It?"

"You know . . . it." Pepper felt like she was having "the talk" with a teenager daughter. She felt her face fill with color.

Her mother smiled. "I'm not so old that I can't still enjoy sex"—Hannah put her thumb and index finger together—"a little." A devilish grin settled on her mother's lips, and Pepper felt nauseous.

Pepper's brow knitted together. "Well, I hope you're being safe. And does Cat know about this?"

"Don't worry, honey. Ben and I have everything under control. You might say we're old pros at this. We are old enough to be your parents, you know."

Ben? Pepper could have done without a name. She sat at the kitchen table, focusing on a dent in the linoleum. Her dad had been bringing in a new refrigerator, and the dolly slipped. She looked around. What was she worried about? This would always be her parent's house. Her dad was everywhere. In the coat hooks he'd put near the back door, in the fancy sink faucet her mother had insisted he install, in the scratches in the brick around the fireplace from the time he'd tried to hang all their Christmas stockings.

"At least you're not living together," Pepper mumbled.

"Not until the end of the summer," Hannah said.

Pepper didn't know how much more she could listen to. Where the hell was her sister anyway? She could do with a little help here. A month ago, she was feeling all in love with Jake, and her mom was having trouble sleeping. Oh, how the tables had turned.

Pepper missed Jake more than she thought possible, and she had never been so miserable. The sadness was like a whisper that surrounded her. If her mother had been feeling anything like she was now, she could understand the need to find someone to fill the void. But how was she supposed to get over the feeling that her mom was cheating on her dad?

Jake and Gordy sat under a cypress tree at a homesite in Malibu seeking relief from the afternoon sun. It had to be one of the best ocean view estates—from Channel Islands to Catalina and beyond—that Jake had ever worked on. With two patios, one covered and one open, and a pool that curved around the entire back of the property like a moat, the owners were sure to host many high profile soirees.

Jake swiped a towel across his forehead. He reached into the cooler for a bottle of water and tossed one to Gordy.

"I'd rather have a beer," Gordy said.

Dry dirt billowed into the still air a half mile down the road, and a minute later, Pete's Audi pulled into the drive.

"Thought I'd check up on you guys," Pete said, bending over the cooler and looking inside. "Anything good in here?"

"Water," Gordy said flatly, "and Coke. Jake's banned beer for a while."

"You're on them pills. I don't need you getting yourself hurt again."

Pete took out a bottle of water and seated himself on the front step. He twisted around and looked from side to side, checking the place out. "Looks good. Glad to see you're still on schedule."

"Yeah, guess it didn't hurt any to have dickwad there laid up for a few days," Jake said, jutting a thumb in Gordy's direction.

"Maybe you could save some money and just have him on call," Pete said.

"Fuck you guys. We're still on schedule 'cause I'm a hardworkin' son of a bitch." Gordy still looked like an overripe banana, and it was hard to take him seriously.

Pete and Jake laughed.

"Damn, Pete," Gordy said, "when're you gonna wash your car back to silver?"

"Haven't had time, but it's sure been nice having it back. Driving Theresa's little car was embarrassing. Made me look unmanly."

"Who do you have to look manly for? You've got a wife at home," Jake reminded him.

Pete laughed, nodding in agreement. "What about you?" he asked Jake. "You make up with Pepper yet?"

Gordy snorted. "Good luck with that. He's been busy with some nurse." Pete's head snapped around. He looked at Jake with raised eyebrows.

"I have *not* been busy with some nurse." Jake gave Gordy a warning look. "We had one date."

"You slept with her—I'd like to remind you that you owe me and Pete fifty bucks."

"I did not *sleep* with her." Jake kicked a small rock. It hit Gordy's shin and bounced off, landing twenty feet away.

"Damn." Gordy rubbed his leg. "No need to get violent. And that's not what you told me."

Jake shook his head and held up his hands. "Okay, she slept in my bed. But we did not sleep together. I've already paid Pete. You'll get yours next week."

Pete raised a hand to stop their bantering. "Does somebody want to tell me what's been going on?

What happened to Pepper? And who's this nurse you guys are talking about?"

"She's no one. I met her when I was taking big mouth here to get a checkup. We went out, had a little too much to drink, and she stayed the night." Jake looked straight at Gordy. "I did not sleep with her."

"Okay. Glad to hear you've still got some sense," Pete said. "So where's Pepper?"

Jake shrugged. "Haven't seen her."

"What does that mean—you haven't seen her?"

"It means he fucked up—"

"Seems to me I had a little help." Jake snapped at Gordy. "I should never have taken that bet."

Pete held up both hands. "Okay, whatever the reason, I don't even want to know. But are you gonna give up just like that?"

"What else can I do?" Jake pulled his T-shirt over his head and dropped it next to the cooler. He dug through the ice and found a can of Coke.

"Do you love her?" Pete asked.

Jake paused. Love was a pretty accurate description of how he felt, but he damn sure wasn't ready to announce it to the whole crew, which is what he'd be doing if he answered Pete's question in front of Gordy.

What Pete said made Jake stop and think. Did he really want to give up so easily? Worse yet, did he want to let some Neanderthal have the only woman who'd been able to touch his heart since Angela died? The thought of another man anywhere near Pepper conjured up images that made him bristle. He squeezed his can of pop so hard soda spilled out the top.

"I just met her. It's too early for love," Jake said. He took a long drink of Coke.

"You've known her long enough to get into her panties and already catch hell." Gordy laughed. He swallowed half a can of soda, then let out a loud belch, and Jake and Pete both stared at him.

"I can see why you might be having trouble with the opposite sex," Jake said.

A blank look covered Gordy's face.

"If you love her, don't give up. A good woman is hard to find, my friend," Pete said to Jake.

Just the thought of looking into Pepper's big blue eyes, smelling the sun in her hair, that clean citrus scent that seemed to form a cloud around her, had him excited. "I guess I could try talking to her one more time," Jake said.

Pete stood to leave. "Good. Maybe Theresa will quit asking me when I'm going to invite you two over for dinner."

The rest of the afternoon couldn't have gone by any slower. With his mind on autopilot, Jake put the finishing touches on the curved entry into the dining room. At quitting time, he was in his truck and headed down Malibu Canyon.

Pepper was relieved that Cat had shown up for dinner. She promised herself she and her sister would get along for her mother's sake, but she'd seen red when she had come downstairs and saw a strange man sitting in her dad's chair. Even though she'd been expecting it, having dinner with the man who was sleeping with her mother was uncomfortable at best. At least with Cat there, she wouldn't have to do much talking. And Cat seemed so damned comfortable with this strange man in their house, sitting in their dad's chair. In her heart, Pepper hoped her mother was happy, but she also hoped Ben would fall off that chair and break a leg.

"Wow," Pepper said, sitting down at the dinner table. "So much food." The corners of her mother's eyes crinkled into a smile. "But I'll do my best to at least taste everything."

Pepper looked around the table from her mom to her sister, avoiding direct eye contact with Ben. It was hard to pretend she was okay with all this change. One, big happy family. Except now, she was an outsider. A thickness formed in her throat. This man was an intruder, and going right along with it, laughing and chatting with him like they were old friends, was Cat. Of course, who was she to object? She'd fallen for a man who'd turned out to be nothing more than a hard hat–wearing liar.

"How's Lucy doing?" her mother asked.

Pepper swallowed a forkful of potato salad. "She's good. She misses you guys."

Her mother reached over to Ben's hand and gave it a light pat. "We miss her, too," she said.

As if he even knew Lucy, Pepper thought.

"Almost as much as we miss you," Hannah said. "Too bad she couldn't have come with you."

"Yeah. Too bad. Maybe next time," Pepper said quietly.

For the next hour, the evening was filled with polite small talk, everyone taking care not to touch on anything too deep, and Pepper silently scolded herself for not being able to relax. Her mother was apparently happy, and she should be happy for her.

"More potato salad, Patrice?" her mother asked. She held the half-empty bowl out to her.

Pepper rubbed her stomach and shook her head. "I'm full."

"Ben?" Hannah offered.

"None for me," he answered.

Hannah excused herself and went out to the kitchen, leaving Pepper, Cat, and her mom's lover alone to carry on the conversation—which they didn't. The air hung like thick fog and Pepper couldn't see any way to cut through it. She quickly found herself wishing she was back home.

A few minutes later, her mother's voice sang through the kitchen door, "Happy birthday to you . . . ," and Ben quickly joined in. Cat smiled delightedly at the fuss, while Pepper blushed at the attention.

"I found this wonderful chocolate frosting recipe and thought I'd try it out on the two of you," Hannah said. She cut a piece of cake for each of them and added a scoop of vanilla ice cream to each plate, except hers. "Lactose intolerance . . ." She patted her stomach.

Pepper thought her eyes would pop out if she ate another bite, but knowing how excited her mother always was over finding a good recipe, she forced a forkful of cake into her mouth. Silky smooth chocolate with a hint of malt tantalized her taste buds. It was like magic, and suddenly, she was no longer too full. A chocoholic always had room to appreciate good chocolate. She ate the entire piece.

For the first time that night, Pepper felt the tension ease. She was probably on a sugar high and had lost all her sense.

Hannah's eyes lit up. "There's more."

Pepper started to protest. She couldn't possibly swallow another bite of anything, no matter how good, but her mother was already reaching through the kitchen door.

When Hannah sat back down, she handed a bright blue package with a white frilly bow to Pepper. Cat had gotten her gift from their mom early: a year of car insurance all paid for. If Pepper recalled her sister's driving ability correctly, it was a gift she suspected would come in handy.

Pepper took her time feeling the entire outer surface of the package. She shook it gently, the entire time fully aware that her mother was sitting on the edge of her chair with her hands clasped together. Whatever was inside rattled and clanged, and she had no idea what it could be.

"Oh, for God's sake," Cat said, "just open the damn thing."

Pepper stuck her tongue out at her sister and slid the ribbon over one end, and then, ever so slowly, she pulled the wrapping open where it'd been taped.

She let the paper fall away and then slid the top off a plain brown box. Her mouth fell open as she stared at what was inside. Sculpting tools. Brand new, professional sand sculpting tools from Sons of the Beach. A lump formed in her throat. Apparently, her mom *had* been listening to her.

"I can't believe you bought these for me."

"I didn't. They're from your sister. The envelope is from me," her mom said, nodding at the white envelope on the table.

Pepper hadn't noticed the envelope, and she was embarrassed at not opening it first. Her grandmother always told her it was bad manners not to read the card first. "Happy Birthday to a Wonderful Daughter," she read out loud. Another envelope fell out, and Pepper gave her mom a questioning look.

"Open it, Patrice," Hannah said, nodding vigorously.

Pepper did, and tears clouded her eyes. Inside were two tickets to the Harrison Hot Springs World Championship Sand Sculpting Competition. For a long minute, Pepper sat quietly, staring at the tickets. Having her mom understand that her desire to become a professional sand sculptor was more than just a silly dream meant everything to her.

"This is all too much," she finally said. "I don't know what to say."

"It's from both of us," Cat said.

Pepper looked at her sister, half expecting to see a smug smile at how clever she was for thinking of something so great, but Cat's face showed nothing but genuine feelings.

Pepper stood and hugged her mother, then went over to her sister and hugged her, too. She could actually feel some of the anger that she'd been holding on to for so long melt away. "Thank you so much," she said, and she excused herself. A minute later, she returned and handed Cat a small gray box.

Cat looked even more surprised than Pepper had felt a few moments before. Maybe they were both growing up.

"Well, *open it,* for God's sake," Pepper said with a smile.

Inside the box was a delicate white gold necklace with three small diamonds in a forever setting that was supposed to represent the past, the present, and the future.

Cat clasped the necklace to her chest. "It's perfect," she said, and Pepper believed her.

Hannah smiled warmly at her girls. "We expect to see some great sand sculptures," her mom said to Pepper.

"Oh, you will." Pepper sat back down and immediately thought about what she would build as soon as she returned to Malibu. She picked up each tool and examined it carefully. There was the SOB loop tool for making scalloped edges around roof lines, the large square tool for making uniform doors and windows, the SOB tiny trowel for creating uniform skinny windows, and miscellaneous other tools. She had a feeling her sculptures were going to improve significantly very soon.

Ben pushed himself away from the table. "I think I'll be going," he said. "I'll let the three of you have the rest of the evening to visit." He took Hannah's hand, and she walked him to the door.

Pepper witnessed their good night kiss. It was more passion than she wanted to see between her mom and another man, and she turned her head away.

She and her mother and sister stayed up late, talking and catching up on everything from the latest fashions to politics, but Pepper's mind was already hard at work building sandcastles. Not once did the talk turn to men, and for the first time in a long time, Pepper didn't dream about Jake.

Chapter 24

Traffic was at a crawl, and Jake had to resist the urge to honk. By the time he pulled up to the curb in front of Pepper's cottage, his road-rage level was a ten, and he had to tell himself to calm down before getting out of his truck. All the way there, he'd practiced what he was going to say to Pepper. The only thing left to do was knock.

The door shook under his hand, and he saw the curtains move. A moment later, the door swung open, and again, Jake found himself staring into Lucy's face. All the words that he'd prepared in some kind of apology-explanation remained like a dry lump in his mouth.

"Pepper's not here," Lucy said. She glanced up at a wreath of red flowers and then looked down at some of the petals that had fallen when Jake had pounded.

"You kinda scared me . . . I thought maybe—" and she stopped. She waved a hand and smiled. "Anyway, she's not here."

"Sorry about the flowers," Jake said.

"Don't worry about it. They were dead anyway."

"Do you know where I might find her? When she'll be home? I really need to see her."

"I'd love to help you, but you'll have to wait a few days. She's gone to see her mom up in Seattle."

Visiting her mom. Jake breathed a sigh of relief. All the images that had been filling his head of Pepper with Bartender Boy breezed out of his mind.

"Didn't she see her mom not long ago? Is something wrong? Anything I can do to help?"

"Nothing's wrong. It's Pepper's birthday, and she wanted to spend it with her family."

Sure. Family. That didn't include him. He didn't even know much about the sister, except that her name was Cat, and according to Pepper, she was the evil twin. He felt bad about missing her birthday, and he swore he'd make it up to her if she'd only let him.

"How much sweet-talking is it going to take to get you to tell me how to find her?" He smiled and gave Lucy a wink.

Lucy blushed nearly the color of her hair. Her nose wrinkled, squishing a hundred freckles together. She looked like a schoolgirl, and Jake decided right then and there that if Gordy ever hurt this young woman, he'd be the next in line to give him a black eye.

"I'm on your side, Jake. I think maybe if you give Pepper one of those winks, she won't be able to resist you. C'mon, I'll write her mom's address down."

"Thanks, Lucy," Jake said as she handed him the address. He gave her a quick peck on the cheek, and she wished him luck. God knew he'd need it. He'd be in Seattle, and it'd be him against three

Bartlett women. Every man on earth could sympathize with that.

Hannah fixed a breakfast of baked French toast topped with fresh blueberries, cubed cream cheese, and chopped pecans. In addition to that, she blended together a concoction of raspberries, strawberries, bananas, orange juice, and vanilla yogurt for the best-tasting smoothie Pepper'd ever had. Cat didn't join them. Smart girl. She, too, was lamenting the gain of two pounds since Pepper had come home. Also absent was Ben. She didn't ask where he was, and her mom didn't offer any explanation. Pepper kinda liked having her mom all to herself.

After eating as much as she could, Pepper pushed her plate away where she couldn't easily reach it. She was stuffed. She'd eaten more in the last couple of days than she'd normally eat in a whole week, and it was scary to think what she'd see when she got back home and stepped on the scale. Surely, the tally would be an extra ten pounds. Hopefully, with a few vigorous workouts, she'd be back to her size six in a few days.

"What do you think of Ben?" Hannah asked Pepper.

Pepper knew exactly what she wanted to say, but it would hurt her mom's feelings unnecessarily.

"He's okay. I'm not particularly fond of gray hair, but he's okay."

"His gray hair is actually what drew me to him. Along with his height. I like a tall man."

Pepper felt squeamish talking about man likes and dislikes with her mom. This was the kind of conversation she'd have with Simone or Lucy. She never knew her mom favored tall men. Her dad had only been just under six foot.

"I like tall men, too," Pepper all but mumbled. Especially when he had dreamy chocolate eyes and thick, dark hair. All six foot, three inches of him.

Pepper and her mom finished their conversation as quickly as she could change the subject, and then she went about helping her mom clean up the last of the breakfast dishes. Just as they stuck the last dish in the dishwasher, they heard footsteps on the front porch and then a knock.

"You expecting someone?" Pepper asked her mother.

Hannah looked up at the kitchen clock over the sink and shook her head. "I don't usually get visitors at this time of morning. Maybe it's your sister. If so, she's too late for breakfast. She'll just have to go hungry," Hannah teased, touching Pepper's arm lightly. "Let's see."

Pepper took one look at the back door and knew it wasn't Cat. Too tall, too broad-shouldered, too perfect. It was a man, and the silhouette was one she'd recognize anywhere. She held her breath as her mother opened the door. Before Hannah could even give the man a proper greeting, Pepper took a quick step forward and nearly sang out his name.

"Jake!" She brushed past her mom, who was showing her full set of pearly whites. "What are you doing here?" The sun came out, birds were atwitter, life was good.

"Aren't you going to introduce me to your friend?" her mom asked without taking her eyes off Jake.

Pepper quickly got hold of her senses. "He's not

my friend. He's just . . . just . . ." Pepper couldn't decide what to call a man who she was utterly in love with, even though he was a damn liar.

Jake's brown eyes twinkled with amusement, and his lips curved into a warm smile. That annoyed her even more.

"He *used* to be a friend," she finally said, lifting her chin. "Used to be."

"Well, let him in, Patrice." Pepper's mom stepped forward and opened the door wide.

"Patrice?" Jake's eyes crinkled in amusement again, and he let out a soft chuckle.

At that moment, Pepper wished she had some duct tape to cover her mom's mouth. She gave Jake a hard glare should he even dare to continue laughing. "Yes, by all means, come in," she told him.

"You must be Hannah," Jake said, turning to Pepper's mom.

Begrudgingly, Pepper introduced them to each other. Jake nodded politely and took Hannah's hand. Then he had the gall to kiss the back of it.

"Nice to meet you, ma'am," he said, and then he turned his attention to Pepper.

"What are you doing here?" she asked.

"I'm here for you. I want you, and whether you're willing to admit it or not, you want me, too."

Pepper tried to ignore the twinkle in Jake's eyes. They were like a flame drawing her in, trying to seduce her, and she had to look away to keep that from happening.

"You couldn't possibly know what I want. If you did, you'd know that I don't want a lying, scheming—"

Jake grabbed her and pulled her to him. She whimpered, knowing what was coming next, and she managed a weak attempt at resisting. The problem was his kiss—so moist, so warm—was all she'd been able to think about since their last kiss. His lips on hers were like a flame burning hot, and Pepper melted into him. Her body relaxed, and the world disappeared.

Until her mother cleared her throat.

Pepper's eyes opened, and she pulled away from Jake. What was she thinking? If it was possible for her to spit fire, Jake would be yelling for someone to call the fire department.

"How dare you?" She turned to walk away, but he grabbed her again.

"Excuse us, ma'am," he said to Hannah. "Your daughter and I need to talk."

Pepper squealed as Jake attempted to lead her out the door. She struggled, leaning back, but his grip was firm.

Thank God Jake wasn't some evildoer intent upon harming them because her mom sure wasn't any help. All she did was stand there all wide-eyed, watching as Jake mauled her daughter. Jake gave Hannah a reassuring smile, and that seemed to calm any fears her mom might have had. His ability to charm her mother infuriated Pepper even more. She continued struggling, yanking, twisting, and pulling, but Jake held on. Finally, Pepper put a foot against his leg and mustered one last attempt to free herself.

"Let . . . go . . . of . . . me," she huffed.

"Suit yourself."

Jake released her, and in her momentum, Pepper took a quick hop backward. She fell to the floor, landing on her butt, and skidded over the hardwood floor, coming to a rest next to the sofa.

Bruised in spirit more than anything else, she sat there seething and waiting to see if anything hurt. It didn't. When she looked up, her mom was doing her best to stifle a laugh, and then there was Jake. He was standing over her with that damn twinkle thing going on in his eyes.

Pepper's eyes narrowed as she took them both in. How could her own mother just stand there in her home and not even say anything while a strange man accosted her? Damn Jake anyway. He'd charmed her mom. She'd been fooled by his smile, just as Pepper had. Poor woman. She didn't even know what had hit her. *Damn it, damn it, damn it.*

If her mom hadn't been there, she'd really give Jake an earful. She'd spew things that he probably had never heard come from a woman's mouth. If she let loose though, her mother would really think Malibu was not a proper living environment, and she'd work overtime to convince her to come back home. Instead, Pepper held her tongue and took a couple of deep breaths. She got to her feet and brushed off the back of her jeans. One look at Jake's gleaming eyes and the upward turn of his mouth was almost enough to make her reconsider giving him an earful.

"You think this is *funny?*" Pepper said, using the most venomous tone she could muster. A quiet snicker behind her made her head snap around like she was possessed. Her mother covered her mouth. "You stay out of this," Pepper warned her.

Pepper felt like she was the butt of a joke, and it was time to put an end to their fun. Any angrier, and she was pretty sure smoke would start billowing from her nostrils. This time, she did the grabbing.

She took Jake's hand firmly in hers and led him to her bedroom. Her mother could protest all she wanted, but this was one time she was going to break the rules and take a boy into her bedroom.

As soon as the door was shut, Pepper spun around.

"How dare you!"

Jake stood so close to her that she could smell the remnants of a mint on his breath. And she wanted to taste it. More than anything, she wanted to feel his sweet lips on hers.

"I dare because I'm not going to be walked out on without even being given the chance to explain," Jake said.

He stared into her eyes, and their gazes locked for a long moment. Finally, she took a step back. It was bad enough he was here in her room. If they kept standing that close, she wouldn't be able to resist him, not when there was a bed calling to them from only three feet away.

"Did you lie?" she asked.

"It's not that simple. There's more to it—"

"Did you lie about who you are?" she pressed him.

Jake shook his head. "Only about what I do. Never about who I am." He ran a hand through his hair. "It was harmless. Gordy and another friend bet me I couldn't convince you—" He reached up a hand and touched her face. "I never expected—"

"Expected what?" Pepper backed away. "To get me into bed so soon?" Her voice faltered, and she swallowed painfully.

"It wasn't about that. We all expected you to be such a stuck-up bitch that we thought it'd be funny to fool you. But you weren't, and then I didn't know how to tell you without having this happen."

"Yeah, I bet it was real funny. Funny getting the stuck-up bitch into your bed, making love to her, making her—" Pepper turned away before the tears that were forming spilled from her eyes.

"Making her what?" Jake asked. He moved up close behind Pepper and pulled her to him. "Making you what?" he repeated tenderly in her ear.

Pepper so wanted to let him bathe her in that tenderness. But the hurt was too deep, and the pain crushed her chest, and all she could think to do was to escape, move out of his reach.

"Never mind. You've explained. You can leave now."

"Not until I finish," Jake said. "Regardless of the lie, everything we did, everything I said, I meant it all."

Pepper didn't speak. She couldn't. She was afraid that if she opened her mouth, all that would come out was a sob. She fought back hot tears the same as she'd fought them at her dad's funeral.

There she'd been, sitting in the church pew listening to everyone say such nice things about Frank Bartlett, things that seemed meant to make a person cry. But she wasn't going to let all those people, most of whom she didn't even know, see her fall apart. Instead, she'd waited until she was alone in her room. She'd hugged one of her dad's shirts and cried. She cried so hard and for so long that she thought all her tears were used up. No one would ever be able to make her cry again.

Boy, was she wrong. Love didn't play by the rules. Pepper bit her lip against the pain. She refused to let Jake see the ache his love caused.

"Okay," Jake finally said resignedly. "Have it your way." He turned to leave, but stopped at the door.

"I was the man of your dreams . . . until you found out the car was borrowed." He reached out a hand and touched her cheek. "Don't let the blue jeans fool you."

Pepper stayed in her room and waited until she heard Jake's car leave. Then she cried.

Chapter 25

What remained of Pepper's summer was filled with sand sculpting and kickboxing and aerobics classes. The Harrison Open Sandcastle Competition was coming up in a couple of weeks, and she practiced every chance she got. The tools her sister had given her made everything easier. "The right tool for every job," her dad always said. He was right.

Pepper considered who to take with her to the competition. Not Lucy. She had flowers to do for a wedding. Not Simone. Paul had come home, and they were getting reacquainted every chance they got. Her mom was so busy with Ben that she didn't dare ask her to go. How would she invite her mom without inviting her lover? She still hadn't managed to wrap her head around that relationship. That only left Cat. Things had gotten better between them over the summer, but they had a long way to go before she'd consider spending a holiday with her.

Pepper sighed. All that would be missing from this huge event was someone special to go and share the experience with her. It would be so much more romantic if . . . Pepper shook the thought away. It wasn't meant to be.

She looked out her bedroom window. The fronds on her potted palms tossed in the breeze, and from the way the sky looked, it was probably a good ten degrees cooler than what the weatherman had forecast for the morning. She pulled a pair of Blue London jeans from a drawer and a long-sleeved T from another. Later, after the sun burnt through the cloud layer, she'd be overdressed, but she'd worry about that then. Right now, all that mattered was getting out to the sand. First things first, though, a cup of hot coffee was in order.

Pepper smelled the flowers as soon as she opened her bedroom door. A heavenly mixture of jasmine, spicy rose, and something fruity that she couldn't identify filled the air.

The kitchen table was covered, and Lucy was off in her own little world finishing five large arrangements that had been ordered for a dinner party that night. She added a sprig of jasmine to one of them, then stepped back to examine her work.

"Beautiful, my dear," Pepper told her. She filled a mug with water and placed it in the microwave, then took down a tin of International coffee.

"I could brew some real coffee for you," Lucy offered.

"No, thanks, I'm in a hurry to get out to the beach."

"That stuff is full of sugar. Go ahead. I'll make some and bring it out to you."

Pepper accepted Lucy's offer and went outside. She paused on the top step, as usual, to see where the high tide line was. She sighed. It'd been a morning just like this when she first brought Jake down to her beach to try his hand at sand sculpting. She'd had such high hopes for their relationship. Unrealistic? She didn't think so. The part that hurt the most was that Jake had taken her to his bed, made love to her with a lie. A man didn't lie to someone he made love to. He might have sex, but he didn't make love, and what she and Jake did was definitely love.

Pepper chose a spot about twenty feet out, assumed a crouch position, and began scooping sand, moving it quickly into a six-foot length. Several minutes later, she finished with the base and then began carving away chunks of sand until reaching the point where she had to slow down to complete some of the finer details. She'd been practicing making mermaids all summer, but she still wasn't sure that was what she would do for the Harrison Hot Springs sand sculpting event. Mermaids weren't all that original, but they were always a crowd pleaser. The added twist was that her mermaid had just been rescued from drowning, and her head was lying in the hero's lap. Was it good enough to win a competition? Not in this lifetime. But it was a start.

She would be there as an amateur to work with some of the best sand in the world, but after this year, she'd have to get busy and attempt some harder projects with a lot more detail.

After an hour of crouching, Pepper felt the strain in her back, and she had to sit back for a rest. Where was Lucy with that coffee she'd promised? She examined the sculpture and tried to see it through the average onlooker's eyes. She could definitely see an improvement in her skill level over the summer, especially since she'd gotten the proper tools. Of course, she'd had plenty of time to practice. Each time, the end result was better, and today, she strove for speed. Another year or two, and she'd be able to contend for real money, not just the fifty bucks here and there that the smaller competitions offered.

Lucy had made a sketch for her to work from, which Pepper had only briefly glanced at before getting started. It wasn't necessary to memorize every detail. She only needed the general idea. But now, she pulled it from her pocket and looked it over more closely. The hero's arms and chest were nicely shaped, each muscle flowing into the other like a gently rolling wave. He had a nice squared-off chin, what some would refer to as chiseled, and his eyes were kind as they gazed upon the mermaid's face. Something struck her as familiar. Too familiar. *Jake!* Pepper's eyebrows drew into a frown. *Lucy!*

As though on cue, the sound of footsteps came up behind her.

"What's this?" Pepper asked, shoving the sketch at Lucy. Lucy's hands were full with two mugs of steaming coffee, but she took a quick glance at the drawing.

"What?"

"Don't give me what. This." Pepper jabbed a finger at the sketch.

"Yes, I think it's pretty good, too."

"It's Jake," Pepper accused.

"Let me see." Lucy handed Pepper one of the mugs and took the drawing. "Y'know, you could be right. What was I thinking?" Her mouth turned up in a little grin.

"That's what I'm wondering. Don't get the idea that this is going to make me miss him."

"I would never—hey, that's pretty good," Lucy said, looking down at the mermaid. "Gee, you're almost a pro." She sat on the bottom step, holding her mug with both hands.

Nice save. Pepper looked at her sculpture with a critical eye. "I've got a long way to go." She stood and brushed sand from the front of her jeans and sat next to Lucy. Together, they sipped their coffee. It was a Taster's Choice moment.

"Just because you make good coffee doesn't mean I've forgiven you for reminding me of Jake," Pepper finally said.

"I know. But you will just as soon as you figure out that you can forgive him."

"Don't count on it." Pepper wasn't in any mood to listen to Lucy talk about forgiveness and second chances and all that crap. "When are you taking those flowers over to the restaurant?"

"Soon as I finish my coffee."

"What took you so long anyway?" asked Pepper.

"Good coffee takes time."

Pepper nodded and she and Lucy sat quietly for several more minutes.

"I'm glad to see you're finally going to do this," Lucy said.

"M-m-m." Pepper gave Lucy a sideways glance. "I might have to deviate from the hero you've drawn."

Lucy smiled. "Mermaid looks good." She took a sip of coffee. "In fact, I've never seen her look better.

Or more well-endowed," she remarked, tilting her head. "This is a family event, right?"

"Of course. I just thought it couldn't hurt, you know, the judges being mostly male and all." Pepper scooted down to the sand and lightly cupped a hand over one of the mermaid's breasts. "She's a perfect size C."

Lucy looked down at her own chest. "Who says C is perfect?"

"Just about every guy in the world."

"Even Jake?"

Pepper shrugged. "I don't know. We never talked about such things. He was too busy trying to keep his lies straight."

"Or maybe he thought you were perfect the way you were."

Pepper got up and faced Lucy, hands on her hips. "Are you implying that I should think he's perfect the way *he* is, lies and all?"

"Isn't he?"

"No, dammit." Pepper spun around and raised one foot, bringing it down full force on top of the mermaid's perfect size Cs. Once they were sufficiently stomped into As, she turned and brushed past Lucy and went up to the house.

"He must be," Lucy yelled after her. "Otherwise you wouldn't be so mad."

Pepper paced the living room. "Perfect, my foot." She continued pacing while remembering how Jake's perfect arms had held her, how his perfect lips had lifted her to higher heights than she'd ever thought possible. She put her hands in her hair and felt like pulling it out. Thoughts like that served no good purpose. What she needed was a shower to wash all the sand off. Maybe if she made the water very, very cold she could also wash Jake's image from her mind. She'd make it frigid, if necessary.

As she started the water, the phone rang, and she waited to see if Lucy was going to run back inside to get it. After four rings, she gave in.

"Hello, sweetie," her mom sang into her ear.

Why the hell was everyone so damn happy? Pepper did her best to sound happy, too—cheerful even—but her mom always knew when something wasn't right.

"What's wrong?" Hannah asked. "Don't tell me you haven't made up with that nice young man yet?"

"*What?*" Pepper shook her head angrily. "How come everyone thinks he's so nice when all he ever did was lie to me?"

"Well—"

"Never mind. You don't even know him."

"Yes, but Lucy—"

"*Lucy?* Listen, I love the both of you, but I need to deal with that nice man on my own," Pepper said. "And stop listening to Lucy. She hasn't even had a real boyfriend since junior high." She ran a hand through her hair and blew out a full breath of air.

"Okay, sweetie. I didn't mean to upset you. I just wanted to tell you that I was sending you some pictures from when you were here."

Pepper immediately regretted snapping at her mom, but she knew if she didn't put a stop to where the conversation was headed, it would probably turn out to be one of those "finding the right man" talks.

"Look, I know you mean well . . . and I know Lucy does, too, but I need to figure this out on my own. How are things there?"

Hannah's voice instantly perked up. "Good. Better than ever."

Pepper suspected her mother's good mood had something to do with Ben, and she did an eye roll. Anger simmered inside her, and she silently swore never to let a man become so important that she'd fall apart if he ever left. Right now, she preferred to think all men were bastard liars.

"That's great, Mom. I'm glad you've been able to find someone. Listen, can I call you later? I've got sand and salt water all over me."

"Sometimes a little love can make all the difference," her mom managed to edge in before Pepper could hang up.

Pepper clicked off and dropped the phone onto the counter. "I'm glad it works for you." She considered taking a glass of wine with her to the bathroom, but being that it wasn't even noon, she settled for lemonade.

A few minutes into her shower, Lucy walked in. At least she assumed it was Lucy, although you never knew in Los Angeles. Pepper took a quick peek.

"I swear, Luce, if you and my mom don't stop discussing my love life—" She shook her head.

Lucy gave her a blank look.

"Never mind." Pepper poured a glob of shampoo onto her palm and lathered it into her scalp.

"What love life? I just wanted to let you know I'm leaving."

"Great. Fine." Pepper stuck her head under the showerhead to rinse. When she finished with conditioning and drying and lathering on a thick layer of lotion, she went to her room and curled up on her bed. In five minutes, she was asleep.

Jake's mouth closed over hers as she desperately fought for air. Her legs were heavy, weighed down and bound as one. She could see everything like it was a movie. But it wasn't. And it was amazing. Blue-green scales covered most of her body and a large fish tail served as her feet and legs. It was horrifying, yet it didn't hurt. Maybe drowning wasn't so bad. Jake held her head in his lap and waited to see if she was breathing before pressing on her chest—

A shrill ringing noise made the image fizzle, and Pepper's eyes popped open. She soon realized it was the phone. She still wasn't in the mood to talk to anyone, but the phone was persistent.

"Are you going to get that?" she yelled out. No response. With a groan, she remembered that Lucy was gone.

It was Brad. Why couldn't she ever resist a ringing phone?

"I'm going over to Catalina and was wondering if you'd like to come along?"

Catalina. Pepper surprised herself by even considering his offer. It wasn't that she didn't enjoy every opportunity to go to Avalon, but the man asking her didn't exactly make her heart tap dance inside her chest. Though he did make other body parts quiver somewhat. He also wasn't a man who'd lied to her and totally ignored her for most of the summer. Since Jake had found her in Seattle, he hadn't made any further attempts to contact her. He hadn't even wished her a happy birthday. If he could so easily give up on them, then she shouldn't have any problem crossing the Pacific Ocean with another man.

"Absolutely. When do we leave?"

"Can you be ready in an hour?"

"Absolutely." Pepper hung up the phone. She lay back down and stared up at the ceiling, wondering what the heck she was doing accepting Brad's invite. A minute later, the phone rang again.

"*Bonjour, chérie,* it is I, the friend you treat like yesterday's leftovers. Didn't Lucy tell you that I called this morning?"

"No. She was too busy trying to concoct a plan to reunite me and Jake. Can you believe she expected me to do a sand sculpture of the man?"

"I have news about your construction man. You want to hear, yes?"

Pepper heard an intake of air on the other end. Simone had just lit a cigarette.

"No. And I thought you were quitting that nasty habit," she said.

"*Chérie,* a *thousand* of these you will wish you had when I tell you what I have been witness to. And what I have seen cancels out our deal."

Pepper rolled her eyes and sunk low into the mattress. "Okay," she conceded. "What's worth killing myself over?" She closed her eyes and waited.

Simone lowered her voice as though she didn't want to be overheard. "I saw your construction man. He was with another woman."

Simone's words were like a gut punch.

"I tell you something else, *chérie.* They were drinking. A lot—"

Pepper closed her eyes and swallowed a sob that lay like a bitter pill on her tongue. "Stop," she said, shaking her head. "I don't want to know what he was doing or with whom."

Simone was quiet for a minute. "I am sorry for you. This man, he has broken your heart, yes?"

Yes, Jake had broken her heart. Even so, she wasn't sure she was ready to admit it to anyone.

"No, not at all. In fact, in about an hour, I'm leaving for Catalina with another man." She paused. "When exactly did you see him?"

"Oh, it has been a while."

"A while?"

"A month or more, maybe."

"And you're just now telling me?"

"Paul, he came home, and we have been very busy. I knew you weren't seeing him anymore."

Pepper did a quick calculation. A month and a half ago, she'd found out about Jake's deception. Boy, he didn't waste any time. It was even possible he was seeing that other woman *before* she'd found out the truth. Pepper swallowed painfully. Maybe Simone was right. Maybe blue-collar men just weren't worth taking chances on. "I've gotta go and get ready." She hung up the phone before any tears came. Jake with another woman? How could he? He wasn't a hero at all. It really had been a dream. And a bad one at that. So it was official. Both she and Jake had moved on to other people.

Chapter 26

Pepper felt like her heart had been punched and left for dead. That lifesaving kiss in her dream was so far from the truth. What a fool she'd been.

All the excitement Pepper normally felt about going to Catalina Island was missing, and she barely remembered the drive to Long Beach. Not even the ferry ride interested her. She just sat in the back the whole time watching the spray shoot up and out of the boat's stern. The high point was a dead whale carcass that provided a landing and feeding spot for seagulls and other carnivorous creatures.

Pepper stepped off the boat and inhaled the crisp, smog-free air. Maybe that was the problem. Probably, she'd been breathing smog for so long she couldn't think clearly anymore. The temperature was a good ten degrees cooler than when she'd left Malibu, and she pulled the zipper up on her jacket. Brad noticed her discomfort, and he put an arm around her. Either that, or he was simply using it as an excuse to get close. Pepper tried to relax into the heat of his body, but what she'd have really preferred was a warmer jacket.

It might be chilly, and she might be suffering from a broken heart, but Catalina did offer one thing that could definitely warm her up—on the inside anyway.

Buffalo milk. Avalon's own heavenly blend of Baileys, Kahlua, vodka, crème de cacao, and fresh banana. A chocolate shake with a kick. A visit to Catalina just wasn't complete until she had one.

Wind whipped Pepper's hair about her face as she and Brad headed into town. The Landing Bar & Grill just off Crescent Avenue was the best place she knew to get a buffalo milk, and it would also provide an escape from the chilly air. The front wall was rolled up like a big garage door, giving patrons a clear view of Avalon Bay. She and Brad sat at the front counter facing the bay, where the sun's rays could help warm them.

Pepper ordered a buffalo milk right away. She wanted to get some alcohol into her so it could go to work on dulling her heartache. Brad ordered a beer.

The waitress returned a few minutes later, and Pepper took a long, slow drink of the silky smooth beverage. It delighted her tongue and moved through her, warming every inch of her body. It'd been far too long since she'd had this tasty treat. Several times, without success, she'd tried to order it back on the mainland, but for some reason, no one had ever been able to duplicate it. Not even the man sitting next to her.

"This is what Catalina is all about," Pepper told Brad.

"Is it as good as the drinks I make?"

Pepper considered his question. "Different," she said. No reason to insult her date. Now that she was here with him, she intended to make the best of it. She finished her drink and ordered another, and the waitress brought it with their lunch. By the time she'd finished half of it, she was feeling better about everything. Including Jake.

A warm glow radiated through her body, and she looked over at Brad, allowing her mind to wander. She closed her eyes and could almost feel the warmth of his body—No! She had to remind herself that it was the alcohol simply dulling her pain—and her good sense. And the warmth she was feeling was simply a combination of the sun and Brad sitting too close.

"Want a taste?" she offered Brad.

He shook his head.

"Is something wrong? You've hardly said two words since we got here."

"I was thinking we'd rent a golf cart—"

Pepper was ready for some action. Screaming around town in a golf cart with Brad the bartender might be fun. It sure beat sitting on those hard stools all afternoon.

"Now you're talking. Do you suppose there's a law against driving a golf cart while under the influence?" Pepper asked him with a giggle.

"Don't worry. I'll be doing all the driving."

Pepper didn't know if that was an insult to her driving or simply his way of saying she wasn't getting behind the wheel while drunk.

Brad paid their tab, and a few minutes later, Pepper found herself on another cold, hard seat, that of a well-used white and blue golf cart.

"Who-o-o ho-o-o," she squealed, holding on for dear life. They took a sharp right out of the parking lot and headed toward Pebbly Beach Road. She'd taken the scenic drive a couple of times, but she didn't remember it being this much fun. Of course, she'd never been drunk before.

They followed the waterfront for a few minutes before turning onto Wrigley Terrace Road, and the golf cart slowed considerably as it made its way up the steep, winding hill. When they finally reached the top, Wrigley Memorial sat on their left. It was closed. Pepper was glad. She wasn't particularly keen on the idea of wandering around Mr. Wrigley's tomb.

They continued on, and soon, they reached the top of Mt. Ada Road, where Brad stopped the cart and got out. He walked over to the crest of the hill, and Pepper remained in the cart. When he didn't return right away, she grew fidgety. She wanted to have some fun. Not the kind of fun she and Jake had on their little adventure, but a different kind of fun would be nice. Pepper climbed out of the cart and walked over to where Brad stood. The fog had finally burned off, and a spectacular view of Avalon with Catalina's famous white casino lay before them. Rows of boats, like toys in a bathtub, were bouncing around in the aquamarine harbor, and the people in town were like little bugs scurrying about.

"I should've brought a camera," Pepper said.

"My mother used to bring me here when I was little. She'd pack us lunch, and we'd sit up here and eat and watch all the activity below." Brad looked over at Pepper. "I think she just liked getting away from my dad. So did I." Brad stared solemnly over the hillside for another minute, and then he turned around and went back to the cart.

Wow. That was deep. She'd just seen a side of Brad that she never knew existed. After that, she was ready for another buffalo milk. Maybe if Brad had a couple, he'd loosen up and quit acting like they were on some death mission.

Pepper relaxed against the seat. The wind licking her hair felt good, refreshing, and she tried to enjoy the ride despite her driver's moodiness. A few minutes later, they stopped again, this time on the edge of a wooded area. Brad got out and walked onto an overgrown path. Stopping for a view was understandable, but what did he hope to see in overgrown brush? Pepper thought maybe he had to pee. She giggled and considered taking a peek. After waiting a respectful amount of time, she thought about going in after him, but then scenes from all the slasher flicks she'd seen flashed through her mind, and she wasn't too sure that would be wise. Too many young women had been killed in the woods—in the movies anyway—for her to feel comfortable following him. She could see the headlines now: *Malibu Woman Comes to an Unromantic Ending on the Isle of Romance.*

Whatever Brad was doing tramping through the bushes, she wanted no part of it. Settling back against the hard seat, she began to examine her fingernails. Boy, was she in need of a manicure. When she got home, she was heading straight over to Malibu Plaza Spa and Manicure.

A few minutes passed, and Pepper wondered if he was ever coming back out. No one took that long to pee. She leaned out one side of the cart and looked down the path. Like a cat, she felt her curiosity getting the better of her. When she couldn't take it anymore, she got out of the cart and moved slowly into the brush. Soon, she found herself surrounded by small graves.

"Aw," she said, looking around the ground at the homemade headstones. She paused long enough to read a few, but it kinda gave her the creeps, and she continued on, careful not to step on any of the graves.

She came to a small clearing and found Brad kneeling next to a small mound of rocks. Oh boy. He glanced up at her and then went back to brushing ironwood tree bark away from the small gravesite. She noticed a small blue rock on his left that said, Gus, 1991–1999. A few feet over from that, another grave was marked by a foot-high cross that had "Freddie Fish, He Drowned" printed across the top. She wanted to laugh, but she was pretty sure that would be disrespectful to those who were resting in peace, even if they were animals. She walked carefully among the small handcrafted headstones, and emotions tugged at her heart. Fresh white flowers rested against one headstone marked, Bonnie, 1985–1998.

Pepper returned to where she'd left Brad; he was still crouching next to the fresh mound of earth. He'd placed a cross at the head of it, and his eyes were closed, as though in prayer. Pepper looked at the cross and saw the name Scratch had been carved into it. She suddenly felt like she'd misjudged Brad. She touched his shoulder, and when he glanced up at her, his eyes glistened.

"My dog," he said. "He died recently. His grave needed a cross. Thanks for coming with me."

Touched by all the love etched into stone, wood, and even plastic, Pepper sobered considerably, and a heaviness settled on her heart. She nodded, feeling awkward, not really knowing what to say. The only pet she'd ever lost was a goldfish, but she could certainly understand how he must hurt.

The wind was picking up, and leaves blew in a restless flurry over the ground.

"We'd better get that golf cart back," he finally said.

In the few minutes it took to get back to the rental place, the wind had kicked up even more, and Pepper held her jacket tight around her. She pulled her hair up into a ponytail to keep it from whipping across her face.

"Looks like you folks might have to stay the night," the cart rental attendant said.

"Says who?" Pepper asked.

"A small craft advisory has been put up." The attendant nodded in the direction of Pleasure Pier on Isthmus Cove.

Pepper shaded her eyes with her hand and strained to see, but it was too far. "I don't see anything." She looked at Brad. "What do you think?"

He shrugged and didn't look at all concerned.

The attendant began to close up shop for the day. "It's likely to get pretty bad tonight," he said. "Better get yourself a room."

Pepper looked both ways down Crescent Avenue. Bison and bricks were all she saw. "Where is everybody?"

"Indoors," the attendant said.

Brad grabbed her hand and began leading her up the cobbled street. Pepper saw that the Landing Bar and Grill had closed its wall. It looked like she might not be getting another buffalo milk. Some fish and salad would have been nice, too. She'd hardly touched her lunch, and all that grieving at the pet cemetery had worked up an appetite.

Brad held her hand firmly and led her along the avenue, and Pepper figured they were headed back to the ferry. That was okay by her. A couple of drinks, a golf cart ride, a peek at Wrigley's Tomb, they'd done just about all there was to do on Catalina. She'd seen enough.

Evidently, Brad hadn't. Instead of taking a left to go back to the ferry terminal, he turned and started up a side street. Pepper went along for a few minutes, but then they came to a Y in the road, and Brad tried pulling her up a very long and very steep hill. She stopped abruptly. She might be a little tipsy, but that didn't mean she was going to go wherever Brad the bartender wanted.

He gripped her hand tighter, and a scary little thought entered her mind. *Stalker.* That's what Lucy had called him.

Pepper pulled her hand free. "Where are we going?"

"No telling how long before the ferry will be running again. We might as well get a room before they're all gone," Brad said.

Pepper laughed lightly and jutted a thumb over her shoulder. "I don't know if you noticed, but the streets are bare. I don't think getting a room will be a problem."

Brad shrugged. "At least we'll have it if we need it."

Pepper considered the hill, trying to decide whether or not she had the energy for that kind of elevation gain with the amount of alcohol she'd consumed. A gust of wind sent chills through her, and she crossed her arms against the cold.

"Okay, but as soon as you get us checked in, we go find some food."

Lucy opened the door to a red-faced man.

"Where is he?"

Lucy tried to push the door closed, but the red-faced man pushed back. She stepped away and wondered if she'd have time to get the lock off the sliding door before he could reach her.

"Where is who?" she sputtered.

The red-faced man stepped inside and looked around.

"That bastard Brad."

Brad? Bastard Brad. Well, that made sense. "Do you mean Brad the bartender?" she asked, still not completely convinced the man wasn't going to turn on her.

"Yeah. Where is he?" The man's face was beginning to go back to a normal color.

"He doesn't live here," Lucy told him.

"I know that. The bastard lives with me and my fiancée. Used to, that is. I'm Vic. Maybe he's mentioned me. Pepper Bartlett lives here though, right?" he said without hardly taking a breath.

"Uh, Pepper?" Lucy looked over at the wind chimes hanging over the bathroom door. She considered going over and fluttering them. "I'm not sure she lives here, either."

The red-faced man gave her a confused look.

"Can I ask what this is about?"

"It's about that bastard screwing my fiancée."

This really did call for at least one wind chime flutter. "Pepper's your fiancée?"

"No. I don't even know her. That's my fiancé." He

pointed to a car at the curb. A Latino woman had her face up to the window. Her face was red, too.

Lucy felt better knowing that Pepper wasn't preparing to get married without telling her, but she was completely confused about what was going on.

"Look, I don't understand anything you're talking about. I just got home and—" She turned and saw a note from Pepper on the table. She picked it up. "Catalina Island?" she mumbled.

"What's that?"

"A note. It's from Pepper."

Vic grabbed it from her and read it. "Thanks," he said, tossing it back to her. He ran back to his car and drove off.

Lucy was pretty sure the red-faced man had just violated some privacy law, and she felt sick for being the one responsible for him finding out where Pepper had gone. Sweat trickled down her back. It felt like someone had just hit her panic button. She had known something like this would happen if Pepper got involved with Brad.

Lucy looked around the room. She should have done more to prevent this trouble. Hang more wind chimes. Insist on keeping the front door painted red. She put a hand over her forehead and tried to think. Only one solution came to mind.

Chapter 27

Pepper sat and waited while Brad got them checked in to the hotel. It was just like in the movies. Only one room available. If she didn't know better, she'd think he had it all planned before they arrived.

The room was ugly, and the painting on the wall, uglier. Some kind of cactus on an orange background. Pepper figured it was probably supposed to look like the sun setting in the desert. The bedspread was the same sickly orange with a little bit of brown thrown in for excitement.

The faucets were beginning to rust. The carpet was stained, but at least she didn't see any cockroaches.

Since she hadn't planned on staying the night, she had nothing to unpack. The only makeup she had was what she'd brought in her bag. Lipstick. That was not going to do. They had to go back to town. While there, she'd get another buffalo milk.

They sat inside a restaurant that looked out over Avalon Bay and watched heavy winds toss the boats around like they were made of paper. Palm fronds threatened to detach from trees and blow away, and only a scattering of seagulls were still in sight hoping for a morsel of food. Saltwater mist swirled through the air, and as far as Pepper could tell, it seemed like the wind wasn't about to die down anytime soon. No doubt about it, she was stuck on the island with Brad for the night.

The barmaid set their food order before them and paused to gaze out at Mother Nature's fury. "Whew," she said. "Hope you guys weren't planning on going home tonight."

Pepper took a big bite from her hamburger. Maybe if she gained twenty pounds in the next hour, Brad wouldn't get any ideas later. She looked over at him.

He was just sitting there, staring out across the water. He was probably thinking about his poor little dog. She could only begin to imagine how she'd feel if she found a beloved pet tangled in its own chain. The thought made her heart melt. She laid a hand on his arm.

"Sorry about your dog," she said.

Brad simply nodded and continued staring ahead. Men like him were hard to read, and frankly, they were more work than they were worth, usually. He nursed his beer, and Pepper downed two more drinks. The more she had, the less she hurt about Jake.

Lucy paced the living room. Pepper's note didn't say if she was with Jake or Brad. But from the way the red-faced man was ranting, she had a pretty good guess. Either way, she couldn't just sit around and wait to tell Pepper that a lunatic might be on his way to find her.

She found Pepper's little black phone book without too much difficulty and located Jake's number under "C" for current boyfriend. Several other names were crossed out, and from the looks of it, Pepper would need a new little black book soon.

Lucy tapped her fingers impatiently on the table while Jake's phone rang. When his answering machine picked up, she started to leave him a message, but then he came on the line.

"Hey, Lucy. What's up?"

"Jake, thank God you're home—" Lucy paused, not exactly sure where to start. She didn't want to alarm him unnecessarily or sound like a hysterical woman. "I'm looking for Pepper. She's not home. She left a note saying she's gone to Catalina, but I was kinda hoping she might be with you."

"If she left a note, I suppose that's where she is. But, no, I haven't seen her in weeks. She's made it pretty clear that she never wants to see me again."

The red-faced man's outburst rose fresh in Lucy's mind, and she felt like she was in a long, dark tunnel. "I'm worried."

"I'm pretty sure Pepper can take care of herself."

Jake could have been shouting in her ear, but all Lucy could hear was the red-faced man yelling something about Brad and his fiancée. She felt light-headed, so she sat down.

"Lucy? You okay?"

Lucy took a deep breath and tried to control the shaking in her voice. "He's with her," she blurted out.

"Her bartender friend?"

Jake was quiet for a moment, and Lucy almost wished she hadn't called him. She liked him and didn't want to cause him any pain.

"Look, I know you hoped she and I would get

together," Jake said. "I tried talking to her in Seattle, but she wouldn't listen. Sometimes, things don't work out the way we want."

"Pepper could be in danger. You've got to find her right away."

"Wait now—I don't think—"

"Jake, *please.*"

"Okay. You've got me worried now. What's got you so upset?"

"*Please!* Just tell me you'll find her."

"If I go to Catalina, she's going to be madder than hell at me for following her, and she's going to be madder than hell at you for sending me. Is that what you want?"

"That's exactly what I want. Pepper doesn't seem to know what's good for her anymore," Lucy shrieked. Jake was quiet, and Lucy realized how she must sound. She took a breath to calm herself.

"Maybe Pepper is with Simone. Have you tried calling her?" Jake asked.

"She's not with Simone. There's something else. I don't quite know how to tell you this," Lucy said. "I'm sure when I do, you're just going to want to hang up and not be bothered by this nonsense anymore. I wouldn't blame you."

"Lucy, just tell me."

"Pepper's gone to Catalina Island. With Brad."

The other end was quiet, and Lucy began to wonder if Jake had indeed hung up. Finally, he spoke.

"It would seem she's where she wants to be then."

"No," Lucy snapped. "She's not where she wants to be. She wants to be with you."

"Lucy, is there something more you want to tell me? 'Cause I've got some things to do."

"Jake, I don't know if I should be thinking the worst. There's this guy . . . very mad. He's looking for Brad." Lucy said, doing her best to control the tremble in her voice. "Something about Brad and his fiancée. I'm afraid Pepper might get caught in all that anger."

Jake knew about that kind of anger from watching Gordy get his ass kicked. "What the hell's going on, Lucy?"

Lucy made an effort to stop hyperventilating, and her light-headedness began to subside. She explained everything she knew to Jake. "She's in trouble," Lucy cried. "I can feel it." Her hands shook as she held the phone. "Will you go find her?"

More silence.

"Jake? You there?"

"Look," Jake said softly, "go lie down. Calm yourself. I'll go to Catalina and call you as soon as I know something. But I'm only doing this for you."

"And I appreciate it."

Lucy got off the phone and looked at the sofa. Lie down? Calm herself? No way was that going to happen.

Anger rippled through Jake when he hung up the phone. He tried to shake it free, but it was useless. He'd done his best to accept the fact that Pepper no longer wanted him, and so far, he'd done pretty good. That didn't mean he didn't want her. It just meant he'd finally learned when it was best to move on. Now this. He scrubbed a hand through his hair.

Along with the anger, he was also worried about what Lucy had been ranting about. Most likely she was letting her imagination run wild. Even though he didn't much care for Pepper's bartender friend, he'd never suspect him of doing anything to hurt her. He thought of Gordy and the beating he'd taken for being with another man's woman. Lucy had talked about an angry man and his fiancée. If Pepper was in the middle of a domestic squabble, she could get hurt. It really wasn't any of his business anymore, but he couldn't allow that to happen.

He felt bad for Lucy. She was Pepper's best friend, and in the short time he'd known her, she'd become important to him, too. He wished he could've convinced her that everything would be all right, that he'd fix everything. The problem was he couldn't even convince himself. He flipped open his cell phone and punched in Gordy's number. After explaining the situation with Pepper, he asked him to go check up on Lucy.

"No problem," Gordy said. "But this wouldn't be an occasion to get my ass kicked again, would it?"

He assured Gordy he was safe and told him he'd call him when he had news.

An hour passed, and Lucy was about to climb the walls. She hadn't heard a thing from Jake. The floor couldn't take too much more pacing. She'd wear a path in the carpet. The thought crossed her mind that she could be wrong. If Jake found Pepper, and she and Brad were having a great time, Pepper might never forgive her.

But what if she was right?

She continued pacing as she dialed Jake's cell

phone. It rang again and again. "Pick up!" she shouted. *"Pick up."* After the fifth ring, he answered.

"Why haven't you called me?"

"I haven't called because I'm not to Catalina yet."

Jake reassured her once more, and she promised again to wait for his call. This time, Lucy went and did the same thing that Pepper always did when her nerves needed calming—she took a bubble bath.

Two hours later, Jake made his way up the plank onto the pier in Avalon. The hair on his neck bristled at the idea of Pepper being romantic on the Isle of Romance with any other man but him.

He paused when he got to Crescent Avenue and looked up and down the street. He had no idea where to start, but in Avalon, it wouldn't be too difficult to find someone. Odds were, if he sat in one spot long enough, he'd eventually see every tourist on the island pass by.

Jake went into a pub and sat at a table where he had a good view of the pedestrian traffic. Unfortunately, with the weather bad and getting worse, Avalon resembled a ghost town. Most of the activity was the island's seagull population, cruising the sky for their next meal.

After Jake had a beer and a plate of quesadillas, darkness began to close in on the town. He hadn't intended to spend the night, but with the wind kicking up such a fuss, it looked as though he'd have no choice. Too early in the year for the Santa Ana, but nevertheless, this was a big enough windstorm to cause significant commotion.

If he had come to Avalon for pleasure, he would have chosen to stay at The Inn at Mt. Ada, a Georgian bed and breakfast that overlooked Avalon Bay. At least that's what he and Angela had planned when they talked about coming here. That dream had gotten lost the same as all the other dreams they'd shared.

The Catherine Hotel, located right in town, seemed a good choice of place to spend the night. No painful memories of long-lost plans. Several golf carts were parked out front, but plenty of rooms were still available.

After checking in, Jake went over to Von's Market to pick up a few personal items, but before returning to the hotel, he walked from one end of Crescent Avenue to the other. The streets were bare, and that only made him feel worse. If Pepper wasn't in town, the only other place she was likely to be was in a hotel room.

Back in his room, Jake showered and then settled on the bed with the remote control in one hand and a can of beer in the other. He flipped through all the channels and found nothing worth watching. He couldn't concentrate on anything but finding Pepper anyway. One thing he was sure of—if Bartender Boy caused Pepper any harm, he was definitely going to use his face as a punching bag.

Time dragged on, and each time Jake looked at his watch, only a few minutes had passed. It was going to be one long night and, most likely, sleepless. Nine o'clock came, and Jake couldn't stay in his room another minute. He grabbed his coat and ended up at the only place still open, the Landing Bar & Grill. He chose a stool near the door to keep watch like some on-duty guard dog, and every now and then, a person would walk by and he'd look up, hoping to see Pepper.

Two hours later, still no sign of her.

Pepper hadn't been in any hurry to go back to the hotel room, especially when she thought about having to climb Mt. Everest again in her sandals, but her belly was full, she'd had plenty to drink, and now she needed some sleep.

"Let's go," she said, sliding off the stool. She wobbled to one side, and Brad reached out a hand to steady her.

"Where to?" he asked.

She smiled sweetly, her eyelids heavy. "Hotel room. Just don't get any ideas." Pepper jabbed a finger into his chest, and it was like poking a slab of granite. Hm-m. Brad the bartender had hidden qualities. Jake's chest was firm, too. If he was here, she'd take him into the bathroom and have her way with him this very minute. She laughed at the thought, and Brad looked at her, confused.

"Never mind." Pepper shook her head from side to side and laughed even louder.

They'd made it halfway up the hill when a hotel van pulled up alongside them.

"Need a ride?" the driver asked.

Pepper eagerly climbed in. She may have had a lot to drink, but not so much she couldn't realize riding up the hill was a whole lot easier than hoofing it in her strappy sandals.

Once they got back to the room, Brad went to take a shower, and she went out on the balcony. Downtown Avalon was one big shadow. A lone palm stood tall and brave against the wind, and several prickly pear cacti were just below their room. She remembered Jake telling her that the purplish red fruit of the prickly pear was sweet and juicy and that if they were left attached while you peeled them, you could avoid getting stuck by their thorns. What she wouldn't give to be there with that lying pig right now. "Jake," she whispered, "where are you?"

She sighed. Too bad no one had ever told her how to date a man without getting stuck by his thorns.

Suddenly, all of Avalon went black, and Pepper let out a squeal. She backed into the room and felt her way to the bathroom door, calling out to Brad. The door opened, and her hand came into contact with skin—damp, warm, hairy. Yuck! Brad the bartender had enough chest hair to weave a blanket. Pepper sucked in her breath and pulled back her hand. How could she not have known? All this time, she'd been flirting with a friggin' caveman.

"All the town's lights have gone out," she told him.

"I've got a lighter," Brad offered. He guided her over to the bed, and she stayed put and waited, not knowing what to expect when she could see. Hopefully, Brad wasn't in his birthday suit. She might have had too much to drink, but just touching that hairy chest had sobered her up enough to know that playing Beauty to his Beast wasn't in any plans she'd ever have. Pepper heard him unzip his bag, and a few seconds later, a small flame brought some light into the dark room.

Brad's face was an eerie mask. Luckily, he was covered from the waist down with a towel. It could have been a romantic moment if it wasn't Brad and his hairy body standing there in front of her.

A few moments later, the room lights started to

flicker, and they slowly came back on, like a dimmer switch being turned up. Brad stood next to her, and she did her best not to stare at all that hair. Yes, she definitely preferred sleek, smooth skin over a gorilla suit.

Pepper caught the gleam in Brad's eyes, and she knew she'd better think fast to nip in the bud any ideas he might have about the two of them hooking up. If he wanted to think there was more to them spending the night together, let him. She'd never hinted she was interested in becoming one of his conquests.

She yawned, feigning fatigue, but as it turned out, all the activity and the buffalo milk really did have her feeling sleepy. She wanted to curl up on one of the double beds, and she even considered going to bed without her nightly shower, but there was just something about going to bed all squeaky clean and waking up fresh that helped each day start off right.

"I guess I'll go take a shower, too," she said, heading for the bathroom. She'd been slightly concerned he'd try to join her, but that fear was soon put to rest. She smelled his cigarette smoke and figured he was out on the balcony.

Brad stubbed his cigarette out on the "This room is a nonsmoking room" sign on the rail of the balcony and tossed it into the bushes. Pepper had yawned. That's what all women did when they didn't want to put out. Why didn't they just tell the truth? Why didn't they just say they didn't want to have sex? And where the hell were all the women that *did* want sex? He lit another cigarette. If she didn't want sex, why had she agreed to come to Catalina with him?

He blew smoke out his nose. Damn women and their games.

The wind had died down somewhat, and the clouds had drifted apart, allowing room for the moon to make an appearance. Tomorrow would be a nice day, and the ferries would be running again. That was tomorrow. This was tonight. Brad knew he might not get another opportunity like this with Pepper, and he intended to make good use of it.

He stuck his head back inside the room and heard the shower still running. Visions of water raining down over Pepper's soap-slickened body made him hard, and he considered joining her, but she'd freak out, and that would probably ruin any chances he might have with her. He reached into his pocket and felt the little bag that contained the two little white pills he'd brought with him. Maybe she'd appreciate them more than Alena had.

Brad went inside and opened the bathroom door a crack. The outline of Pepper's slender body showed through the shower curtain. He felt his blood pulsing, and he started to push open the door, but stopped when he heard a creak in the hallway outside their room. At the bottom of the door was a shadow. He held his breath and waited, and finally, the shadow moved on. Brad pulled on a pair of jeans and went to the balcony. A minute later, the dark form of a man appeared on the walkway below. Brad stepped to one side and flattened his body against the rough stucco wall. At one point, the man paused and glanced up at their balcony, and Brad could see his face under the lamplight. Son of a bitch. Pepper's

friend. What the hell was he doing here? No doubt
Lucy had put him up to coming here to look for
Pepper. Still, he had some nerve following them to
Catalina. From what Pepper had told him, they
hadn't been seeing each other for a while.

Brad smiled. Nothing to get worked up about, he
told himself. He'd used fake names on the register.

Jake's shoes landed on the floor with a thud, and
he rubbed the soles of his feet. Avalon might not be
very big, but it had a lot of hotels, and he hadn't
done this much walking since he and Angela spent
their weekends hiking.

Riding a golf cart in his search for Pepper would've
been less painful, but he figured he'd stand a better
chance of spotting her if he were on foot.

A list of the island's hotels lay next to him. He
picked it up and crossed off all the ones he'd already checked. No one by the name of Brad the
bartender or Pepper Bartlett had checked in to any
of them. That didn't surprise him. One thing was
sure, with the ferry service shut down, if they were
here, they'd still be here come morning.

Jake lay on the bed, staring up at the ceiling. What
possible reason could Pepper have for coming here
with Brad? Hurt was the only thing he could come
up with. He'd hurt her, and she'd come here to lick
her wounds. The real surprise was that she'd come
here with a guy like Brad. He was the kind of man
she might engage in a little innocent flirting with,
but to date seriously? Not a chance.

Jake considered what Lucy had told him. If it was
true that Brad had fooled around with another
man's fiancée and that man was out to get Brad,

why would Brad come to a place where there was no escape? Stupidity was the answer to that one. Where would he go to get away if he had to? Into the hills? Jake shook his head. All Brad would find up there was a herd of bison and a whole lot of scrub brush, and if he went far enough, he'd eventually come to Wrigley Ranch. Then what? Did Brad have plans to ride off into the sunset with Pepper? That was reason enough for Jake to punch the guy out.

Chapter 28

Pepper stirred. A hand softly caressed her hair, and she smiled at its warmth. "Jake," she whispered. Her eyes fluttered open, and the desert print with the sickly orange-colored wall as its backdrop stared back at her.

"Jake?" she said again, raising her head. She put a hand to her hair where she'd felt his touch. Disappointment washed over her. She didn't need to look. It wasn't Jake who'd been caressing her hair. Pepper swung her legs off the bed, and she jumped up, spinning around in one furious motion.

"What the hell are you doing?"

"You looked like an angel . . ."

"Look, just because we were forced to spend the night together doesn't mean it's going to lead to that."

"I didn't intend—"

"Don't play stupid," she said.

Brad looked amused. "Do you need a cup of coffee?" He got up from the bed and poured her some of the complimentary brew.

Coffee wasn't going to fix the mood she was in.

It'd take something a lot stronger. Like maybe more buffalo milk.

Brad handed her the cup, and their eyes met. Pepper took a sip, but quickly spit it back out.

"That's not coffee," she said. "That's untreated sewer water."

Brad laughed. "It's not that bad. Drink up. I'll buy you a better cup when we go to town."

Pepper tried another sip and set the cup down.

"How about I add a little more sugar and creamer?"

Pepper got up and went to the bathroom. When she came back, Brad had doctored the coffee so that it at least resembled something she could drink.

"Here," he said, handing it to her. "Try it again."

He'd made the effort to be nice, so Pepper took one large swallow, hoping that would be enough to satisfy him. Choking and sputtering, she set the cup down and backed away, holding up her hands. "No more. Please. I'll wait for something better."

A few minutes later, she felt all fuzzy, warm, and cozy. And she hadn't even had any buffalo milk yet. She looked over at Brad. She'd never noticed how sexy his eyes were. They must be his secret weapon with women. Then she remembered all the hair beneath his shirt. Maybe she could overlook a bit of hair.

"Brad," she said softly, "I'm sorry. I didn't mean to push you away so abruptly a while ago—"

Someone knocked, and Brad put a finger to his lips. He gently pushed her toward the bed, and she stepped back and fell, landing half on the floor, half on the bed. "My head," she cried. "I'm bleeding." She reached up and felt something wet. Her fingertips were bright red. "Look," she said, holding out her hand.

"Housekeeping," a woman said from out in the hall.

"Later," Brad shouted.

He crouched next to Pepper. "Jesus, you've gashed your head. Wait here. Let me get something." He returned with a warm, damp towel.

"Jesus," he said again. "We better get dressed and take you into town."

Pepper had other ideas. What was a little cut when she was feeling so good? "Let's not." She grabbed Brad's hand and pulled him down next to her.

He pulled the towel away from her head. It was soaked red. "I think we better go see if there's a doctor in town."

"Let me go take a look." She got up and went to the bathroom and saw that Brad was right—she might need a doctor. She giggled. It didn't even hurt, but she was beginning to feel light-headed.

Adrenaline surged through Brad. He hadn't intended for Pepper to get hurt. He managed to get her dressed, but it wasn't easy, all those buttons and straps and hooks. Women wore the damndest clothes. Bras, cute little panties, shoes with tiny little straps. He didn't have a lot of experience putting women's clothes back on, just taking them off. And it didn't help to have her nakedness staring him in the face either. For the first time, that didn't matter. Getting Pepper downtown where someone could take a look at that nasty cut was the only thing he cared about right then. He got her dressed the best he could, and they went outside to wait for the shuttle.

"Maybe we could go get some breakfast," Pepper mumbled.

"Maybe," Brad said. "Depends."

"On what?" Pepper asked.

"On how you feel."

"I feel fine," she said. "Just fine." The shuttle picked them up a couple of minutes later, and Brad helped her on. Once they reached the center of town, Pepper whispered into his ear, "Buffalo milk?"

The town doctor fixed her up, and in an hour, she was as good as new. The cut turned out to be minor. "Head wounds tend to bleed profusely," the doctor had told them. Pepper even asked for some food, and the doctor said they could go but that she had to take it easy the next couple of days.

Brad rented a golf cart so that Pepper wouldn't have to walk, and he found a couple of small cafés that looked like they were about to open, but she wanted to keep looking. They continued down Crescent Avenue toward Catalina's famous casino, and finally, they stopped at a small booth with a hand-painted sign above it that said Casino Dock Café. Brad looked at his watch. They had plenty of time. The ferries wouldn't be running for a couple more hours. After they ate, he'd still be able to go back to the pet cemetery and visit Scratch's grave.

A cool breeze washed over her face, gentle and refreshing, and Pepper felt a lot better. She was feeling more like herself with each passing minute. Everything had been a blur since she drank that awful coffee in the room. She didn't know what'd happened. Probably it was a combination of not drinking enough water and too many buffalo milks.

Brad ordered breakfast for her without even asking what she'd like. She didn't care. She was so hungry she'd have eaten bison meat, which, she was sure, they probably had.

As it turned out, she had to be satisfied with bacon and eggs on an English muffin, along with another cup of bad coffee. The food wasn't too bad if you didn't mind clogging your arteries.

In a few hours, she'd be on a ferry on her way back to the mainland. She could already hear Lucy saying, "I told you so." It might be better not to tell her about her little adventure on the Isle of Romance with Brad. Besides, this would be the last time she'd go anywhere with him.

"C'mon," Brad said, taking her hand. "We've got a few hours until the ferry leaves. I'll buy you a little something to make up for your head." Pepper closed her eyes and pretended it was Jake's hand she was holding

They went further down the beach until they came to an area where tables had been set up with handmade jewelry, clothing, and other trinkets for souvenir shoppers. Beyond the tables, several men were setting up band equipment on a large wooden stage. Directly in front of the stage was a barbecue pit, and inside was a good-sized pig. Somebody was going to feast tonight.

People milled about slowly as though recovering from a previous night of too much partying. Some carried cups of coffee, others cans of beer.

Brad let go of Pepper's hand, and she turned to see what had drawn his attention away from her. She should have known. A tall, dark-skinned woman, hair glistening black under the morning sun, was hanging turquoise jewelry at one of the booths. She smiled, and her cheekbones rose up to her eyes, making them almost disappear into the fleshy mounds. Her teeth flashed white behind full, painted lips, and she had a light-hearted, girlish laugh. From the way she'd catch a man's eye and smile, it was obvious she was aware of the luring effect she had on the opposite sex.

Pepper glanced over at Brad. He was mesmerized by the dark beauty. Not that she cared one ounce. She was through with men for the time being. She laughed quietly. Men just didn't get it.

"What's so funny?" Brad asked.

Pepper waved a dismissive hand. "Nothing," she said, but Brad had already turned his attention back to the woman, who now beckoned him with her full smile. Caught in the spider's web. If that had been Jake the woman was trying to reel in, Pepper might've been inclined to grab his arm and drag him away.

Jake. She wondered if she would ever again feel his strong arms around her. Or have him hold her and make her feel safe. Pepper closed her eyes and remembered the love they'd made at Imperial Beach. The memory was so intense that Pepper barely noticed when Brad walked away.

The woman continued hanging her silver and turquoise trinkets on small hooks, all the while giving Brad that look. It was a look that only another woman would recognize. Pepper continued to watch the woman in action. The nerve. What if Brad were her boyfriend or husband? How dare she?

How dare *he*? She was Brad's date. Sort of.

That was it. She wasn't going to waste another

second wondering if she should give Brad a try. Pepper glanced around. She wasn't interested in hanging around and watching their pathetic little dance of seduction. All she needed was a ride back to town. Maybe she'd do a little shopping. Get some real coffee.

A golf cart approached, and Pepper looked back at Brad. He was busy trying to pull his tongue back into his mouth. She raced over to the golf cart and hopped on the back seat as it slowed.

"Into town, please," she whispered.

"Sorry, ma'am. This ain't no taxi," the driver said.

"C'mon. You're going that way anyway." She looked over her shoulder.

The golf cart crept forward, and Pepper turned to look one more time. Brad's eyes met hers, but it was too late—she wasn't in any mood to listen to any more lame explanations about anything.

"Go! *Go!* For God's sake, go!" Her voice was a shrill shriek as she pounded a fist on the back of the seat. The startled driver finally got the idea, and the cart picked up speed, and Pepper's heart thudded as she watched Brad jump into the golf cart they'd rented.

"What the hell's wrong with you? Put the fucking pedal to the metal," she yelled into the driver's ear.

The golf cart stopped abruptly, and Pepper had to grab both sides to keep from going head first over the bench.

"Get off," the driver said.

"What? Are you crazy?"

"I told you this ain't no taxi."

Pepper glanced back. Brad was gaining ground, and in another ten seconds, he was next to them.

"Off," the driver repeated.

Pepper slumped in her seat.

"Where are you going?" Brad asked. He held out his arms like he really had no clue what was the matter.

Pepper stuck her lips out into a pout.

"Don't tell me you're jealous," Brad said with a laugh. "I was just looking at what she was selling."

"Yes, I could see that. And I'm not jealous. Certainly not of her with you." She crossed her arms over her chest. "Let's just say I'm fed up with men."

Brad gently took her by the arm and pulled her from the golf cart. The driver pulled away slowly, shaking his head and muttering something about domestic squabbles. Pepper shook her arm free.

"I thought we had an understanding," he said.

Pepper stopped cold. "Understanding? Brad, I never meant to give you the wrong impression. Our understanding is that you make good drinks and I drink them. That's as far as it goes."

"You willingly came here with me."

"Yeah, and it was a mistake. I'm in love with another man." Pepper heard herself say the words, and they stung. Had she blown it? Was it too late to let Jake back into her life? "I'm sorry. I feel bad about giving you the idea—"

"Forget it," he said, rubbing the back of his neck. But Pepper could tell things had permanently changed between them. She shifted from one foot to the other. A group of people passed by, hurrying toward the casino, where a movie would soon be starting. Brad reached up to Pepper's cheek and rubbed it lightly with the back of his hand.

"I need to find out if Jake and I have a chance."

"What about him lying to you?"

Pepper suddenly had a bad taste in her mouth. Lucy's words of forgiveness made her swallow it away. "Everybody deserves a second chance."

Brad nodded. "Will you at least go down to the pet cemetery with me?"

Jake sat on a bench a block away from the casino and pulled out his ticket back to the mainland. Departure time, one PM. He still had a few hours to find Pepper. He ran a hand through his hair. He'd looked everywhere, checked every hotel. He'd even had Lucy check with Simone to see if she'd heard from Pepper. She only confirmed what they already knew. Pepper had come to Catalina with Brad.

His stomach protested its emptiness, and he looked up and down Crescent Avenue for a place to get something to eat. Across the street was a booth that had just opened its shutters, and the smells coming out were actually appetizing. He started toward it, knowing that at any minute the entrepreneur might choose to close up for a couple of hours or a full day because he had something better to do. That seemed to be the way most of the locals ran their businesses in Avalon.

Jake ordered a coffee and a ham and cheese breakfast sandwich, and five minutes later, his order was placed on the counter. He dropped some change into a little wire tip basket just as a golf cart whizzed by. Jake turned to watch as it sped toward town. As soon as he glimpsed the passengers, he knew one of them was Pepper. Another cart whizzed by with a man and a dark-haired woman aboard. Jake dropped his sandwich into the nearest waste bin and strained to keep his eyes on both carts. A golf cart had just pulled up at the café, and Jake confiscated it, saying "Police business." After all, he'd seen that line work in plenty of movies.

"Sorry, I need to borrow this," he told the young driver. He pulled a twenty from his pocket and shoved it into the boy's hand. With any luck, it was enough to keep the kid from calling the police—at least for a few minutes.

Halfway down Crescent Avenue, he caught sight of Pepper again. The cart rounded a corner near a wooded area, and Jake mashed his foot against the pedal, but the small engine was at its limit. Christ, he could almost get off and run as fast.

A block out of downtown, Pepper's cart slowed and came to a stop at the edge of a wooded area. The other cart with the man and woman stopped far enough back that they wouldn't be noticed, and Jake figured that it was the red-faced man Lucy had spoken of. Jake stopped even further back and waited.

Brad and Pepper got out of their cart, and Jake saw what looked like white gauze on Pepper's head. It sent a chill through him. If that bastard had hurt her . . .

Pepper and Brad disappeared into the brush, and the couple from the other cart followed them. Jake motored up to the wooded area and followed the same path. A quiet reverence came over him as he looked around at all the small graves. It was like being in a library where if he dared make too much noise, someone would come out and "shush" him. A twig snapped under his feet, and adrenaline coursed through him. He had to fight to keep himself from running after Pepper.

Being among all the tiny graves gave Pepper the ooly goolies just the same as the day before. She crossed her arms and tried rubbing away the goose bumps.

Brad knelt on the ground before Scratch's grave and attempted to right the cross he'd put on it the day before. It had fallen over. He pulled a hunting knife from his backpack and quickly whittled a sharp point on the end, and then he struggled to push it into the ground, but it was hard clay. Pepper shuddered as he began to stab the knife blade into the dirt. After a minute, he'd managed to cut a hole big enough for the cross to slide into easily.

After a few minutes, he got up and went over to another grave.

"Duffy?" she read the name on the marker.

Brad nodded. For the first time since she'd known him, Pepper saw a hurt in his eyes that she never expected to see. Not from him anyway. Reactively, she touched his arm.

"He died a long time ago."

"What kind of dog was Duffy?" she asked.

"Just a dog." Brad glanced at some of the other graves and knelt again, rearranging rocks, pulling grass. "People forget," he said.

Pepper looked from one grave to the next, then back at Brad. He reached up and wiped the corner of one eye with his sleeve, and Pepper hoped he wasn't going to break down bawling. She didn't want to feel obligated to try to comfort him.

"I'm sorry," she muttered. She shifted uneasily

from one foot to the other, wondering how long she was going to have to stand among all the lonely little graves.

A twig snapped behind them, and Pepper almost jumped into Brad's arms. They turned as another couple pushed through the brush. Brad didn't exactly look thrilled to see them.

"What are you doing here?" he said to Vic.

The woman with the man glared at them with a look that could kill. Pepper wanted to tell her not to worry—she wasn't interested in Brad. Whatever the three of them had going on, Pepper didn't feel at ease being a part of it. She backed away from where Brad stood, giving them their space.

"I thought you were my friend," the man said to Brad. "Course, friends do share, don't they?"

"It wasn't all me. One night when you were away, I woke up to find her in my bed," Brad tried to explain.

It was more than Pepper wanted to hear. Another one of Brad's romantic escapades. How the hell had she gotten into the middle of this?

Vic looked none too happy with Brad's explanation. He moved toward Brad, and Pepper moved even farther away.

As much as she didn't want to be involved with Brad, she also didn't want to see him get hurt. She looked around the ground for some kind of weapon, if it became necessary. She had no idea what this man and woman were capable of.

Pepper quickly glanced around for Brad's knife, and she saw it at the head of Duffy's grave. One small leap, and she could have it. But so could Vic. She looked at Brad and frowned, averting her glance sideways toward the knife. He inched in that direction.

What the hell was Pepper doing? Instigating a knife fight? Jake figured he'd seen enough. He thought it might be good to make an appearance before anyone decided to use the hunting knife. He stepped into the small clearing.

"Shit," Brad mumbled. "What are you doing here?"

Pepper felt her heart leap.

"I came to take Pepper home," Jake said.

She looked over at Brad. "We can't just leave him."

"Brad can take care of himself," Vic said. "Just ask him."

Brad nodded. "You go ahead. This is my mess," he told Pepper.

"Are you sure? Your friend seems pretty mad."

"Yeah, it's all right."

"Wait," the dark-haired woman spoke up. "Don't you want to hear what your boyfriend has been up to?"

All eyes were on Pepper.

"That motherfucker drugged me." Marta ran over to Vic. He tried to push her away, but she clung to his arm. "We'd just got done eating some Thai, and I went to bed. Before I knew what hit me, I was feelin' all good, and I wanted you, but you weren't home."

"Brad was the next best thing, huh?" Vic said.

Good all over? That's how Pepper had been feeling after drinking the cup of coffee Brad had given her. She suspected Brad deserved an ass kicking.

He could fend for himself. She couldn't get back to Malibu fast enough.

"C'mon. Let's leave these people to their soap opera," Pepper said to Jake.

Jake took her hand, and Pepper looked defiantly into Brad's eyes. "Don't expect to see me at Beachside anymore."

She and Jake walked back through the brush, and Jake stopped just on the other side. He squeezed her shoulders.

"I'll be right back," he said.

"No." Pepper grabbed his hand. "Whatever is going on back there, I don't want you to have any part in it." And she sure didn't want Jake knowing that she suspected Brad of drugging her. Anything Vic and his girlfriend did to Brad would be nothing compared to what Jake would dish out.

Jake shook his head. "I'll be right back. We can't leave him back there with those people and that knife lying on the ground."

"Why?"

Jake looked in her eyes. "Is there something you want to tell me?"

Pepper shuffled from one foot to the other. She looked at the ground. "No."

"Then wait here."

Jake left Pepper standing there, and she waited for about ten seconds before following him.

As soon as she stepped into the clearing, she caught a glint of metal in the sunlight. Vic had Brad's knife, and he stood poised to fight. Pepper watched in horror as Jake moved slowly toward the two men. It was like a scene from a movie. Grown men fighting with a knife right before her eyes.

"You don't want to do anything stupid," Jake said to Vic.

"Stay outta this," Vic said.

Vic's eyes were full of hate, and it looked to Pepper like he really did want to do something very stupid. He stared at Brad. Brad didn't look too happy about the situation, but he didn't look mad. His face was void of expression. Empty. Pepper had seen that look before. It was the same as she'd seen on her mother's face the day her dad died. It was almost enough to make Pepper feel sorry for him. Obviously, Vic had been a good friend, and now that friendship was forever broken.

Pepper touched Jake's arm. He didn't seem to notice. His eyes were fixed on the knife in Vic's hand. She wanted a hero, but she didn't want him to do anything heroic enough to get hurt.

The next thing she knew, Vic charged Brad like a bull and sunk his head into his chest. Brad gushed air and fell backward onto the ground. Pepper's pulse raced. She had to find a stick or something—anything—to help Jake if Vic turned on him as well.

Brad got to his feet, and Vic rushed him again. He lost hold of the knife, and the two men fell to the ground, punching and kicking. Jake jumped in and pulled Brad off Vic. Vic punched Brad in the stomach while Jake held him, and Pepper didn't think that Jake had meant for that to happen.

She scoured the ground and saw the knife just inches from the ball of manflesh, and she kicked it to one side to prevent something worse from happening.

A large hunk of wood caught her eye, and Pepper quickly surmised that it was big enough to do some serious damage if need be. She picked it up and readied herself for a strike. Fists flew, bodies twisted. She couldn't focus on any one man for more than a few seconds. Finally, Jake broke away from the other two. He had mud and dried leaves in his hair, as did Brad and Vic. If it wasn't so horrifying, she might've laughed. Instead, she screamed.

"Stop!"

Marta screamed too, "Kill him!"

Everyone looked in their direction. Pepper stood over the two men, wielding the log, shifting from one foot to the other.

"Just stop!" Pepper said again.

No one moved, but Pepper saw Vic take a quick look around. He was looking for the knife. This was craziness. Knives and fighting—trying to kill each other? She stuck out a foot and kicked the knife farther away just as Vic lunged for it. His fingers grasped the air between her and the knife, and with a shriek, she brought a foot down on his hand.

"Fucking bitch!" Vic rolled to one side, holding his injured hand. After only a second's hesitation, he lunged again.

Pepper tossed the log aside. Screw the log. She was a kickboxer, for crying out loud. She knocked Vic backward with one sharp kick to his chest, then her foot swung up hard to his chin. A huff of air escaped from Vic's lungs as he slumped to the ground. She quickly positioned herself for another kick, but it wasn't necessary. Everything went quiet. Not even a twitter of birds in the trees. Vic opened his eyes and tried getting up, but he sank back to the ground and became still.

Only then did Pepper notice that everyone was standing there, staring at her.

Jake clapped his hands briefly. "Way to go, Wonder Woman." He stepped toward her and put both hands into her hair. "A woman who can kick ass on a man kind of turns me on," he said.

"I could've been killed," Pepper said. Her hands were trembling, and she felt as though her heart would burst from the adrenaline. What a friggin' rush.

"That's not what it looked like from where I stood," Jake said.

Pepper felt herself blush. She'd surprised herself, but she was glad to know she had what it took to protect herself.

"You okay?" she asked Jake.

Jake shook his head. "Not unless you tell me what I want to hear."

"What's that?"

"You know . . . c'mon, say it."

Pepper's forehead wrinkled. "You're the man of my dreams?"

Jake shook his head. "That, too. But that's not it."

Pepper was pretty sure she knew what he was getting at. She looked into his eyes and saw what she'd seen the first time they made love. He loved her.

"I love you, too," she said.

"Oh God, Vic," Marta screamed.

Jake and Pepper turned. Brad was crouched next to Vic, and he didn't seem to be doing so well.

Jake pushed Brad to one side and put a finger to Vic's neck. Blood seeped out from under him, and Marta's face turned to horror.

Jake rolled Vic to one side. Pepper gasped. Red covered the back of his shirt.

Jake pulled open Vic's shirt and wiped away the blood until he saw the source. It was a puncture wound about the size of a dime. He looked over to where Vic had been lying and saw a broken grave marker. The end of it was bright red.

"Dear God, I've killed him," Pepper cried.

Jake pulled out his cell phone and tossed it to her. "Call 911 or the operator or whoever it is you call on this island."

She did as she was told, but didn't take her eyes off Jake as he worked to save Vic's life. She'd never seen anyone in such control or working so purposefully, and she stared in awe at the man she loved performing a miracle.

Avalon Emergency Services picked up Vic, and as soon as Jake knew that he would live, he and Pepper were on the Catalina Express headed for home.

"I could've killed him," Pepper said. "I may never kickbox again."

Jake held her close. "But you probably saved Brad. It was an accident." He pulled out his cell phone. "We better call Lucy. She's been worried about you."

Pepper groaned. "She'll never let me hear the end of this."

"I won't either." Jake grabbed both of her arms. "You make me crazy, but I love you. No more running off with other guys."

Pepper looked into his eyes and saw the love she'd been waiting for her entire life. "No more," she said. She was quiet most of the ride home, but finally, she had to know how Jake knew what to do to save Vic's life.

"That was some miracle you performed back there."

Jake gave her a blank look.

"You want to tell me where you learned to do that?"

"It was nothing," Jake said. He rubbed a hand across the back of his neck.

"That makes two lives you've saved." She studied Jake as he fidgeted in his seat. "What? Have there been more?"

Jake sighed. He loved her. If they had any chance at a future, he was going to have to come clean. "I'll tell you everything if you'll promise not to run away ever again."

Pepper felt sick. What surprises were left? How many lies had he told her? "I promise," she said weakly.

Jake took a breath and told her about Angela and how he'd been a doctor in Portland, Oregon. She remained quiet for several minutes, pondering all that he'd told her.

Finally, he put a finger under her chin and looked into her eyes. "What now?"

"Now," she said, "I guess I'll have to learn to live with having a doctor for a lover."

"Perhaps," Jake said. "I never thought I could go back. But maybe . . ."

Pepper felt bad about Angela. She could even understand why he hadn't wanted to go back to work for a while. But to give up being a doctor? If it was really what he wanted, she'd have to let it be, but maybe he wouldn't object to them *playing* doctor and nurse once in a while.

Chapter 29

With summer just about over, Pepper had only one more matter to tend to. It was time for the Harrison Hot Springs World Championship Sand Sculpting Competition. And Jake was going with her.

Feeling giddy as she packed her new tools, Pepper imagined the sculptures she would see built with some of the best sand in the world. Even after practicing all summer, she knew she still couldn't compete with the Masters, but that day would come soon enough. She was sure of it.

The flight to Canada took them sailing through clear blue skies, and for once, Pepper was glad to have a window seat. Snow-covered Mt. Baker and the Cascade Mountain Range were visible in all their glory, and she'd never imagined how spectacular the sight could be at 32,000 feet.

Jake got them checked into their hotel, and when they walked into the room, Pepper was delighted to see a dozen pink roses sitting atop the dresser—from Jake, of course.

While he took a shower, Pepper sat on the edge of the bed and unpacked her bag. She lined up her sculpting tools neatly on the bed, like a surgeon about to perform surgery. She wondered if this was how Jake felt when he prepared to operate.

She couldn't have been more proud that Jake had decided to go back to practicing medicine. It seemed such a waste to have that gift and not use it.

Pepper picked up a straw used for blowing away loose sand that Lucy had attached a string to so she could wear it around her neck just like the pros did. She slipped the string over her head and pretended it was a medal for best sculpture.

She was ready to give it her best, that was for sure, and she'd come up with the perfect idea for a sculpture. Instead of the perfect size-C mermaid, she'd chosen something unique. One day while watching Gilligan in Jake's backyard, the brown pelican had waddled to the top of a mound of dirt and stopped, his gaze focused straight ahead as though he were looking out to sea. Pepper had gone home that night and had Lucy draw some sketches. The mound became the back of a whale, and Gilligan, a hitchhiker with binoculars. All she needed now was to smell the salt in the air and feel the grit of sand between her fingers. She spent a long minute daydreaming how it would look, until someone knocked at their door. She opened it to the smiling faces of her mom and Ben.

"Hi, sweetie," Hannah said, whisking into the room. Her mother wore a sundress splashed with yellow pineapples and orange tangerines and a floppy sun hat atop her head. Dark sunglasses completed her Audrey Hepburn look.

Her mother was positively beaming. "Their room is nicer than ours, don't you think?" she said to Ben.

Ben nodded. He seemed uncomfortable, and

Pepper felt ashamed that she hadn't made more of an effort to make him feel welcome into their lives.

"What are you doing here?" she asked her mom.

"I invited them," Jake said behind her.

They all looked toward the bathroom. Jake finished mauling his hair with a fluffy white towel and then threw it back through the bathroom door.

"I figured they might want to see how talented you are."

Hannah took Pepper's hands. "It's okay, isn't it? Our being here?"

Pepper glanced over at Ben, who was still standing quietly near the door. Her mother obviously loved him, and she'd managed to forgive Jake. Maybe it was time for all of them to get on with their lives.

"Of course," she said, pulling her mom close. Ben's face lit up when she approached him, too. It was like a weight had suddenly been lifted from her heart, and Pepper swore she could feel it swell with love.

The sun was shining, the water glistening, and the sand perfect. Pepper completed her sculpture in the time allotted, and even though she didn't place, she felt like she'd won something even better. Her family was healing.

After spending hours in the sun bending, digging, and carving, what Pepper needed now was a warm bubble bath. Jake had other ideas. He insisted that they walk down the beach to look at all the other sculptures.

"They'll still be here later. Let's go clean up, get some rest," Pepper said, tugging at his arm.

Jake resisted, pulling back. "How about now?"

"Yes," Hannah said. "Let's look now. They might all get washed away."

"Believe me," Pepper said, "they aren't going anywhere. They'll be here for a couple of weeks. I *need* to get out of these clothes. I *need* to get cleaned up."

"Soon," Jake said. "Walk with me." He squeezed Pepper's hand and pulled her gently along.

Pepper could see she wasn't going to win this one. She reluctantly stepped forward, but kept looking back, trying to keep track of her mom and Ben. They strolled slowly along the beach, weaving through the crowd of onlookers, holding hands. It made her smile. Her mom was going to be okay.

After several minutes, Jake stopped. "Look," he said, pointing.

An ocean of people stood in front of her. Everywhere she looked, there were adults and children standing, walking, playing.

"What?" she asked, her brow furrowing against the bright sun. She put up a hand to shield her eyes.

Her mom and Ben caught up to them and stopped, looking in the direction Jake was pointing. Hannah brought a hand to her mouth, and the corners of her eyes crinkled into a smile. Pepper thought she might cry.

"What is it?" Pepper demanded. "What am I missing?" She stood on her tiptoes, but still, she couldn't see above all the heads. All she could make out was a very large arm with a fist raised high in the air. The rest of the sculpture was hidden from view by dozens of people milling about. Finally, Pepper squeezed between her mom and Ben, and what she saw made her breath catch. The sculpture was a larger-than-life Superman, and he was holding a bride's hand. His other arm was reaching into the sky as though he were about to take off in flight. Beneath the sculpture was a huge sign, also made of sand, that said, "Marry me, Pepper!"

The muscles in Pepper's chest tightened around her heart, and she could feel it swell so large it hurt. This time, it was a good hurt. She turned around to face the person responsible for her physical condition, but he was gone.

"Where is he?" She asked her mom.

"Who, dear?" Hannah asked.

"*Who?* Who do you think? *Jake.* He was here—"

Ben nudged her and pulled her over in front of him. She could barely see between the two people who were standing in front of them, but what she saw made a tear form in the corner of her eye. Jake was on bended knee next to the sculpted "Marry Me" sign, and he was holding a small box. When their eyes met, she thought her heart would melt like warm chocolate.

Her mom gave her a gentle push, and she moved forward as people stepped aside to let her through.

She stood in front of Jake, unable to take her eyes off the tiny box. He opened it, revealing a dazzling diamond ring, and Pepper put her hand to her chest. Her heart beat so fast she felt she might swoon or need mouth-to-mouth resuscitation.

"Marry me, Pepper," he said to her in front of thousands of people. "Marry me, and let me be your hero."

Tears clouded Pepper's eyes, and she couldn't speak.

"I'll take that as a yes," Jake said. He gathered her into his arms and kissed her, and she melted into his lips as though no one else in the world were there. When she finally caught her breath, all that came out was, "Wow."